In Mourning

Accusations From The Grave

J. K. Grueber

MYSTIC RIDGE PUBLISHING, LLC

The characters and events portrayed in this book are fictitious. Any similarity to real persons, living or dead, is coincidental and not intended by the author.

Mystic Ridge Publishing, LLC

Mysticridgepublishing.com

ISBN: 978-1-965796-17-7 (Ebook)

ISBN: 978-1-965796-18-4 (Paperback)

ISBN: 978-1-965796-19-1 (Hardcover)

Cover design by: J. K. Grueber, Bruce Sanderson, Anne Graff, Andrew Grueber, and William Grueber.

Contributing cover photo and editor: Bruce Sanderson, Sanderson-Decello Design, LLC.

Printed in the United States of America.

By J. K. Grueber

The Envy Series:
COLORS OF ENVY: A Paranormal Romance Mystery
FACES OF ENVY: A Paranormal Romance Mystery
ECHOES OF ENVY: A Paranormal Romance Mystery

The MacDade Brothers Mysteries:
EXPOSED IN SHADOWS: He Who Plays.
A Paranormal Mystery Rekindling Lost Love
EXPOSED In The CROSSHAIRS: He Who Rides
A MacDade Brothers Paranormal Mystery
EXPOSED By The RIVERSIDE: He Who Lives
A MacDade Brothers Paranormal Mystery

The Vampire Tales:
Cursed At Conception: The Vampire's Henchman
Damned By Death: The Vampire's Hammer

The Whistlebrook Mysteries;
Mourning Child: Letters From The Grave

$Dedicated$

To my oldest brother,
Andrew Charles Graff.
1940 – 1958
They say that only the good die young and I've believed that idiom
throughout my life.
Though I knew you only briefly,
I've felt your presence watching over all of us from above.
Until we meet again, know that you are remembered.

Prologue

Wiping hot tears with his fists, he sniffed and forced a sob down his throat. Crying. Someone else was crying, too? He held his breath, listening, straining to hear the sobbing within the furnace sounds. Both of his fists dropped behind him into deeper shadows, pressed between the cold stone wall and his inflamed backside. Sparks flashed down his legs, hurting all the way to his toes. Bruises thumped in his arms, too. Nanny Briggs had grabbed him, hard. A sob lodged in his throat; he bit into his bottom lip to keep the sound from escaping. More tears flooded down his cheeks. Shaking his head angrily, he barely lifted his fists to clear his eyes when the whining sob froze him. Someone was hurt! He knew those sounds. Someone hurt—but down here? Sniffing softly, he sidled from the wall, nearer the doorway. Mommy would be awful mad if she found him down here—but that wasn't Mr. Beers crying. Almost sounded like mommy crying.

Forgetting his misery with his thought, he sniffed again, dragging his shirt sleeve over his face to wipe his nose and clear his eyes. Only after he lowered his arm and stood peering out into the shadowy hall, his muscles gripped with a thought of Nanny Briggs finding his soiled shirt sleeve. Not even the furnace roar drowned that sobbing, and he heard another voice. A familiar voice.

Dr. Cullugan always talked in a low, careful voice when moving the Residents, and they always moaned in pain, too. Like Mommy moaned now, straining to form words. Or was it Mommy? And why was Mommy in pain? Why was she down here? Hurt!

Panic squeezing his stomach, he hurried within the shadows to the doorway and poked his head carefully into the hallway. He never went too far, never too far into the shadowy halls. Never even all the way to the first furnace room. Mommy said it was dangerous. She told him to stay out of the basement, stay out of Mr. Beers' way. 'Don't you go pestering—'

"D-Do. It!"

His muscles gripped; he stood frozen. Sounded like Nanny Briggs, and if she caught him in the wine cellar, she'd surely 'tan his hide' with her wooden spoon, again. His breath caught in his chest, constricting his lungs before the voice softened, defeated, almost whining, "Just d-do it... Get it o-over."

"All right then," Dr. Cullugan spoke quietly, barely audible within the natural sounds. "Just relax then."

If that was Momma, she was hurt. Hurt bad! He could hardly make out her muffled voice, and Dr. Cullugan sounded the way he always sounded when talking to the old folks just before they went to greener pastures—whatever the dickens that meant. Whistlebrook had plenty of green fields in summer, except Mommy no longer let cows roam over the hills, like Nanny Briggs said cows and chickens roamed the fields. Not even the stray cats stayed long. They just up and disappeared. And the boy had a funny feeling about those cats disappearing the way they did sometimes. Nanny Briggs always put out a saucer of milk when those strays came—

A violent sob echoed in the shadows, halting his thought of cats and Nanny Briggs. Mommy was hurt, and he knew where Mommy and Dr. Cullugan were! Just two doors away, in that room that was always locked.

The door stood open enough to let a strip of light cross the gray painted floor, brightening the jagged walls.

"A-are y-you sure no-nobodies g-gonna know?"

"If you're having second thoughts, perhaps we should—"

In the muffled voice, the boy heard a determined 'no.' And no longer thinking about the prickly burns under his britches, he peeked into the shadowy hallway. It looked like a cave with dull light bulbs dangling far apart, barely touching the gray, cracking floor. That door was open and Mommy was in there with Dr. Cullugan. How could he think about his backside when Mommy sounded so awfully hurt? And maybe she would keep Nanny Briggs from swatting him if he made her feel better, like he made the old folks feel better. They always smiled at him and patted his head when he sneaked into their rooms, and he always knew which rooms to enter, which hands needed holding. Mommy needed to feel better, now, and if Nanny Briggs swung that spoon at him, that was just fine, too.

Gathering his courage, he swallowed the last sob and lump, hiked his britches, and fixed his shirt sleeves at his wrists. Mommy would want to see him properly dressed. Cautiously, he leaned and looked out into the hallway. Better not to get in Mr. Beers' way. That big fella sure liked to flop his big-brimmed hat down on a guy's head, but if he ever got to swinging something, it was likely to be a hammer or one of those long pipe-wrenches he wore on his belt. Warily, the child peered down the hallway, eyeing the long black gaps between the dull circles of light. If a fella wasn't careful, he could end up butt over bean cups with all the loose bricks and cracking mortar between those circles of light. Reconsidering, he nearly changed his mind. The voices mixed, almost drowning out in another clink and clatter as another furnace fan ignited. His attention caught the thin stream of light spiking through one of the pitch-black patches. That was the room all right. Just two doors away, and Mommy needed him. He could reach that door quick enough. Drawing a breath, he stepped hesitantly, inching into the dull glow of the nearest light. Worried sure whether he liked being in the dark or the light—he stood another second, heartbeat racing, more tears threatening the corners of his eyes.

If Nanny Briggs came down here...? With his thought, he shuffled into the shadows, not foolish enough to think he could disappear in the shallow darkness. The voices were barely audible, just muffled sounds, but he recognized the difference in pitches, and Dr. Cullugan's voice chanted steadily, now. Drawing breath, Kip began sidling along the wall. Nanny Briggs told him about monsters, about how trolls lived under bridges like the one in the back lawn, about how trolls liked little boys even better than Billy goats. And ghouls, too! He wished he hadn't thought of the ghouls. Sidling through the shadows, his attention swung front and back, peering and darting into the cobwebbed beams overhead and searching every shadow. Mommy said there were no such things as monsters and ghosts, but Nanny Briggs—

Dr. Cullugan's voice became clear, now. Less than a half dozen steps from that strip of light, Kip halted, listening to the low lulling voice. "Just relax now... That's it. You're doing fine... You'll be a little woozy for a little while. You'll have to rest... You have a room in town, don't you...? There now. That's it. Lie still, now."

Confused, he listened to the moaning reply, recognizing that sluggish sound, like the old folks moaning even after the nurses offered pain medicine to stop their wailing or cursing. What would Mommy need a room in town for anyway? She was going *away!* Going to Greener Pastures! No! She couldn't leave him here with Nanny Briggs! Hurrying the last steps, he reached the door and slid his fingers into the thin opening, nudging the door open—

His body froze. His mind and attention riveted.

A blinding circle of light reflected on a raised ivory knee and thin shin. Paisley-printed blue cloth gathered at white hips resting on a metal table. One small barefoot stood on a slight metal ledge, with a wide leather belt holding the limb in place. At the end of the table, Dr. Cullugan hunched forward, white light highlighting his silver-gray streaked hair. A small metal table stood at his side, nearly level with the manacled foot. No other light entered the room, and for a split second, he thought of that puppet show Mommy had taken him to see, A spotlight on the puppets. Not puppets. *Not puppets!*

Cold fear doused him, shuddering his frozen limbs as his focus locked on Dr. Cullugan's red-gloved hand shifting toward the metal table. A red glob plopped into a small metal basin; the sound amplified in his throbbing ears. Dripping red, the medical prongs reflected silver sparks, shivering, suspended. A splatter of red—*red paint!*—splattered the white leg, trailed down the ivory jittering shin. In slow motion, in stopped time, the red vein spiraled around the thin calf, skittered down the back of the ankle, and dipped off the bare heel.

"Almost done, now, you're doing fine. Just relax," Dr. Cullugan spoke through a mask covering the bottom half of his face. "This might pinch a little... There now," he said in finality and settled back on his feet. Lifting his hunched shoulders, turning...

As the metal prongs passed the bloody shin, a gasped moan halted Cullugan's motion, just a pause, a stopped second.

From the metal prongs, a dripping red glob suspended, and that wasn't paint, not paint at all. *Blood!* Blood dripped off the wicked scissor prongs, splattering the metal table and jittering foot, but the thing caught in the prongs jittered, too. And in flashing milliseconds, the child recognized the outline of a tiny human head between the blunted metal prongs. A tiny, bloodied arm swung in open space, aglow under the wash of blinding light. A single leg—a single bloodied leg jiggled above the tray, and in a blinding flash, he understood why that first glob had struck him dumb.

A tiny leg. A tiny red leg! *MOMMMY!* His silent scream echoed through his reeling mind. *MMMOOOMMMY!* The plop resounded in a vacuum as the glistening red glob dropped into the metal pan with a wet thump. A sound escaped his constricted throat. In slow motion, Dr.

Cullugan turned as a round, ashen face lifted at the far end of the metal table.

"Oh-my-God—" Dr. Cullugan breathed, his voice amplified as he started turning from the table, bloody hands and gaping bloody forceps extended.

Part One

The Will

Chapter 1

Funeral!

That single word erupted in Kip Patterson's mind, resounding under an instant whirlwind of confusion. His focus cleared, his thoughts twisted as a shadowed collage of yellowed pictures, fading and peeling, came into focus in his line of sight. Images from his childhood. Alone in his windowless, childhood room, he'd cut and pasted these faces and pictures on every sallow blue wall. Directly in front of him, a magnificent white—yellowed—stallion reared against a midnight sky; its white mane thrown across the front wheel of a red bicycle; its front hooves landing upon the prow of a speedboat. The boat ran over a child's face, obliterating the soft chin. A man smiling around the butt of a cigarette rose from the bicycle's banana seat as if mounted on a wall plaque. On and on, the scenes of his childhood flowed, and the sight of a hearse near the ceiling brought him full circle.

A funeral.

His bedroom. His childhood bedroom. Not his immense bedroom with an incredible view of the Pacific Ocean through an entire wall of floor-to-ceiling windows. His home now stood on a ridge above the shore. Rather than curtains, living emerald vines rose at either side of the windows, creating an illusion of a forest. A scent of earth and hibiscus woke him, more by its absence. The crafted scent of potpourri didn't mask the musty, familiar smell filling his lungs.

Automated, Kip untangled himself from a blanket, one brought from the recliner in the next room. He still wore his jeans and flannel shirt, both disheveled. In a splotch of lamplight from the living room, he found his shoes resting neatly at the bottom of his bed, and with a lucid flash of the previous evening, he knew he hadn't removed his own shoes.

So, which kind soul had braved his insanity to remove his shoes and cover him?

At the sight of JD Mulden, just another face from the past, dozing on the recliner, a magazine lying open about to slide off his lap, Kip smirked and nearly huffed a laugh. Good old JD. A real friend, not letting the mouse out of the trap this late in the game. For the past four days, the illusion of lasting friendship had sustained them, but the game had ended with a phone call. JD, former ally and only friend of the Prince of Whistlebrook, had posed as a Colorado Forest Ranger when, in fact, he was a DEA agent in league with the Justice Department to hang a certain entrepreneur. For what exactly, Kip hadn't discovered, but he could guess with one too many government contracts under his belt.

Silently, Kip collected his garment bag, carrying it into the communal bathroom, and remembered to lock the door to avoid another odd encounter. Flashing a thought of a stranger, an attractive, brunette stranger holding a towel as he stood dripping outside the shower door, he shook his head, stifling a smirk. Only in Whistlebrook Nursing Home, his childhood haunt, could a fellow run headlong into a stranger while tending to his personal ministrations.

Before stepping into the shower, he glanced at his watch, verifying 9:05—hopefully 9:05 a.m., although he hadn't passed a window yet to confirm the time of day. Poised momentarily, he identified the distant hum of activity from industrial appliances to copy machines and typewriters.

Office hours had begun. A.M., then. And in another hour, Mr. Calfactor would take his final ride.

Showering and dressing quickly, Kip aligned his schedule for the day's activities. First, the funeral. Naturally. He couldn't possibly leave Whistlebrook without attending one more funeral. After which, he would return and collect his bags—along with the dancers and hats as his mother proposed in her pre-postmortem missive.

Bullshit. He'd lived without his hat collection, and he would take only the Wallendorf figurine with him. He could take his bags to the official reading of the Will and head for the airport from John Madison's law offices.

Passing through the broken door of his suite, he fleetingly recalled shattering the knob plate under a quick kick last evening. The old wood hadn't held up to his moment of madness, but then, he'd mastered his talent for destruction.

Already amused, Kip dropped his garment bag onto the nearest chair and caught JD's start, meeting his gaze. "Sleep well?"

"Shit, I must have conked out," Mulden said quietly, and his stark gaze intensified. "Are you uh...? How you feeling today?"

"Fine. You?"

Tense, JD studied him, trying to read through his vacant grin. "What happened last night, Kip? Why did you blow?"

"Ask the sun why it shines, JD," Kip answered and glanced about the room before focusing on Mulden. "There's a closet full of hats in that room. Take them if you want them. The dancers—aside from the one under the dome—take them and give them to your sister—"

"Kip," JD interrupted soberly. "I don't think you're thinking this out—"

"On the contrary, JD. I have," he said simply. "What you don't take will become the property of the new owners as of 4 p.m. Frankly, there's a small fortune in this room, and the new administration will likely trash them." Looking into Mulden's troubled gaze, Kip commented, "Our paths shouldn't cross again, JD, but thank you for being here."

"What the hell does that mean? Shouldn't cross?"

The scrambling device rested in his pocket in the guise of a transistor radio, compliments of Frank Culver—another of the late, great Marilyn Patterson's minions. Palming the contraption in his pocket, he engaged the on switch. His gaze unwavering, his voice lowered an octave so it wouldn't be overheard through the door. "Do not cross me, JD. Accept that as sound advice from someone who does—occasionally—enjoy skiing in Aspen."

Mulden's wheels were spinning, his gaze held steady. "How long have you known?" he asked carefully.

"Long enough to appreciate your talent, my old friend," Kip answered evenly and started toward the door as JD pushed swiftly afoot. Halted, Kip studied Mulden's tense gaze. "You'll find some plastic covering the hats. Use it to wrap the dancers. I'll send someone with a box—"

"Fuck those dancers. We need to talk," JD stated.

"My dear old *friend*, there's absolutely nothing we need to discuss," Kip said simply, his focus abstract. "I've been screwed by government whores before. I just hope they're paying you handsomely for services rendered. I certainly enjoyed every second of it. Now, if you'll excuse me? I have a funeral to attend."

"What happened to you, Kip?"

"Seems to me, I could ask the same of you, JD, but frankly, it doesn't concern me. Stay out of my social circle and I'll stay out of yours."

"I didn't lie to you," Mulden said evenly. "I came here as a friend—"

"JD," Kip interrupted, looking into the tense hazel eyes. "You're fired. I'll see that Carolyn prepares your severance pay—"

"I don't want your fucking money!" Mulden snapped. "I didn't stay here because I was being paid—"

"Oh, that's right. Severance pay might look like a payoff. Too bad, really, but I suppose you'll have to settle for the hats or nothing at all for your time and trouble. Now, if you'll excuse me—"

At the start of motion, Kip's hand flew, blocking the grasp, catching Mulden's wrist. Without a conscious thought, Kip stepped and twisted, rolling Mulden over his back into the center of the floor. Not losing an instant, he followed. As startled as JD, Kip halted on Mulden's chest. Fifteen years ago, he wouldn't have stood a chance at besting JD Mulden, wrestler, weightlifter, All-Star sports material. Holding JD's neck in a firm grip between his thumb and forefinger, Kip glared into the startled hazel eyes, his own the color of ash. Mulden knew the position, knew enough to remain very still. "I didn't spend those three years in a sanitarium, JD," he said quietly. "But it was a sanctuary of a nature with few distractions, and I'm not the docile little introvert you once knew. Now, be nice and sign the register when you leave within the next thirty minutes. I don't think you'd like to explain to your superiors why you've been arrested for trespassing. Go quietly, and they need only know that your mission was a failure. Create any problems for me, and I can guarantee you'll need a new career. I can be a real bastard when I'm angry, and I am angry."

"You always—were—too—damned—fast," JD struggled with his words. His muscles had relaxed into the twisted position. "Let's talk, damn it! You're—In—Trouble. You need—my help!"

"Goodbye, JD. Be gone when I get back." In a swift, easy motion, Kip found the pressure point to short-circuit Mulden's nervous system. His hazel eyes widened for an instant and rolled back in the socket; his head lulled. Releasing his grip, Kip pushed onto his feet, muttering a curse. He really hadn't meant that end.

Stepping over JD's feet, Kip picked up his black brimmed hat, passed through the door, and closed it behind him. Kitchen clatter and business machines converged in the hall; a subtle lurch at the thought of food veered him toward the offices. He strode into the secretarial pool in time to see

Angie slice her finger, utter a short breath, and pop her index finger in her mouth. A paper cut. Business as usual.

Carolyn glanced at Angie indifferently, then shifted her attention to him with a quick, worried smile. Her soft blue eyes darted down and up; her smile brightened, "Good morning, Mr. Patterson."

Angie's stricken gaze darted to Carolyn, then Kip, before she snatched her bleeding finger from her mouth and grabbed the sheet of paper from her typewriter roll.

"You spoke to Bill," Kip realized, looking to Carolyn.

She nodded with a bemused shine in her eyes. "He's informed me that we are currently under a new administration, sir. Is there anything I can do for you?"

Drop the 'sir' for starters. "Actually, yes. In about 10 minutes, send a couple of boxes to my room and see that a security guard escorts JD Mulden to his car after he packs whatever he wants to take with him. Any messages?"

She glanced down, sliding three switchboard sheets from under the phone and handing them to him.

Morgan had called last evening; the block print indicated Frank Culver's handwriting. Father Jordan—8:30 a.m. M.B.—Marsh Baxel—9:15 a.m. *5:15 a.m. California time?* He would return Marsh's call from a payphone. His gaze shifted to the window, half expecting to see a blizzard through the sheer curtains. Looking to Carolyn, he asked, "How are the roads?"

"Just wet. It's almost 40 degrees," she said and smiled more at his unbidden disgust. "You California boys just don't appreciate a heat wave."

"Personally, I'll take forty-foot waves any day," he admitted. "Tell Mrs. Feeney, I'll see her around lunch. Imagine Bill's already come and gone?"

She nodded as her eyes clouded with a thought. "I heard things got out of hand last night. Are you all right, hon?"

"Fine," he said absently, feeling strangely numb as he turned and strode into the alcove, passing into the office. He entered only as far as the coat rack, where he vaguely recalled leaving his long cashmere coat. At least he'd remembered to pack a few winter threads when hustling to catch his flight less than a week ago.

Marilyn Patterson was gone. Truly gone.

Pulling his coat on, he stood momentarily, fumbling in his coat pockets for his keys while scanning the office in the morning light. The room still felt cold. Empty. As empty as he felt as he uttered, "Goodbye, mother."

Automated, he passed through the second exit door from the office, avoiding the secretarial pool, and avoiding the kitchen a second time by cutting through the lobby.

Fifteen years later, and his body still reacted to the smells coming from the kitchen. . .

One after another, those funerals had piled up. Six of them that Kip knew of. Six of his friends. Except he hadn't considered Mr. Hammond a friend. As if cobwebs stirred in an attic, Kip remembered a distant internal battle of grief and relief when he stood at Mr. Hammond's casket. Hammond had been one mean old man in his latent prime, never missing a chance to swing his damned walking stick, and later his flat hand.

Too swiftly, Kip recalled standing at another gravesite, and it was the face of Denton McDaniels in that crowd. God, that same timeframe. One of the *away* funerals, he recalled, but no name accompanied his thought. One of the special cases. Those years, those events were too cluttered, but Kip remembered meeting the classy blond-haired man, shaking his hand, and looking into the pale blue eyes that had appeared so stricken with grief. Not grief, but shock, Kip realized fifteen years too late for it to matter. Denton McDaniels had recognized him, had said something, asked something.

You're Marilyn Patterson's son?

"Damn it," Kip uttered and yanked open the car door, sliding into the driver's seat. Denton McDaniels. On two to three separate occasions, Kip corrected while flashing another memory glance of the Basilica at St. John's Academy. Denton McDaniels had stood in the shadows, in the gathering to witness his bastard's Baptism. Marilyn hadn't even bothered attempting to make the trip for that most auspicious occasion, but old Denton had flown in from Boston.

Ironic, fifteen years ago, that might have meant something to an astute, introverted teenager. Having some connection, however remote, to another living soul who'd think enough of him to make a trip, to stand in witness? One of the Brothers had stood as his Godfather. One of the nuns had stood as his Godmother. Strangers. Always strangers and stand-in relatives. Having a father would have been different. A novelty.

If his mother's third letter could be believed, McDaniels was, in part, responsible for that seminary sojourn. Must have cost him a bundle to pull that off, getting a non-denominational accepted into that holy fraternity. Kip had spent hours of private instruction, in addition to the required classes. Before the end of his sophomore year, he'd learned enough to be Christened into the Catholic faith, and Denton McDaniels had stood in witness, nearly lost in shadows toward the rear of the church, maybe hoping to be seen and recognized. More likely, hoping to see Marilyn Patterson, but that dear lady had too much on her agenda to be worried about a son's spiritual growth.

Mechanically, Kip navigated the Buick, making a three-point turn at the kitchen dock and following the lane to the highway. Always something had taken precedence—just as this alleged father seemed to hover in the shadows on at least three separate occasions. How many other times had Denton McDaniels stood in the shadows? That funeral was the beginning—that was the day Denton McDaniels had learned that his affair had borne fruit. And five weeks later, Marilyn called him. In desperation?

Chapter 2

Showered, dried, and dressed, Kelly Mulden stood in the small bathroom on the second floor of her parents' house. Looking in the mirror at her reflection, she contemplated having a heart-to-heart chat with the stranger staring back at her. Until a week ago, she'd believed her life was in order. Engaged to a decent enough man—an honest man. He'd treated her well when he was around. He was downstairs right this minute, chatting with her mother and younger brother, not a care in the world for at least another two days. Four days. Christmas vacation. Christmas morning, he would be in the hospital, waking on a cot no doubt, while she would be here, waking in her childhood bed as she had every year. 'Perfect in every way,' she'd told JD, regarding Richard Whitman, but somehow that seemed more like wishful thinking.

Heart to heart. If she married Richard, she'd spend the rest of her life taking second chair to the medical profession. If she spent a single night with Kip, she could spend the rest of her life hoping for a repeat performance. And if she didn't spend a night with Kip, she'd likely spend the rest of her life wondering—*what if*? What would it have been like? What might have been?

Well, at least she answered one question. She wasn't marrying Richard. Whether she returned his ring, now, or after Christmas, remained the only question in her mind. She hadn't lied or fabricated the second thoughts she'd confided in her mother. She'd never survive as a doctor's wife, waiting by hearth and home for her husband to find time for her. And she was dang tired of feeling like her profession was a hobby. Granted, dance wasn't a matter of life and death, but it was her life. She'd spent hours—a lifetime of hours, stretching her muscles to peak endurance, repeating the same steps a thousand times until every move slid into the next. She'd transformed that profession into a business, a relatively successful business. Months ago, Richard had suggested that she should keep her studio after they were married, as if humoring her, condescending to her whim, or granting her permission. She'd need to take time off to bear his children, of course...

The wedding was truly off.

Next question.

Should she throw caution to the wind and truly pursue Kip Patterson? Or should she let the clock run out and wave a fond adieu to the tail feathers of whatever jet carried him away? He wasn't a man willing to make any commitment, and in his current state, he was vulnerable. All too well she recalled holding him in that living room last evening, feeling the grief ripping through him. God, the strength in those arms, the violence. Even in retrospect, her muscles gripped with the memory of him spinning in a perfect dancer's spin. The kick was more of a Karate move, but the grace of that explosion had knocked her for a loop. God, the man could move like lightning! First rage. Then pain. Then total control. He hovered on a fragile edge, a dangerous edge.

And the question of JD remained.

How many times over the past few days had JD warned her to steer clear of his old pal? Too many. Common sense alone told her she should heed her brother's warning. Whatever had brought JD across the states had nothing to do with comforting an old friend in need. He was on assignment involving the State Department. And if she remembered correctly, that branch of government generally investigated organized crime. Racketeering. 'Not a player.' But what did that mean exactly? The State Department obviously thought differently, or her brother, with an extensive background in law enforcement and combat training, wouldn't be in Randall.

What the hell had Kip gotten himself into? And was there any truth about whatever charges they were apparently attempting to bring against him?

In serious reflection, Kelly reviewed every moment she'd spent watching him, and a single moment held, stop-action in her mind—him, standing alongside that limousine out at the cemetery, a black-brimmed hat slung low, gangster-style and tipped at an angle to conceal his face as he spoke to another suited gentleman. He could have stepped right off the silver screen from the scene of an old gangster movie. Cloak and dagger. And she shivered with the memory of last evening when he'd lifted his lashes to catch her sitting across the desk from him.

Annoyed suddenly, Kelly shook off the reflection and focused on her spooked eyes in the mirror. As much as she'd love to dismiss her worries, she too easily imagined Kip Patterson in league with high-class criminals. He was smart. And undoubtedly, wealthy. From his Italian silk suit to his shoes, he'd screamed money. And in a heartbeat, she recalled her visit on Friday afternoon—blue jeans, a baseball cap, stocking feet, and a flannel shirt. Granted, even that flannel hadn't slid off a department store rack, but he'd appeared all too casual ... and *sexy*.

What did gangsters wear to lounge?

"Dang it," she muttered and pulled her gaze from the mirror, turning, leaning at the edge of the sink. Did she truly believe Kip was up to something criminal?

'Setup.'

For a long moment, she stared into the past, recalling the few times she'd seen him and JD together in this house, and the first day she'd seen him sprang readily to the foreground. Her heart had stopped as Max, their golden retriever, had slammed the lanky, blond-haired stranger, pinning him to their front door. That day had become her undoing, and she couldn't even recall what had zapped her heart. The fright in his pale blue eyes? The wide-eyed wonder as JD snagged Max's collar and rescued him from being mauled—by a wet tongue? The tailored black suit ... a tailored three-piece suit. He'd just come from a funeral, Kelly remembered absently. He'd always been coming or going from a funeral over the short duration of his and JD's friendship. And she'd ached for him even then.

Well, she'd been in love. And her memory was slightly skewed by that misty-eyed affliction. No help there. Even Al Capone had been a boy at one point in his life. The man she'd met a week ago in that fancy dining room ... she'd seen him take the hands of those old women and watched as those elders had received swift care to recover their dignity at Kip's command.

And he sent her away last evening. Not for lack of interest. Out of respect for his old friend? Or to keep her out of harm's way? Something happened yesterday evening. She'd heard him send JD to check the security, and JD hadn't come home the previous night.

As if her thoughts materialized him, she heard the footsteps outside the bathroom and launched into motion before fully grasping the reason. Yanking the door open, she stepped into the hall just as JD pushed his old bedroom door inward. "JD?"

Halted, he looked over, and Kelly had seen that heated shine too often recently not to recognize the temper barely restrained behind his hazel eyes. "Morning," he said with a subtle edge.

To hell with burning new bridges. She needed answers, and JD had them. Moving forward, she started, "We need to talk."

"I'm in sort of a hurry, Kell," he said as he pushed into his room, apparently intending to pull the door closed in his wake.

She caught it first, halting the action. Surprise flickered in his eyes; her own held steady. "We need to talk," she repeated, more quietly.

Unreadable, he held her gaze an instant before glancing past her, then nodding, stepping aside to let her enter. "Maybe we do," he conceded in a low voice.

Pushing the door shut behind her, she studied his face momentarily, noting the weariness as well as the tension. He'd combed his hair recently, but his clothes remained disheveled and wrinkled. The flannel was haphazardly tucked under his belt. "I'd like to know what's going on," she began simply.

"As in?"

Nothing easy, she realized, and considered the ramifications. To hell with ramifications. At most, he would be furious with her, and what difference did that make? A tentative trust. He'd always been her favorite big brother, but she hadn't liked him much for quite a while. She was tired of walking on eggs. Holding his gaze, she spoke quietly, keeping her voice just above a whisper, although she doubted anyone could overhear them through the solid oak door. "As in—I know you didn't come here just to comfort an old friend, JD. I'd like to know what Kip's being accused of and why you're here."

If he was surprised, it didn't show. For the second time, Kelly felt as if she looked into the eyes of a stranger, but this one's face was a whole lot more familiar. "Exactly what are you asking me, and who told you Kip's being accused of something?"

No holds barred. "Actually, you did," she answered.

"Excuse me?"

"I overheard you in the den Saturday morning," she said bluntly, and read the first flash of genuine emotion, though it wasn't comforting. He appeared angry. "I heard enough, JD. You're here in some official capacity, and Kip is under investigation by someone. I've never questioned your profession. God knows, you've slipped in and out of here for years."

"What exactly did you hear, Kelly?" he asked in a barely restrained civil tone. "And who else have you told?"

"I haven't told anyone, anything," she admitted quietly. "Not mom or dad. Not Kip," she added and glimpsed enough of his doubt to wonder if he might accuse her of lying. "I heard you mention the State Department and—and that Kip's not a player," she added, and for the briefest instant, she wondered if she knew this brother at all.

Shaking his head, he turned from her and meandered a step as if orienting himself in a strange room. Odd, they were surrounded by children's paraphernalia, from football and baseball pennants on the walls to cartoon characters on the quilted bedspread. Not exactly the atmosphere one might expect for the nature of this discussion, and maybe that detail touched JD as well. He wore a faintly haunted smile when he turned. "You were at the Home last night, Kell. You're telling me you didn't mention this to Kip?"

The accusation was there, masked behind his faint smile. "Assuming you're on the right side of the law, do you really think I'd compromise your position by mentioning it to a man I hardly know?"

Far more critically, JD studied her, and in slow stages, something akin to admiration crept into his eyes. "What were you doing there last night?"

"What you weren't doing, JD. Comforting an old friend," she answered, and belatedly thought about biting her tongue. The soft sarcasm and accusation had filtered through loud and clear, hitting its mark and freezing her brother's tentative acceptance. This was going all wrong. "The fact is, when Kip left here, I had a feeling he was close to the edge. He is hurt. Maybe a lot worse than he wants anyone to realize. He told me he and his mother weren't close, at least not for several years, and maybe that's what's hitting him."

"You were in his private suite last night when we heard that crash?"

"He kicked a wall," she verified.

JD studied her momentarily, and a kink crept into his mustache. "Temper tantrum, huh?"

Somehow, she failed to see the humor, especially with the memory of Kip vibrating, holding back a sob inside his mother's living room. "You know, I was ... I was sort of hoping you were there to help him, JD," she admitted quietly, recalling those overheard words when JD had sounded as if he were defending Kip despite the bitter edge in her brother's voice when speaking on the den phone. "That's one of the reasons I kept my mouth shut, but—"

"Kell, you need to drop this," he interrupted, all traces of humor gone, now.

"You've been warning me to stay away from him, but that's not going to happen," she said bluntly.

"On the contrary," he stated. "That is going to happen. You have a decent fellow downstairs who seems to adore you—"

"I'm not marrying him," she stated, more confidently, now, than two days ago when they'd first chatted in the kitchen downstairs. "I've already made up my mind to return Richard's ring. Whether I do it today or after Christmas remains the only question, and don't even think about blaming Kip for this. The only thing he's guilty of is being an exceptionally good flirt."

"Honey, you don't know the half of that," JD stated with an edge. "You heard him yesterday. Women mean about as much to him as houseplants. And believe me, I have reason to believe that entire discourse. He's not the same little kid we knew—"

"You have the advantage of having known him, JD," Kelly stated. "And about him," she added quietly, watching her brother's stopped pose. "I have the advantage of not giving a damn what he was, or is, for that matter. I happen to like him, and whether you approve or not, if the opportunity presents itself, I intend to get to know him a whole lot better. Now, unless you'd like me to start asking questions elsewhere, why don't you tell me exactly what you do for a living when you're not posing as a Forest Ranger from Colorado?"

"I can't answer you," he said bluntly.

"Bullshit," she stated in soft anger. "What—FBI? CIA? Are you a Federal Marshal or something?"

"Kelly—"

"JD, you can either trust me to keep your confidence, or you can leave me hanging, and I will most definitely try to find the answers on my own," she said smoothly, refusing to consider the impotence of her threat. Well, and maybe it wasn't an impotent threat. She had friends in Philadelphia, beginning with the daughter of a state senator in her student group. Bolstered with the revelation, she held JD's haunted gaze. "I'm not bluffing, JD," she said quietly. "I've been driving myself nuts for two days trying to decide how to approach you with this question without erecting another wall between us. God knows, I love you, brother, but I'm damned tired of walking on eggs with you. A simple question. Are you on a government payroll?"

"Yes," he answered quietly, his wheels spinning behind his steady gaze. "And that's about as much as I will tell—"

"You're investigating Kip," she said bluntly. "Do you believe he's guilty of whatever he's being accused of doing?"

"Kelly—"

"JD, we have two options here," she said quietly. "You can leave me in the dark and go on about your business, in which case, I'll most definitely attempt to help Kip by myself. Or you can tell me what the hell's going on, and I'll have the perspective to make a sensible choice. Either way, I won't repeat whatever you tell me, not even to Kip, without speaking to you first. As much as I know I already like him, you're still my brother, and I won't break your trust."

"Kelly, for your sake and mine, I'm asking you to stay out of this," JD said quietly.

"Why's he under investigation?"

"I wouldn't tell you—"

"Fine," she stated, irritated beyond belief, her gaze heating. "Keep your secrets, JD. But don't ask me to stay out of this. As far as I'm concerned, you're as much of a stranger as he is," she stated. "You both stepped out of my life more than a dozen years ago. And guess what, bro? I'm not eleven years old anymore. In fact, I truly am all grown up, which means I have a choice. If you can't even tell me whether you're here to help him or to arrest him, then I guess I'll just have to trust my instincts to believe he's not guilty of whatever bullshit the government is trying to pin on him. Since you're obviously a member of that government, and that's more fucking important to you than either friends or family, then screw you. I will see Kip again, and I will be in his corner when whatever the hell's going on here hits the fan." Turning, reaching for the door, she managed only to clasp the knob before JD caught her arm.

"Listen to me, damn it," he started.

Spinning on him, she lanced him with her gaze. "I'm listening."

"This isn't a goddamn fairytale, Kelly. Kip Patterson is not Prince Charming, and I don't want you anywhere near him—"

"Are you finished?" she asked.

"No, I'm not finished," he stated crisply, his voice at a lower pitch, his gaze steady. "I didn't come here to burn Kip," he said. "I came here to help him, even though he could be in some pretty deep shit. I don't want to have to worry about you, too, Kelly. Stay away from him and let me do my job."

She considered the words for half a second before asking, "Does he know you're here to help him?"

A flash of anger passed through his eyes. "Doubt he believes it," he stated quietly.

"Does he know you work for the government?"

More annoyed, JD eased his hand away. "Yeah. He knows," he said as he turned, reaching for the buttons of his flannel shirt as he started across the room. His suitcase still rested open on the dresser, half empty, or half full, depending on one's attitude.

Kelly moved with him, reaching the end of the dresser as he sorted through the meager stack of rifled clothes. "Who do you work for, JD? What branch?" she asked and caught his fleeting, annoyed glance. For a moment, she doubted he'd answer.

Sighing, he tugged off his shirt and looked over, the lines of tension more prominent under a sweep of unkept waves. "Look, Kelly, there really isn't a whole lot I'd feel safe telling you for your own good. The fact is, I'm on loan. Something like a sabbatical, you might say."

"You're really not a Forest Ranger," she grasped. "And Kip figured that out sometime yesterday."

"Tell me something," he said quietly, searching her now. "When you were with him, did he say anything about me?"

Considering, she remembered, "He doubted you'd approve of me being there, and he said he valued your friendship." Noting her brother's more critical thought, she asked, "What are you thinking?"

"That he's probably guilty as hell," JD stated simply. "And I really will appreciate it if you stay out of this."

"Guilty of what?" she asked.

"Did he happen to mention his profession?"

"An entrepreneur," she remembered.

"Yeah, he's enterprising as all hell," JD said with a ring of disgust. "Which entails a world of sin, but what exactly he's guilty of remains to be seen."

"You're not telling me anything."

"Because I don't have a helluva lot to tell, Kelly," he stated in irritation. "Being an entrepreneur isn't illegal, and the problem with this joker is all too simple—he's a fucking genius. Even if he's not playing by the books, I doubt he'd leave an open trail to nail his ass."

"Have you considered that he's really not guilty?" she asked, feeling a lot like the dumb partner in a comedy routine. It would help if she knew exactly what she was talking about.

"If I didn't believe that to some remote extent, I wouldn't be here," JD stated as if questioning her foolishness for asking.

"You realize, you're not making a lick of sense, right?" Kelly asked. "Two seconds ago, you decided he was guilty... Oh, never mind. Since we're on the subject, why don't you tell me what he's supposed to have done?"

He collected his thoughts, looking at her without the abstract gaze. "All right, you want it straight?" he asked, apparently reaching a decision. "Someone has the hair-brained idea that he's embezzling from the Home. For the obvious reason, that's a stupid idea, seeing as how he stands to inherit Whistlebrook. The catch comes in here—the Home is on a steady decline. Now, the big problem. The decline appears natural. No proof of tampering. Next, a bigger problem. I'm here."

That final statement should make sense, but Kelly failed to make the leap. "Why, uhm... why exactly is your presence a problem?"

"I met Kip fifteen years ago and hung out with him for a little over a month," he said bluntly, holding her gaze. "Now, less than twenty-four hours after his mother passed away, somebody already knew enough about Kip Patterson to make a phone call and have me pulled off another assignment. Because they knew he and I were friends way back when. And they had the clout to manage that. So, the question is this. What the fuck am I missing?"

"I'm really not getting this," Kelly admitted quietly.

"That's making two of us, honey," JD stated irritably. "I was about ninety-nine percent sure that Kip pulled the strings to bring me here. Why, I hadn't quite worked out. Now, though, I'm not sure that's true, and that makes me a whole lot more nervous."

"What uhm...? What did you mean when you said he's not a player? What kind of player?"

"I really should have been a helluva lot more careful on that phone," he said offhandedly and sighed, shaking his head. "Drugs," he stated simply and held her gaze. "And that part is bogus. Kip's loaded. Granted, he travels in some interesting circles, but he's not part of any drug cartel. Having said that much, I'd have to admit, I'd know if he was. I mentioned I'm on loan. I didn't mention that whoever pulled me into this probably suckered my bosses into believing Kip's a high-rolling player in the trade."

"Damn," she said abruptly, looking at her brother in a whole new light. "You're DEA."

"You, sister, are way too quick on the uptake," he said grimly. "And I hope the hell you meant what you said about keeping my confidence."

"Oh-my-god," she muttered, realizing abruptly that her brother had chosen one extremely hazardous career. "Undercover."

A faintly amused glint sparked his eyes. He smirked and shrugged.

"You couldn't be something simple like the CIA, huh?"

"Simple," he mused.

Leaning a little more heavily against the dresser, Kelly gazed at this fellow, realizing she honestly didn't know him very well, and what was worse, none of them did. But it made sense. All the missed birthday parties, anniversaries, and graduations. In his profession, he couldn't simply take a day off or fly home for the holidays. If he worked undercover, he couldn't risk even making phone calls or sending cards. Shaking her head, she panned her gaze over the bedroom where he'd spent very little time, and suddenly, she felt like crying again.

His hand came to rest on her shoulder, his voice quiet. "Hey?"

She blinked the sting away and looked into his far more compelling gaze, remembering the boy, recognizing the nobility of the man. "I feel like I owe you a million apologies, JD," she said quietly. "I haven't been the most forgiving soul."

"You don't owe me anything, Kell. Just don't keep hating me, and we'll call it square."

"I don't hate you."

"Hell, I hate myself sometimes," he said with a smirk, but his eyes clouded as he scanned the room. "I forgot what it was like to come home."

Impulsively, Kelly turned and wrapped her arms about his shoulders, drawing him into an embrace as she swallowed a lump. "God, I have missed you," she uttered as his arms came about her, returning the fold.

"Back at ya, sis."

Chapter 3

Lost in thought, Kip turned between the stone pillars of Misty Haven Cemetery and followed the wet sheen of gray pavement ascending the slope. Only after he rolled to a stop near the level plateau, did he realize—Mr. Calfactor was to be buried at St. Matthew's Cemetery, at least a twenty-minute drive.

Uttering a curse, Kip scanned the vacant hillside. Appreciating the heat blowing from the dashboard vents, he watched the sway of barren branches overhead. Less than a week ago, he'd stood half freezing on this blustery hillside, listening to a Catholic priest—Fr. Jorden—touting Marilyn Patterson's accomplishments and wishing her a fond adieu. Blowing snow, then; dark clouds billowed across the sky, now. More like rain clouds than snow, and wouldn't that just figure? At 40 degrees, it would probably rain and then turn to ice later. A warm-weather driver's worst nightmare. Sleet.

Even driving. Even that most natural of all rights of manhood had been delayed and nearly denied him. And he suffered because of it. Then Marilyn wondered why he never visited at Christmas? He'd almost killed Marsh Baxel when the fellow had tried teaching him to drive on *dry* pavement. While waiting for the tow truck to pull Marsh's Vette out of a ditch, Marsh had vowed to hire an instructor with nerves of steel and offered to pick up the tab, provided Kip never asked him to ride with him when he acquired his license.

Marilyn was right in that letter. He blamed her for a long list of things. She should have taught him to drive or at least authorized the seminarians to teach him. No, huh uh. That would have been too easy. She liked leaving him trapped, where she could visit at her convenience, her discretion. And Fr. Benedict had accused him of stealing Brother Nathaniel's old Chevy and dipping it into the sacred font at the foot of St. Joseph's shrine. They'd found it outside the friary doors, nose first in the font, as if he could have driven across the compound. Fat chance! But he'd spent a month washing and waxing their fleet of holy chariots—as penance for a crime he'd never committed.

His vacant gaze caught and held on the new stone and patch of uneven snow-dusted soil. Two ruby-glass perpetual candles stood sentinel-like in front of the shiny marble. Several plastic flower arrangements danced in the wisps of wind that lifted loose snow and sent mini funnel clouds spinning past the monument.

Unconsciously, Kip twisted the ignition key, ignoring the slight resistance between his icy thumb and forefinger, as he lifted his foot off the brake pedal and groped for the door handle. Slipping from behind the wheel as the engine silenced, he stepped into the wind and his sole skidded on a patch of icy pavement. He caught his balance on the door, cursing the snow and the cold wind that swept from the valley and dropped the temperature several degrees despite the sunlight pouring between barren branches. He should have remembered how cold this hillside could get at this time of year. January would be worse—more bitter. God knows, he'd shivered through enough funerals, despite a pair of thermal underwear beneath his suit slacks on enough blustery mornings to judge the climate here. On a funeral day, the caretakers salted the paved lanes several times. He should have remembered that detail when passing between the pillars onto the snowy lane. He might have realized he'd reached the wrong cemetery sooner.

Pulling his coat flaps together, already shivering against the wind battering his pant legs, Kip fumbled the buttons together as he tramped into the crusted snow. The footprints had iced over, forming uneven ridges on the downslope. He stepped into the unmarked snow, sinking his hands into his pockets.

Already shivering, he reached the headstone marking the new grave.

MOTHER

Marilyn Patty Patterson

July 5, 1922 -

Kip made a mental note to call Fitzpatrick and ensure that he consigned a mason to fill in the second set of numbers.

His focus shifted to the aged stone alongside the new marble. The stone had weathered like all others in this ancient cemetery, turned black and slung low, sinking into the earth. Wind had torn the snowcap, leaving chunks of ice in the pitted granite. Snow mounded, covering the dates near the ground, but the words were visible at the top.

Beloved Father

Ronald Elijah Patterson.

For thirty years, Kip had believed himself to be the son of an octogenarian. He'd imagined his father in every ancient face within the Home, and he'd forever feared questioning the improbability.

A face swam from the black depths of his subconscious, freezing him more completely than a winter blast. Thin and long in the face, lines like volcanic cracks in her jaundiced skin. Her skeletal fingers had locked in vice grips on his pudgy arms, digging into his muscles and sending fire into his shoulders. 'You wicked little morning child!'

With an uncollected back-step and shudder, Kip shook Mrs. Brigg's echoing screech from his mind, and jolted at a very real, inhuman screech. Goose bumps ignited at the nape of his neck as his attention spun.

In a half turn, he froze, watching and hearing the continued squeal as a stone cross projectile gouged the rented Regal's rear fender. By reflex, Kip started a step and a stride, sliding on his smooth soles. Way too late. As if an angry spirit rested behind the steering wheel, the Buick broke from the mason-cross arm and lurched toward the second row of stones descending the slope. In a shattered second, Kip understood defeat. Sliding and catching himself from a fall, he watched as the car rode one wheel up a slanted headstone and crunched its rocker panel with a violent scream, metal folding. Now, it would stop. Surely it... *Ohhh.* "Shit."

Where freewheeling momentum failed, gravity and a steeper slope joined forces. The rocker panel continued its piercing scream, folding as three wheels dragged it across the squat stone. The rear driver's side wheel rolled up the stone and remained airborne for a few seconds as the red beast reared sideways.

The moment of no return. With a vengeance, the Buick plunged, bounced, and leaped across a virgin white runway, then nose-dived between two immense black stone family monuments.

In slow motion, Kip gauged the car's direction. Undoubtedly, it intended to reach the tree line an acre below. Several considerable stones dotted the hillside, and one immense, ornate St. John stood boldly in the face of disaster. Another squeal of metal bending against stone echoed on the wind, and for an instant, the Regal appeared to halt. No such luck. The car bounced back on its heels and plunged forward with renewed vigor. A swell of steam burst from the front end as granite assaulted the undercarriage.

Crouched, Kip watched the rear end buck over a smaller desecrated cross as the front grill lunged toward St. John. "No!"

Yes, he realized an instant later. A corner of the front bumper slammed into the saint's pedestal stone base at an angle, and in slow motion, the car lifted and twisted. Dropping to both knees, Kip watched the undercarriage flash angry silver streaks as momentum tipped it up and over. St. John vanished momentarily within a cloud of steam. Glass shattered. Window and doorjamb snapped with screams, and the *god-damned-Buick* broke free of St. John. Taking a chunk of masonry arm, the car continued down the slope on its smashed hood. Sliding, spinning, bouncing off and over several more stones, it reached the open slope and sledded unhindered to land with a dying battle crunch against tree trunks and tangled vines.

Billows of steam flowed through barren branches, caught the breeze, and disintegrated across the white slope. A faint hiss carried on the breeze, and for an instant, Kip thought he heard a near-human, inhuman laugh.

In several slow-moving seconds, Kip backtracked the visible path of the rental's descent. Tire tracks marred the snow where the momentous journey had begun, casually slipping off the icy lane. In a flash of memory, Kip recalled merely lifting his foot off the brake and turning off the ignition while stepping from the car. He hadn't waited for that tiny click of a steering wheel lock or engaged an emergency brake. The damn keys were probably still in the ignition. Or lying on the ceiling, by now.

"Goddamn it," he uttered into the wind and again turned to survey the steaming ruins. A four-mile walk to Whistlebrook, where he would need to call a tow truck equipped with several hundred feet of cable. Kip's gaze staggered over a half dozen destroyed monuments, tallying the damage and obvious distress of loved ones who would need to be notified when he replaced or repaired their family monuments and headstones.

"You win, Marsh," he uttered as he pushed off his knees and onto his feet. "I'm hiring a limo and driver first thing in the morning."

With a cursory glance at his mother's headstone, Kip turned and started walking up the slippery grade toward the lane. *Conspiracy, huh? What was that move?* His mother capitalizing on his eccentricity, enlisting an army of spirits and striking from the grave, now, too? Bad enough, she'd been talking to him in those goddamn letters from the grave.

Obviously, he'd pissed her off by holding her responsible for his poor driving skills.

Shaking his head, he groped in his coat pockets and found his cigarettes as he reached the slick pavement. Wind whispered through squat hedges and stones, scraping branches overhead, and again, he heard a soft, ethereal laugh. Turning his back to the wind, he cupped a flame under the brim of his hat and managed to light a cigarette. Cold air and cigarette smoke stung his throat; cold wind snapped at his fingers; his slick-soled shoes—designed for walking into dinner parties or funeral homes—skidded unmercifully on the wind-frozen pavement. The Buick had been a decent car. Its tires had certainly held the pavement on the upward climb better than his shoes, and its descent had undoubtedly been an impressive display of perseverance.

By the time he reached the stone entrance and started along the gravel edge, his shoes sinking in road-ash and slush, Kip decided to call Edna from the first house on the route. A little stone French design, he remembered. Unfortunately, he hadn't noticed a 'For Sale' sign tilted on its axis in the front lawn. With a glance at the unmarked driveway and desolate, blind-covered windows, Kip continued walking. Only a few cars passed, and he imagined the drivers' sick sense of humor as wet splatters speckled his pant legs.

Haunting visions swam to the surface of his memory. Walking to and from school. Running, not walking, he corrected silently. When he reached an age to avoid the bus odyssey, he'd become a runner, running the two miles to Randall Middle School, then high school, running home every afternoon. A hard rain or a bitter wind were welcome companions against the alternative of being tripped or shoved or laughed at while trying to reach an empty seat. He'd lost count of how many of his books sailed from bus windows or into mud puddles, or how many silent tears he'd shed in the privacy of his collage-covered hideaway.

A morning—mourning child—a morbid child.

The driveway was plowed; the walk shoveled. Stomping ice from his shoes, Kip walked to the split-level's porch entrance and breathed a sigh of relief at the sound of voices, television voices, coming through the picture window. In a few words, he explained his need for a telephone to a stout woman in a bright red housecoat, reflective of the season.

Repeatedly, she pulled at her uncombed hair and smiled nervously as she invited him into the landing, eventually letting him ascend the steps to a modest living room where her phone stood on an end table.

An immense fir tree stood in the center of the picture window. Tinsel and popcorn strands clashed beautifully on the long-needle pine. A fireplace mantle held four furry red stockings with children's names scripted in glitter.

Christmas—two days from now—Kip considered while listening to the sensuous voice in his ear. Mechanically, he offered Mrs. Feeney's extension. For years, that switchboard voice transferred his calls, and it occurred to him that he'd never seen the woman's face or lent her a thought before Morgan's comment several days earlier. Like so many other aspects of his Home, the operator remained just another fixture he either blindly accepted or ignored. Like old Mr. Gerald, the slightly maudlin gardener who'd once given him a baseball cap from Yankee Stadium—

"I'm sorry. Mrs. Feeney doesn't seem to be in now. Would you care to leave a message?"

"Try the kitchen extension if you will."

"One moment, please."

—Or old Mr. Beers, who'd taken care of the maintenance for years before a younger man, Simon something, had taken over five years ago. So many people. So many new faces.

"Kitchen. What can we do for you?"

Another stranger? Not a stranger! "Jason?" *Jason King. The home's first King.*

"Speaking," the young voice hesitated.

"Why aren't you in school?"

"Uhhh, it's uh...Christmas vacation."

"Oh." *Shit!* "Is Mrs. Feeney there?"

"Uhhh, no," Jason answered hesitantly, possibly starting to recognize the voice. "She hasn't been in yet today."

The red-robed woman danced nervously in the center of her splendid living room, smiling as she puffed her mussed brown curls.

"Do you have a car?"

"I ... a pickup."

"With you?"

"Sure—"

"Good. You're being temporarily promoted. Get your coat, your keys, and get in your pickup. Make a left at the main entrance and keep driving until you see me. If you reach Maple Haven, turn around and come back. You'll have missed me. And do *not* tell anyone why you're leaving or where you're going. Understood?"

"Got it," Jason said with a hint of excitement in his young voice. "See you in a few minutes."

Amused, Kip began lowering the receiver. Hearing the clatter and a second click, he halted the receiver and lifted it to his ear. *Silence. Shit. Paranoia.* Dropping the receiver into its cradle, he spotted the woman's nervous, darting eyes. "Thank you immensely, luv," he commented and turned to the steps.

"Do you want a cup of coffee—or hot tea—while you wait?" she stammered.

"Thank you, no," he said as he continued down the brief staircase, preoccupied as he stepped into the cold. He walked as far as the mailbox, where he cupped a flame to a cigarette and stood, watching cars pass while looking into abstracts. Edna Feeney—not in the kitchen? Not in her room? Shit, she could be anywhere. He should have just paged her, but this would work out just as well. No sense worrying her.

Not quite five minutes passed before Kip spotted a pickup slowing and a turn signal igniting. On the surface, the 1965 Chevy lacked appeal. Still, the engine rumbled a healthy sound, and somehow, the vehicle matched the rough edges of its driver, who wore his curiosity within a strained sobriety. When the truck stopped, Kip strode around to the passenger door, not surprised when the door squealed and dropped nearly an inch as he pulled it open.

"I'm just starting on the body work," Jason said by way of an apology, his curiosity on hold to a flash of embarrassment.

The interior was clean; the gauges and dashboard were original. Kip started pulling the door shut, needing both hands at Jason's suggestion to "lift and pull." Amused, Kip caught the lively, brown eyes. "Home, James," Kip commented and noted King's increased amusement and bewilderment.

"Did uh—" He paused while twisting to check the highway, backing out. Glancing at Kip, he continued, "Did you have car trouble? I mean, do you need a tow or something?"

"Yes, on both counts," Kip answered.

"I have some chains in the back if we have to pull it off the road or something."

"Oh, it's certainly far enough off the road," Kip answered and caught a flash of Jason's glance as he shifted gears. "Good driver, are you?"

"My dad would say, no," he mused. "But I've never even dinged a bumper."

"Are you bragging?" Kip asked.

"Uhhh … no. Well… yeah, maybe," Jason huffed with a wiry glance, his profile sobered. His glance returned, concerned, "You uh… Did you wreck? I mean, are you okay?"

"Fine. Unfortunately, I can't say the same about my rental, which serves it right for leaving me stranded."

"Uh, do, uh … did you…?" Jason hesitated, collecting his thoughts before glancing over with a sober, reluctant smirk. "You didn't just leave the scene of an accident, did you? I mean, did you call the cops or anything?"

"Yes, technically, and no," Kip answered, enjoying King's growing curiosity and building concern. "Neither will be a problem. The Buick can do no more harm where it is, unless it decides to detonate, which, I'd imagine, I'd have heard by now if that were its ultimate plan."

"Where the heck is it?" Jason asked as he slowed down, shifting gears, approaching Whistlebrook's main gate.

"If you truly must know, it ran over St. John and it's currently resting on its hood in peace—several pieces, in fact. And if not for the trees, it would be swimming halfway to the Ohio River by now. So, tell me, are you interested in being my chauffeur today?"

"Uhhh—" He pulled through the pillars, glancing over. "I could probably borrow my dad's LeBaron."

"This is fine," Kip said simply. "Drive around back."

Chapter 4

Leaving Jason in the kitchen to wait, Kip returned to the private rooms, not surprised to find the dancers still on the stands. Automated, he changed into dry shoes, jeans, and a sweater before moving about the room, collecting his discarded clothes and personal items. Carefully, he lifted the Wallendorf prima donna from her tomb, swathed her in one of his shirts, and laid her in the center of his larger suitcase. Bringing his wallet from his pocket, he brought out a laminated card and, in a few swipes, unlocked his mother's bedroom door. Nothing had been moved or touched as if he expected otherwise. The curtain hung haphazardly over the wrecked closet just as he'd left it last evening.

Without the burden of nostalgia, and slightly amused at his apparent destruction, he brought the Family Album from the top shelf of the closet and, on impulse, snatched the silver-framed picture of Maria Van Alt on his way out. Maria Van Alt, his mother, poised magnificently in a ballet stance to mimic the statue. Both the album and photo he tucked into his suitcase, wedging the album at the bottom so it wouldn't be affected by any careless luggage handlers. On impulse, he moved into his childhood refuge, ignoring a tug of memories. Mulden hadn't taken the hats either, by no surprise. JD hadn't returned to renew childhood bonds. Lifting two hats from the closet, Kip returned to the living room, pulled his bags together, donned the English gentleman's cap, and moved his belongings into the hall, leaving the second hat lying on his coat.

Carolyn's telephone voice echoed in an undertow of at least two hammering typewriters; the sounds reached him before he entered the office. The tension in Carolyn's swift gaze and her abruptly curt tone as she dismissed the caller alarmed him as he approached her desk.

Already lifting a small stack of messages, she tried forcing a smile. "I didn't expect you back so soon, but I'm sure glad to see you, hon. This phone's been ringing off the hook—"

"Have you seen Mrs. Feeney?" he asked.

Her thought shifted at light speed. "No, actually, I haven't. I left a message in the kitchen. She hasn't answered my call. I was going to have her paged—"

"Do it, and when you find her, tell her I'll see her at the attorney's office." He accepted the notes, thumbing them sideways and recording the names. M.B. again. Morgan again. Fr. Jordan had called. Mr. Fitzpatrick had called. John Madison, Mark Frances, and several other familiar names, whom he could contact from California.

"Bill hasn't returned yet," Carolyn said lightly. "You could use the office—" She seemed to remember the 'new administration' abruptly and smiled as she finished, "To answer them."

He might answer one or two, but not from Whistlebrook. Glancing at the notes, Kip snared Carolyn's gaze. "You're coming to the reading, aren't you?"

"I'll be there, hon."

"See you then," he commented and turned, catching a fleeting glance of Angie and tossing her a wink before striding out. At least that was one mystery he wouldn't need to solve; he couldn't care less why he scared the devil out of that woman—or a half dozen others.

As he strode down the hall, he suffered a nagging twinge and thought of Mr. Louten, the Parkinson' s-afflicted fellow who'd inadvertently started the chaos to ensue over the past two days. He should have remembered how the aged often suffered paranoia. Not unlike his mother, whose blasted letters had become a testament to her decline. He'd nearly destroyed the blasted Home over her conspiracy theories and delusions. Three days. She'd sent him on a three-day blitz and almost sent him off the edge, believing that the residents were all in danger. Murder, for god's sake. She'd alluded to murder, and he'd nearly bought into it after his Saturday excursion in the Spring Chicken ward.

He'd seen Mr. Calfactor on the west wing and identified the dark gray shroud closing about that bed, stretching over the quilt like floating gauze. The fellow was dying. *Peacefully*. But Elsa Taylor? The shroud had hovered about her, but not to the color of coal, more like ash—

No. He was not buying into that conspiracy bullshit again. One meltdown was enough to last a lifetime.

No repeat performance, thank you very much, mother.

Dismissing his thought to visit the lounge and ultimately Louten and his cohorts, Kip yanked on his coat and tugged the garment bag strap over his shoulder. If he never saw another forbidding aura, it might be too soon, and there was no need for any parting amenities. The old regime was gone. He knew none of the present regime well enough to feel remorse at parting, and he certainly didn't owe them anything, least of all a farewell.

Odd, how that thought persisted, following—chasing him through the hall and into the kitchen—as if he were leaving unfinished business. Barely sparing a word for Edna's assistant, Kip forfeited his larger case to Jason's proffered hand and handed him the spare hat—a pilot's hat, rather than a chauffeur's cap. In a momentary lapse, Kip stood at the door, scanning the kitchen of his childhood. An immense exhaust fan above the stove had once roared, drowning out the sounds of banging doors, clanging pans, and shouted orders.

"Where to?" Jason asked when they were both seated in the cab.

"The restaurant of your choice," Kip commented absently as he scanned the sloping lawns. With the rising temperatures, the landscape melted into a wet sheen, as if a glossy veneer had swelled over his childhood.

Once and for all, he'd put Whistlebrook behind him, along with all the painful memories, the faces of his childhood—the Family Album. As the truck sped beneath barren branches, melted splatters dropped on the windshield, and in his mind, Kip heard the plop and snap, remembering the walks—and runs—down the long driveway, remembering the sound of raindrops hitting the brims of his hats. Always hats.

The impressions of his youth had haunted him in blinding flashes, always to be pushed aside. In California, in the private forest scents of his terrarium, he'd let himself wander through his subconscious images one last time before tucking Whistlebrook into the Family Album within his mind. Perhaps then, he'd reach the inner peace, forever evading him. Perhaps then, he could find a house to call home and stop living a nomad's life. In Ireland, possibly. But then, with Catholicism wrapped like an albatross around his neck, he might be better off in a more neutral setting. Too well, he knew the fanaticism of the PLO, and a man of financial means could too easily become a marked man.

Switzerland—neutral territory. *Snow.*

Bermuda—*the Devil's Triangle.*

Puerto Rico—*militia.*

Australia! Australia, with its mountains and shores, its climates ranging from winter winds to tropical heat. A land overflowing with opportunity.

***

Preoccupied, Kelly strode from her room, catching the sound of shower water as she passed the bathroom door. Doubtful that her brother would stick around too long. He'd admitted his intention to contact Kip, and apparently, JD remained in contact with someone who knew where to find him. Briefly, JD mentioned 'Prince Charming' throwing him out of the

Home. If the flicker of amusement she'd witnessed in her brother's eyes was any indication, he was nearly as amused as he was annoyed with his old pal's reaction. But in the next moment, JD had sobered to mention that if he found evidence to suggest Kip was running some illicit scam, he wouldn't hesitate to take appropriate action.

Could she really remain on the sidelines? Could she, as she'd told JD, steer clear of this entire ordeal until her brother either confirmed or cleared Kip of guilt? The problem, as JD had attested, was the absence of evidence; however, someone had pulled strings to initiate this investigation. Kip had made some enemies, and undoubtedly, her brother hadn't entirely confided in her. The basics remained obvious, though; JD was worried.

"I thought maybe you went back to bed, darling," Richard said as he swept off a kitchen chair, stepping into her path.

Before she even glanced at her mother or younger brother, Richard's arms swallowed her in an embrace. His head ducked to capture her lips, blurring the edges of her vision with his dark, neatly cropped hair. Cookies. She smelled cookies baking, belatedly recalling her mother's mention of needing help baking them. God! Was she honestly thinking about baking cookies while locking lips with the man she'd agreed to marry? Weird. Very weird, this epiphany. If this were Kip, with his wild blond waves ... *stop it!*

Retracting from the kiss, Kelly looked into Richard's heated eyes, and she suddenly felt awful. And just a little guilty. She'd kissed Kip last night, and she most assuredly would have done a lot more if he hadn't chosen that last moment to become chivalrous. Protecting her virtue, undoubtedly, but she'd have forfeited that commodity in a heartbeat, and she'd found Richard, already asleep on the living room couch, when she'd returned. He awoke long enough for her to pull out the foldaway couch and make his bed, not even asking where she'd gone. Did he trust her? Or was he so sure of himself? And therein lay another odd thought.

Ever since she'd agreed to wear his ring—after the fourth or fifth time he asked—he'd behaved as if he were the only person in her life. He never asked about her instructors or students. And on those rare occasions when she shared an anecdote from a particularly entertaining day, he listened as if indulging a child. Or worse, he made some offhanded comment as if preoccupied, not unlike when she'd mentioned JD's arrival on the phone a few days ago. He'd surely known how much JD's arrival had meant to her.

'Oh, that's nice.' Indulgent. Preoccupied. Not truly interested.

Last night, the instant the long lashes lifted off his gray eyes, Kip's focus had never wavered despite the plethora of thoughts haunting him.

Richard still held her, his arms linked at the small of her back, his head tipped, and a smirk planted on his lips. "I think you're even more beautiful today than you were yesterday, darling," he said with a catty smile.

Clueless, she realized absently. She stood, looking up into his soft blue eyes, reading the heat there, thinking about another man, and Richard was clueless. She didn't feel guilty at this moment. Instead, she stood poised on the verge of anger and annoyance, as much by the trapped pose as by her mother and brother in witness. A practiced move, this big romantic display—perhaps for her family's benefit, although he'd trapped her like this alone in her apartment occasionally. Especially when she had something else on her mind, as if he couldn't bear sharing her attention. Once, not long ago, he'd nearly barred her departure and caused her to open her studio late because he had the morning off.

So, what was this game, now? A show for her family? Or worse, his way of invading and claiming her every thought with the sole purpose of becoming her one and only focus? And why did she suddenly feel used? Rather than flattered by this blatant display of affection?

"I need a cup of coffee," she decided abruptly and skimmed her hands off his shoulders, where she'd mechanically rested her arms. A reflexive response. A programmed response to indulge him when he wanted a hug or kiss. Sidestepping, she glimpsed her brother at the table, not entirely amused by his rolling eyes and puckered lips. Mike the clown. Shaking her head, she moved to the counter, glimpsing her mother's more critical glance. Kelly could almost hear Patty asking, 'How much longer before you talk to Richard?' Patty didn't need to ask where Kelly had gone the previous evening, but if her mother held her to account, nothing showed in her eyes then, or now.

In an odd moment, Kelly realized neither of her parents was altogether fond of Richard. They accepted him and tolerated him for her sake. Richard had lost points months ago when he showed up late for the dinner Kelly had planned for her parents to meet him, and she'd made excuses for him, although he admitted to merely falling asleep. 'He's been on call for a few days,' she remembered telling them, right after waking him with a phone call. What she had failed to mention, but had grasped within seconds of speaking to him, was that he'd forgotten the dinner plan despite her reminding him of her parents' arrival several times. To Richard's credit, he apologized a million times—

Afterward. After her parents had left.

That evening, after he'd trounced into the apartment, sitting down to a cold dinner, he'd offered only an apology for being late and making his excuse to extrapolate on a horrific workload over the past five days. Wisely, he hadn't mentioned forgetting the dinner engagement altogether, and he might not have mentioned it afterward, if Kelly hadn't called him on that tiny detail. Oh, and he offered his excuse then, pouting with a sheepish smile while elaborating on his exhaustion during each of her half dozen reminders. She'd nearly returned his ring that evening. In fact, she'd removed it two seconds after bidding her parents a safe drive, but he'd made her feel guilty for being mad, for not being more understanding. After all, he couldn't help it if his profession demanded his undivided attention. How did she expect him to remember something like a dinner engagement when he rushed from one emergency to another?

Oh, so reasonable, and she'd fallen for it after a few tears—on his part—and a beseeching claim that he'd forget the medical profession and become a carpenter or something less demanding, if only she would marry him.

Damn, what a ditz, Kelly nearly muttered aloud and shook herself from the distraction barely in time to accept the bowl of cookie dough her mother thrust in her direction. Cookies. God. Belatedly, Kelly realized she'd been standing for several seconds, merely gazing through the kitchen window into the overcast sky above the backyard ... a steel gray, like the color of a particular pair of stunning eyes—

"Make yourself useful, dear," Patty said offhandedly. "Fill the next tray, will you?"

With a quivering smile, Kelly recovered, "I take it you weren't kidding about baking today?"

"You did say you intended to help," Patty confirmed with a shrug.

At a glance, Kelly identified the nutty white dough for butterballs, JD's all-time favorite Christmas cookie. Her brother could wipe out an entire batch in one sitting as a kid. No wonder her mother had started with these.

"Before I forget, hon," Patty said as she poured powdered sugar into another bowl. "Bryce called last night after they got home." As much as her mother tried, she couldn't quite succeed in sounding lighthearted as she continued, "He and Shelly made dinner reservations for this evening. They want to take us all out."

A belated engagement dinner, Kelly realized and glanced over, reading the confirmation and distraction in her mother's faintly troubled eyes. Undoubtedly, Patty had attempted to counter that invitation for the obvious reasons, but she couldn't have declined without setting off a riot of alarms in the Mulden clan. "Where are we going?"

"Le Chateau," she answered with a hint of wiry Irish humor.

The fanciest blasted restaurant in Randall, if not within thirty miles. Naturally, her brother chose an extravagant place to celebrate his only sister's engagement. The fact that she hadn't even begun making wedding plans should have told her more than she cared to know. Only halfheartedly, she'd called a caterer and two banquet venues, asking generic questions. But despite Richard's occasional persistence, she hadn't even settled on invitations or made a date with a parish priest, much less decided on a hall. Heck, she hadn't even decided whether she wanted to get married in Randall or Philadelphia, or in the church where Richard was baptized, a couple of miles from his parents' house in South Carolina. Well, to be honest, she hadn't even truly considered getting married in Georgia. She'd met Richard's parents exactly once—at a dinner he hadn't forgotten to attend—in a restaurant near his hospital.

Somewhat violently, Kelly rolled the wad of dough into a small ball between her palms and slapped it onto the tray on the counter. She had three more in place before she noted the velocity had flattened the neat little balls, making them look more like sugar cookies. By no surprise, she caught her mother lifting one and watched her roll it between her palms, reshaping the dough into a ball. Lifting her gaze to find her mother's lifted brow and bemused smile, Kelly shook her head, likewise amused, idling, "Butterballs, huh?"

"The operative word is 'ball,' dear," Patty mused.

Richard chose that moment to step behind Kelly and grasp her hips. For a heartbeat second, Kelly remembered Kip's hands, skillful hands, drawing her against his long, solid length. Somehow, Richard's touch and his head lurching over her shoulder failed to provide the same effect. "What can I do to help, darling?"

Go back to Philadelphia, she nearly spoke aloud and bit her tongue, looking up sideways as she reached for another wad of dough. "If you really want to help, you can start by washing your hands."

Rising from the table, where he'd undoubtedly rested to sample the dough, Jimmy commented, "She's given you a way out, Rich, and if you know what's good for you, you'll take it and get while the getting's good."

"Where do you think you're going, James?" Patty asked in a mocked tone of authority.

"I just remembered, Billy wanted me to call this morning."

"Brat," Kelly stated a half second before JD came through the kitchen archway, appearing far more collected and awake. Their gazes connected a second before his focus dipped like a laser beam to the dough in her hands. A flicker of a smile quivered his bearded lips, and for that tiny reminder of the past, Kelly was oddly relieved. He was home. Perhaps, truly home for the first time in years. Amused, she watched him gravitate toward the end of the table and snatch three of the still-warm balls. "Those aren't ready yet," she stated.

"So, you say," he mused and popped one of the balls in his mouth, his gaze darting to scan the entire kitchen, not omitting Richard already at the sink, washing his hands. Unreadable, his gaze skipped over Richard and landed on their mother with a wink.

"Hey, JD, if you don't have any plans, Pete and I are probably going up to the mall this afternoon. You could come along," Mike offered, hopefully.

"Couple errands I have to run," JD said offhandedly.

He had to find Kip, Kelly grasped, torn between several thoughts even as she witnessed the disappointment in Mike's eyes.

"Yeah, maybe tomorrow, then, huh?" Mike said and strode from the kitchen, reacting like all Mulden males, copping an attitude to cover his hurt.

With an entirely new perspective, Kelly realized her older brother wasn't nearly as insensitive or immune as he always appeared. She glimpsed the flash of sorrow in his hazel eyes, and the regret was still visible when he glanced in her direction. She understood. God, in heaven, she understood at last why JD kept his distance here, and she had a funny feeling that he was having a lot of second thoughts about his chosen profession.

Like a perfect idiot, oblivious of the tension spiraling in the room, Richard arrived at her side, presenting his hands as if he'd just scrubbed for surgery. "Scrubbed and ready," he said with a wry smile.

At any other time, she might have found his antics amusing, but too many thoughts crowded her mind. Handing him a wad of dough, she collected some of her own and demonstrated the fine art of rolling dough, setting it more carefully on the pan. An instant later, the doughball disappeared under a quick, clever hand, and she did find that amusing as she caught her brother's feigned innocent smile. "Now, that one really isn't done yet," she stated.

"So, you say," he said and popped the raw dough in his mouth with an arrogant smirk and wink. Looking over Richard's shoulder, he commented, "Keep up the good work, doc."

Undoubtedly in heaven, Patty mused, "You could wash your hands too, dear."

"Gees, ma, I would, but the chances of one of those trays actually making it into the oven are about zip to none," he said and picked up an abandoned coffee cup from the back of the sink, sidling to the coffeepot. "I think I'll just get my coffee and make good my escape."

Not before swiping several more cookies off the end of the table, Kelly noted and shook her head, smiling when she caught him winking again before he strode out. If she wasn't absolutely sure this entire ordeal was a deliberate ploy to appear relaxed, she might be far more amused. Theatrics. She'd become privy to a remarkably fine-tuned talent, which accounted for her brother's success as well as his safety in any number of situations. That last wink had carried just a touch of conspiracy.

He'd promised they'd talk this evening, promised to confide in her as soon as he knew one way or another about Kip's situation. Marilyn Patterson's Will would be read this afternoon, and if JD was right, the shit would hit the fan sometime shortly thereafter. Unless Kip left town in advance.

Kip wasn't going to call her. He hadn't promised, knowing he wouldn't follow through.

Rolling yet another wad of dough in absent motion, Kelly wondered if she should consider that a good sign or a bad one. Either way, she would lose. At some point in the very near future, Kip Patterson would board a plane, and the chances of ever seeing him again were extremely thin. Just the thought of letting these moments slip through her fingers wrenched her heart. She wanted to go to him. The same emotion that had set her into motion a week ago tugged at her now.

God, the choice. To run and find the only man who'd ever truly turned her head and slammed her heart? Or to betray the promise she'd made to her brother to steer clear until the situation was resolved?

Merry-freaking-Christmas, she nearly uttered aloud.

"You went to see him last night, didn't you?" Richard interrupted quietly.

Distracted, Kelly looked over, abruptly more attuned to the hint of temper in his eyes, though he wore one of his more woebegone smiles. A poor-me smile.

"That fellow, Kip, I mean," Richard said quietly as he tortured a ball of dough in his soft hands.

"Yes," she answered bluntly, honestly, half expecting to face outrage or jealousy. Her gaze steady, she saw something else altogether. Something akin to annoyance and speculation, as if Richard couldn't decide exactly how he should feel about this situation. At least he'd awoken to a problem, but this confrontation, with her mother in witness, could have waited a bit longer. At least until Kelly decided how to handle it on top of everything else.

"Kelly, I have to be honest," he said quietly, his brow furrowed. "I'm not sure I like the idea of you going to see that fellow. I know you probably felt you had to, I mean, with him leaving today and all, but...? You're not planning on seeing him again, are you?"

Odd, very odd. Richard sounded at this moment as if he were addressing a child who'd chosen an improper playmate. Or worse, a husband who had every right to decide who his spouse should and should not see. Was he so blasted blind—or self-assured—that it never even occurred to him that she might truly be thinking about sleeping with another man? Much less, falling in love with one?

"I mean, he seems like a nice enough guy." Richard continued on ever-thinning ice. "A little too arrogant if you ask me," he said in a somewhat lofty note. "I can see where some females might find that attractive. Your niece was certainly smitten with him," he said, and quivered a soft smile as if he found Abby's obvious adoration rather cute and excusable. After all, the girl was only sixteen. *Certainly not old enough to have any good taste in men.* "But truly, darling," he said with another flicker of wisdom across his troubled brow. "I don't think he's the type of person I'd want to get to know."

Uh-huh. And did Richard suddenly see them becoming good friends? Her, in the kitchen making dinner, while he and Kip sat smoking cigars and drinking before-dinner cocktails? As she tried to decide between his audacity and insanity, Kelly glimpsed her mother's peculiar gaze past Richard's shoulder. By expression alone, Patty found this rather one-sided conversation almost as bewildering as it was uncomfortable.

Belatedly, Richard seemed to realize Kelly's silence, and his gaze landed more critically. With a sheepish grin, an almost self-deprecating huff, he continued, "I'm sure that came out all wrong. I know he's your brother's friend and all, and ... I didn't mean to sound critical, darling. I gather he's a rather good friend of your family. If ... well, if you haven't done it already, I suppose we could add him to the guest list."

Well, the moment had come. That last swipe was a wee bit too pompous, and this was certainly not the first time Richard popped off with that condescending tone. Dropping the final doughball on the filled tray, Kelly glanced at her mother. "Could you put those in, Mom?" she said offhandedly. Not awaiting a response, she landed her gaze on Richard, "We need to talk."

Chapter 5

Restaurants in Randall were limited. Was it any wonder that Jason, with his sixth sense, pulled into the not-too-crowded parking lot of Le Chateau, where John Madison had recommended lobster only two evenings past?

"I was in here once," Jason said as he pulled into a space near the entrance. "The food's pretty good and it's probably the kind of place you'd dig."

"It's fine," Kip commented absently and tugged the door handle.

"I could wait out here," Jason said hesitantly.

"I'm buying. Join me," Kip stated and shoved the door open against a squealing protest of worn hinges. Not quite noon on a Monday morning, no reservations were necessary. The lean maître d', familiar from Saturday evening, recognized Kip on sight and escorted them to a comfortable booth within the shadowy dining room. "Coffee," Kip said as he dropped his coat onto the bench and looked to their escort. "A phone?"

"Near the restrooms, sir."

Naturally. Too much to hope for phone jacks in Randall. Disgusted, Kip backtracked to the entrance and found a surprisingly private built-in phone booth in the elegant hallway. Only three calls would he return, beginning with Marsh Baxel. Two rings later, Kip cursed the answering machine and hung up. Next, Dr. Mark Frances, to whom he owed an apology, wasn't answering his phone, but his answering service offered to page him. *Strike three and you're out.* Kip listened to John Madison's secretary apologizing while fielding Madison's call. Annoyed, Kip hung up, thinking about the smoking rental capsized at the bottom of Misty Haven Cemetery. Finding the Randall Police Dept. number in the book chained to a ledge under the phone, Kip dialed, grateful to hear a live voice. Police Chief Ed Cartel's voice erupted on the line seconds later. Cartel, like most of Randall's prestigious citizens, had attended the funeral, and after personal amenities, Kip explained the nature of his 'accident' to which Cartel breathed an audible sigh of relief.

"We just got a fire call on it," Cartel rumbled. "Somebody across the river spotted the smoke—"

"Good God, it caught fire?" Kip asked with a fair amount of amusement bouncing into his voice. Seemed fitting. Death by cremation.

"Steam," Cartel corrected. "But the trucks rolled. We were about to run the plates," he barely paused. "You say it's a rental, then?"

Pulling out his wallet, Kip offered his California driver's license number, his current address, and the rental agency information. "Forward the property damage report to my L.A. address, Captain, and give Mr. Rugby my personal apology, if you will." Rugby would be awfully busy contacting those families, repairing those stones—

"Not planning on sticking around here then, eh?"

"Few things to take care of in L.A.," he answered evasively and, after finalizing details concerning the car's resurrection, politely terminated the call.

One more call, he should make one more call. Hand resting on the receiver, he remembered the flash of hazel eyes, an image he'd tried shoving from his mind several times in the past few hours. Kelly. Damn it! 'Promise me?' No promises, he remembered and repeated silently, withdrawing his hand from the receiver. Whatever power this young woman held, he would do well to ignore it—ignore her. But god, that was hard. He needed only a fleeting thought of her livid eyes and the warmth of her hands to heat his blood. In another time, another place. Maybe in a week or two, he would arrange a layover in Philadelphia. Damnit! Impossible! Not only was she engaged, she was the little sister of a man he'd just struck from his list of acquaintances. For her sake, he needed to steer clear of her. And wasn't that just a weird twist? *For her sake?* Since when had he ever given a damn what was suitable for someone else? On principle, he should pursue this lovely young lass, and to hell with her brother—Mr. Undercover DEA Agent. God, those eyes, long legs...

Preoccupied, Kip returned to the booth across from King. His coffee had cooled, and Jason had, no doubt, memorized the leather-bound breakfast menu. In a swift scan, Kip decided and flopped the menu aside, catching the eye of a passing waitress.

"Think I'll settle for a cinnamon roll," Jason decided as he set the menu aside.

Between ordering and waiting for delivery, Kip repositioned himself to lean against the interior wall, skidding his tennis shoe onto the leather-cushioned bench as if he were resting in his private booth in Whistlebrook. Only after spotting Jason's amused glint, Kip realized his pose and abstracted thoughts. Far too late for proper etiquette. Besides, a restaurant without a phone jack didn't warrant a tuxedo-manner despite the queer glances he received from the increased flow of lunch clientele. Most wore business suits and carried briefcases or newspapers at their sides, probably, to claim the overpriced meals as a business expense and tax write-off. At his thought, Kip found the irony and amusement, winking to a woman who scoffed, apparently offended by his lack of finesse. Her disdain vanished into a dissipated smile. Probably, a secretary to a local politician, he considered while watching her shapely legs pass, and a moment later, recognized the state representative in her wake.

The politician started past, scowled, then froze and wheeled, thrusting his hand with a winning 'mourning' smile. "Mr. Patterson, I almost didn't recognize you. How are you?"

"Fine. You?" Kip asked, barely shifting to shake the hand over his knee.

"Good. I was just thinking about you this morning. I'd imagine you've been kept pretty busy, putting things in order. I know this is probably the last thing you want to think about right now, but you could probably use a distraction. My wife and I are having a few people over on Christmas Eve. We'd love to have you join us."

The politician was right. It was the last thing Kip wanted to think about. He'd fairly succeeded in ignoring tinsel, glitter, smiling Santas, and nativity scenes, which seemed to smother him suddenly. "Prior commitment, but thank you for the invitation," he managed politely.

"Well, if you change your mind and you can arrange it, have Carolyn call me at home."

Jason's initial amusement slowly drained into dumbfound at his recognition. His gaze followed the politician, returning to Kip with a stunned, bewildered amusement. "Was that who I think?"

"Imagine so," Kip said absently and watched King glance in Mike Fischer's direction.

Shaking his head, Jason stifled only part of his amusement and awe. "You're wild, man. You probably play golf with the President on the weekends, too, huh?"

"Actually, I only met him once," Kip mused. "No golf. It's a boring sport."

"You uh... You really aren't keeping the Home, huh? I mean, you're really taking off today, huh?"

Considering his packed bags in the pickup, Jason didn't need any further verification. Curiously, Kip studied the boy's disappointment as he appeared to await an answer. "Disturbs you?"

"Guess it does," he said honestly, toying with his cup of hot tea, shrugging, smiling lamely. "Think it'd be pretty cool working for you," he commented. "That stuff? I mean, the old folks calling you 'the Prince.' I thought it was sort of funny," he paused with a wayward glance from the booth. "Like a fairytale, ya know?" he said with a more reluctant smile. "But the thing is, you really are like a prince or something. Man, you just walk into a room and it's the way you look at people," he shrugged, visibly uncomfortable; perhaps, nervous behind his smile. "It's like you look at people from a distance, but you're willing to forget you're out of their league." He shrugged again, glancing away, less confident. With a hint of apology, he commented, "That's not a put-down, ya know? And I really do think it'd be cool working for you."

"Did you like my mother?" Kip asked absently, watching Jason's amplified sorrow and discomfort.

"I ... I only saw her a few times, but yeah. She was a neat lady," he said solemnly. "I mean, shit, she looked over my application personally, and the only thing she asked me at the interview was if I liked Randall High."

"Your answer?"

A smirk haunted his lips, his eyes brightened with an amused glint as he glanced away, no doubt, hoping to see their waitress arriving. "Guess I uh. . ." His attention returned. "I was pretty nervous, ya know? And she hit me with that question like you did—like out of the blue—and I sort of snapped—I'm a senior. She got this smile, like she knew I couldn't think of anything good to say about school."

"She hired you because you didn't like high school?"

"I don't know why she hired me," he mused. "She just told me to report to Mrs. Feeney on Monday after school." His gaze clouded, lowering to toy with his cup of tea. "I was only there for a week, ya know? But uh ... I felt it, too. I remember I was getting ready for school when my mom told me. Guess it was on the radio." He looked over solemnly. "School got delayed because of the snow, so I went out to the home. Mrs. Feeney," he shrugged, his mood falling toward dismay. "Figured I could help out in the kitchen or something."

Their waitress interrupted them then. Kip motioned his stacked platter toward Jason and took the cinnamon roll instead, already doubting his ability to eat. Under protest, Jason began eating. In silence, Kip managed only a few bites, nudged the plate aside, and shifted his refilled coffee in front of him. In a few days, maybe in a few more days, he could put the memories and mourning away. The sooner he departed from Randall, the sooner his life could return to normal.

Only shortly after noon, and he had several more hours to kill. Across from him, Jason finished his last bite of toast as Kip commented, "The old theaters are closed here in Randall. Where's the nearest cinema?"

"The mall," Jason answered curiously.

"Matinees?"

"Sure."

"Buttered popcorn sounds appealing," Kip decided and shifted on the bench, lifting a wallet from his back pocket. Dropping a ten on the table, he slid from the booth. Lifting the bill and his coat simultaneously, he glanced at Jason. "Let's go catch a flick."

Amidst the rush of Christmas traffic entering the mall, Kip briefly reconsidered his decision. Jason drove well, avoiding the bumpers and fenders of erratic drivers in front and back, and finding a parking space not too far from the four-screen cinema. A long line of teenagers crowded the ticket counters, and they barely stepped into line before Randall's 'center' in his letter jacket, attracted hearty calls from pimple-faced boys and several over-made-up teenage girls. Odd, Kip thought of Kelly Mulden. Half-heartedly, he considered stepping out of line and finding a phone to call her before cursing his insanity.

"Thought you had to work today?" one boxer-built boy said while slugging Jason.

"I uh... I did," Jason mused and shrugged, glancing to Kip, then his comrade. "Me and my boss decided to play hooky and do a movie."

If not for a sudden prickling sensation, Kip might have found the boxer's doubt amusing. Perhaps it was just the crowd and voices, excited voices reaching a steady crescendo of static, not unlike the subdued voices in the Oak Room a week earlier; perhaps, a latent effect of nostalgia creating visions of a single face within the crowd—pale blue eyes intent, an enigmatic grin. Unconsciously, Kip scanned the two lines of faces and the expansive lobby in search of a shadow, an image. Instead, he glimpsed a man near the glass doors. Too sharply, the fellow riveted his attention to feign interest in a movie poster on the window. Even before continuing his vacant scan, Kip realized the poster faced the sidewalk—the images and words were backwards. He barely shifted his abstract gaze and caught another glimpse of the poker-faced, trench-coated man looking in his direction. The same fellow had rested in a hotel lobby a few days earlier.

No DEA training behind this character. This one had FBI written all over him despite his dark blue knit hat and tennis shoes. Tennis shoes below dark blue polyester slacks? No finesse.

Dropping a twenty on the ticket counter, Kip flashed a glance over the billboard that compared nicely to the plastic marquee in Stones—Victor A. Calfactor. Reading the times rather than the titles, Kip bought two tickets for the nearest designated showing. Handing Jason a ticket and his change, he commented, "Buy some popcorn and sodas and find us a seat near the door?"

Without waiting for agreement, Kip located the payphones and stood behind three teenage girls who took turns speaking with a fourth on the line. Not surprisingly, trench-coat navigated a path to the phones and stood, reading another poster. At least this one faced him, Kip mused as one of the girls glanced over her shoulder. Her eyes shot back briefly with a nervous flush and smile before she wheeled about and whispered discreetly to her companions.

In record time, she disengaged the call and turned to him, smiling, "Sorry we took so long."

"Quite all right, luv," he commented and sidestepped to the phone, tuning out their whispers as he plunked coins into the slot and dialed O. At the nasal voice, he recited the number, reversing charges, not reacting as the answering machine came through. The operator suggested he try again later. As the dial tone erupted in his ear, he spoke just loud enough to be overheard. "Meet me at the airport in an hour. Gate thirty... Fine... Don't be late."

For a split second, as he hung up, he considered dialing a second number and nearly cursed aloud. Damn those warm hazel eyes and that smile! Whatever this blasted infatuation—shit. Those were Mulden's words, 'She's infatuated with you.' Forcing a smile to the three clustered youngsters, Kip strode to the tuxedo-dressed ticket attendant, handed over his ticket, and followed the line headed for the proper theater entrance.

***

"What do you intend to do? Just close your studio and move to Hollywood, or what? Is he going to move here, now that his mother's passed away and he has a geriatric home to run?" Richard asked arrogantly.

Leaning against her dresser, studying Richard from a distance, Kelly suddenly wondered how she had convinced herself that she could be in love with this pompous ass. He stood, as if posing for a men's magazine, his hands hooked in his hip pockets by his thumb, looking at her the same way a parent might address an unruly child—as if he was angry, but intended to give her time to see the error of her ways.

She lost track of how many times she'd denied that Kip was responsible for her change of heart, but Richard just wasn't getting it. All the reasons that had piled up over the past several months, from the forgotten dinner to meet her parents to his indifference to her studio, had fallen by the wayside in his mind. Like a dog with a bone, Richard was convinced that Kip Patterson was the single reason behind her decision to break their engagement three days before Christmas, and she was getting damn tired of denying it. In fact, she was beginning to suspect that Richard was right—for all the wrong reasons.

'What does this say about our relationship, Richard?' she'd asked the first time he mentioned Kip. 'When you're convinced that I'm breaking our engagement for the first handsome guy to cross my path?' That question had remained unanswered, countered only by another accusation. But suddenly she heard her own words. God knows, Kip wasn't the first handsome guy to cross her path, and not the first man to flirt avidly with her. As little as three weeks ago, a single male parent of one of her students had stuck around after a recital rehearsal and asked her out to dinner. Paul was a good-looking guy, not a lot older than her, and a successful businessman, but she hadn't even considered accepting his dinner invitation. And she'd already been suffering several serious reservations about marriage that evening, an evening when she'd needed to remind her *exhausted* fiancé that she had a recital in one week. First, she'd needed to explain why she was still in her studio well after 10 p.m. Richard had forgotten entirely.

She could always tell when he'd forgotten something of importance in her life, and in reflection, she realized how often she heard that brief hesitation and 'Oh, that's right. I'd—' Which was generally where he remembered to restrain the word 'forgotten,' a half second too late. In her opinion, there could be only two reasons for his forgetfulness. Either he honestly didn't give a damn about what was important to her. Or he never listened when she spoke, as if her words were too shallow to be heard and remembered. After all, he had dealt with life-and-death situations. Once, only once, he'd admitted aloud that her career didn't compare with his, and he'd stumbled over recanting his words, bungling the extended explanation until she'd nearly decked him.

Now he stood here, believing himself somehow superior to her, as if she didn't have enough God-given-intelligence to decide what was best for her.

As if he thought that his permitting her to keep her studio in Philly would be a determining factor in their union.

For the very first time, Kelly realized exactly why her words meant so little to him—he truly believed himself mentally superior. She was a dancer, after all. He was a budding doctor with seven or eight years of education under his belt.

"Is that it then?" Richard asked with a lofty note. "You're planning to move back here? Maybe move in with a bunch of little old ladies and give dance lessons between changing bedpans? If that's the case, darling, you really do need to think about this. Even if he only has a half dozen or so geris, they'll need your undivided attention. Believe me, I know what's involved with geriatric home care—"

"You condescending son of a bitch," she said softly as her temper rose in quick degrees.

"I'm not condescending," he stated. "I'm trying to make you see reason, for God's sake, darling. I can certainly see him talking a good line, but I can't imagine you'd be foolish enough to fall for it."

"I'm beginning to think I have a knack for falling for just such a thing," she said with a soft edge.

Pompous ass that he was, he failed to feel the dart. "I'm only saying that you need to think about this. For God's sake, he as much as said only yesterday, he has no intention of settling down with one woman. Whatever he said or implied to convince you that he'll suddenly settle down with you, you can rest assured, it's not going to happen. I've seen men like him all too often, darling. Oh, they're smooth operators—"

"You know, Richard, it's occurred to me that you really are a pompous ass," she said bluntly and watched him take that hit as if deflecting a fly, barely flinching. The measure of his arrogance was truly startling. And enlightening. Until this moment, he'd seemed like the perfect man. Always so kind and sensitive, always feigning to be so gentle and understanding. Willing to forgive her. Forgive her for suffering doubts, and constantly reassuring her that they could make a marriage work. Always so fucking reasonable and thoughtful enough to bring her flowers the day after the recital, claiming he wanted to hand them to her in person rather than have them delivered. When the truth was, he'd forgotten the recital entirely. A fact she discovered when he called her late that evening and said, 'Oh, that's right, that was—' *This evening.*

"I just don't want to see you throwing our life away for nothing," Richard continued. "Can't you see that? Guys like Patterson are a dime a dozen. They get their kicks playing with women. We have a life, darling," he said in a lowering, softening tone, starting forward. His award-winning pout came into play, apparently misreading the signals and coming into her territory to begin—as he always began—the soft touch after a few heated, reasonable blows. "We're meant to be—"

"Parted," she stated, and he halted his advance, appearing annoyed for an instant. "And you're wrong, dear," she continued. "Men like Kip Patterson—men who truly say what's on their minds—are scarce. Unlike those of you who believe most women are idiots and don't have enough sense to decide how or with whom they might spend their lives. God knows, I'd take the guy who's honest enough to simply state—let's go to bed—over the jerk who'd try to wheedle his way into my heart with sweet-talk and fake charm."

"So that's what this is about," Richard said in a haughty voice. "He's asked you to go to bed with him? What—dear God, last night," he stated and feigned to appear offended, or shocked with the lofty tilt of his head. "Good God, you had sex with him," he said as if the possibility had only now crossed his mind.

Sooner or later, he had to reach that conclusion, Kelly considered. Too bad it wasn't true. "You haven't truly heard a word I've said, have you?"

"Oh, I hear you," he said in a descending tone and turned, raising a hand to swipe through his hair as if he either needed a distraction or intended to scratch his scalp. Shaking his head as if disappointed, rather than furious, he stood a few steps away before turning again and looking at her speculatively. "Well... Well... It doesn't matter," he decided in the oddest tone to date. More completely, he turned and crossed his arms over his chest. "I'm not about to say I understand this. I did give you more credit, Kelly, but it truly doesn't matter. Obviously, you made a mistake, but that's no reason to throw your whole life away—"

"You sanctimonious son of a bitch," she hissed softly.

"One of us has to be reasonable—"

"Reasonable? You as much as accuse me of being a slut and stand here proposing to forgive me my transgressions like a goddamn priest granting absolution, and you consider yourself reasonable?" she stormed, truly stunned and outraged by his audacity. "Get the fuck out of my room," she stated shortly and pushed off the dresser, no longer either tired or controlled. Her Irish temper had just reached its peak. For one incredible instant, she caught herself searching her near-empty dresser for something to throw or use to strike a telling blow.

"Kelly, for God's sakes, I'm not the one—"

The light rap of knuckles intruded, and Richard cast an annoyed glance toward the door.

Fairly ready to strike, Kelly sent a likewise heated shine, parting her lips to snap a 'Get lost.' Too late.

JD pushed the door inward without invitation, his gaze fleeting off Richard indifferently and landing on Kelly with far more concentration. "Everything all right in here, sis?"

"No. Everything is not all right, in here," she snapped and started toward the door.

"Everything's fine," Richard stated with a lofty, deeper pitch, his anger far more apparently directed at JD. "If you don't mind, my fiancée and I are having a discussion."

"This discussion is over, Richard," Kelly snapped and spun her hot glare on him. "And for the last fucking time, that applies to our engagement and wedding plans as well. If you hurry, you can be back in Philadelphia or halfway to Georgia before it gets dark. Take your pick, but I want you out of this house, out of my life, now, and that *is* the end of this discussion."

"I can't believe you're willing to throw your entire life away over a one-night stand!" Richard stated, then shot daggers at JD, who'd meandered another step into the room. "You know what this is about, don't you? It's about her sleeping with your old pal," Richard stated shortly. "Apparently, your dear old friend took advantage of my fiancée last night, and now she intends to throw away her entire life because of it!"

"Think you better slow down, doc," JD said in a quiet voice.

"If you had any sense, you'd help me reason with her," Richard stated hotly. "Granted, I don't like this one damn bit, but I don't intend to have some leche ruin our entire life."

"That's nice of you, doc. A real noble gesture," JD said in a slightly quieter voice.

Suddenly, Kelly's mad paled in comparison to the green tornado brewing in her brother's concentrated gaze. She took a step toward him, but Richard, unwisely, took a step in JD's direction as well.

"I do intend to have a talk with this *friend* of yours," Richard stated. "And I don't give a damn if he is grieving. That doesn't excuse the fact that he took advantage of your sister when I'm sure she only meant to offer him a shoulder to cry on. If you're any kind of brother, you'll take me to see this fellow, and we'll get this mess sorted out—"

"Richard!" Kelly snapped. "That's about enough!"

"Stay out of this, Kelly," Richard stated and closed another two steps toward JD. "Your brother and I will take care of this—"

"Kell, let me ask you something, here, just out of curiosity," JD said in a deceptively conversational tone. His posture betrayed his readiness. He stood barring the door in a casual pose. "Did you sleep with Kip last night?"

"JD, for God's sakes," Kelly snapped, irritated that he even asked. "Not you, too!"

"That's sort of what I thought," JD said and leveled his no longer indifferent gaze on Richard. "Where the fuck do you get off treating my sister as if she's a secondhand slut off the strip, asshole?" he asked in a far lower, lethal tone. "Or some brainless twit to be taken in by a smooth-talking Casanova?"

Richard arched slightly, as if slapped. "Excuse me?"

"Even if she had slept with my old pal, which she didn't, she's old enough and smart enough to make that decision—and buddy, that's a decision she has every God given right to make without facing your fucking righteous indignation." JD moved forward, seemingly without taking a step, and Richard took a step back from the advance. "Where the fuck do you get off thinking you have the right to pardon her for infidelity? Or for that matter, thinking she doesn't have the God given sense to hand you your fucking ring. As I seem to have heard rather clearly, the lady's told you the gig is up," JD stated, and his hands lifted, locking on Richard's sweater, lifting him easily. "What part of get the fuck out of this room, this house, and her life, didn't you understand, doc?"

"JD!" Kelly snapped and moved forward, catching her brother's sleeve with an instant vision of JD sending Richard sailing off the second-floor landing. "Just let him walk out—"

"Get your hands off me," Richard snapped as he clasped JD's wrists, apparently waking to the genuine physical threat in front of him.

"Not quite yet, doc," JD stated, nearly nose to nose with him, now. "I have this funny feeling that you think my little sister's a pushover. Like maybe, you just wanted a pretty trophy wife to wait on you hand and foot, and I'll tell you, that kind of guy really pisses me off. That kind of guy puts on a nice show for the public eye. A lot like you've been doing in this house for the past two days, then treats his lady like she's a piece of shit behind closed doors. He doesn't really respect her, let alone love her. Sort of figures she's dumb as dirt, a lot like you were doing here a few minutes ago, when you were willing to forgive her for infidelity.

"Now, the problem is, if you even attempt to come back into my little sister's life, or if you have any inclinations toward making her life hell in any way, then see...? I'd have to make a trip to Philadelphia. And I want us to be really clear on this, Richard, if I had to make that trip, I'd probably have to break your fucking jaw for starters. Now," JD spoke while lowering the fistful of sweater without backing off even slightly. "Why don't I help you get your starched undershorts in your bag, and we'll get you pointed in the right direction?"

Belatedly, Richard seemed to grasp the full measure of his danger and looked suddenly as if he might cry. His gaze shot to Kelly, torn between fear and anger. "Kelly—"

JD yanked the sweater, starting a backstep and a turn. "Don't make this any more ugly, pal. The lady made her decision, and maybe you were too busy being righteous to have heard. The wedding's off."

"Kelly!" Richard tried again as JD swung them both toward the door. "We're not—"

"Just go, Richard," she said flatly, and glanced at her mother as JD nearly propelled Richard in that general direction. Feeling oddly bad—maybe for having JD doing her dirty work, or for her mother standing in witness to this ugly scene—Kelly turned away from the door as JD sent Richard into the hall.

This wasn't exactly how she'd intended to break her engagement, but somehow, she wasn't as upset over the result as over the means to the end. How could she have been so damned stupid to fall for all of Richard's sweet talk and fake charm? God! She felt like an idiot. In less than two days, her brother had pegged Richard, and probably every other member of her family had seen him for what he was. An arrogant, pompous prick. Tears came unbidden, but those had nothing to do with the lingering sounds of heavy footsteps descending two flights of steps. The door snapped shut, muffling the angry words, and Kelly wasn't surprised when her mother touched her back.

"Are you alright, honey?"

"I have t-to be the wo-orld's biggest idiot," Kelly professed on the brink of a sob. Straining, swallowing, she blinked away the tears and found her mother's eyes. "I'm sorry," she said softly.

Likewise, straining against a moist shine, Patty consoled, "Honey, there's nothing to apologize for."

Kelly nodded, "I was going to marry that jerk."

For a half second, Patty strained, then a smile quivered on her lips; her eyes sparked with mischief behind the shine. No one could ever accuse Patty Mulden of being anything but full-blooded Irish to find the blasted humor in any situation. "No, you weren't, sweetie," she said lightly. "If you were, we'd have already gone shopping for your wedding gown, and we'd certainly have spoken with Fr. Jordan by now."

"I-I was thinking about g-getting married in Phillie," she heaved softly.

"Fat chance," Patty said with a ring of amusement, forced, but relieving, nonetheless. "As I recall, you once professed you'd have a huge wedding in St. Matthew's. Think you had ideals toward draping white lace and red carnations the length of the pews."

"Oh, God," she huffed, shaking her head, forcing the new rise of a sob down her throat. She'd once professed that fantasy, about the same time she'd fallen crazy in love with the curly blond-haired boy who'd graced their front door wearing a suit that looked like a tuxedo to an eleven-year-old. "Life sucks," Kelly decided as the tears erupted with a mere thought of how miserable she would be when Kip Patterson departed her life for the second time.

The time for jokes had passed, and mother's intuition kicked into high gear. Patty tugged Kelly into an embrace, and despite her slight size, her arms were as sturdy as ever. "Sometimes, I guess it does, sweetie," she said quietly.

"I-I can't b-believe I l-let JD get into this mess," Kelly heaved against her mother's shoulder, and that thought only quickened the tears.

"If I know your brother, he doesn't mind a bit, dear," Patty said in an offbeat note, too wise to mention JD might be having the time of his life. "He always loved coming to your rescue."

Unspoken. There were always so many unspoken words regarding JD, and Kelly wondered, in an odd moment, if her parents were a little more privy to her brother's occupation than they let on. She hadn't asked JD earlier whether any others knew, and she had a feeling she needn't bother. Either her parents knew, or suspected, that their third-born son wasn't half as irresponsible or negligent as everyone else believed. All too easily, she recalled how often they defended him, and likewise, their genuine distress on several occasions. Belatedly, Kelly understood. They were usually less concerned about him missing a gathering than what might happen to him in those dreadfully long absences.

By the time the knock intruded, Kelly and Patty were sitting quietly, commiserating silently, side by side on the bed. Even as Patty extended an invitation to enter, Kelly pushed off the mattress and began moving toward the door. How could she have doubted her brother for all these years? She needed only a glimpse of his genuinely concerned eyes to know how deeply he still cared, how much they still meant to him.

"You alright, Kell?" he asked hesitantly.

Without reservation or estrangement, Kelly wrapped her arms around him for the second time in only a few hours and welcomed the strength of his return embrace. "Thanks, bro, b-but I'm sorry," she stammered at his shoulder. "I didn't... I wouldn't have wanted you to..."

"Hey, can it," he said offhandedly. "What are big brothers for if not to defend the honor and virtue of their little sister every once in a while?" Despite the teasing tone, he was sincere. "I'm just glad you wised up, sis, but I have to admit, I'm a little disappointed. The son of a bitch didn't even try to sucker punch me," he stifled his chiding as she eased from his arms, and his eyes emitted a more sober shine. "You ... you really don't intend to take him back, do you?"

"Not in this lifetime," she assured.

"Glad to hear it, sis. I'd hate to think I just ruined your life."

"Huh?"

"Honey, I think I just sent the fear of God into that asshole, but I think he's just pompous enough to try getting you back. If that happened, you'd most definitely have trouble with his in-laws, and that wouldn't make for a happy union."

Richard's in-laws. She shook her head, managing a smile. *The Muldens.* "I don't intend to tempt his in-laws," she said smoothly. "And ... thanks for not making me feel like the biggest fool afoot, JD."

"Sometimes we all land in a situation we have a hard time getting out of," he said with a far deeper meaning behind his words. "If we're lucky and smart, we wise up before it's too late, and as far as I'm concerned, you just did. As long as you don't take this too hard, that's what counts."

"I ... I'm glad you were here," Kelly said honestly. "Even if I was afraid you intended to throw him down the steps."

"Thought about it," he said with a smirk, a shrug. "Figured mom and dad didn't need the hassle, and him being a doctor and all, he probably knows all about lawsuits."

"You reeeallly didn't like him at all, huh?"

"Truth?"

"Preferably."

"He lost my vote about two seconds after he introduced himself as Dr. Richard Whitman the Second, as if he was born and bred southern royalty." His eyes sparking with mischief, he commented, "But I'll tell you, sis, I had a blast watching him flinch every time I called him Rich or Doc. The man definitely lacked a sense of humor."

"You, brother, are a shit," she said bluntly. "But a wonderful shit."

Chapter 6

"Great movie," Jason said en route to the pickup. "Where to now?"

"Find the courthouse, I'll direct you from there," Kip answered distractedly, and if Jason said anything else, Kip hadn't heard. Around and around, his thoughts spun, rereading his mother's letters in his mind, reviewing conversations, reminiscing, and running the financial figures over and over. 'Stealing our residents blind.' Those words had continued to pulse inside his head along with a final 'unpaid' invoice in a randomly selected file. Ellie Baker, a not-too-sexually, sexually aggressive resident. Mr. Louten's message, 'The Prince is in danger ... destroying the castle.' Mark Frances, evasive, had seemed convinced of a conspiracy inside the Home, and Bill Bickerman allegedly knew nothing of the other options and stipulations within the Will. 'Formalities,' he had alleged. And Frank Culver had spent countless hours resorting to measures against his moral judgment in search of facts, evidence, and a villain. And JD's struggling breath, 'You're—in—trouble.'

And every time Kip fleeted a thought of Mulden, the face changed in his mind, and he thought of those long, slender limbs melded against him. God, he loved the feel of that young lady! She would be a tempest under the sheets. All that grace and symmetry in motion.

Still lost in the abstract, Kip directed Jason into the private parking lot of Madison, Cummings, and Wade Law Offices. Several familiar cars crowded the lot. Drawing from his thoughts, Kip scanned the lot, unconsciously searching for Edna's old, reliable Nova, cursing his foolishness. Edna had probably ridden with Bill or Carolyn, possibly Frank Culver, who had likely driven the new Whistlebrook Security truck, which was presently parked across the lot. Mark Frances's Mercedes stood in a far corner space alongside Carolyn's Porsche. Several Lincolns—including John's—filled the three rows.

"Should I wait out here?" Jason asked hesitantly.

"There's a lobby inside," Kip answered, preoccupied as he strode around the truck and passed between two Lincolns on route to the modern two-story. The building contradicted John Madison's style and old-fashioned principles. Stepping through the glass doors, Kip spotted four suited men grouped near a small bank of chairs to his immediate left. Their faces were familiar only by a remote sense of having seen them sometime recently. The funeral home, no doubt.

The oldest man nodded, but Kip barely returned a glance before John's mid-aged secretary hustled from behind her cluttered desk, hurrying to a doorway on the left, exasperated as she stated, "This way, Mr. Patterson."

Unless someone had changed the designated time, he wasn't late, which he verified on an old advertising clock behind the desk as he veered toward the secretary. The door cracked open on a low fusion of voices, all falling away and staggering into silence even before he stepped into the fluorescent glow.

Suddenly, it struck Kip as bizarre.

The way John had spoken of this event, Kip had expected more strangers in the room. Instead, he faced less than a dozen familiar faces collected around a long, wide conference table. Bill and Carolyn sat side-by-side at the far end of the table, their backs to the outer wall. A gray day-glow emanated from between the curtains. The windows faced a park that separated the law offices from the county courthouse, with its ancient stone walls barely visible through the spiked, bare branches. A vacant chair waited between Bill and Frank Culver, who eyed Kip a little critically, probably reflecting on the previous evening. Three aging head nurses occupying the chairs nearest the door halted their conversation; two offered cautious glances and smiles. Mark Frances, John Madison, and a slightly junior partner, Attn. Wade stood across the room near a second entrance. The *good doctor* Frances carried a hint of swelling within his mountaineer-bearded lips; his blue gaze held steady with a fair amount of tension and concern in evidence.

Turning his attention to Carolyn, whose slender face aged subtly with her tension, Kip asked, "Where's Mrs. Feeney?"

Lines deepened across her brow as she answered, "She never answered my page, hon. No one's seen her. I had one of the girls try her room. Are you alright, hon? The police—your car—"

"Fine," he answered and shifted his gaze to Frank. "The Nova?" Was it still at the Home?

"In the garage," Frank answered tensely. "I figured she rode over with Bill."

"Kip," John interrupted. "We have a few minutes." Motioning and glancing toward the far door, he commented, "I'd like a few words with you before we begin."

Shrugging out of his coat, Kip eyed Mark Frances, commenting, "I owe you an apology. Wrong place at the wrong time sort of thing. Sorry."

Mark nodded, faintly amused. "Obviously, you were upset."

Dropping his coat over the nearest chair, Kip strode behind the two aging nurses and joined Madison, striding into the office reflecting more of John Madison's style. Dark oak shelves lined with books, leather wing-backed chairs, silk cloth shaded lamps, and a collection of framed certificates and awards intermixed with family portraits of wife and children on every available wall space. Not unlike Marilyn's office, Kip noted, without the feminine undertones.

With tension engraved on his cultured face and emanating from his careful actions, John waved Kip toward one of two receiving chairs in front of the wide desk while moving behind and into a rich leather swivel. Madison turned his attention sharply to a thick legal brief on his desk and tipped open the coverlet. Almost heavily, he leaned back in his chair, looking across the desk with a lawyer's neutral gaze. "You've made your decision?" he asked.

"My suitcases are in a pickup truck outside. Imagine so."

"Three days ago, you sensed a problem. Have you satisfied your doubts?"

No games today, thank God. John Madison was playing by Marilyn Patterson's rules to remain nonpartisan. "As much as I feel necessary," Kip answered. "Financially, I will neither lose nor gain, regardless of either option."

"I tend to disagree with you. Whistlebrook's capabilities to turn a profit—"

"—Is not my problem," Kip finished evenly and held Madison's gaze. "Dollars and cents are not an issue, Attn. Madison. Financially, Whistlebrook is stagnant, and to turn it around would take an investment in the future, which I'm not willing to devote."

"You're afraid of it, aren't you?" John asked quietly. "Not the financial risk. It's the emotional risks scaring the living daylights out of you. The thought of not filling your mother's shoes adequately, of facing the tremendous responsibilities—"

"And if I were?" Kip asked evenly. "In my shoes, with the financial freedom of choice, tell me, what would be your decision, counselor? Accept the albatross and spend thirty years chained to that white elephant or walk away free?"

"I am not in your shoes," John said quietly. "And frankly, I don't envy you, because, simply, I wouldn't want the emotional ties you have to that monolith. That property's been in your family for nearly a century. You are emotionally attached, and I understand your need to walk away. I'd like to ensure that *you* are aware of what you're doing and the reasons behind it. Frankly, Kip, you could accept Whistlebrook and put it on the market six months from now. And I believe you're aware of that. You're far too intelligent not to have spotted the loopholes in the options your mother gave you, and yet, I need to wonder why you haven't mentioned them."

Kip's thoughts halted, his gaze held steady, seeing into the lawyer's eyes. "Are you telling me that those 'loopholes' were deliberately built into the Will? At my mother's request?"

"Your mother's known for years that you were emotionally hurt in the Home," Madison said temperately. "Emotionally and physically," he said delicately. His gaze steadied. "As much as she loved Whistlebrook and hoped you'd battle and face your horrors over the past three days, she also wanted to give you the freedom to vent your rage. I was hoping we wouldn't have this conversation, but such is life," he said with a sigh and leaned, lifting a sheet of legal-sized paper from within his folder. Bringing it in front of him, he glanced down its printed side, then bent and slid the form across the desk. "You'd better read that."

Another Last Will and Testament, Kip realized as he caught sight of the single-page document. Oh Grand! Another—Last Will and Testament—recorded a single day *after* the Will he'd read three days ago. *Oh God! After!*

This was the official, legally binding Will.

'I, Marilyn Patty Patterson, being of sound mind and body, do hereby bequeath my worldly possessions to be distributed as follows:'

In the following lines, the names coincided with the faces presently collected in the conference room, apart from Mrs. Feeney, whose inheritance in the first paragraph jumped to fifty thousand. In the final section, Marilyn Patty Patterson bequeathed the remainder of her properties, stocks, bonds, savings, and trusts to her single living heir ... without options, contingencies, or conditions.

Chapter 7

A game! A goddamned game!

Setting the paper on the desk, Kip pushed off his chair and paced to the window. Fumbling in his shirt pocket, he found his cigarette and cupped a flame between his steady palms. With his exhale, he cast his gray gaze through the glass, not surprised to notice streaks of rain slicing down the pane. "Why the game, John? Why did she play the fucking game with me?" he asked calmly despite the turmoil raging through his mind.

"I'm not convinced it was a game, Kip. A deception, yes, and I'm not altogether certain of her motives."

Looking over, leveling an icy glare, Kip lowered his voice. "Spare me more lies, Attn. Madison. As my recently acquired attorney, I expect you to uphold your oaths; otherwise, frankly, I will have you disbarred. How did she convince you to become a part of this—*deception*—and what was her motive?"

"You're every bit your mother's son," Madison said quietly, a faint grin on his lips. "Frankly, by your same method of persuasion, far more gently. She possessed information that could have jeopardized my career and credibility, and it's rather ironic, considering it concerned a certain birth certificate and marriage license."

"She threatened to expose her deceit to discredit you, and you bought it? Try again, sir," Kip said evenly.

"Your mother was dying, Kip," Madison said in reserve. "I've spent twenty-five years loving her and in awe of her. If I allowed her to believe that her threat secured my allegiance for infinity, that's my business. As for her reason, I hoped you'd supply me with that answer. That you can't is not only annoying, but also alarming. I'd honestly believed she'd have revealed something to you."

Kip turned his focus to the window. Bickerman had seen the dummy Will; he knew nothing of this second Will. Looking over, Kip wondered, "How many people know about this, obviously, authentic Will?"

"Mark Frances, I believe, Edna Feeney, myself, and now, you."

Edna knew? And yet, as she told him the story? Their discussion afterward? Shaking his head absently, Kip concentrated, "Courthouse records?"

"Only one Will was recorded, Kip. This one."

Bill Bickerman believed the fraudulent document; he'd seen it before. In this new document, Bill received a stipend of ten Gs. No employment options or guarantees. In fact, no one received options. Mark Frances. Mark was named executor on the official document, and he knew about all three. He'd lied last evening.

In a single motion, Kip turned and moved to the door, one of two that opened to the conference room. Again, silence dropped; Kip found Mark seated near the front of the table. "Come in here, will you?"

For a large man, Frances moved with impressive grace, pushing from the armed chair and striding forward as if he'd merely awaited the summons. As surely, he had. His gaze shifted to Madison with the question; Madison nodded; Mark turned and met Kip's gaze as the door closed. "Congratulations."

"Don't fuck with me," Kip said calmly. "Last night was an accident, but my temper's on the rise."

"Control it," Mark said simply, unamused this once. "I don't need the aggravation of trying to prove you competent, and Bill won't be a happy man when he leaves here today."

"Possibly that's her motive," Kip said absently. "If I were proven incompetent, who would gain?" he asked John.

Mark spoke before Madison could answer, "I don't believe your mother intended to drive you off the edge. The opposite seems more appropriate."

Looking again into Frances's sober gaze, Kip stated, "Explain."

"I've been trying to find her reason for months. But it's only occurred to me over the past week, and listening to you from outside that door last evening... You truly haven't been home in fifteen years. You haven't spent a single day—much less a night—in your home. You never came to terms with the past. Whatever her method, she seems to have succeeded in keeping you there long enough to confront your childhood fears."

"Again. My question, doctor," Kip said bluntly. "If I buckled under the stress of this odyssey?"

"Obviously, we'd be tied up in litigation for a millennium," Mark said quietly.

Looking to Madison, Kip stated, "Legal procedure? Precedents?"

"Someone would have to contest the Will and attempt to have you discredited or committed to a mental facility."

Bickerman? "What would become of the Home in that event?"

"Would depend on the nature of your incarceration," John said thoughtfully. "As the single surviving heir, no one could truly lay claim to the property. It could become a matter of state sale, and eventually, the proceeds could be placed in trusts. But, I doubt we need to consider this."

A legal corporate raid. The Home is to be sold. "I'll be damned," he said matter-of-factly and dragged on his cigarette, passing between both men. At the desk, he lifted the Will and turned, leaning and again glancing down the page. 'A sheep in a wolf's cloak.' The players were obvious. *Surface obvious,* Paranoia! Even if Bill attempted to contest the Will, he'd need more evidence. *For Chrissake, I* am *the only heir.* A stipend of ten grand for ten years of devoted service? Financial restrictions, secured position. Marilyn Patterson hadn't trusted Bill, and her instincts had generally hit the mark. Could she have anticipated Bill's participation in a raid? Had she deliberately given him ammunition?

At the buzz of the phone intercom, Kip leaned mechanically, punched the button, and lifted the receiver. Still contemplating the Will, he said, "Yes?"

"Uh...? Attn. Madison?"

"Yes?" he said absently before realizing the words were in question form, not a statement. *Shit!* "Hold please." Faintly amused at the curious faces, Kip held the receiver toward Madison. "Believe this is for you." By no surprise, since this was John's office.

Madison came forward, accepting the receiver, starting around the corner of his desk. "Lesli?"

"What are you thinking?" Mark asked as he settled onto the arm of the nearest chair.

"Put him through," John stated and sidled, holding the receiver to Kip. "For you, after all."

Lifting the receiver in time to hear the line engage, he asked, "Yes?"

"Young Mr. Patterson?"

John Fitzpatrick. "Yes. Go on."

A low tension passed through the line, reaching into the low voice. "Have those results you wanted. Your suspicions were confirmed. Abnormal levels. Toxic levels, young sir."

Abruptly tense, Kip maintained a surface calm. The stakes had just taken a violent leap inside his mind. "I see."

"Don't think you do, sir. I talked to Tony Cellini about a certain Mr. Seratti. Seems the gentleman might not have slipped away of his own accord. He was flushed an abnormal red—the flush that comes with an Atropine overdose." Fitzpatrick hesitated, then pushed on decisively. "Out of respect for your mother, sir, I never reported that episode a lot of years ago, but you better know, if any more come in like this, I'll be talking to the DA. Know your intentions are good, but—"

"Back up, sir. Episode—elaborate," he stated cryptically, and heard Fitzpatrick's hesitation. "Explain, if you will, sir."

"Fifteen years ago or better," the aging mortician said carefully, sighing in his tone. "You, sir. You can't go administering medication to those folks," he said heavily, fatherly advice in his tone. "Know how hard it is, you having to watch them suffer, and after just losing your mother and all? But you leave the medicating to the doctors from here on."

A new wave of tension—and horror raced into Kip's mind as he heard his mother's words. 'If you had a nervous breakdown before or after those cocktails were doctored.' *Brompton Cocktails*, he understood, a mixture of morphine, cocaine, and several other barbiturates to relieve the suffering of the terminally ill. Not lethal, in proper doses.

Murder? His mother thought him a murderer?

"Oh my God," Kip uttered softly. His mother. Mr. Fitzpatrick. *Murder.* Covered up *murders!* Fifteen years ago. Murders that they suspected *him* of committing? Fifteen years ago, she'd sent him away.

A violent wave of nausea swept through his system, rocking him, shaking him as he stared into abstracts. His mother believed *he* doctored pain medicine and murdered several residents? "How—how many, sir?" Kip asked in a low, strained voice, his focus cast toward the dark blue carpet beneath his black shiny shoes.

"What was that, young sir?"

"How many?" Kip asked tensely. "How many then?"

"Two," Fitzpatrick said carefully.

Two. Two that Bill Fitzpatrick knew about. Two deaths. The mortician had covered up two murders out of loyalty to Marilyn Patterson, no doubt, with her promise that this would never happen again. And fifteen years ago, she sent her son away into a controlled, ecclesiastic environment. He hadn't come home. She hadn't permitted him to return home. Holiday vacations, the two summers of his sophomore and junior years, he'd spent with the brothers, learning Latin and Catholicism. To pay for a crime?

With another violent cramp, Kip dropped his hand with the Will in its grip and steadied himself against a physical sway. A voice spoke in his ear, but he couldn't decipher the words within a reeling fog. In slow stages, he recovered enough sense to utter thanks and managed to land the receiver in its cradle. Murder. Two murders fifteen years ago. At least two murders, now. Fifteen years ago ... six people had died. Six terminally ill residents had passed away within days or weeks of one another. Five, oh, God, counting his mother, five people had died in the past week. Murdered?

'Know how hard ... seeing them suffer.'

Mercy killings. Fitzpatrick believed they were mercy killings then and now. But neither the police nor a jury would see it that way. No statute of limitations on murder. *Oh God! Not just committed! Incarcerated for life in prison?*

"Kip? What was that all about? What's wrong?" Mark asked.

DEA. Justice Department. Federal agents.

And the option—his way out—had never existed!

Looking over to John Madison's inquisitive gaze, Kip asked, "That paper option? Was there any truth to any of it? Could the home be sold today?"

Madison appeared dismayed and alarmed. "It's based on facts. The contracts are dupes. There are possibilities."

"Damn it," he said absently, not feeling well at all as he glanced down at the Will in his fist. "Bitch," he stated.

"Kip—" Frances started carefully.

"Don't *Kip* me, doctor," he said as he lanced Mark with a cool glare. "I was just starting to like her—"

"She loved you—"

"You don't know the *half* of it, doctor, or then, too, maybe you do," Kip stated as he studied the good doctor's eyes. Malpractice, that was the word his mother had used. A malpractice suit over the near-death of her son. He'd been beaten up in school, Kip remembered absently. His blood had spilled from his mouth, a great pool of blood, and he'd almost died in Randall High's cafeteria. And there, his memories twisted. Distorted and out of order. He remembered looking through a dark cloud, his talents reversed. He'd known himself dying more than once in that sojourn.

JD Mulden had moved into Randall during that time, appearing off and on. JD had come into Kip's visions of those last days at Whistlebrook. Mulden ... what had he said a few days ago? Something about his first day of school, the cafeteria food. A funeral. He was constantly vomiting after funerals. But that wasn't exactly true. The vomiting had only started then, during those few weeks. Physical battle against mental. His mother had insisted he visit Dr. Blake. They talked about dying and anger, and an incident in school. A dead fish had become the catalyst, and he'd suffered a wicked temper tantrum. He'd become so damned tired of the bullying, always backed into corners and bullied. And people were dying; his sixth sense had abandoned him. The gray clouds lingered over his entire home, but no longer darkened around the dying. The deaths were taking him by surprise. Shock and grief. Mrs. Ramsey—

"Kip?" Dr. Frances clasped his arm, jolting him from his memory.

Forcing away the whirlwind, Kip cleared his focus, concentrating on the present to find both men watching him worriedly.

"What the blazes was that call about?" Mark asked.

Call. Damnit! Fitzpatrick! Murder! The memories. Damned the memories dredged from the slush in his subconscious. "Business," he said absently, and pushed onto his feet, looking to Madison. "Are you ready to read the Will?"

Madison hesitated, then nodded, accepting the document Kip handed to him and lifted the folder. "Gentlemen," he said while motioning to the door.

A few others had entered the conference room. Edna Feeney wasn't one of them; however, JD Mulden had gained access to the room and stood near the door, his gaze piercing past the shoulders of the two men from the lobby. Tense, Kip slid into the chair alongside Madison, who stood at the head of the table. Mark settled into the next seat. Glances ricocheted about the table.

When had he last seen Edna Feeney? Yesterday? Not yesterday. Saturday night in her room. Last night, he'd heard her television through her door, and this morning—

A hand landed, clasping Kip's shoulder, jolting him, and by no surprise, JD leaned down. By force, Kip willed his reflexes still and refrained from reacting, other than tipping his head to receive a hissed whisper against his ear.

"Smile, asshole, or we'll both fry," JD said calmly. "You even think about knocking me out again, and I'm putting your ass on ice in an 8 X 10. Smile nice and nod like we're old *pals*."

Kip glanced up, nodded with a faint, unamused grin.

"Good," JD whispered again. "Now, as soon as this is finished, we're going to find someplace we can talk in private, and unless you like stripes, you'll hear what I have to say. Smile nice and nod."

Less amused, Kip smirked a grin and nodded. Lifting a hand, catching Mulden's leather lapel, Kip pulled him down to whisper, "Did your friends enjoy the tour of the airport?"

Mulden glanced at him with stifled amusement. "You bet."

"If I could have everyone's attention, I believe we're ready to begin," John spoke in a standard pitch and waited for the silence. "As you know, we're gathered this afternoon to hear the last bequests of Marilyn Patty Patterson. As some of you may already know, there has been some confusion regarding the Will; however, the situation has now been resolved. I hold before me, Marilyn's Last Will and Testament as recorded on the 23rd day of July in the year 1987." Madison produced a large manila envelope from his legal brief.

Unconsciously, Kip glanced at the envelope to Madison's concentrated gaze, instantly wondering if the man had deceived him again by the document he'd read in the office. Madison broke the seal on the envelope and took his time, extracting several legal-sized envelopes, each one sealed and labeled. Madison's gaze shifted as he began disbursing the envelopes, starting with Bill directly across from Kip.

"As we all know, Marilyn was an extremely complex woman. A friend, a leader, a woman of unparalleled energy and compassion." Madison handed an envelope to Kip, then gave one of the three remaining to Mark, keeping the last two in hand. "You each have before you an envelope. Marilyn asked that we all receive her parting thoughts in a personal manner, for which we all knew her so well. If we could all just take a moment."

Following Madison's example, Kip lifted the envelope, preparing mentally for another whiplash effect. Already tense, he ripped the edge and blew into the end of the envelope. Unconscious of his action, he extracted the folded sheets of paper, catching estranged glances from Mark, Bill, and John Madison. Belatedly, Kip realized how often he'd seen his mother open her mail in the same fashion. All three men turned their focus sharply, and Kip caught a lingering glance from Carolyn before she smiled and turned her attention to her letter. Dropping his attention, he unfolded the three pages. The first was handwritten in an oh-so-damned-familiar script. Every muscle tensed at the sight of it.

With an effort, he read;

My Darling Kippen,

Someone in this room is your enemy, as he or she has been my enemy.

Oh God. Here we go again.

I know that you and I have passed like ships in the night, but do not ever mistake that for indifference, my darling. You have always been my candle in the darkness. There are so many things I would like to tell you, but a telephone never seems quite fitting, and the distance I've put between us is far too painful.

By the time you read this, I hope to have dealt with the problem I'm facing. Do not fault me, or you, for my inability to pick up a phone on this 23rd day of July. I would simply rather not have you involved for your own well-being, and perhaps my opening statement is a preemptive measure—or a terrible omen. (I cannot bring myself to change that sentence.) I feel that when you read this, you will understand, either in the past or present tense, the nature of those words.

I have always admired—and been awed by—your incredible ability to grasp the impact of information. I truly should call you. How I would love to see you analyze this information. Indeed, no surprise to me that you are a financial wizard. My God, you're not even thirty. I am so proud of you.

Now then, darling, if you must finish this for me, read the compiled data I've enclosed for your eyes only. And please, darling, forgive me if John's been forced into implementing the phony papers I had him prepare. If I don't stop this in advance, I hope to have roused your interest and perhaps upset our enemy through that ruse. Watch the reactions as my bequests are read. Possibly, we'll get lucky, and their eyes will turn red with rage. By the way, darling, I do hope you decide to take the helm. Whistlebrook has needed its prince as much as I believe its prince needs his castle.

P.S. I'm counting on you, darling. Clean house, or tear it down—no regrets in either case. A Patterson built it, and by God, only a Patterson has the right to destroy it. My Blessings.

Love Always and Forever

Mom

Not the words of a paranoid woman. Angry, perhaps, but sane beyond question. With his thought, Kip glanced to the silent readers, then turned the letter facedown and raced his scan down the columns on the two following pages. On the first, she'd listed names, admission dates, and death dates—year and month. Names, beginning financial assets, end balances—all in negative numbers with a final column designating unpaid balances to Whistlebrook. Rita Hamilton, the name he'd spotted two days earlier when perusing her files, hadn't been the exception—he recognized her name on the list. Forty-one names, beginning with the death date, October 15, 1976, and ending with the death date, June 4, 1987. The total outstanding balance was mind-boggling. 41,258,987. Without a doubt, the accounting firm had used those losses to Whistlebrook's advantage, but what of the families who'd lost their inheritances? A combined total of over 250 million in assets?

The second compiled data sheet contained several similar family names, and Kip realized it consisted of the prime beneficiaries and the alleged losses. Good God, it was no wonder this was for his eyes only. Frank Culver hadn't accumulated this information by sitting in hedges or perching in trees. Government records, financials, and alleged private banking reports. Therein lay the evidence and mystery. In nearly every one of the forty-one cases, the monies were channeled into the hands of the surviving relatives, then appeared in denominational differences over three years. The terminally ill were being robbed, the surviving families were benefiting, and in an endnote, Marilyn had handwritten: (When confronted, those with an asterisk presented evidence of living wills—lottery winnings—Vegas jackpots—can you believe? But numbers don't lie.)

Numbers never lie. 250 mil in unaccounted funds; 248 mil in combined capital gains.

On the third sheet, 32 employee names appeared, with employment dates ranging from March 1971 to May 1987, and these were apparently considered questionable in light of Frank's investigations. March 71 coincided with the first victim's arrival date.

Could it have truly begun as early as sixteen years ago?

Only a little over a dozen of the thirty-two names remained in Whistlebrook's employment, and was it a coincidence? About half of them occupied this room. Surprisingly, Carolyn McAnthony had made the list. Guilty by default? Or had his mother found some dirty laundry in Carolyn's closet? Bill, too, by no surprise.

In abstracted thought, his gaze caught briefly on a date—9/72 to 2/73. Francis a.k.a. "Franny." His own departure date, 10/72.

Folding the papers, Kip noted that only Mark Frances and John Madison had finished reading. Mark sat with his hands gripping the empty envelope, the page in his lap, his expression strained. His moist eyes stared vacantly toward the window beyond Bill's tipped head. John was far less controlled, though he brought a handkerchief from his suit pocket and wiped discreetly at his eyes. Leaning, Kip elbowed Mark and watched him jolt as if waking from a trance. Tipping his head, he signaled Mark to lean and, using Mulden's method, whispered, "Are you alright?"

Mark's head staggered back, his watery eyes seemed oddly surprised as he nodded and leaned, whispering, "Fine. You?"

Hearing his own words repeated back to him, intentionally, Kip cast Mark a glance and a nod, then sought Mulden with his gaze. Naturally, JD stood only three paces away, leaning against the wall, watching him. With a tip of his head, he signaled Mulden forward, ignoring JD's faint surprise as he accepted the gesture and leaned down. Across the table, Carolyn sniffed and stifled a sob; someone down the table followed her example, mimicking the sound. Kip whispered to JD, "Reposition discreetly and record the faces and impressions at this side of the table over the next ten minutes. I'll explain later."

JD nodded and dropped a hand on Kip's shoulder, offering a reassuring clasp for any interested party to notice.

Papers rattled and crinkled as more people sniffed and stifled breaths. Frank Culver wiped at his eyes unashamedly, and not surprisingly, JD moved along the wall, emerging at the far end of the table, where he sidled up to Frank and leaned in to whisper. Frank nodded, and Kip glimpsed the watery eyes along with his dogged nod. JD glanced at Kip, too, and nodded with a grim smile before backing to rest against the window. Without a doubt, Mulden had perfected his acting abilities.

A true artist. The prick.

John Madison cleared his throat with an effort. Reflection lingered in his solemn, strained features as he scanned the faces. "Marilyn will be missed," he said quietly and turned his focus to Kip. "She was an incredible woman," he said directly and received several murmured agreements while turning his attention to the task at hand, lifting another sealed envelope. Leaning, he handed it to Kip. "Will you hand that to Dr. Frances?"

By action, Kip agreed, catching Mark's dreading glance as he accepted the document.

"As executor of Marilyn's Will, Dr. Mark Frances, will you open that and read aloud its contents?"

'Was Mr. Patterson on that floor this evening?'

Unbidden, Bill's words echoed more clearly than John Madison's statement, and Kip remembered wondering why Bill had asked. And several days ago—Friday morning in the kitchen—Bill had mentioned Dr. Blake's records. Dr. Carmine had seen Dr. Blake's records, and there could be no mistaking Bill's fear over the past few days. *'He could be dangerous.'*

Not financially dangerous! Bill truly meant *physically* dangerous.

'Did you see Mr. Patterson on that floor this evening?'

The floor where one of the three residents had died. Not *died* for Chrissake! Two people *murdered?*

Abruptly, Mark's off-the-wall comment about 'competency' was no longer even remotely amusing, and God almighty, he couldn't *remember!* His stomach twisted in a violent lurch. He could not *remember* those five weeks clearly! And what if he'd doctored those drugs? He knew the chemical mixtures for a Brompton Cocktail. At thirteen, he could have doctored the drugs and known the results!

Beside him, Mark Frances unfolded the document. Across the table, Bill Bickerman rested with a lingering fond glaze in his eyes, even managing an assuring, faint grin toward Kip's glance. *'Bill won't be a happy man.'* And someone had doctored the meds, repeating a fifteen-year-old crime—a crime Bill Bickerman knew about! Knew at least enough to question Kip's whereabouts the previous evening! Not 'a happy man.' An unhappy man with suspicions that John Fitzpatrick could confirm and validate!

A goddamn murder charge! A setup! If the only heir to Whistlebrook was framed and convicted of murder. The Home would be tangled in litigation for years. 'The Prince is in danger ... someone wants to destroy his castle.'

And him!

As Mark cleared his throat to begin, Kip choked, "N-o. No—okay?" When Mark's attention pivoted, Kip swallowed a breath, rising tears to his eyes, shaking his head. "I-I'm *not*—fine. I-I can't handle this! I-I need a minute!" With tears spilling from his eyes, he pivoted his chair toward Madison and pushed to his feet clumsily. If Mark read that Will—the *authentic* Will—Bill Bickerman would cry allegations! Catching a fleeting glimpse of John's bewilderment, Kip shook his head. "Please, a minute—" He strangled the words and completed his clumsy stride, pushing into John's office with Mark following and Madison's words echoing in his wake.

"If you'll all bear with us for a moment."

Part Two

Enlightenment

Chapter 8

Deliberately, JD had stuck close to home, and despite his offhanded remarks and bantering, Kelly had sensed his ulterior motive. If he'd asked, she might have admitted that Richard was not the type of guy who'd barge in with a shotgun, but considering the kind of people JD apparently dealt with daily, she knew the futility. Having him around to snag cookie dough and hot-off-the-tray creations had truly been fun, but she'd recognized his tension growing as the afternoon wore on. Not to mention, he'd received and placed a dozen calls in the den. More than once, he'd sauntered into the kitchen, appearing more relaxed than his eyes indicated. Kip. Without a doubt, his thoughts and communications concerned Kip, and by no surprise, JD had changed from his flannel shirt and jeans into a decent shirt and jacket before departing. Saturday. Possibly, during one conversation or another on Saturday, someone mentioned that Marilyn Patterson's Will would be read this afternoon.

Considering the absence of relatives, Kelly suspected it was a formality, and for the first time, she wondered whether Kip would even consider staying in Randall.

Yesterday, maybe during dinner? No, before dinner, her father had made some comment about the inheritance, and JD had spoken offhandedly, mentioning, "He'll probably put it up for sale ASAP. Think he has too many memories there.'

Some of those memories had slammed him last evening. Pausing, staring blindly at her image in her dresser mirror, Kelly remembered those moments in his mother's room. His anger and sorrow had exploded in controlled violence. Absently, she shoved another lock of hair into the masterpiece unfolding atop her head. Sticking another bobby pin in place, she nearly cursed aloud. Why the hell even bother fixing her hair? The only reason for this family gathering in a five-star restaurant had evaporated. Or exploded. Studying her reflection in the mirror, she shook her head, feeling and watching the smirk sliding into her rouged lips. The Mulden clan.

Why even be surprised?

Half expecting to receive the third degree from her oldest and most practical brother, Kelly had called Bryce at his office to suggest they cancel the dinner reservations. Honestly, after the heart-to-heart and chummy conversations between Bryce and Richard only last evening, she'd thought Bryce would find a dozen reasons why she should reconsider her engagement to the prospective doctor.

Instead, in true Mulden nature, Bryce had commented, 'Guess that's one less seat we'll need at the table.'

'Bri, we really don't have any good reason to go to La Chateau,' she'd repeated, doubting he'd heard his words. When he was busy—which was always the case—he became something of an absent-minded professor. Unlike her former fiancé, however, Bryce never missed a thing regardless of his preoccupation. He was one of those rare individuals who could study a blueprint, imagine the building, and still arrive on time for any scheduled event—whether attending Bryn's soccer practice or showing up for a meeting with his engineers.

'Nonsense, Kelly-girl. We'll celebrate your un-engagement,' Bryce had said, sounding entirely practical. 'Tell the folks we'll be there around five and Kelly...? Smart move. Hope you're not too disappointed. See you in a bit.'

Insane. The entire Mulden clan was insane, not excluding her middle brother, Jeremy, who'd called from Kentucky to offer his congratulations over her disengagement. 'Heard he was a pompous ass anyway... Sorry, I can't be there to celebrate with you, but we'll be home in a couple of days. As wily as all other Mulden males, Jeremy had ended the call on another practical note. 'So, sis, if you don't have any plans for the un-honeymoon, how about planning on visiting our way for a while sometime soon?'

They were all nuts, she had decided years ago, but she loved the devils just the same. Even Mike had feigned disappointment for a half second, likely judging her mood, then sped into a running dialogue, offering ten million reasons why he was thrilled with the news and following up his words with about ten million reasons why Mr. Right-eous was all Wrong. 'So, what do you say I phone Pete and tell him you need a date for your un-engagement party?'

'Thanks so much, Jim, but I think I'll enjoy my un-attachment status this evening and pay fitting tribute to all the jerks in the world.'

Possibly, therein lay her reason for taking time to dress to the nines. When she'd tossed the new black dress in her garment bag, she'd been thinking about a funeral, but about two seconds after pulling the dress from her suitcase a week earlier, she'd reconsidered. Not a chance she'd wear that slinky black cocktail dress to a funeral. Too short, too shimmery, too form-fitting, and far too slight with the thin straps over the shoulders. She'd turn heads without a doubt, and God pity the first male to send her a lewd stare or whistling breath.

***

By the time Kip reached John's desk, every trace of tears had evaporated. Panic lingered in internal tremors as he rifled through the two folders with one hand, clearing his watery focus with the other. Where was it, damn it! Where was that damned bogus Will? Security. In that Will, Bill's position had remained secure. The man would have no reason to open a formal investigation! Security. Bickerman's position in the home was his vice!

Mark had followed Kip to the desk; his hand landed on Kip's shoulder, his confusion apparent in a glance. "What—"

At a glimpse of the Will in Mark's hand, Kip lifted his gaze sharply and focused clearly. "You can't read that Will, Mark. It's a match—a match to send Whistlebrook up in flames."

"Wha—"

Madison entered the room with Mulden on his heels, and even before the door snapped shut in their wake, their sorrow transformed into doubt and bewilderment. Suspicion flew into JD's hazel eyes before they reached the desk.

"Kip...?" John asked. "Are you...?"

Flashing glances between them, Kip leveled his gaze on Mulden. "Why the hell didn't you stay in Aspen?" he asked angrily.

"Because a friend of mine needs me whether he likes it or not," JD fired back clandestinely. "What the hell was that act about?"

Only more annoyed, Kip backhanded the stack of papers, sending them sailing off the desk. "Hysterical," he stated and shot a volatile gaze at Madison. "My mother trusted you, but I'm not at all sure I do. In fact," he glanced at Frances and Mulden. "I'm not too sure I trust *any* of you," he realized with his anger rising. "I have been manipulated and deceived, and if I didn't know better, I'd *swear* this is some sort of ultimate payback designed exclusively to throw me into a mental tailspin, and at this juncture, I wish that were the case!"

"What did you mean about a 'match,' Kip?" Mark asked carefully.

Murder! For God's sake! 'I don't know what lengths these people will go to.' Her second letter. Shaking his head, Kip scanned the clutter of papers on the floor, then lifted his focus to Madison. "Where's that goddamned Will you showed me Friday?"

"Per your mother's request, Kip, it no longer exists," John said carefully.

Stunned, Kip gazed at him. "The options?" *Please, tell me—*

Madison's apology enhanced with his nod. "Dr. Frances is holding the only Will in existence, although I have reason to believe there's at least one duplicate along with the recorded pages."

"Thought of everything, didn't she?" he snickered his disdain, again shaking his head as he shook a cigarette from the pack already in his hand. Catching the filter under his mustache, he dragged a flame into the tobacco. A subtle tremor slid through his palms.

A nervous breakdown? Not far off, thanks, mother!

Sighing an exhale, Kip looked at Madison with genuine dread. "Don't imagine an heir's ever contested a Will to forfeit his legacy?"

Madison smiled slightly. "Not to my knowledge."

"Care to tell me what's going on?" Mulden asked.

Turning his thoughts inward, Kip gazed into abstracts as his subconscious waded through the added input of Marilyn's latest script. Numbers don't lie. Forty-one residents were robbed over the course of twelve years. Thirty-two employees are suspects. Fifteen-year-old murders repeated.

Why did you ask, Bill? Why did you suspect that I visited that ward last night? Who—who the hell gave Bill that ammunition? Why had Bill seen Dr. Blake's confidential files? What the hell did those files contain?

'The old fruit cellar ... archives.'

The archives. Only two keys existed. One was kept in the safe, and Bill had access to the safe.

"Damn it! Snap out of it!" JD stated.

Blake's files. The archives. Thirty-two names.

"Kip," Mark started.

Looking to Mulden, Kip commented, "Don't imagine I could walk out of here without you, could I?"

"You're catching on," JD mused.

With a disgusted sigh, Kip turned his focus toward the window, momentarily watching a curtain of water spilling down the pane like a thick layer of tears. The trees beyond the glass melted into a collage of fading, fusing color, reminding Kip of his childhood room.

"Damn it," Kip uttered, his focus clearing. His mother had believed he'd suffered a nervous breakdown, but did she truly believe him capable of accidentally or intentionally murdering at least two of their residents? His friends. *Damnit, I can't remember!* He cried silently, angrily, before a more immediate thought tugged at his consciousness. An enemy. His mother believed the enemy would be in the room when her Will was read. Bickerman then? Bickerman had asked the nurse on the ward; his voice was careful, troubled — not panicked — when he asked whether Kip had gone onto the ward.

Damnit. Security.

Bill's vice was job security, and the Home was his security. Bickerman's loyalty was to Bill Bickerman, and he wanted Whistlebrook under his thumb.

Back to the reactions in the room. Concentrate. 'Watch their reactions.' The Will needed to be read, the fire controlled, and Bill Bickerman could be controlled. Three days prior, in the kitchen, Bickerman had forfeited his threat of an 'assault charge' to secure Whistlebrook.

The Will needed to be read, reactions monitored and controlled.

Breathing another smoky sigh, Kip leaned and crushed his cigarette, finding Mulden's intent gaze. "Record what you see when the Will's read."

"Am I looking for anything in particular?"

"A red glow," Kip answered offhandedly and turned his gaze to Mark. "Ready to read?"

"You said—"

"Forget what I said," Kip said evenly, glancing at John, then the door. "Let's try this once more, shall we?"

If only auras could announce guilt or else volitions, but nothing was ever easy.

Over the next ten minutes, as Mark read the final words and bequest, there were reactions, but none without merit or sincerity. The colors swirled in rainbow waves from one body to the other. From brilliant crimson to glowing orange to black and green, the mist swelled over the heads and spread, one into another. No help there.

For the first time in weeks, if not months, Kip utilized the talent that generally lent him insight across a boardroom table and assisted in most negotiations, but the auras here remained too convoluted for quick interpretation.

All three head nurses appeared bewildered and flushed. Mrs. Cross, close to retirement age, broke into muffled sobs, and one of the others, Margie Morone, comforted her while struggling against her choked voice behind a cloak of yellow and purple. Compassion and purple. Carolyn maintained her poise despite her visible sorrow, which she concealed behind a haze of pink and blue, a combination of compassion and insight. Bill Bickerman showed early signs of surprise; his dark eyes riveted on Mark. Confusion etched across his brow, folding slowly into anger; his twitching cheeks flushed in outrage, and his eyes darted between Kip and John Madison, his color flowing red in spiraling waves.

As the final words spilled from Mark's bearded lips, Bill's tension snapped; his focus leveled on John Madison. "That's not her Will," he stated sharply, barely restraining his tone. "That is not—and never has been—Marilyn's request, and I would like an explanation, John."

"Bill, I can understand your surprise—"

"Just tell me—" Bill's gaze leveled on Kip, close to glowing. "How did you manage it? How did you manage to change her Will?"

"Excuse me?" Kip asked quietly, dueling Bill's gaze with practiced indifference.

"Don't you play innocent with me!" Bill stated. "That's not the Will you showed me three days ago! Your mother made provisions. She secured the Home's future! She didn't want it left to your bungling hands! She wanted the Home to run smoothly in her absence! That—was her dying wish. Not this! It's absurd!" His gaze shifted to Madison. "How much has he promised to pay you, John? How much did it take for you to draw up this *forgery* and turn your back on Marilyn?"

"Bill," Carolyn said quietly, touching his arm, drawing his angry gaze, her own confused. "We've all been under a lot of stress, but do you realize what you're saying?"

"What I realize is that a *crime* has been committed here," Bill stated, not willing to be appeased. His gaze shot to Kip. "And I will not stand still for this! Your mother wouldn't have turned the Home over to you, no-strings-attached. She worked too hard to keep it running smoothly to leave it entirely in your hands!"

"She might have been counting on you to help me of your own accord, Bill," Kip said quietly, his focus intent despite the abstract quality of his gaze.

Haltingly, Bill seemed to consider the words before he realized his precarious position, along with the improbability of his continued affiliation with Whistlebrook. His dark eyes hardened; no trace of his infamous smile touched his flat expression. "I will get to the bottom of this," he stated and looked at Madison. "I don't know how—or why—you helped him with this insanity, but in the interest of Whistlebrook, I intend to retain an attorney, and I will see that you—"

"Bill," Kip interrupted, stopping Bill partway out of his chair. "Sit down and be quiet."

"I am not going to sit back and watch you ruin your mother's life's work," Bill stated. "I will not allow you to squander away her estate as you've squandered thousands—if not millions—over the past ten years!" His gaze shot to Frances. "And you! Why am I not surprised that you'd be involved in all of this? You think I don't know about your relationship to him? I never understood that attraction—what you held over her—but it all adds up," Bill stated. "All of these years, you've tried convincing Marilyn to bring him in. I wouldn't be surprised if you arranged all of this! You'd like nothing better than to have your bastard son at the—"

"Bill!" Mark stated sharply, his gaze bouncing off Kip to Bickerman with his anger unmasked. "I think that's enough!"

"Oh, that's right," Bill sniggered and shifted his hostile gaze to Kip. "You don't know that—"

"Mr. Bickerman," John stated in a curt, commanding tone. "I believe I've heard enough of your hysterical rambling and accusations. The Will, which we have all just heard, is, in fact, the only duly recorded and authentic document. The document you claim to have seen for the first time on Friday afternoon was one of a half dozen that my agency had prepared for Marilyn. Except for financial allotments to all of you, she decided that her only son was more than amply qualified and well deserving of her accumulated assets, his inheritance.

"As an attorney, sir, I should advise you that should you continue in your present dissertation, Mr. Patterson would be well within his rights to bring personal legal charges against you, and in the interest of Whistlebrook, I'd advise him accordingly. I suggest, you consider, sir, you have no legal—or financial—claim to contest or question these proceedings."

Watching Bickerman's knotted pulse, Kip decided and interrupted in a quiet tone, "Bill?" When the blazing eyes shifted, he continued, "I understand your concern for Whistlebrook, and as sole owner and temporary administrator, I'm obligated to tell you—you are, presently, in jeopardy of losing what little ground you have beneath you. Frankly, sir, sit down and be quiet, or I may be forced to ask for your resignation in the Home's best interest."

"I will not—"

"Bill," Kip stated without lifting his tone, concentrating his focus. "As you pointed out, sir, my mother spent her life and energy in Whistlebrook. I will not permit you—an assistant administrator—or anyone else to destroy her legacy. Obviously, bearing in mind her considerations on early drafts of her bequests, she felt you were an important asset. I value her intuition despite what you may believe, sir. But if you should prove her wrong at this junction and threaten Whistlebrook's stability during this transition, I will have you replaced."

Behind his rage, Bill's wheels began to turn—both bewilderment and surprise flashed like neon before he grasped the intensity of Kip's gaze and forfeited his outrage to dumbstruck disbelief.

Carolyn McAnthony rested back in her chair, smiling faintly, not even slightly surprised at the transformation or the echo of Marilyn Patterson's countenance and intellect. Frank Culver, too, appeared mildly amused, though his dark eyes carried a mist of nostalgia; no doubt, remembering the queen. Behind Culver, JD stood with his arms crossed, leaning casually against the wall, his gaze amused despite a lingering intensity. Mark Frances wore an unmistakably smug expression; his blue gaze conveyed only assurance and approval. Past Mark, Mrs. Cross strained against another sob, and Margie Morone patted her shoulder, whispering comforting words which appeared to fall on deaf ears.

Unconsciously, Kip's gaze shifted past Mark, seeing the nurses huddled together while he suggested, "Carry on if you will, doctor." *Mrs. Cross—1971 to present.* Her short, graying hair, held in place by a stiff perm, shook back and forth. Her rounded cheeks blazed with a bright red flush between swipes of a stark white embroidered handkerchief held in trembling fingers. Arthritic fingers. Kip suffered a pang of sympathy as he noticed the swollen bulge of her knuckles. So many of the residents sustained that horrific affliction in their brittle joints, and more than a few night moans could be attributed to that unearthly pain.

Madison had again turned to his legal brief, extracting an ample collection of documents. He and Mark Frances had been busy this afternoon. The bulk of the forms concerned the transfer of Whistlebrook; all of which, John rifled together and slid in front of Kip with a wily grin. "You may have writer's cramp before we're finished. If you'd like to begin looking over those, Dr. Frances and I will see to the personal allotment of funds."

In what could pass for random scans, Kip introverted the legal jargon, lifted one of several pens on the table, and began signing the documents. Questioning one, he turned it onto the pile without his signature and continued at a rapid pace. By the time Mark signed the last of eleven checks totaling more than one hundred thousand dollars in bank drafts, Kip had reached the last of Whistlebrook's transfers.

As Mark began distributing the allotments, Kip moved from his chair, passed behind John Madison, and stopped behind Bill, who ducked as if cowering from a physical blow. Not amused, Kip gripped Bill's shoulder, leaned and whispered to him, "Take a few days off, Bill. Your stress level's peaking. The business office is officially closed now through Christmas." He started to lift, impulsively leaning again. "Merry Christmas." Pushing off, ignoring Bill's dumbstruck surprise, he moved to Carolyn, leaning, accepting her fingers, which came over her shoulder to squeeze his hand. "Take a holiday, luv. I'll see you next Monday. Merry Christmas."

"Kip," she said softly, wearing a combination of fondness and concern. "If you need me, call me, all right?"

"Thank you," he said, bypassing an empty chair and leaning, dropping his hand on Frank's shoulder, whispering, "First order of business, Frank. Find Edna. She bought the house on Adderly Lane. Know where it is?" At Frank's nod, Kip whispered, "Check there on your way home. If she's not there, turn Whistlebrook upside down."

Frank nodded, conveying his concern in his dark eyes, a concern Kip mirrored. Edna Feeney wasn't a woman to miss an appointment, and certainly not *this* appointment. Something was very wrong.

Patting Frank's shoulder in a sign of assurance that he didn't feel, Kip turned to JD, offering a grin with even less assurance. "I need a break and a drink. Care to join me in John's office?"

"Love to," Mulden said with a natural grin and light tone.

A few spectators took a casual interest, and for the first time, Kip realized at least two undercover government agents stood in attendance, along with representatives of civic groups and charities awaiting Marilyn's posthumous contribution. Barely glancing to record the strangers' faces, Kip turned, catching a more than casual glimpse of Mrs. Cross's glassy eyes—bloodshot eyes falling away from him, dropping sideways into a tissue as if in shame. *Or was it fear?*

***

Taking an extra second to check her makeup, twist a wisps of curls from the bundle now perched on her head, Kelly collected the sheer black shawl to cover her shoulders, and stepped into her high heels.

Less than a minute later, Kelly strode down the steps and caught her father's rapid second glance. Amused, she watched his dark blue eyes slide down and up, and saw the curve of his mustache as his eyes lit with genuine delight and subtle relief. Of all the Mulden males, this one was the crème de la crème. Hugging Patty under his arm, he ducked his head conspiratorially, whispering, "Think we'd better try tracking down a few more of our sons. We're going to need a whole blasted battalion to fend off the sharks this eve, m' dear."

Patty's eyes sparked with amusement and delight, approving wholeheartedly as she skipped her gaze over Kelly's ensemble. "Your father's right, sweetie. You look absolutely stunning."

Guaranteed to boost the ego, Kelly mused silently and caught even her younger brother, generally the cad, speculating as he surveyed her ensemble.

"Good thing I didn't phone Pete," he muttered as he tugged on his navy jacket. "Either the poor guy would have tripped over his tongue or incinerated at the sight of you." With a spark of amusement, he added, "Nice getup, sis."

Ten minutes later, Bryce and Shelly arrived and, like all others, judged her level of distress before launching into banter. The un-engagement dinner party was off to a roaring head start, and the only pall over the affair was the absence of JD. Technically, unbeknownst to him, he had earned the position of guest of honor for his heroic participation in what they unanimously agreed was a monumental carriage of justice. Mike was the most dismayed, having missed the ordeal, which he would have enjoyed seeing, if not assisting. "The guy was a jerk, Kell," Mike had professed at least a dozen times. "Believe me, you deserve better..."

Despite all the outrageous comments designed to prohibit her from dwelling too deeply on the regret they expected her to suffer at any moment, Kelly couldn't quite dismiss a sense of foreboding, and Richard was no part of her thoughts. If she didn't hear from JD by the time this dinner engagement ended, she would either track him down or find Kip. With every passing minute, she caught herself worrying just a little more with no sound reason for her growing unease.

Chapter 9

Mrs. Janet Cross—1971—South Wing. *South Wing now*, Kip corrected as his internal mechanics kicked into high gear on route to Madison's office. In 1971, she'd worked in the East Wing. He remembered her as a younger woman, in her early forties, stout in nature and build, with the leadership qualities her position demanded. Hardcore, the way Marilyn Patterson always liked her nurses, especially those on the East Wing. That group needed to be hardcore to survive the emotional stress. Janet Cross had been tough, tough enough to scare the hell out of a thirteen-year-old prince. What was it? What single thread of memory? A patient...? An obese patient, her stomach swollen with a tumor, tubes protruding from beneath the sheets. The woman had been moved to the East Wing, but she'd dwelt in Spring Chicken Lounge before that, and Mrs. Cross had visited—Mrs. Ramsey? No, something was wrong with that memory. Janet had visited the lounge, but not to visit a tumor patient—

In a fleeting instant, Kip drew the memory from the past ... Mrs. Ramsey, a kindly elderly woman whose brittle fingers had worked tirelessly crocheting a checkered quilt which even now lay on the bed in Kip's college-covered room. For hours, he'd held the weave of cotton on his splayed fingers as she worked on that quilt, 'For someone special," she'd told him, alluding to one of her grandchildren as the recipient. On his eleventh birthday, she'd given him that wondrous quilt to his surprise and delight. How he'd loved them, all of them, but some more than others.

And Mrs. Cross, head nurse on the west wing, had threatened to blame Kip for the elder woman's mishap, a mishap that might have contributed to the old woman's demise several days later. He'd heard Mrs. Ramsey's scream the moment he'd stepped onto the fourth floor, pushing the evening snack cart, and he'd found her clinging to the side of her bed, sliding in her own excrement. Even now, he remembered that wicked smell and the searing pain of his torn intestines ripped through his memory. The beginning, he knew now. The beginning of what was nearly his own end. At three hundred pounds compared to his one-twenty, catching her had almost killed him, and set off a series of events to send him from his home.

Not once in fifteen years had he confronted that elder nurse about that incident, and this wasn't to become the exception. Some memories were better left buried.

"All right," JD interrupted the memory, halting within arm's reach in front of Kip. His inherently deep voice lowered to a menacing octave. "No more games, Kip."

Clearing his focus, Kip lit a cigarette and spoke with an exhale of smoke. "It seems to me, I have more right to make that demand than you, sir. I'm not the one in Randall under false pretenses."

"I won't deny I'm here in a semi-official capacity," JD said soberly, his gaze intent. "Had I known about your mother, I would have come regardless. The fact that I was pulled in—officially—is secondary. Your sources are good, and to tell you the truth—"

"Novel idea. Truth," Kip commented, faintly amused at Mulden's spark of anger.

"—that bothers the hell out of me, because for the simple reason," Mulden continued darkly. "That qualifies a few of the allegations against you."

"Isn't this rather unorthodox in your profession? Rather like compromising your agency and your mission."

"I'm well aware of the risks I'm taking, but I took this 'mission' for personal reasons and in doing so, compromised my agency a week ago. Now, let's drop the bullshit," JD stated bluntly. "I came here to help you because I don't believe—despite your indifference over the past few days—that you are guilty of whatever illicit dealings are going on in Whistlebrook."

Absently, Kip looked toward the window. Only last night, he'd dismissed the conspiracy idea, but numbers don't lie. The list—the list of beneficiaries. At the extent of those searches, Frank would have needed months to compile that data—and Marilyn's list was the missing link. "Numbers and facts," he said absently. Abstract thought had forever carried him into fantasies, and fantasies were built in wandering minds—minds floating on morphine or atropine—minds with physically induced frailties.

"What about numbers and facts?" JD asked.

Kip focused on Mulden's tense gaze. "I've built my life on numbers, JD. Numbers and concrete facts don't change, don't lie or deceive, which is far more than I'd credit to most living, breathing entities."

"Look, I don't blame you for being pissed," Mulden said lightly. "But you need me whether you like it or not. Too much of this shit doesn't add up, only starting with the fact that three nights ago, you seemed to believe your mother wanted Bill Bickerman to run the Home. You were dead set on signing it over to him—"

"Ah, that's right. I made you privy to certain details under the guise of friendship. Tell me, old friend, were you wired? Do you have a microphone under your shirt right now? No, I don't suppose you do since you've blown your cover—"

"Goddamn it, knock it off. I wasn't wearing a fucking wire and—no, before you ask—I didn't know your mother's office was wired—which, by the way, did not originate in my office."

"You truly should have stayed in Aspen, or should I say, South America, since we've dropped theatrics for the moment?"

"Information like that doesn't engender my trust," Mulden said with a visible shift in attitude; not a glimpse of his old smile touched his bearded lips.

"Another novel idea, old friend. Trust," Kip commented without affect, his gaze steady. "And I think we've wasted enough time sparring. At the moment—" As he spoke, he shifted on his feet, starting toward the second door. "We have—"

"Hold it! We're—"

By reflex and instinct, Kip pivoted, not fully conscious of deflecting the intended grasp. In one motion, Kip clasped the wrist and spilled Mulden over his shoulder, following. Resting, halted, and faintly stunned, Kip rested on Mulden's chest, looking down on the lax, unconscious face for the second time in a single day. Three concentrated years of daily training, a lifetime ago, had paid off. "Damnit," Kip uttered and halfheartedly considered slapping Mulden awake. Impulsively, he pushed to his feet, moved to John's desk, and tore a sheet of notepaper from a pad near the phone. Leaning, he wrote briefly, 'You really shouldn't grab people like that, old friend. Clear your head and meet me at Whistlebrook.' Striding to JD, Kip tucked the note into his limp hand and stepped over the splayed agent on route to the door.

The archives. Somewhere in those damned 'archives' evidence existed, evidence of a fifteen-year-old crime, evidence of an enemy dating back twelve years ... or fifteen years? Mrs. Cross—1972.

Damnit! 1972.

Striding through the corridor, Kip passed into the modern reception area, appreciating Jason's sharp glance. In an instant, the boy dropped his magazine aside and rose.

Madison's secretary looked over, too, lowered her gaze, then lifted it sharply. "Mr. Patterson," she said haltingly, and shuffled pages on her desk. Lifting a note page, she started out of her chair as Kip veered to her. "You had a call—she wouldn't leave her name." With an odd nervous smile, she glanced at the note while handing it to him. "She wanted me to tell you—you look good in a towel—and she said she'd be waiting for you."

At a glance, he read 'Le Chateau' while motioning King toward the door. On impulse, he turned his gaze to Leslie. "If anyone enquires, you never gave me a message. Right?" The last thing he needed was a hostile Mulden barging into a five-star restaurant.

"Right, sir," Leslie said and winked.

"Don't you need your coat?" Jason asked, while taking a step toward the door ahead of Kip.

Not California! Blasted rain rather than snow, but still cold. His coat rested in the conference room with at least two government agents standing guard, and returning to Madison's office—to the possibility of Mulden stirring—held no appeal. Disgusted, Kip motioned Jason out, already dreading the downpour. Breaking from beneath the awning, he knew the futility of remaining warm and dry even before he trotted across the parking lot. Drenched, he stood a moment as Jason fumbled anxiously with his keys and opened the passenger door. At least he had dry clothes on hand. Stepping into the cab, already shivering, he swept his wet hair into a '50s style and began manipulating his suitcase as Jason scrambled into the driver's seat.

"Where to?" Jason asked.

"Le Chateau," Kip decided, and flopped open his garment bag between them before pulling his dripping sweater over his head.

***

Of all the people Kelly would have enjoyed seeing within the crowded entry of Le Chateau, Richard Whitman was the absolute last on the list. Somehow, though, she wasn't entirely surprised to find him already seated at the reserved table. JD was right. Richard wouldn't forfeit his fantasies without a fight, and apparently, considering JD's hostility, Richard had chosen the path of least opposition. The idiot! Did he think JD was the exception to the Mulden clan rule? The two eldest males in the present company would think very little of lifting Richard by the scruff of the neck and escorting him, rather rudely, from this fine restaurant. Richard was pushing his luck. If they escaped this evening without an old-fashioned donnybrook, Kelly would consider Richard extremely lucky.

With a few stifled steps, the clan nearly halted en masse, and by no surprise, her father moved to her side, dipping his head near her shoulder. "Your call, sweetie. Would you like us to remove this fellow?"

The nerve of this idiot to turn up here, apparently thinking himself safe within the public setting. He sat, bold as life, already holding a tumbler—probably, brandy—on the table in front of him, though he set it aside quickly and rose at the sight of the advancing party. His gaze fixed on her alone, he seemed suddenly desperate, his tense eyes watery in the subdued light. A strained smile affected his soft lips—another pout that suddenly grated on Kelly's nerves. How dare he come here with every intention of apparently making a scene, if not another appeal for forgiveness? He should be in Philadelphia by now!

"Mr. Mulden, Bryce," Richard said as the two crowded him, nearly backing him into the aisle. His gaze fleeted sharply, desperately. "Kelly...?"

Darting her gaze between her father and brother, both of whom appeared all too ready to grab Richard, Kelly shook her head, warning them away from a physical confrontation. "Let's just sit down," she said smoothly and sent her mother a reassuring glance, stepping aside to let Patty and Shelly reach the chairs between tables. A coward, Kelly considered. On top of all his other attributes, Richard was apparently a coward, coming here, ensconcing himself at this table where he wouldn't likely be tossed on his ear. Or pompous, to believe he had every right to be here waiting, expecting to win her undying appreciation for his clever tact.

With a scathing glance as he moved closer, reaching for her coat, she stated, "Just sit down, Richard."

"Darling, I know you're angry, but I needed—"

"Just sit," she hissed, barely able to control the venom in her tone. She wouldn't offer this idiot the satisfaction of creating a scene in this restaurant, but maintaining civility might truly pose a problem.

"You look fantastic," he said lamely and stood aside, looking at her with a beseeching, pouting smile.

With a glare, she backed Richard from reaching for her chair, and on her opposite side, Mike clasped her chair in proper gentlemanly form. One glance into her younger brother's heated blue eyes and she knew the powder keg simmering. "Be civil," she said discreetly.

"You're asking a lot, sis," he said quietly and slipped into the chair at her side.

Richard moved into the chair he'd occupied directly across from her, perhaps feeling safe with Jarred Mulden taking the seat alongside him.

Big mistake, Kelly might have mentioned with a glance at her father's heated eyes, too visibly tense despite the subdued lighting. If Richard so much as made an untoward remark, the fellow would need dental work. For her father's sake, Kelly forced a smile, her eyes conveying the silent message to her father. *Let it alone. Let him alone.* Dinner, however, might be extremely short.

"Mr. Mulden," Richard spoke in a strained, low tone. "I uhm ... I'm sorry for intruding like this—"

"Out of respect for my daughter, I won't assist you to the door," Jarred said with a tip of his head, his dark blue eyes intent. The smile that every Mulden male had inherited, a wiry twist of dark whiskers that could never be mistaken for friendly, tipped her father's lips. "But don't push your luck here, Richard. I know my daughter broke off her engagement with you this afternoon. I don't know the details, but I know she has her reasons. Frankly, I think you showing up here is in bad taste."

"I needed to see her, sir," Richard said, sounding desperate, his gaze shifting across the table. "Kelly, I realize how wrong I was this morning. I'm sorry," he said in a soft, near pleading tone.

At the opposite end of the table, the waitress arrived and began taking drink orders. Grateful for the distraction allowing her to avoid Richard's pitiless plea, Kelly placed her order for coffee, although a double of anything sounded pretty good.

Chapter 10

By the time the '65 pulled in front of Le Chateau, Kip was straightening his tie and collar. As an afterthought, he rooted in his bag, found a comb, and managed to untangle the wet strands. At a glance, he read Jason's laughing eyes, mirroring the boy's amusement. Eccentric. He truly was becoming eccentric, changing into a three-piece suit in the cab of a moving pickup truck. Shaking his head, he turned his attention to tugging the door open. White tracer lights decorated the canopy, countering the onset of dusk shadows and holding back a blowing rain.

"Think I really *will* wait out here this time," Jason mused.

"Nonsense. Park the limo and come inside. Get a cup of tea at the bar. I'm not sure how long we'll be. Doubtful we'll have time for dinner."

"I could uh ... go get my dad's LeBaron. I mean, if you're going to be picking up ... needing a backseat—"

Amused, Kip commented, "Just park and come inside." Stepping out of the truck, he sobered before reaching the frosted glass door. A half-sister. After thirty years, he was about to officially meet a half-sister.

Moving through a crowded lobby, Kip caught echoes of Christmas carols from a banquet room and suffered a momentary bout of claustrophobia as bright red and livid green closed around him. Christmas. Christmas parties. Christmas dinners. One large party clustered about the maître d's station, and as Kip waited, he heard reference to a wedding, a Christmas wedding. Excusing himself, he sidled next to the pedestal and snagged the tuxedoed man's aloof gaze. A gentleman's gentleman, Kip mused. "Someone's expecting me—Kip Patterson."

"Of course, sir. This way," he said without a glance at his waiting list.

Definitely a Christmas crowd. Kip followed the maître d' into the shadowy, candlelit atmosphere, a festive setting. Reserved laughs and giggles erupted; clinking glasses and silverware cut through the air, scissoring china plates. A soft, symphonic rendition of "Deck the Halls" muffled the words within the hum of voices. How much had she palmed the maître d to get a corner booth in the busiest season—barring Valentine's Day—of the year?

His question disintegrated as he slid into the rear bench seat; his gaze locked on the blue eyes watching him. A half-sister, his mind snapped, remembering those brief seconds in the bathroom and his moments of vulnerability. A smile played on her lips, rising into her candlelit eyes. She was beautiful. Her shiny, dark hair glistened, swept and folded into an elegant style. A low V-neck dress exposed a small fortune in diamonds within fine, delicate gold chains. Diamonds flashed beneath the sweep of hair against her slender neck. Her eyes—long black lashes framed her eyes in remarkable contrast to her light complexion, and for a moment, Kip had a sense—a distant sense of having seen her before ... before Friday. Sometime in the past—

"Could I bring you a cocktail, sir?" the maître d asked.

Glancing at her half-empty glass, Kip nodded to the gentleman, "A Scotch and water and another for the lady."

"A Pernod," she said aloofly, barely acknowledging the maître d. Her eyes danced with mischief; her voice softened lyrically, "I wondered if you'd accept my invitation."

"How could you possibly doubt it?" Kip mused. "I generally have the pleasure of an introduction before wearing a towel."

Her eyes sparkled. "You weren't wearing a towel, darling."

"As I recall, I attempted to rectify that blunder," he countered, mirroring her mischief, wondering how long she would continue this charade before enlightening him, wondering if she *would* enlighten him.

Her gaze trailed over him with a familiar appraisal. "You're a handsome man in—or out of—a towel, darling."

"You're a beautiful woman, luv," he said lightly, glimpsing the motion outside the booth. At a glance, he spotted the short-skirted waitress advancing through the shadowy aisle. What possessed him to take a second glance? His focus was drawn to the magnificent candlelit eyes. Hazel eyes swamped in long, thick lashes, her brunette curls flowed in a shimmering cascade over her bare shoulders. His heart skipped a beat, his inanimate smile warmed with his quickening pulse, and he parted his lips to speak. Never was he more grateful for a waitress stepping into his path, breaking the connection just as Richard Whitman had started to pivot his head. God Almighty! Randal was such a *small* town! Kelly Mulden and her fiancé here—of all places in the universe—and they weren't alone. Jarred and Patty Mulden, Bryce and his wife, Shelly, all scattered about the center table within the shadowy light. What was it? What was that odd sense of heat rising into his mind as he turned his attention to finding a cigarette pack in his jacket? He should be only happy for Kelly Mulden and grateful that she'd taken his advice!

Then why suddenly did he consider dueling Richard Whitman...? Escorting him through the frosted glass doors, walking twenty paces, turning, firing. Damnit! Kelly Mulden was not his type! Not his concern! She deserved Whitman, a love-sick puppy foolish enough to brave blizzards and ice storms through mountains in a *fucking Datsun! I can't even keep a* parked *car safe on an icy road, and God knows, the Buick had needed its front end aligned after skidding into a few curbs and snowbanks on Friday morning!*

What the hell am I doing?

Shaking his head, exhaling smoke through his smirked grin, Kip focused on the deep blue eyes across from him. Someone was trying to frame him for murder, recreating fifteen-year-old crimes that he could neither deny nor confess to committing. Presently, he sat across from a half-sister whose existence he'd never even imagined before three days ago, and who appeared intent on flirting with him. He had a DEA agent waking up in an attorney's office, probably issuing a warrant by now; he had just inherited close to eighty million dollars, which he neither wanted nor needed ... *and I'm pissed because I can't drive in the snow to rescue Kelly Mulden, whose only real problem is probably an unhealthy infatuation with me?*

"I'd love to know what you're thinking, darling?"

With a sardonic amusement, he shook his head, lifting his drink and catching an uncontrollable glimpse of Kelly's averted profile—magnificent. "Trust me. You'd rather not know," he commented, looking into Marion's blue eyes while lifting his glass. "A toast, possibly?"

Maintaining her smile, she lifted her glass delicately, meeting him halfway. "To what should we toast?"

"Communal baths," he mused.

"Cheers," she agreed with a comfortable laugh in her voice.

With a swallow, he collected his thoughts, sobering within his vacant smile. "As much as I love a good mystery, luv, do you think we might formally introduce ourselves soon?"

Still amused, she answered, "Humor me, darling. Let's order dinner first. I'm absolutely famished."

His lack of interest in food nearly started a protest before he reconsidered. He couldn't even recall when he'd last partaken, let alone anything of substance. Possibly not since Friday evening before going out with JD. He'd skipped dinner at the Muldens' and barely made an appearance at the ladies' luncheon ... cold chicken in the kitchen—

How gracefully she'd slipped into his arms, fitting onto his lap, her fingers sliding under his collar. A taste of peppermint lingered in his mouth, a scent of strawberries. His gaze drifted, catching on her hazel eyes before she cast a deliberate gaze, almost forcefully, to the man seated across from her. *Whitman wasn't even wearing a suit,* Kip noticed while glancing over the dark, wavy hair facing him—the idiot wore another sweater with a shirt collar clashing miserably. *I changed in a truck ... Damnit! Stop it!*

Withdrawing his attention, he scanned the menu briefly and set it aside, concentrating his gaze on Marion McDaniels-Smithfield. In one blinding instant, an image came to him: a dark, floppy hat, blue eyes—piercing blue eyes—leveled at him with an intensity that sent heated flashes through his body. A sense of doubt and insecurity—vulnerability—swept through his mind more vividly than the vision. Unconsciously, he pulled away from that feeling, dropping his gaze. Not in years—not in a dozen years or more—had a woman's touch intimidated him, much less her gaze. As a child, he'd suffered insecurities around strangers—men and women, children and adults alike, until they reached resident age.

JD Mulden had initiated that change ... Jenna Scottsdale. Sweet, not-so-shy Jenna ... He hadn't entered the seminary chaste or disillusioned himself that he could live a life of celibacy.

"Could I take your order, sir?"

Preoccupied, Kip ordered the Lobster as John had recommended three evenings past, then, on impulse, stopped the waitress from turning. "There's a young man at the bar wearing a Randal High letter jacket, take his order and put it on my tab. Also, that party behind you? Send them a bottle of your finest champagne ... on the house, so to speak. Understood?"

"Yes, sir," she said while glancing at the Mulden table. "Will there be anything else?"

"That's all for the moment," he said absently and caught Marion's curious gaze. With a faint smile, he tipped his drink in a silent toast, but the roller-coaster of nostalgia hadn't ended. Nor would it ... not with the weight of Whistlebrook falling into perspective. The option ... had he fallen so readily for that deceptive option, ignored the apparent discrepancies out of desire? Once and for all, he'd allowed himself to believe he would be free of the Home and the past to haunt him. No option existed. The Home was, now—officially—his burden, and how easily he'd accepted that albatross. Perhaps, though, not so easily. Stopping Mark Frances hadn't been entirely an act. The panic had staggered him from that room, the sudden hot flood of tears ... He'd recovered by the time he reached the desk, his conscious mind overruling his subconscious hysteria.

'...Aa Patterson built it ... only a Patterson has the right to destroy it. My Blessings...'

"You are a man with a great deal on your mind," Marion interrupted in a soft, lyrical voice. "Forgive my boldness, darling, but I know you've just come from an attorney's office. The public reading of your mother's Will." Her eyes carried a hint of sorrow. "You have my sympathy for the loss of your mother. I understand, she was an incredible woman . . ." She paused, studying him with her soft gaze. "I can't help wondering about your preoccupation, though ... You've not been robbed of your inheritance, have you, darling?"

The intensity of her gaze contradicted her soft, forced grin, and abruptly, annoyance flooded him. Annoyance over this game. Annoyance that she chose this time in his life to confront him. How long had she known? When had she learned of her father's infidelity and the bastard son of her legitimate father? With anger rising in his gaze, he asked quietly, "Why are you here, Marion?"

For a split second, her blue eyes faltered in surprise, then brightened with laughter. In passing seconds, her expression wavered with a contagious, giddy amusement. Stifling a tiny laugh, she lifted her wine, not losing him in her gaze as she sipped a few swallows.

Not amused, Kip watched her, more curious than he cared to consider. Of all the reactions he might have anticipated, to see his half-sister battling a giggle hadn't made the cut. Maintaining his grin, he watched her set the glass aside, wondering how many drinks she might have downed before his arrival.

"Oh, darling," she stifled a laugh. "I wish I remembered to bring a camera when I see you. You wear such wonderfully innocent expressions."

Silence had always served him well. He waited, watching her quivering smile and dancing eyes. Eventually, hopefully, she'd be sober enough to answer his question. Too few coincidences existed in life, and too many recent jaunts down memory lane had carried him back fifteen years...

Fifteen years ago, when Denton McDaniels came into his life. Fifteen years ago, when a chaotic chain of events had changed his life forever ... and Dr. Frances was right. Before his return to Whistlebrook a week earlier, Kip hadn't dealt with the past. Not once had he consciously faced the anger and pain of his childhood. With firm resolve, he'd erected a mental block, prematurely forcing Whistlebrook and his mother into the Family Album and never visiting long enough to open that black silk cover.

If she'd asked—if she'd ever asked him to come home, what might have been his answer?

'You're going! And that's final!' *Her words echoed inside his mind, her eyes raged across the top of her oak desk, burning him.* 'The arrangements have been made—'

'Like a funeral!' *His words dropped to a low cadence that had remained his adult voice forever. In startled shock, she'd stared at him as he'd continued in his changed voice,* 'You've made arrangements ... I didn't die, but you're burying me anyway, huh, mom? So, okay. You want me dead and gone? I'll go, but I'm not ever coming back either.' *Trembling with anger, he'd pushed from the chair in front of her desk and sidestepped.*

'Kippen James! Sit down! We're not finished! You—'

'Oh, yes, mother,' *he said as he shot a level glare at her.* 'We're finished. I should have figured this out years ago. You never wanted me around. You never wanted a son created by that old bastard. You've just been waiting for a reason to fire me like one of your employees. We're finished. Just pretend I'm dead. It shouldn't be too difficult. You never knew I was alive. I'll go be a priest. It's gotta be better than a fucking Undertaker!'

"Kippen!"

Jolted, he shot his focus across the table, momentarily trapped within a vision of his mother's stricken eyes and the echo of her voice. Disoriented, he recognized the brunette, hearing her soft voice, reading her curiosity. Tearing his gaze away, he knocked a long ash off his cigarette and reached for his drink.

"You looked lost for a moment, darling. Are you alright?"

How many times had someone asked him that recently, like a 'hello, how you doing?' 'Hello—are you alright?' And always the shadows of doubt lingered behind the gazes. Marion McDaniels-Smithfield was no different, spying him through regal blue eyes.

How he envied other people's eyes, so full of livid color and life. His own were dead, as empty and colorless as a winter sky, and that vacuum could be intimidating, like looking into the eyes of a dead man ... or the aura of a dying man.

"God, those eyes," Marion muttered as if hearing his thoughts, dropping her focus, fumbling with an enameled cigarette holder. She snapped it open with her red nail and extracted a long, thin cigarette. When she had it lit, she blew a stream of smoke at him. Her pursed lips quivered, threatening more laughter. "Now, tell me, darling. How much more than my first name do you know?"

"Enough to wonder why you're here," he said without affect.

"Cryptic," she smiled, appraising him through laughing eyes. "I've heard you love to talk in riddles, but then, I hear many contradicting rumors about you." She paused for another drag off her cigarette, possibly hoping for a comment.

Offering nothing, Kip waited, watching her. A faint, familiar soft laugh echoed out of a chorus of 'O Come All Yee Faithful' and momentarily distracted him. At a glance, Kip glimpsed Kelly Mulden's graceful hand float to touch her brother's sleeve alongside her. Her eyes ... how they caught the candlelight, and her smile played across her shadowed features, at once compelling. For an instant, her eyes landed on him, and despite all reason, when the instant passed, he suffered an instant ache. Deliberately, so it appeared, she drove her attention into the conclave at the table and mouthed some words that brought a familiar Mulden chuckle into a chorus of '... yee of Be-eth-la-hem.'

Barely, he shifted his attention when he glimpsed the waitress arriving at the Muldens' table with the bottle of champagne and six glasses. Kelly's eyes shot to him, and for one crazy instant, he knew a smug satisfaction at averting his gaze before her focus found him. Marion was truly a beautiful woman—probably not much older than him, which didn't matter one way or the other. Morgan LaMont was thirty-nine, a sleek thirty-nine with long lean muscles toned to perfection by daily workouts and regular visits to health spas—

"Denton McDaniels," Marion said quietly. "Do you know him, darling?"

"Personally, no," Kip answered honestly; his focus riveted despite his practiced indifference.

"Come now. Surely you've met him," she said with a wry smile.

"Met him, yes," Kip answered evasively, waiting, offering nothing in his gaze.

Doubt and curiosity rolled into her eyes like a slow incoming tide. Her smile lingered by force. Her amusement nearly vanished. She tapped her cigarette, knocking off an ash with a jittery forefinger. Momentarily, she wrestled with her thoughts, no doubt, trying to decide if he knew the family tree.

He enlisted only her first name—not Mary as she'd signed the register—and he'd only alluded to knowing anything beyond her name. If she chose to acknowledge family ties, so be it.

Apparently reaching a decision, she looked over and barely started to speak when the waitress arrived, flipping open a portable stand and lowering a tray off her shoulder. Annoyed, Kip watched the aloof young woman use a hand-cranked pepper shaker on Marion's salad. Impatient, he waved the pepper away, not particularly interested in the salad, much less the dressings and rolls cluttering the table. He should have waived dinner completely. By now, JD Mulden had probably called out the militia and God knows what Bill Bickerman might be contemplating ... and Mrs. Feeney was missing ... and a killer—

"Excuse me a moment, luv," he commented and slipped from the booth, catching a fleeting glance from Kelly. He had no way to pass unnoticed. Noting Kelly's deliberate attempt to ignore him, he needed only a split second to wonder how he'd offended her before realizing he hadn't called her. In the next instant, he witnessed Jarred Mulden's double-take and startled smile. Damnit, no way to just ignore them. With Jarred Mulden's glance past Kip, he probably expected to see JD. With a respectful nod and smile, Kip paused at the table, flicking his glance past Whitman, acknowledging each Mulden in a glance before fixing Kelly with a deliberate gaze under which her estrangement crumbled into a hurt, soft smile. God, she was magnificent! She'd done something with her hair and makeup, and even in his limited view, the shimmery cloth ignited a wave of vibrations through his system. In an odd moment, the restaurant emptied, sounds muted behind the pounding in his ears. On every other occasion, her physical attributes had struck him dumb; in her present ensemble, she was magnificent—the cover of Vogue, magnificent!

God! What he would give for a taste of peppermint at this moment!

***

Insanity! No other word could quite cover the riot of emotions raging through Kelly's system with those gray eyes holding her for an eternal instant. Even with several moments to prepare for this encounter, she hadn't anticipated the instant heat flashing through her.

"Lethal," he said in a soft, low voice to send tingles down her spine. Only a haunted smile touched his mustached lips.

In a split second, Kelly forgot all the reasons why she should be annoyed, or hurt, or indifferent to him, considering the distinctly feminine hand that Kelly had glimpsed inside the booth. Instead, she recalled that catty conversation from a week earlier and smiled slightly, glancing down at his all-too-capable build, enhanced within an impressive Italian silk suit. God! The man could do sexy with a twist to spin any sensible female's head. "Likewise," she said and connected with his gaze, enjoying the brief flicker of amusement under his long lashes. All too easily, she remembered last evening, his distress, his pain inside that living room, and the last of her resolve shattered. Her heart—and eyes—softened, searching him, and they might as well be alone in this restaurant for as swiftly as the world receded. Nothing—not one thing else mattered. She barely parted her lips to speak—

Richard's hostility reached its peak at that moment. "Mr. Patterson," he started as he began shoving his chair backward as if to rise.

Kip's gaze flickered, rather indifferent as well as curious.

"Richard," Kelly stated, abruptly awake to the possibilities. At a glance, she read Richard's volatile gaze, not sure whether to be more annoyed, startled ... or worried. With a fleeting memory of wood and plasterboard buckling, she knew Richard was biting off more than he could chew. Suddenly more alarmed, her attention pivoted to Kip.

"Richard," Kip said in such a benign tone that he might have been mentioning the weather. He hadn't moved, but something in his expression had changed, darkening. Either he'd spoken to JD or he possessed an exceptionally keen sense of trouble. His gaze pinned Richard, halting him from vacating the chair more effectively than Kelly's attempted warning.

The fleeting seconds offered Richard a moment to reconsider this confrontation. Appearing outraged, he remained seated, impressively glaring at Kip as he stated, "I'd like to speak to you—outside."

Of all the reactions she might have expected, the flicker of a smile—a very dark, mischievous smile on Kip's lips, in his eyes—halted Kelly's intention to intervene.

"Don't suppose you brought a checkerboard, have you, Richard?" he asked in a near-musing tone.

Damn him for sounding so whimsical, as if he truly found this situation amusing, and he was no dunce. He surely grasped Richard's outrage. For a man who'd spent at least a few moments kissing another man's fiancée, he appeared less than affected by Richard's jealousy. Had it truly been no more than physical contact? Had it meant so little to him that he would be only entertained by this confrontation?

Suddenly, Kelly wasn't entirely sure how she felt about Kip Patterson. God knows, he could stir her blood ... but was she truly willing to settle for a one-night stand? Could she forfeit her morals for one quick, exciting romp in the sack? Had Richard truly pegged Kip from the onset? And her, for that matter. If she'd stayed with Kip last night, would it have meant so blasted little to this fellow who stood, willing and ready to engage in whatever duel Richard chose?

"No, I didn't bring a checkerboard," Richard said in a low, seething tone, rising again or making the motions to rise. Both of his hands touched the table as if to shove off.

"Then I suggest you remain seated, Richard," Kip said in a suddenly calmer tone. "I haven't the time or inclination to humor you with a backyard brawl at the moment," he continued, and the humor vanished from his eyes. "A word of advice, though, lad, if you fully intend to marry such a stunning young lady, I suggest you either control your temper or invest in dueling pistols. You, sir, will need them regularly."

With his words, his gray eyes shifted to Kelly, and something in those eyes conveyed far more than indifference despite the curtain dropping over his emotions. "If you'll excuse me," he said and winked, then flashed his gaze to the others at the table. "Nice to see you all again," he stated and lanced Richard only once more before turning and striding toward the entrance.

Silence. At their table, a silence had dropped. The reason for her and Richard's falling out seemed, suddenly, blatantly clear. More so with Richard glaring menacingly at the retreating figure before landing his gaze on her, attempting to soften the twitch in his cheek.

Oddly calm again, Kelly gazed across the table, deciding once and for all that she hadn't made a mistake to follow her heart. In those parting words, Kip hadn't only restored her dignity—apparently unaware of her no-longer attached status—but he'd also repaired her faith in him. For her sake, he'd made light of that duel until Richard had pressed the issue. Without a doubt, Kip had covered a world of temper behind that quiet warning, not entirely betraying the fact that he would gladly meet a challenge at another time. Getting to know him, breaching that impenetrable wall he erected could take time, but suddenly, she was far more certain of that possibility.

"Kelly," Richard started, perhaps, only now waking to the rather pensive, subdued silence at the table. "I'm—"

"Behaving like an idiot?" she asked quietly, holding his gaze in the firelight.

"I love you," he said irritably, leaning forward as if they might share an intimacy. His hand reached across the table, palm open as if he expected Kelly to clasp his fingers. "I know that was probably foolish, but I'd only meant to clear the air. I had time to think, darling, and I realize my accusations were unfounded—

"Richard, do me a favor," she said with a touch of indifference, unconsciously snatching a page from Kip's book. "Don't say another word."

"Kelly, for God's sakes, at least let me explain—"

At her side, Mike leaned rather casually on his forearms and looked over at Richard. "Hey, Rich?" he said offhandedly, a thin smile on his lips. "Mr. Patterson might not have time for a backyard brawl, but I wouldn't mind meeting you outside for a tumble."

"Michael," Jarred said in a low warning tone, but his gaze had shifted toward Richard. "After hearing that my son had to escort you from the house this morning, Mr. Whitman, I wasn't happy to find you waiting here for my daughter, and honestly, I don't like thinking this could become a habit with you."

"Mr. Mulden, I assure you, I didn't come here for any trouble," Richard said carefully. "Rather the opposite. When your son intruded this morning, Kelly and I were just having a bit of a rift, but we could have worked it out if he hadn't barged in. I just wanted to speak with her in a neutral atmosphere. I truly don't want to cause any trouble, and I was afraid if I came back to the house, your son would have started something. If I could just talk to Kelly alone for a little while, I'm sure we could work this out. It was a misunderstanding, sir," he said placatingly.

"I assume it had to do with Kip," her father said lightly, his gaze steady on Richard, tilted at a conversational angle.

"Yes, it did," Richard answered stiffly. "I didn't appreciate him flirting with my fiancée yesterday afternoon," he continued. "And I didn't much care for it a few moments ago."

"A few moments ago, my daughter wasn't your fiancée," Jarred said quietly.

Kelly heard about enough of this. "Richard," she stated shortly and drew his critical gaze. "I think you're right. We need to talk." Passing her father a reassuring glance, she pushed off her chair and stepped into the aisle, not awaiting Richard, although he hurried to rise with her.

Chapter 11

Sidestepping through the crowd in the waiting area, Kip nearly muttered another curse with the thought of Whitman's ill temper. What the hell did she see in that pompous ass? She could indeed find better. The man was apparently an idiot—or lacking in self-confidence. Well, and maybe the fellow wasn't such an idiot. If the circumstances had been different last night, Kip would have welcomed Kelly's company. In fact, were he honest with himself, he regretted sending her away. Obviously, she wasn't as happy with that jerk as JD had professed, or she wouldn't have come to visit an old friend despite her good intentions to offer comfort.

God, but the lady possessed interesting twists. Innocent one moment, blushing like a schoolgirl, and heating him the next.

Muttering another curse, Kip reached the payphone, and for several unaccountable seconds, he couldn't remember who he meant to call when slipping from that corner booth.

Edna Feeney. The Home. Murder. Frank should have reached the Home by now and hopefully found Edna. Forcing his thoughts into order, Kip placed the call, bypassing the reception desk, and let the phone ring a dozen times before dialing the front desk.

Mike Dorsen offered a friendly, "Merry Christmas. Whistlebrook."

At least the castle hadn't crumbled. "Is Frank Culver in?"

"Sorry, he's not in this evening."

"Mike, put me through to Frank if you know where he is," Kip said evenly.

"Uh, Gees. Sorry, sir," Mike stammered. "I uh … uh, sir? I don't know where he is. I could page him."

"He is in the Home, then?"

A husky voice came into the background; Mike tried muffling the mouthpiece and voices. Unmistakably, JD stated, "Give me that fucking phone!" An instant later, he snapped, "Where the hell are you!"

"Calm down, I haven't left the country," Kip mused, oddly relieved despite Mulden's rage. Unfortunately, with JD on the line, Kip thought about Kelly again, sidetracked to that moment when she smiled across his mother's desk last evening. Muttering, he recovered his thought. "Have you spoken to Frank?"

"I haven't seen Frank! I'm going to kick your ass from here to—"

"JD," Kip said haltingly and awaited a pause. "Find Frank Culver and help him locate Edna Feeney. No one's seen her since Saturday evening. I'll page you when I get to the Home." Hanging up, he held the receiver momentarily and lifted it again, tossing another quarter into the slot. After three rings, Marsh's answering machine picked up. Annoyed, Kip listened to Marsh's formal out-of-character message, resembling a mechanical voice. 'Our mutual friend is unavailable. Calls will be returned in the order received. Begin now!' "Have you taken a holiday?" Kip asked and hung up.

Pushing from the phone booth, he nearly stepped into an immense woman, excused himself, and sidled around her. In the lobby, he passed near the bar entrance and glimpsed Jason's navy blue and gray jacket at one of the tables against a dividing wall. King wasn't alone; his young female companion laughed at something he said. The youngster had an impressive confidence —the kind that comes naturally at eighteen, when the whole world is still a playground and childhood dreams are on the verge of becoming a reality.

What lent him the second glance? Radar? Intuition? His gaze slid through the glass doors in time to see Whitman clasp Kelly's arm. They were standing under the portico, their faces illuminated in the twinkling white lights, and she wasn't happy. Without considering his action, he veered. Outside, she yanked her arm away and backed a step, turning toward the entrance, and Whitman snatched her arm again, halting her. Pushing through the door as she spun on her intended, Kip heard the soft, angry voice.

"That's enough! For God's sake, Richard, grow up!"

"Is there a problem here?" Kip asked quietly and locked gazes with Whitman as the man's eyes flashed pure fury.

"This is none of your business," Whitman stated shortly. "I just hope the hell you're satisfied," he continued while stepping back.

On a practical note, Kip understood this fellow's hostility, though to be honest, he couldn't recall initiating any move to create this scene. In rapid clicks, he recalled Kelly's admission only last evening—her childhood crush. Had she mentioned that to Whitman? Hell. If this character figured out what had nearly transpired last evening, he had a right to be peeved. Jealousy, however, was an ugly vice. Besides, if Miss Mulden loved this creep, she wouldn't have visited him last evening. *Docile, contented fish don't bite.*

"If you think for one damn minute I'll sit back and let you get away with this, Mr. Patterson, you have another thought coming," Whitman attested, though he stood back a few sensible paces. His gaze flashed to Kelly. "Are you coming?"

In a side glance, Kip read her faintly disbelieving gaze.

"No, I am not coming, Richard," she stated shortly. "I'm going back inside, and if you have half the intelligence you're so fond of boasting, you won't follow me."

"We aren't finished with this, Kelly," he stated, looking at her with a heated shine, refusing even to glance in Kip's direction. "I'll call you tomorrow," Richard snapped and spun on his heels, stalking into the pouring rain.

Not entirely sure what to make of this, Kip spied the lovely lady who appeared only more troubled and tense than any moment passed as she watched her intended striding away. Damn, she was still stunning. Mona Lisa-stunning, with the faintest trace of a smile on her lips, one slightly tucked as if she might be chewing her gum. Her arms crossed, hugging herself, undoubtedly, to ward off the chill. The idiot had dragged her out here without even thinking to lend her his sweater. Without a thought, Kip slipped off his jacket. She was apparently not ready to return to the din inside. As he slid his coat about her shoulders, he looked into her startled eyes. Tears shimmered on the surface, reflecting the twinkling white lights, and she suddenly appeared lost. "Are you alright?" he asked and nearly uttered a curse at how mundane he'd considered that question not long ago.

"I uhm ... yes," she stated collectively. With a tainted smile, she looked at him, straining softly. "I think I owe you an apology, Kip. You didn't deserve that."

"He doesn't deserve you," he said without a thought, his gaze searching now. "But if I'm responsible for this, then I'm the one to owe you an apology. If you like, I'll have a chat with him."

She huffed a soft humph, nearly a laugh. "Out in the backyard?"

"I'll try civility first," he offered, grateful for her stab of humor. She truly was a fascinating young woman. Bold as brass one moment. Soft and sensuous, the next. Just catching a breath of her soft perfume ignited a riot of thoughts, and the shimmer of light dancing off her wispy hair drew his attention. Unconsciously, he lifted a hand and touched an errant curl off her brow, his gaze locking on her stunning eyes. Far too swiftly, he could be drawn into those eyes. And like every other blasted moment in the past week, this wasn't the right time. There might never be a right time to carry through with all the wild images spiraling in his rampant mind.

"Truly, luv," he said quietly, willing himself not to be drawn into her shimmering hazel eyes. "If this is, as it appears, about last night, I will have a chat with him and set him straight."

"What would you tell him, Kip? That nothing happened between us?"

Damn, that would be tough, and what was worse, it would be a blatant lie. She'd come to him, and if not for his anger with JD, if not for the blasted turmoil in that wretched Home, something most assuredly would have happened between them and her fiancé bedamned. How to answer her without reducing those moments that seemed too important in his mind? "If that's what you want me to tell him," he replied quietly, searching for an indication in her expressive eyes.

She shook her head slowly, her gaze fleeting toward the glass doors. "We'd better go in," she said offhandedly and started a turn, then looked up, halted. "Don't talk to him, Kip. This is my problem, and I'll deal with it. With him."

In an odd moment, he realized how swiftly he might truly come to her aid, even if it meant flattening Whitman and making the idiot listen to reason. Peculiar, if not weird, this latent protective streak rising in him. Physiological attraction? Hormonal? Something to do with grieving and all the damned memories breaking loose inside of him? All that shit about being the Prince of Whistlebrook. Was this some fantastical nobility rising?

His thoughts carried him to the door, catching it, holding it for Kelly to slip past him. Unwittingly, his hand touched the small of her back, escorting her through the crowd. At the entrance to the dining room, she slipped his jacket off her shoulders, offering him a faint smile. "Thanks for the use of your jacket. And your timing," she added quietly.

"Anytime, luv," he said, more honestly than he cared to admit. Jacket in hand, he walked her as far as her table and glimpsed several pairs of curious, mildly relieved eyes as he held her chair. On impulse, he leaned and brushed a kiss on her cheek, winking as he caught the slight twinkle in her eyes. "Later, luv," he said lightly and continued toward the corner booth.

By now, his half-sister probably believed he'd ditched her, not that it mattered. Whatever this fascination—infatuation—with Kelly Mulden, the affliction was apparently limited to her alone. Barely acknowledging his dinner companion, collecting his thoughts, Kip managed a few bites before shoving the salad aside and lighting a cigarette. If he had any good sense, he'd drive to the airport, board the first available continental flight, and enlist his troop of attorneys to sort out this mess. The option had been based on fact. Selling the Home would, in fact, solve the problem. Or would it? Either way, Att. Brad Sinclair would have a field day unraveling this web.

An enemy with the patience to persist for more than ten years? The financial clout to manipulate legal documents and disburse 250,000 dollars with enough people on the inside and outside to collect the required information, from confidential financial statements to physical and family histories? Whistlebrook's confidentiality was legendary. Marilyn Patterson took pride in her patient anonymity. Even the goddamn names were frauds. Mr. Rodgers—

William Rodgers had been one such character. Kip hadn't even known the man was a member of the President's cabinet until the fellow's funeral. According to hospital records, Rodgers was listed as a successful architect before his premature retirement. At least a dozen patients on the present roster were likely labeled under fictitious titles. Elsa Taylor's bird-like features came readily to mind as he remembered the information that Marsh had delivered only last evening. Kip's instinct had been on the mark. She was a widow from Richmond, Virginia. Her husband had built a respectable business, which their single heir had already begun to squander.

Whistlebrook's internal records network resembled an octopus with its head cut off. Upon entry, names were altered and coded. A Mr. Doe might have records in every wing, but Mr. Doe's past life remained separate from the details that only Marilyn Patterson could mesh with records retained by the family.

Kip had known them. Eventually, their stories had enlightened him, or out of trust, they'd confided in him. Rodgers had been an exception. The fellow had arrived at the Home suffering latent stages of his illness, barely a shell of his former self. Horrible, a true horror, seeing a man of his prominent stature waiting, degenerating, in the prime of his life—

'What are you doing in here!' the coarse voice shouted from the past.

Blindsided by the memory, Kip remembered wanting to shout, 'Trying to stand up!'

Through a layer of unemotional tears, he glanced at the woman in the doorway. In front of him, Mrs. Ramsey—all three hundred pounds of her—lay safely on the bed, but if he released the bar in his white-knuckle grip, his knees would buckle. Fire spread through his groin and into his legs; sparks flew through his abdomen, piercing his chest, taking his breath away. Not even his fear of Janet Cross could start him moving—

"Sir? Was everything all right with your salad?"

Bouncing a glance to the waitress, Kip nodded absently, catching a studied glimpse of Marion before looking at the Lobster lowering in front of him. And abruptly, he was not at all hungry. Halting the plate partway, he noted the young woman's abrupt worry. "Did my driver—the boy at the bar—order anything?"

"Just a soda, sir," she answered.

"Good. Send that out to him," Kip commented. "And bring me a cup of coffee."

Her aloofness wavered in bewilderment. "If you'd like—"

"Just the coffee," he cut off abruptly and turned his focus to his startled half-sister. "Eating Lobster is rather like eating a vulture, you know."

Marion glanced down at her plate, apparently relieved by her prime rib. "Your dinner manners leave something to be desired, darling."

Sounded like his mother—*darling. Damnit!* "Beef's generally safe," he commented idly. "But you truly shouldn't order it raw, luv. Salmonella, you know? If not bacteria, parasites often carry in the bloodstream. And one can never be too careful about one's blood."

Her souring expression froze. Her eyes leveled on him and in the space of ten seconds, brightened in livid amusement. "Riddles, darling? Or insight?"

"Insight, I should think," he mused. "Certainly, you'd prefer not to contaminate your bloodlines."

Her gaze held, transfixed, her words guarded. "Parasites shouldn't concern you, darling. Cancer, though, cancer in the blood can be devastating to the body." Her eyes shone intently, and suddenly, her smile froze, aging her appropriately. "Cancer can be hereditary," she said quietly.

The curtain had dropped, and she hadn't chosen 'cancer' randomly. She knew about the conspiracy eating away at Whistlebrook?

Her gaze dropped as she lifted her steak knife and fork, slicing into the thick slab of meat. When her attention returned, she lifted a delicate bite skewered on her fork. Her amusement lingered. "Perhaps, we should discuss the ecosystem," she said lightly. "Far less grizzly over dinner."

"The ecosystem, by all means. Symbiotic relationships or Darwin's theory, luv?" *Survival of the fittest?*

In slow, elegant motion, she placed the beef chunk in her mouth, savoring the taste while studying him thoughtfully. She'd abandoned her seduction; sophistication wore well, manifesting in her entire liquid motion. "Symbiotic," she said lightly.

"Commensal, mutual, or again, parasitical?"

She eyed him critically despite her soft smile. "We shouldn't make the mistake of categorizing too critically. All three have a substantial vestment in the ecosystem."

Nature's balance, he agreed absently, but this wasn't a discussion about ecological balance, and Marion McDaniels-Smithfield hadn't asked about his inheritance without a reason. Symbiotic—mutual advantages? *What the hell are you trying to tell me, lady? What do you know?* "Possibly we should—"

At a glimpse of motion, Kip halted his words and lifted his attention as the suited gentleman halted warily outside the booth. State Department? The man wore a tailored suit, stiff tie—not one of the clowns who'd inevitably tailed him from Madison's office.

With a careful, low voice, the intruder stated, "Forgive me for interrupting, sir. I'm Philip Forrester, manager here at Le Chateau. It has come to my attention that you may have found our cuisine unsatisfactory again. I've taken the liberty of removing your entree from your bill, sir," he paused, stepping aside slightly to let the waitress deliver coffee. "Mrs. Patterson was a valued patron. My deepest sympathies, sir. If you'd prefer another entree, I can assure you, I'll see that it's prepared to your specifications at no charge to you."

Annoyed, or merely amused, Kip couldn't decide. He should have known by the tailored suit—not State Department issue. Across the table, Marion smiled, undoubtedly, amused. Randall was too damned small! Studying the distraught manager, Kip commented, "Mr. Forrester, as much as I appreciate your concern, don't dismiss your chef on my account. If you'll excuse us, now?"

"Yes, sir," Forrester said and looked to Marion. "Ma'am, forgive my interruption. Is everything to your satisfaction?"

"I'm far easier to please than my friend," she mused. "My compliments to your chef."

"Thank you, madam," he said and bowed away gracefully.

Marion restrained her giggle, darting glances from the booth to note several very quiet tables, now. Her focus returned, bright with laughter. "Where were we, darling?"

"You were about to tell me why you're here," he said lightly.

"But I thought that was obvious, darling," she said smoothly, splitting her attention to dab sour cream on her baked potato. "An introduction seemed long overdue." Her attention sharpened; her smile animated. "Don't you agree?"

"How long have you considered an introduction?" he asked.

"On and off for years," she said offhandedly, busy with her steak knife again. Her eyes shifted, distractedly, sprinting to Kip in silent appraisal. Savoring another bite, she eyed him directly; laughter lines crept into her temples. "I really must know, darling. Did you know who I was Saturday?"

"Why?" he asked without affect.

Her smile was a ruse, not quite hiding her tension. "Simply, darling, if you didn't—which I believe is the case—then you are in far more trouble than I was beginning to realize."

"Are we about to drop the facade?"

"As much as I've enjoyed sparring, darling, I don't think we have a choice," she said with a faint echo of a sigh. Setting her fork aside, she lost the last traces of her seduction and glanced vacantly outside the booth, then returned her full attention with a refined countenance. "Come over here, wayward prince, rightful heir to the throne."

She wasn't referring to Whistlebrook. Smoothly, he slid from his bench seat, sidled, and slipped into the space she provided. A scent of soft perfume, an imported perfume, came more readily to him than the aroma rising from the plate of prime rib between them.

Her eyes rose to spy him, a lingering contrast of estrangement and concentration. "How much do you know about your lineage, darling?" she asked quietly.

"Far less than I need to, obviously," he answered while sliding his arm behind her across the thick cushion headrest. "Talk to me, Marion. Tell me a story."

"You're going to make me a promise first, young prince," she said soberly, her concentrated gaze unparalleled. "I will give you the key to the castle, but you must never use it against me."

"Far too cryptic, luv. Elaborate."

"I'm well aware of your financial independence," she said quietly. "You don't need the McDaniels' fortunes any more than your recent inheritance. And not without a degree of admiration, I understand you've risen in social circles as a power in your own right—young, well-informed, and calculated. At the risk of wounding your ego, I should tell you, not all your life was left to fate—or chance. Commensal," she said, her intensity unmasked within her gaze. "A union of sorts. To your benefit."

***

A soft scent of imported cologne lingered in Kelly's awareness as she attempted to concentrate on the conversations around her. After assuring her family that Kip hadn't dispatched Richard in some medieval—or Victorian age—duel, and convincing Mike that he hadn't—once again—missed a dandy brawl, she'd fallen silent.

No matter how many times she attempted to dismiss the thought, she couldn't stop thinking about the moment Kip intruded outside, striding through the glass doors and coming to her rescue—like a knight in shining armor. When Richard had clasped her arm the first time with every intention of escorting her to his car, where they could talk without freezing, she hadn't exactly felt threatened. Or maybe she had. His reasoning had been sound. He'd brought his coat from the back of his chair—and in retrospect, she realized he meant to take her from this restaurant the moment she'd agreed to talk privately. Whether he failed to collect her coat deliberately or in negligence, she couldn't decide. Still, the chill had certainly provided him a good reason to demand her company in his vehicle. The second time he grabbed her arm, the threat had definitely enhanced. He'd fully intended to carry her off to some remote place for their *discussion*.

A budding doctor—a healer, she repeated for the hundredth time in a very short time. What had she expected? He intended to pound her to pulp to see reason? Not his style. But he most definitely had intended to batter her emotionally without the prying eyes of her family. How could she have been such an idiot? For months, he'd enlisted those same tactics. First reason, then hints of accusation, then soft understanding to beguile her into believing herself unreasonable. When he couldn't win her over with sympathy, he played on her guilt, making her feel as if whatever 'rift' came between them was entirely her fault.

Only half in tune to the attempted banter around the table, Kelly noticed the manager visiting the corner booth and zeroed in on the soft, low voice when Kip had responded offhandedly about not firing the chef. Funny, she should hear the whispered words from the tables around her, catching the name 'Patterson' spoken a time or two. Who was that female in the booth with him? Morgan? Had the woman flown in from California to repair the 'rift' between them? Any woman with half a brain would make that flight. But then, any woman with half a brain and a warm heart would have flown with him a week ago.

Well, apparently the 'rift' had cleared. Kelly glimpsed him sliding into the booth at the woman's side. With the high-backed booths, they remained hidden, now. And for a half-second, Kelly suffered a pang of jealousy before she countered that errant emotion. Despite what she felt for him, she couldn't delude herself into believing he suffered a similar condition of heart. He liked her. That much, she knew. Whether alone or in a crowded restaurant, when his gaze landed on her, she sensed his undivided attention. A casual interest? Intrigue, perhaps? Or was he gifted with a strange power to enthrall women with a single glance? Too readily, Kelly recalled him stooping alongside Abby over that checkerboard, undoubtedly, in tune with the girl's adoration, but too much of a gentleman to play upon Abby's emotions. That stupid game had become a dueling field, and Kelly smiled faintly, recalling her thought that Richard lost the instant Kip stooped down. Kelly had needed only a glance at the board to know Richard had lost with Kip's first move. He played those next moves if only to torment Richard.

Grateful for the waiter's interruption, Kelly vowed not to think about Kip again, but no sooner did she begin cutting her steak when she glimpsed motion down the aisle and noted him lifting his jacket from the opposite booth. Leaving alone? He appeared preoccupied, but his gaze shifted toward her, and a smile flickered on his mustache. Whether he would stop again--he was too much of a gentleman not to stop again.

"Mr., Mrs. Mulden," he acknowledged, then touched Kelly's shoulder, sending a tingle through her flesh, which had nothing to do with his chilly fingers on thin fabric. Leaning, he spoke discreetly, "I'll be in town another day or two. If you change your mind about that chat, call me."

She nodded, her heartbeat leaden as he brushed another chaste kiss on her cheek, until she caught his gaze on the rise. Not entirely indifferent, his eyes conveyed an odd implication—as if he added 'that chat' as a formality—and she hadn't admitted to breaking the engagement with Richard. Kip was gone before that final thought touched her mind.

"Now, that guy's a class act," Mike said quietly, a smile playing on his lips as Kelly found him watching her. "And he's definitely interested in you."

"Male insight?" she asked lightly.

"Hell, doesn't take a rocket scientist here, Kell," he said lightly, enjoying himself. "The rest of us might as well be invisible every time he gets within three feet of you. Now, level with me—what did he do to your X? I know he didn't just let that guy walk away."

In an odd moment, she reviewed those seconds outside and a tiny smile quivered on her lips. "On the contrary," she said quietly. "That's exactly what he did."

"Come on, Kell," Mike persisted, amused. "There's more to this. I can tell. What did he say or do?"

"Absolutely nothing," she assured and held Mike's questing gaze. "He didn't have to do a thing," she added. "He just showed up."

Mike parted his lips to coax, then seemed to realize exactly what she'd said; his eyes lit with a glittering amusement. "He just showed up, huh? And Dr. Richard took to his heels."

"Exactly," she mused and lifted a bite of steak, glimpsing her father's likewise amused eyes. Sparks.

Chapter 12

Preoccupied, Kip found Jason just finishing his Lobster, and with little more than a hand signal, they waded through the crowd in the lobby. Rather than wait beneath the canopy as Jason suggested, Kip motioned him ahead and trotted into the downpour.

'The key to the castle,' Marion McDaniels-Smithfield had said a half hour ago, but very little of her ensuing story could be of use to him. His half-sister had simply verified the information that Kip had accumulated over the past several days. Earnestly, she'd elaborated on her family tree, admitting that the fortunes amassed by a great-grandfather had been diversified and expanded by a grandfather, now controlled by her father and an uncle.

Her knowledge of Kip had begun—not surprisingly—fifteen years ago, when her father had taken an unnatural interest in a particular Nursing Home proprietor and her son after attending the funeral of a family friend. 'William Rodgers,' Kip had supplied, and Marion had offered him a queer look. 'No, I believe his name was Montgomery. I know he held a position in the President's cabinet. I recall thinking not many years later, he would have been a part of Watergate if he'd lived.' With her words, Kip's memory had clicked into high gear, remembering his surprise when reading William

Rodgers' actual name on the funeral marquee. Anonymity shouldn't have surprised him. By the time Marion McDaniels attended Montgomery's funeral, rumors of her father's brief affair had transcended thirteen years, and a shy, handsome youngster bore a striking resemblance to pictures of Denton McDaniels in his youth. If expressions could be trusted, she found the entire sordid affair incredibly romantic and deliciously scandalous—a proper credit to the visages of her class. With a pleasant conspiratorial shine in her eyes, she envisioned a dozen more brothers or sisters who might someday come knocking on her father's door. In the next breath, she dismissed her suggestion, assuring Kip—as it would seem—that he was the result of her father's one and only infidelity.

Shadows had fallen over her eyes as she spoke of her mother, who'd passed away twenty years earlier. 'Sad, really,' she said quietly. 'Only after my mother became ill did she and my father realize that they truly loved each other. But isn't that always the way? One never knows what one has until it's gone. Had they stopped bowing to their social graces sooner, they might have shared a much happier life together...'

In silence, Kip listened to her outpour, confused by his decision to sit through her nostalgia. He hadn't interrupted, although, in retrospect, his thoughts had drifted more than once to imagine a pair of warm hazel eyes. Marion McDaniels-Smithfield, without her coquetry or mystery, was a lonely young woman who'd lost her own true love six years earlier in a car accident on a wet Boston highway. She had two daughters who spent most of their time with a nanny. 'By their preference,' she seemed to believe. She had a sister she rarely visited, and almost at once, she dismissed further discussion. Apparently, a falling out some years earlier. Her life revolved around Denton McDaniels and managing his household while pursuing her own discreet affairs.

When she, at long last, returned to her mention of cancer and trouble, the details had become sketchy, but she seemed to believe her father—his father—was worried about him.

Only two salient facts played heavily on Kip's mind as he stepped into the pickup's cab.

One: Denton McDaniels might have been responsible for the Justice Department's interest. According to Marion, he had several contacts within that branch of government, and as much as three months ago, he'd made some discreet calls on Marilyn Patterson's behalf.

Two: 'At the risk of wounding your ego, I should tell you, not all of your life has been left to either fate or chance.'

Commensal. He'd received the benefits of their relationship, while Denton neither lost nor gained a thing.

Uttering a curse under his breath, Kip watched the blur of colored lights reflecting on water-streaked glass. Marion's comment had confirmed his belief that Denton McDaniels had remained a shadow in his life. How many times had Marsh stood in dumbfound, watching mysterious wheels turning financial tides from swinging votes in Congress in their favor to incredible sums of money joining forces? 'A guardian angel,' Marsh had once professed.

'You don't need the McDaniels fortunes any more than you need your recent inheritance... Promise me you won't use the key. I don't want my mother's name dragged through the dirt,' Marion had said at one point.

'Any more than I'd want my own mother's memory soiled,' he'd agreed. 'I'll make no public—or financial claims—to your inheritance.'

She'd smiled, then, a little sadly, a little fondly. 'I'd often thought it would have been nice to have a little brother. I should have sat down with you years ago.'

This morning, if not days ago, he'd known he couldn't walk away so easily. Whether he wanted it or not, Whistlebrook was now his sole responsibility. The safety of his residents rested in his hands, and damn the game Marilyn Patterson had played at the cost of two lives. As early as September, she'd wondered 'what lengths' her enemy would go to. She should have contacted the authorities, and to hell with her suspicions about her ill-begotten son. He could have endured a paper-chase investigation.

Murder!

Euthanasia!

A decrepit face flashed through Kip's mind's eye. Death. Every night, he'd fallen asleep with 'death' hanging over his head within an image of a poster protesting 'Euthanasia.' That poster still hung on the ceiling above his pillow in his old room, and Kip could just imagine a prosecuting attorney mentioning that tidbit of evidence against him.

At the sight of the stone pillars and lighted sconces passing slowly, Kip commented, "Pull up in front." By the time he collected his suitcases, Jason had stopped at the main entrance. Bringing his wallet from his jacket, Kip thumbed two hundreds from the fold and handed them sideways. "Thank you."

"I uh... shit. I don't need all that," King said as he handed the bills back, his expression amused within a wash of gauge lights. "I had a blast."

"Put it towards your college tuition," Kip said lightly and waved the money away, clasping his bags instead and reaching for the door handle.

"Hey, uh? You want me to help with those?"

"Thank you, no," Kip said absently, his thoughts divided abruptly as he scanned the lighted Oak Room windows. A Monday evening. Still early enough, visitors occupied the lounge,

"Uh... Thanks, ya know? I mean for the dinners and everything, and if you need me tomorrow, I promise, I'll borrow Dad's LeBaron," he said with a laugh in his voice.

"We'll see," Kip commented and forced the door open with a lift and shove before dragging his luggage from the cab.

The office windows were dark. A faint glow touched the curtained windows on the second and third floors. The rooms directly above the administration wing still housed ambulatory residents. A dozen or more couples who could afford to live in the semi-controlled environment enjoyed the freedom of the grounds while sharing the benefits of communal living. Most worked within the Home, either in the snack shop and cafeteria or at the courtesy shop on Two West. Mrs. Conners, who manned the reception desk throughout the day, occupied one of the third-floor suites. An age-old story, her husband's death had left her a meager social security check, most of which went toward her medical coverage in the event she'd need a room in another part of the Home. So many came here, and so few had Marilyn turned away by choice.

Lost in thought, Kip pushed through the glass doors, barely noticing Mike Dorson, who stood behind the reception desk. Veering toward the executive wing, Kip glanced toward the Oak Room doors. An echo of piano sounds and muffled voices reached him, swaying him with nostalgia for those familiar sounds. His attention split, darting to the semi-concealed doors beyond the staircase in time to see JD slow his trot to a walk. Halting, Kip read Mulden's tension, and his system lurched with a thought of Edna Feeney. *Found? Had Frank found her? Was she hurt?* Mulden's expression heralded trouble. "JD, what's—"

Holding out his hands as he strode within reach, Mulden started, "Let me help you with those—"

Distracted by his alarm, Kip reacted automatically, handing a bag forward. Far too late, he recalled the last seconds in Madison's office. In his split-second illumination, Kip started shifting the suitcase to block. Knuckles power slammed his ducking jaw. White splashes ignited as he staggered, losing hold of the smaller suitcase. The weight of the larger case, combined with Mulden's continued momentum, tipped Kip's balance. JD hadn't neglected his karate training, merely perfected it with a few practical improvisations attributed to his occupation.

With his arm twisted, his fist driven into the nape of his neck, Kip heaved a breath of aging carpet while blinking away unemotional tears.

At close range, JD whispered, "Give me a reason not to lock you up."

"Not—guilty," Kip heaved and swallowed a salty taste of blood.

"Lame, my old friend," JD stated. "Very lame."

"Hey—uh," Dorsen faltered. "You—uh—Mulden—"

"Back off!" JD snapped at him and leaned down, whispering, "I owed you that. Now, if you come up nice and easy, we have a problem to discuss." Barely awaiting Kip's struggling nod, JD rose swiftly, untwisting his arm and backing away a safe step.

In no hurry, Kip picked himself partway up to rest on his hip, pausing to work sparks from his jaw and knuckle a drip of blood off the corner of his mustache. Naturally, JD wore an honest glint of amusement in his hazel eyes. Dorsen stood frozen a safe distance away, his stricken gaze darting glances off Mulden to Kip—then to the door as Jason King burst through. Young King shot his focus off JD down to Kip, back to Mulden, and slowed his stride as he forfeited his fury to bewildered curiosity.

"Need a hand up, Mr. Patterson?" JD asked solemnly.

"Didn't—" *Damnit!* Touching his jaw and swallowing another wad of blood from his inner gum, Kip ran his tongue over the broken skin. Mulden only appeared more amused, and, honestly, Kip shared the humor. Clearing his focus, he spied Mulden's innocent concern. "Didn't I—fire you—once today?"

"Twice," JD said soberly.

"Strike three. You're out," Kip said and glimpsed Dorsen recovering enough to start toward Mulden, apparently choosing his loyalties. "Mike, back off," Kip said haltingly.

JD's glance lent no doubt about who would hit the floor first. His arrogance was genuine; his smile less than friendly as he eyed Dorson.

In one fluid motion, Kip rose, noting JD's stance and attention shift in a split second. Sincerely amused, Kip leveled his gaze on the wary hazel eyes. "A truce, Mr. Mulden?" he asked while offering his palm.

Hesitantly, JD stepped forward, although by his manner, he expected to be thrown. His grip firmed; his tension held steady. "Truce."

"Problem?"

JD glanced toward the glass doors. "Outside?"

To avoid being overheard, Kip understood but flashed a thought of the frigid rain and the damp chill already settling into his bones. He'd left the jamming device in the PRIVATE suite. Darting a glance toward the administration hall, Kip leaned to collect his suitcases. Rising, he tossed the heavier case to Mulden, amused when JD staggered a half-step under its weight.

"Christ, you carrying a fossil collection?"

"Encyclopedias," Kip mused and glanced at Jason as he started for the hall. In a flash of thought about the boy's intention to rescue him, Kip decided, for a youngster, King was quick, and depending on what JD might say, an extra pair of hands might be helpful. "I may need you after all. Stick around if you will."

"No problem. Think I better go park my truck, though."

Through the glass doors, the headlights angled unnaturally across the parking lot, suggesting King had started to pull out when spotting Mulden's attack. Nodding absently, Kip continued into the administration wing. Even in a hurry, the boy had apparently engaged the parking brake or slammed the truck in gear to keep it anchored to the pavement.

Within the living room, Kip found the transistor lying on the stand where the telephone had rested. He paused to turn it on, then began peeling off his suit jacket while looking to Mulden. "Our conversation's secure. Where's Frank? Mrs. Feeney?"

"You really don't know?" Mulden asked as he settled onto the recliner's arm, his attention strained.

Pausing, Kip looked into the angry hazel eyes, flashing an instant thought of Kelly Mulden and shoving it aside by force. "I wouldn't be asking you if I knew."

"Frank's in surgery."

Frozen, doubting, Kip studied Mulden's calculated gaze. "If you're..." Mulden was neither joking nor lying. Tension spiked through Kip's systems. "Details."

"Where'd you call from?"

"A goddamn restaurant," Kip stated icily. "And I don't appreciate your implication. What happened to Frank?"

"His truck went off the road about a mile down Adderly Lane," he answered evenly, still watching closely for a reaction. "Unofficially, they think he hit an ice slick. More unofficially, there might have been another vehicle involved."

Not an accident, damnit! No accident, and Edna? Details! Concentrate! "How—how did you find out? Who contacted you?" *His allies? His office?*

"The police called here about ten seconds after you hung up on me," he answered with a flash of renewed anger.

"Surgery," Kip said absently; his fingers moved mechanically down the buttons of his vest. "How bad is he?"

"The hospital wouldn't say. Just that he was already in surgery when I called."

"Mrs. Feeney?" Kip asked in his low undertaker's voice. *Tell me you found her! Don't tell me she was in Frank's truck—*

"I paged her, and I had Mike let me into her rooms. Nothing looked out of place," JD said with a distracted thought. "Tell me what's going on here, Kip."

"You said I was in trouble. I needed your help. Elaborate."

"Regardless of what you believe, I didn't come here—accept this assignment—to burn an old friend, but don't mistake that. If I thought for one damned minute that you were embezzling, I'd nail your ass. As it is—"

"Embezzling," Kip said as he peeled off his shirt. Bickerman had said those words in Madison's conference room.

"Embezzling or laundering. The evidence is there, despite the red tape and bureaucratic bullshit. I don't know the totals, but I know a helluva lot of money's coming into the Home and disappearing. With Bickerman's outburst at the reading, I don't need to guess to figure out who fingered you. Lucky for you, someone high-up has enough sense to doubt your need to embezzle, and I've already nixed the laundering idea. Now. Your turn. What's going on? Who'd want to run Frank off the road—why—and while you're at it—"

McDaniels. McDaniels had come to the rescue, but had the man enlisted JD Mulden by coincidence? Stepping out of his wet shoes and socks, Kip considered the possibilities as he dug a dry change of clothes from his suitcase.

"What do you know, Kip?"

"Not enough, obviously," he said vacantly while stepping out of his slacks. "Embezzlement's a fair assessment of what's happening." *Could Mulden truly be trusted?*

The wheels of time turned back, and for an instant, Kip stood in the Spring Chicken Lounge, leaning precariously against a window, swaying with the heavy dose of sedation Mark Frances had ordered. *'You bring that young scallywag this way for a visit,' the elder commanded.*

Disoriented, Kip suffered a hot sting of tears, remembering Irish McGuire, remembering the day he'd taken JD into the Spring Chicken lounge. Not once in thirteen years had Kip walked through the halls of his Home with a friend in tow. What had made him more nervous, anticipating Mulden's reaction to the desperate atmosphere or the leers he received from the residents? Both had vied for time in his still slightly foggy mind. With his natural charisma, JD had accepted the introduction, and Kip had relaxed enough to smile just a little. And how Irish's olive eyes had danced with joy—and life—on that afternoon and later.

'You mark my words, lad, that scoundrel knows the value of friendship.'

An ache raced into Kip's chest as another memory swam through his mind. More tears threatened his eyes as he groped for his jeans, avoiding JD's gaze. Irish had known—as Irish had known all things—Irish had known Kip would not return. The old man had known they'd never see each other again in life. 'She's sending me a-a—' Kip hadn't been able to finish. As he had a thousand times, he'd rested on the end of Irish's bed, and the reality of his mother's decision settled in his inflamed mind. As always, he'd run to Irish McGuire with tears he couldn't shed in front of Marilyn Patterson, threatening to burst.

Without much effort, Irish had leaned forward and drawn Kip into an embrace. 'Word travels in these ol' halls,' the elder spoke in a voice thick with emotion. 'Thinking it's safer you do as yar momma says, now, laddy. When things settle down, she'll be begging you to come home.'

Safer, Irish had said so long ago. *Safer.* Not *better.*

"Damnit!" News did travel in the Home. Something truly had happened in the Home fifteen years ago, but Irish hadn't held Kip to blame. The elder had never once alluded to the possibility of Kip's guilt.

"Your wheels are spinning," JD said in a careful, low tone. "Care to tell me what you're thinking?"

Trusting Mulden. That question had stirred the image of Irish. If not JD, who would he trust? Frank in the hospital—in surgery, for God's sake. Edna missing. Fifteen-year-old crimes repeated. Repeated? Or recreated? Could he afford to believe the same perpetrator still existed?

1972.

"Damn it."

"Kip!" Mulden stated sharply.

Effectively jolted, Kip glanced at JD, belatedly thinking to wipe the blur from his misty eyes. Uttering a curse, he sidled and stooped at his suitcase. Without consciously considering his decision, he slid his hand into the concealed slot of the larger case and extracted his mother's letters. Pushing to his feet, he sorted through the folds, putting the letters in the order he'd received them. Turning, he handed them to Mulden. "Read those and you'll know as much as I know. The first letter I received was on Friday, after I attempted to sign away my inheritance on a bogus Will. Those last two, Madison delivered this afternoon in the envelope my mother left for me. Believe what you will, Mr. Mulden, but before Friday, I had no idea the castle—or its queen—were in jeopardy."

Hesitantly, JD accepted the letters.

Kip turned and sidled, lifting a shirt from his suitcase. Mechanically, he dressed, turning over the details of the past three days—and ancient history. No dry shoes. Without conscious consideration, he strode into his bedroom, digging a pair of Army boots from the closet. Like almost everything he'd owned, one of the residents had gifted him the footwear—a fine addition to the field jacket and camouflaged cap that one of the staff nurses had given him. Unconsciously, he brought the cap off the shelf and found the jacket where he'd left it hanging fifteen years ago. Hats had remained his first true love, but he'd accumulated almost as many jackets throughout those early years. He could be anyone, anything.

The second or third time JD had invaded this room, uninvited, the arrogant bastard had begun rooting in the closet, tossing various hats on the bed and landing a half dozen on the floor. 'What do you call this one?' he'd asked and made some offhanded comment about Kip's strange collection of clothes, likely too polite to criticize the odd motif.

Standing at the closet, Kip remembered those moments as if through a fog, and a smile played on his lips. He hadn't even worn a pair of blue jeans until beginning his freshman year. *Undertaker.* Throughout elementary and middle school, he'd dressed as if he were attending prep school, and instead, he'd ended up at a seminary.

***

The un-engagement party had gone well, despite the odd turns, until Kelly caught her first glimpse of the woman slipping from the corner booth. If this were Morgan, Kip was a fool for dumping her. That was

Kelly's first thought as she stole a discreet glimpse. The brunette wore a look of class to complement Kip between her diamonds and sleek, sophisticated style. On second thought, though, Kelly wondered at her assessment. Would a woman of this apparent caliber settle for a few months of bliss?

Dumb question.

In an odd instant, the woman glanced over the Mulden table, and for a brief second, Kelly caught her eyes. No venom. Merely curiosity and a pleasant smile. Kip had sent that bottle of champagne. Had he mentioned an engagement party? An 'un-engagement' party? Could JD have mentioned that? No. In an instant, Kelly remembered the quiet advice Kip had offered Richard about 'intending' to marry her.

Where was JD if not with Kip?

What the hell was going on?

Preoccupied, Kelly suffered through the last moments of the meal, grateful when the others rejected dessert and, apparently, privy to her mood, decided to end the evening early.

One way or another, she needed to find out what was happening, and if JD wasn't home, she knew where to find him, along with the answers. Enough games. She needed to discover the status of that investigation as much as she needed to know if Kip was genuinely interested, or if he'd been playing games with the phone calls and those catty quips. Once and for all, she needed to sit down with that gentleman and have a serious conversation. God knows, she'd visited that Home last evening for just that reason, and he'd derailed her without half trying with a few embraces, a few kisses which had nearly sent her over the edge. They hadn't spent more than a minute or two chatting.

If this were a purely physical attraction, then she...? Well, she would get that out of the way and move on.

Practical. Sensible reasoning.

Stepping through the glass door in time to see the mystery lady tipping the valet and sliding into a rather plain economy car, Kelly's attention was riveted momentarily. Darcy somebody? JD had mentioned the name Darcy, and this was definitely not her business! But a fleeting memory of that overheard conversation halted her thoughts yet again as she pulled her long coat together against the chilly air. Her brother had also mentioned another woman. For God's sake. Three women. *Four* if she included herself.

Did she truly want to become another notch in this fellow's belt? Or to get involved with a man who appeared to be a female magnet?

Once more, Kelly decided. She would approach him only once more and let the chips fall where they may. She owed it to herself to investigate the possibilities ... and to satisfy her blasted curiosity.

Chapter 13

Drawing from his reflection, Kip donned the field jacket and noted that it fit him better now than fifteen years ago. To a nostalgic echo of a kitchen fan and laughter, Kip stepped into the living room, snapping off the bedroom light.

JD cast him a blind glance, but his attention froze in a startled double-take. His concentrated glaze faltered; a grin quivered on his bearded lips. "Christ, that's the same getup you wore the day we went fishing."

Apropos, Kip mused, "Really?"

"You know, it just hit me," Mulden smirked. "You really don't look a helluva lot different than you did the first time we met, except maybe you got taller and a little more arrogant."

Glancing at the papers in Mulden's hand, Kip lost the last vestiges of nostalgia. "Are you finished reading?"

JD glanced down at the third letter; his gaze sobered dramatically. "Not quite."

"Bring them along," Kip commented and strode to the door, glancing at the jamming device. Sidling past Mulden, he lifted the transistor. Frank Culver—first order of business. Get Mark Frances to the hospital to check on Frank, then try Marsh again. And God help Baxel if he wasn't there to answer the phone this time. By now, Marsh should have compiled a list of at least forty-one names, along with the financial stats from the past five years. And that list would have arrived via McDaniels, Kip realized in a stopped instant.

Just how deep into this mess was this estranged father? Fifteen years. Everything dated back fifteen years. To Denton McDaniels' enlightenment. How far could this fellow truly be trusted? How reliable was the information Marsh would supply?

Numbers. Figures don't lie. But how neat those numbers jived.

A bogus Will? Bogus financial reports?

Where the hell did this game begin and end?

At least two people had been murdered under this roof, and this was a bad time for Marsh to become unavailable. Not like him at all despite the holiday.

With his mind sorting and sifting, Kip strode into his mother's office and dialed Mark Frances's home number before settling into the chair. On the third ring, Mark answered. Mechanically, Kip told him about Frank's accident and asked him to enlist his clout to check Culver's condition. Without hesitation, Mark agreed and promised to call the direct office line as soon as he had something to report.

JD had settled into one of the receiving chairs, starting on the fourth set of letters as Kip dialed Marsh's business number. At the start of the recorded message, Kip uttered a curse, disconnected the call, and dialed the number Morgan had left for him—the cabana. After a dozen rings, he disconnected the call but held the receiver. Breaking his own golden rule, Kip dialed Baxel's home phone number. Not once since the beginning of their association had he dialed Marsh's home number, remaining steadfast in his decision to keep their relationship strictly professional, with no illusions of friendship despite the long hours they often spent together. No answer and no answering machine, which was Marsh's pet peeve. He claimed he answered enough phone messages in the office; he refused to put a machine in his apartment.

Dropping the receiver into its cradle on the phone base, Kip leaned back. Vacantly, his gaze drifted to the windows as he scanned internal abstracts, his focus shifting from images of Irish McGuire and a young JD to more recent visions of Marion McDaniels-Smithfield aglow in candlelight and a flashing image of a white-haired sophisticate with a cultured, compelling voice. A father, thirty years too late. A shadow in his life, a shadow that had manifested fifteen years ago.

What was his earlier thought about coincidences?

No coincidences in life.

With his thought, Kip leaned slightly, lifted the receiver, and dialed the number from memory. Across the desk, Mulden continued reading; his expression pensive as his focus sprinted across the lines of the computer printouts. Several rings pinged Kip's ear before a stately, unfamiliar voice erupted, "McDaniels' residence. To whom would you like to speak?" A butler. Marion had mentioned a butler. Damnit, with JD here, Kip would rather not say the name aloud. "Your employer, sir, if he's available."

The man hesitated; no doubt, considering hanging up. "Your name, sir?"

"Kip Patterson," he answered evenly.

"Hold one moment, please. I'll connect you."

More than a moment passed, nearly a full minute, before the familiar voice slipped through the line. "Hello, Kippen?"

"You have thirty seconds to give me a reason to trust you, sir, or I'll break a promise I made an hour ago and send you one hell of a Christmas present." Which would only begin with a Federal investigation into conspiracy.

Denton McDaniels hesitated.

"Counting, sir," Kip said quietly, ignoring JD's startled gaze watching him from across the desk.

"Your mother trusted me, lad."

"Evidence."

Again, McDaniels hesitated. Tension transcended the distance.

"Twenty," Kip commented idly.

"I have a duplicate of your mother's Will naming you sole—"

"Not good enough, sir. Fifteen." *How well do you work under pressure, Father? That's my forte.*

A brief pause, then, "Justin David Mulden is an undercover agent who's there to see to your safe—"

"More reason to doubt than trust. Ten, sir."

"What can I say to you, lad? How much do you know about—"

"Two—five—zero, sir. Five seconds."

A stopped pause, then, "You're my *son*!"

"Ancient history, sir. Four—three—"

"Irish McGuire!"

Irish McGuire? What the hell did Irish McGuire have to do with Denton McDaniels? Nothing! Just a name recited to stop the clock. "Zero. Expect—"

"He was like a grandfather to you," McDaniels intruded hurriedly, then slowed. "We spoke at great length. Through him, I came to know you—your idiosyncrasies, your ambitions, your desires. In the third grade, you ran to him. A birthday party. Your tenth birthday," McDaniels paused. His voice thickened as he continued, "A grand affair. Balloons, clowns. A tremendous cake. You were heartbroken, and Irish held you as you cried. He loved you, and through him, through hours of listening, I came to understand and admire the son I'd so wanted to claim.

"Trust me, lad, I am not your enemy." Heaviness lingered in his voice. "God knows, I've tried finding the force at work within Whistlebrook. I've had a dozen private investigators working on various sundry leads. I've tapped government sources in turn. I've tracked and investigated literally dozens of suspects, from bereaved families dating back twelve years to acquaintances who might have a personal motive—all to no avail."

"The individual cases. By what method are the funds transferred?"

"Each case varies from a deceased family member acquiring power of attorney and dispensing funds, to the victims simply liquidating through legal living Wills. The only consistency is that in each case, Whistlebrook is the only actual victim, and in several cases, legal documentation showed that Whistlebrook's claims had been satisfied."

Something wrong. Something in McDaniel's voice, his tone. Why did he sound as if he were reading from a script? A part of the game? Fifteen years ago, McDaniel's had helped to arrange a seminary school. *Think, damnit.* "What documentation?" As if he needed to ask. The information Mulden held had come through Denton McDaniels.

"From canceled checks endorsed to Whistlebrook to copies of Whistlebrook's billing statements showing accounts paid in full. Frankly, lad, the nature of this crime is that there is no visible crime. The monies appear to have transferred into the Home's accounts, then simply vanished—"

"Canceled checks. The banks?" Those were questions any sensible man would ask under these circumstances.

"Conveniently, the teller numbers were accurate, the initials illegible and untraceable, and eventually, most of the funds appeared in one form or another on the tax schedules of an heir."

"My mother considered me the master of this game."

"In its brilliance, yes," McDaniels said quietly.

"And you, sir?" Kip asked in an equally low tone. "How did you fare in her suspicions?"

"Not well at the onset," he admitted. "Your mother seemed to believe I had a personal motive dating back thirty years."

"You convinced her otherwise," Kip prodded without affect. Something wrong. Offbeat. Out of sync. *What was this fellow's game?*

"I understood her logic of thirty years ago, and I had nothing to gain by destroying my son's birthright. Any more than I had a right to confront him and negate his past as he knew it to be."

"Evidence on your behalf, sir?"

"Pardon me?"

"How did you convince her?" Kip asked directly.

McDaniels paused for a long moment, sighing heavily when he answered, "You were my proof, lad, and I would appreciate not recounting—or detailing—that evidence. Suffice it to say, she understood. I had neither motive nor contempt for the past—"

"Your discreet meddling in my financial success," Kip said, and McDaniels hesitated, startled. "Marshal, yes?"

"Lad, I don't—"

"Answer me, sir," Kip said softly, his abstract focus trailing along the window curtains. The rattle of glass under pattering rain and wind barely offered a nuisance within his vaporous thoughts. Just how much of his success must he attribute to McDaniels?

"Do not question his loyalties to you, lad. Unwittingly, yes, he's benefited both of us—"

"How did you locate him? When, sir?"

McDaniels sighed in a practiced gesture to buy a moment of thought. When he spoke, his voice carried a reflective note. "Thirteen years ago, I watched my seventeen-year-old son climb into a taxi. I stood in a bus terminal and watched him board a bus destined for Chicago. By the time the bus reached Chicago, I'd enlisted a trusted guardian to look out for him. A month later, I knew at least part of his plans for his future. A few days later, he entered a commune and sought spiritual peace through a Zen practitioner—a Zen master, I believe he was called. Should I continue?"

McDaniels had known? And never bothered to enlighten Marilyn Patterson over those three years? "Tell me—what did my mother say when you told her where I was?"

"I never told her, lad," McDaniels said with a fair amount of regret. "Even if I'd wanted to, after she discovered the trouble you encountered in the seminary, she refused to have any more to do with me. She held me responsible for that travesty, and perhaps she wasn't wrong. Belatedly, I apologize. At the time, I believed you would prosper in that environment."

Enough history, thank you. "Marshal tried reaching me this morning. Do you know what information he possessed for me?"

"I availed him of information about the names you requested," McDaniels answered without pause. "All of which your mother received months ago, I might add."

"Wiretaps, sir. What do you know?"

"Excuse me?"

"Are you responsible for the listening devices throughout this Home?"

"No," McDaniels said with a fair amount of alarm in his voice. "Are you positive—"

"My mother didn't trust you, any more than she trusted me, sir." Leaning, Kip dropped the receiver onto the telephone base, then settled back in his chair, closing his eyes against the strain of his vacant stare. Denton McDaniels wasn't his enemy. If anything, the son of a bitch was exactly what Marsh had unwittingly called him—a guardian angel. And Marilyn Patterson had died, not trusting him either. Perhaps, she'd believed they were in league against her.

"Don't suppose you want to tell me who you were just talking to, huh?" Mulden asked lightly.

"Not particularly," Kip answered absently.

"If you suspect him—"

"I don't," Kip interrupted without affect. "But yes, he's involved. For now, his name remains anonymous." *Mrs. Feeney needed to be found, and the residents required protection.*

"These names," JD said while rustling papers on his lap. "I take it most are employees. I recognize a couple names."

"They're all employees or were at some point. All of whom are being used," he said absently.

Mulden considered momentarily before commenting, "You aren't guessing. Being 'used?' Not the key player?"

"One might be," Kip said absently. Frank Culver's accident was no more an accident than the deaths within this Home were attributed to natural causes, and Kip's chest tightened with a thought of his mother's demise. With her medical history, no one had doubted the probability of a massive coronary. Had she come too close? Had she found her enemy?

"M-my guess is no," he stammered slightly, forcing himself to concentrate on the conversation, on Mulden who studied him intently. For a split second, Kip remembered those moments in the restaurant and outside those glass doors. *Damnit!* He couldn't afford to keep falling prey to reflection or fantasies! "Thi-is is coming from an—an outside source. Too much money involved." *And those numbers added up too damn neatly! Still, embezzlement? Who in the Home?*

'One classy lady that Carolyn. Her old man's loaded,' Frank had said last evening in the security booth.

Kip hadn't needed to ask. Sam McAnthony was an avid financial player. Not quite on a scale to match Morning Sun Enterprises, but the fellow drew a respectable income from the commodities trade. Carolyn hadn't been married when she arrived at the home fifteen—again, *fifteen* years ago. An office assistant, a gofer, with a pair of legs to send a thirteen-year-old into a tailspin whenever she leaned over a desk in one of her mini-skirts. "No, damn it," he uttered. Not Carolyn.

Yes, damn it. 1972 to the present.

'You could use Bill's office,' she'd offered Friday morning when he'd returned to the Home, and he'd spent most of Friday in the PRIVATE suite, returning calls, talking to John Madison. He'd handled affairs that he would have typically conducted in his mother's or Bill's office. Only this morning, 'use the office—' She'd stopped and smiled as if remembering his position of temporary administrator. *Or had she considered the broken wiretap in this office?* No, damn it! *Yes, damnit.* In Madison's conference room, Carolyn hadn't appeared surprised, not shocked like Bill when Kip had transformed, forfeiting the whimsical Playboy image that he'd cultivated on every prior visit to Whistlebrook. Carolyn had known him, but then, she'd become the liaison between him and his mother.

"Damn," he uttered, realizing that was only more evidence against her. She *had* become their liaison. She always knew where to find him, how to reach him, and she probably knew as much about the Home as Marilyn Patterson. "Goddamn it," he uttered, remembering how she'd squeezed his hand, smiling warmly, 'If you need me, honey, don't hesitate to call.'

'Someone in this room is your enemy. Watch the reactions as my Will is read.'

The reactions had come. Carolyn had appeared only slightly surprised, tempering Bill's outrage—

'Clean house or tear it down.'

How many others?

Automated, Kip pushed from his chair and started around the desk. Mrs. Janet Cross had been mortified, unable even to look him in the eyes. Halted, he leaned against the desk, unconsciously fishing his cigarettes from his pocket, looking into abstracts as he shook out a butt and held a flame to the end. He needn't open the drawer to the employee file. He'd read the information two nights past ... Mrs. Janet Cross, hired in 1971, widowed since February 72. Her husband had died in the Home. Currently, she holds the head nurse position on the Summer Floor, also known as 'Spring Chicken,' on the fourth floor.

And Margie Morone, starting date—November 1972. She'd begun as a nurse's aide while attending nursing school. She'd graduated in May 1973 and currently held the head nurse position on Autumn Floor Three ...

And the third nurse in that room, Larowski, held the head nurse title of Winter Floor Two.

"Goddamn," he breathed with an exhale of smoke. "You had them—" *Not one name on the list, Goddamn it! All of them! Every Goddamn one of them! Even Bill, the little fucking weasel!*

If not directly, Bill had indirectly aided and abetted this endeavor. Dr. Blake's records. How easily Carolyn could have mentioned those records. She'd worked here at the time, a young office assistant—

The 'archives,' damn it.

How many times had Kip thought about those damned 'archives' that Frank offered to show him? Archives consisting of the compiled personal information, the culmination of Frank's investigations. Unconsciously, Kip had avoided that bit of sleuthing, and he was still trying to postpone that ordeal.

"Damn it," Kip said absently. The last place he wanted to go ... *the goddamn basement.* At the mere thought of it, his muscles gripped. He couldn't even remember the last time he'd descended into the basement. Even if she'd enlightened him about her blasted archives, he would have ignored her. *Thanks a helluva lot. You couldn't put those files somewhere simple.* Like in the damned attic where she'd always stored the heads of the octopus. "Goddamn it."

"One helluva conversation we're having," JD intruded. "So far, let's see? Three or four 'damn its,' and we're up to about that many 'goddamn its'."

Looking over and down at JD's critical gaze, there could be no illusions of humor despite his casual words.

"You going to tell me what you've just figured out, or do we play twenty fucking questions?"

Army fatigues for Chrissake! Demanding war on ghosts, now? *Not eccentric, Mother, thanks a bunch.* If he wasn't certifiable before his arrival last week, he was certainly nearing that end.

"Earth to Kip—"

"Knock it off, I'm not falling for any more goddamn nostalgia," he stated and cleared his focus to study Mulden as more concrete wheels began turning. "You're back on my payroll, right?"

"Oh Christ, here we go again," Mulden said with a hint of genuine disgust.

Ignoring him, Kip leaned and opened the center drawer of his mother's desk, extracting a yellow marker and flashing a thought of how often he'd seen his mother enlist a highlighter on official documents, from correspondence to medical records. Handing the marker to JD, he continued evenly, "There's a copy machine in the next office. We'll make a couple of copies of that employee list, one of which we'll give to Mike." He checked his watch while continuing. "In about ten minutes, visiting hours will be over, after which, no one's coming through the front doors. Or any other door for that matter." Damn it, he might need Dorsen elsewhere. With his thought, he lifted the receiver and handed it to Mulden, who accepted it cautiously. "Ask for Angie. Ask her to come in for a few hours. Offer her double-time if she'll man the reception desk."

"Wouldn't it make more sense if you called her?"

"She wouldn't come," Kip said simply. "She's afraid of me."

"Can't imagine why," JD commented as Kip punched the digits to Angie's home. "Don't suppose you'd like to tell me what we're—" The phone was ringing. In a few words, JD enlisted Angie and, in record time, leaned and dropped the receiver into its cradle. "You just don't know how to talk to women," he smirked. "She's on her way. Now what the hell—"

"We're securing the Home," Kip said bluntly. "Discreetly, you and Jason need to visit each of the floors and remove anyone whose name is on that list. Ignore the janitors—they won't come in until nine. Orderlies, nurses ... be sure to get them all at once. I don't want anyone left to chance. Check the work schedules at the nurses' stations. Start on the second floor and work your way up. Escort them, JD. Make sure they're out of the building before you go to the next floor."

"I'm starting not to like the way that sounds or the way you look, and a few of the things your mother wrote ... And Frank's accident... And I'd have to be an idiot not to know you're worried about Edna. If these people are dangerous, maybe it's time we call in—"

"There are currently eighty-eight residents in this facility, JD," Kip interrupted calmly, his gaze steady. "Unless you can assure me that you're calling in eighty-eight escorts—each one personally trained on medication, dosage, and treatment of the elderly—I won't allow you to turn Whistlebrook into a circus to remove these parasites. I'll either have your discreet assistance, or you'll be the first person escorted from my Home."

"You know, you've been threatening to evict me since the first day I came here," JD said, sincerely annoyed despite his tension. "It's getting mighty goddamn old, old friend."

"My way, JD, or I'll expect you to leave quietly. And I don't think you have enough physical evidence for a search warrant."

In a heartbeat, JD considered options and alternatives before uttering a curse and pushing onto his feet, meeting Kip at eye level. "I'm back on your fucking payroll," he stated, leaving no doubt that he wasn't entirely comfortable with his decision. "Where will you be while I'm doing this surgery?"

"Spelunking," Kip answered evasively, refusing to buckle under a wave of nausea. "Before leaving each floor, there's one more thing you'll have to do," he considered absently. "Speak privately to the respective nurses in charge and have them dispose of any pre-mixed or pre-measured medications. Have them open new cases or cartons where applicable. When Mark Frances calls, I'll leave a message for him to come in, and when he comes, have him personally check any patient whose condition's declining radically—"

"Oh Christ," JD hissed softly. "Last night—even for Whistlebrook—three in one night—that's what you said. And you weren't just suffering from a bad case of déjà vu."

"When the Home's secure, you can call in whatever troops you feel are necessary, JD, but unless you intend to take full responsibility for the eighty-eight lives you'll be jeopardizing by setting off too many alarms, you'll keep your suspicions to yourself at the moment."

Anger swept across Mulden's eyes and stiffened the muscles beneath his neatly cropped beard. The total picture had come clear. "I had a bad feeling when I saw you a week ago, you were going to be trouble—"

"Funny, your sister—" —*said something similar. Damnit!*

"Yeah? My sister! That's exactly the trouble I was worried about a week ago," JD said in an irritated voice and stifled his anger. "Let's get the Home secure. Then—we'll talk about my sister."

Far easier to think about his sister, Kip considered as he took a step to follow, halting with his second thought. He would need a key to access the archives. "How about making those copies? I'll meet you in the lobby," he said simply and turned to the desk, sidling to reach the safe as JD continued through the door, uttering inaudible curses under his breath. If the information in the archives was so delicate, why the hell had his mother kept a key in the safe? A safe that at least Bill knew the combination to unlock? In quick turns, Kip freed the tumblers, already doubting his need to search the archives. Unless he was wrong about Carolyn and Bill, he doubted he'd find any incriminating evidence.

Dropping to one knee, he removed the infamous folder to begin this odyssey and moved several stacks of papers about in search of the key. No key on the first shelf. Dropping more solidly to his knees, he pulled a stack of business-sized envelopes from the jeweler's shelf and slid his hand into the narrow slot. His mother's arm might have fit in the narrow slot; his own halted at his forearm. And he doubted removing his jacket would help. Pivoting on his knees, he brought the flashlight from the desk where he'd left it last night, then leaned again and cast the beam into the shelf. "I'll be damned," he uttered absently as he spotted the shiny key in the deepest corner. Maybe there was hope for the archives, after all. Shifting on his knees, he brought a ruler from the center desk drawer, turned back to the open safe, and fumbled for several seconds, nearly standing on his head to take aim and drag the key out. No way Bill would have found the key; he would have needed to lie flat on the floor to see it.

***

For the third time in under a week, Kelly strode across the parking lot, grateful to have found a space close enough to the main doors to avoid getting drenched. What exactly she would say to Kip, or to JD, whose rental occupied a space three cars from her own, she hadn't decided. Pushing open the industrial glass door, she had an odd thought about a little boy. And not for the first time, she wondered about Kip's childhood, living here in a geriatric home. Although the lobby resembled a parlor, the plastic runner, signage, and reception desk conveyed an institutional ambiance. Unlike last evening, when the young receptionist had remained engaged with several visitors, the desk was empty, sparing her the need to announce her presence.

With the sound of muffled laughter echoing from the open oak doors across the lobby, Kelly judged her luck holding. Without pausing at the desk, she strode to the administration doors and pushed through as if she had every right to invade that private domain. Well, and this was his home, after all, and bore resemblance to entering an apartment building, if one ignored the placards designating office spaces.

At the junction that led to his private space, she started down the hall, but at the muffled male voices, she halted. Only last evening, Kip had directed her into the cove near the main office, where she'd remained out of sight until Kip cleared her way—not that it had mattered. JD had known she was there.

And this was her brother's voice.

Without a conscious thought, Kelly stepped into the shadowy cove and stood contemplating her advance. She couldn't hear their words, but she identified both voices. Considering her brother's mention of his eviction this morning, she realized they'd apparently mended fences. Holding her breath, she heard the mumbling curses as her brother emerged from the opposing door, and standing in the shadows, she identified the sounds of a copy machine kicking to life. Should she slip through this second door? Or wait a few moments? If she heard Kip — JD was alone, still grumbling or cursing. The copy machine completed its cycle. Only distant sounds drifted from the lobby, more muffled, and in an odd moment, Kelly considered the shoddy security. This was supposed to be a secure building. How had she passed through that lobby for the second time without notice?

The thought fleeted away as she heard footsteps and drew back against the shadowed wall, watching her brother's shadow pass on the wall directly across from her. Frozen, she listened to the scrape of his soles on the carpet, a pause in his stride, and held her breath. Likely, he'd return and step around the corner at any second. But seconds turned to hours before the parlor room sounds amplified as JD passed through the administration door. Breathing a sigh of relief, she waited another few seconds before deciding she was an idiot.

Nearly muttering a curse, she sidled from the cove and glanced toward the administration door, then strode into the secretarial area. At the office door, she hesitated, contemplating the need to knock. She hadn't knocked last evening. Last evening, however, she'd knocked on the PRIVATE door before chancing a peek into the office. Well, she knew Kip was in the office and apparently alone. The element of surprise. To hell with propriety.

Testing the doorknob, half expecting to feel it catch in her hand, Kelly jolted when the door started opening in front of her for the second time. Already tense, expecting to find him standing in front of her, she skimmed her gaze toward the empty office chair turned at an odd angle behind the desk. To the odd scraping sound, her attention dipped, halted on the lamplight shimmering on a swatch of blond waves. Surely he wasn't sitting on the floor.

Beckoned by her curiosity, she started forward, tilting her head as if to peek around the side of the desk, thinking he might have dropped something and bent to retrieve it. He wasn't sitting on the chair and bent over, however. The chair was empty.

He knelt in front of an open safe.

Chapter 14

Looking down at the key in his palm, Kip shook his head absently. If this was the key to the archives, his mother truly had needed a lesson about hi-tech. Doubtful, a search of the archives would bear fruit. Anyone interested in extracting information from the archives could have engaged a pair of metal snips to the lock. Possibly, removing the parasites would be enough. If he just fired the entire staff and started over, he wouldn't need to go spelunk—

He started to rise, to turn. A glimpse of motion, the scrape of a sole on carpet! Pivoting on boot leather, he lost his balance and sat down on his hip as his attention shot skyward. For a full five seconds, he felt like a five-year-old with his mother catching him invading her private domain.

"Uh…"

Kelly Mulden, for God's sake! His heart skipped a beat, and his breath returned in a gulp. Belatedly, the humor struck him. She had—without a doubt—just scared the hell out of him.

Her attempt to appear serious, as she apparently intended, failed. A smile quivered in her sensuous lips as she realized her effect, an effect that too readily quickened his heart even before she offered an innocent, "Hi."

His attention riveted. His focus slid off the twinkling hazel eyes, taking his fill of her shimmering brunette curls caught in a halo of soft colors reflected from the Tiffany lamps—or so he chose to believe. Far safer to judge the natural effect of light than to consider the brilliant kaleidoscope glowing around her. She still wore that soft, low-cut black dress, and despite her long black coat, which concealed the curves, his imagination heated to the memory of her bare shoulders aglow in La Chateau's candlelight. Standing less than three feet away, not even the shadows behind the desk offset her slender calves and the promise of long legs behind that bulky black curtain.

"Dammmn," he drawled softly, lifting his gaze to study her face. She wore another of those half-hitched smirks; amusement enhanced in her emerald eyes. The lady possessed a wicked sense of humor and a fine, quick wit to know her effect—both the scare and the heat. How the hell had she gotten past her brother? Or had she? In a sharp glance, Kip verified JD's absence and then met her gaze. "Hi," he responded in delay.

"Was uh...? Was that Morgan with you at the restaurant?" she asked, conversationally.

Or all business. Kip couldn't decide.

"No, that wasn't Morgan," he answered with the humor taking a turn in his mind. Was she jealous? *Idiot.*

"Successful fishing trip then?" she asked lightly.

"Not in a manner to which you're referring," he heard himself answering, doubting his sanity. Why in God's name was he attempting to dispute her obvious conclusion? Explaining himself? But damn, she was direct. "Did you happen to pass your brother in the hall?"

"That alcove works pretty well," she mused. "I'm sort of glad he talks to himself."

Faintly amused, Kip imagined her ducking into the shadows a second ahead of JD. One helluva DEA agent if he couldn't even catch his sister hiding around a corner. At the soft scent of her perfume, Kip lost his thought of JD. What was she doing here? "Did Whitman hassle you again?" he asked in a quieter tone.

"This isn't about Richard," she said smoothly, looking down at him with a coquettish tip of her head to suggest curiosity, but her eyes remained intent. "I may still care for Richard," she said carefully, quietly. "But I realized I can't marry him. I'd only make him extremely unhappy."

"I doubt very much you could make any man unhappy, luv," he said sincerely.

Rather than comment, she stepped forward and lowered slowly, meeting him at eye level. One delicate hand rested on his raised knee to balance her precarious stoop. "No word games or fantastic one-liners, Kip," she said with a soft, all-business tone. "I'm not a fish accustomed to being reeled in by professional fishermen. I tend to spot them a mile away. I'm twenty-seven, not eleven or twelve, and puppy love only goes so far... I gave Richard back his ring this morning. I'd only be humoring him if I married him, now."

The lady knew how to cut to the chase. Mesmerized, he held her compelling hazel eyes.

"I'm something of a realist despite whatever JD might have told you. Right or wrong, I'd rather be here with you for a little while than keep wondering what it would be like to know you."

For all the practical reasons—his own indifference to women and lasting relationships heading the list—he thought he should say something. This once, not one single word came readily to mind. Too easily, he remained lost in her soft hazel eyes and long lashes, fascinated by the curve of her lips even as sobriety echoed in her words. No one-liners. She was, without exception, the most stunning young woman he'd ever met.

Abruptly, she closed the distance, tipped her head, and brushed a kiss on his lips, pulling away before he could react. Settling onto her heels, she smiled slightly, "That was sort of all I came to tell you. I'd like to stay, but if you want me to go—for any reason other than Richard or my brother—I will."

"Richard—nor your brother—are of any concern to me," he said honestly, feeling slightly like the victim of a hit and run.

"But?" she anticipated.

There was a 'but. Several 'buts,' in fact. A murderer ran loose in the home. Mrs. Feeney was missing. Frank Culver was in surgery. He needed to secure Whistlebrook. He'd already wasted more time than he could afford. In one motion, he rolled onto his knee, caught her hand, and carried her afoot with him. Looking into her magnificent hazel eyes, he decided, "I have to ask you to leave tonight, Kelly. But I can't give you the reasons. Suffice it to say, it's no lack of interest." An understatement, he considered even as he continued, "Unless you change your mind between now and tomorrow—" He lifted his hand, slipping his fingers into the nape of her neck, and tipped her head as he lowered his lips to hers. No peppermint. A tangy taste of spearmint awakened his mouth as their breath mingled. Too quickly, a wave of anticipation raced through his veins. With an effort, he pulled away, heaving a soft curse and breath. Dumbfounded by his reaction, he decided, "I *will* phone you tomorrow."

She smiled slowly, laughter rolling into her livid hazel eyes. "I think I believe you this time."

"You should. I don't make idle promises," Kip commented soberly and slipped his hand from her neck, detaching himself against his will. *Damn! This was hard.* She was no longer engaged. She'd dumped the dork. *For him?* He was vain enough to believe that possibility, and oddly grateful, for whatever reason. Suddenly, JD's parting shot and irritation made far greater sense. A smirk slipped onto his lips uncontrollably. "If you'd like to avoid your brother, remain here for a few moments. I'll stop back to let you know when it's clear."

"Guess we shouldn't give him an ulcer just yet," Kelly mused and stood on her toes, brushing a kiss on his lips. "I'll wait here."

Part Three

The Archives

Chapter 15

Entering the lobby in time to see Mike striding from the glass doors with a set of keys rattling in his hand, Kip caught a flashing glance of JD's gaze. Something in that intent glance lent him cause to wonder if Kelly's presence had truly gone unnoticed. Piano sounds no longer emanated through the French doors, but a faint echo of voices lingered in the lobby. Stopping two steps from JD and Jason, who stood at the desk, Kip caught another subtle flash of Mulden glancing toward the executive wing doors. When their gazes connected, no doubt remained. JD knew his sister was here. No time to discuss Kelly. "Did you brief Mike on our endeavor?"

"My credibility isn't what it used to be," JD commented. "And I doubt you're too high on his list."

Probably right. Readily, Kip remembered standing on his mother's desk and his flippant interchange with Bill Bickerman. Wariness haunted Mike's eyes as he halted a few steps away.

Far too easily, Kip imagined Dorson longing for a sight of Bickerman and days gone by. The next few moments would not improve his mood. "We have a problem, Mike," Kip said evenly, leveling his gaze on Dorsen's darting eyes. "As of five o'clock this evening, I became sole owner and proprietor of Whistlebrook. I am officially—irrefutably—your new employer. As the new administrator—no longer *acting* administrator—I'm offering you an option to remain in my employ, in which case you will follow my instructions to the letter over the next several hours, or you can hand me your keys, walk out those doors, and return in the morning to receive your severance pay. The choice is yours, but I should tell you, the next couple of hours may seem a bit chaotic, and I don't have time to waste. I need your answer, now."

Dorsen considered only a moment, glancing off Mulden and King, deciding abruptly, "Guess I'll stay employed." He barely paused for a breath. "Have you heard anything else about Mr. Culver? Do you know if he's okay?"

"I haven't heard. Hopefully, Dr. Frances will call here shortly. How many security men do we have on duty tonight?"

"Just two others—Ted Short and Rick Franklin."

Neither name appeared on the list, thank God. "As of this moment, you're promoted to Assistant Chief of Security, second only to Mr. Mulden. You'll take your orders either from him or directly from me. You are—in effect—third in command of this Home, and should you find yourself unable to contact either of us, I'll expect you to use your own judgment in dispatching my orders beyond this point. Is that understood?"

His attention riveted, Mike nodded, "I understand."

"Angie will come in soon to relieve you; however, for the time being, I want you to remain near this entrance. As of this moment, except Dr. Frances and Angie, no one is to enter the Home." With his words, he glanced at JD, barely lifting his hand and receiving the copy Mulden handed to him on cue. Handing the copy to Mike, he continued quietly, "I'd like you to look over that list. Over the next hour or so, anyone on that list within the Home will be quietly escorted to the exits by JD and your recently promoted associate, Mr. King. I don't expect trouble, but if, for any reason, one of these people attempts to regain entry, you'll see they're denied. In a few moments, I'm transferring the switchboard system to manual and routing all calls through this desk. The intercoms will remain functional, but you will undoubtedly start receiving calls from staff. You'll tell them we're experiencing technical difficulties and expect to have the phones repaired soon. No outside calls are to reach the floors. Only in the event of an extreme emergency will you—or Angie—transfer or place an outside call on behalf of anyone in the Home. Understood?"

"You're going to shut down the phones. No calls in or out unless somebody has a serious need," Dorsen nodded as his attention slid down the page, then lifted abruptly. "You're firing all of these people?"

"Let there be no misunderstandings, Mike," Kip said calmly. "I am taking extreme measures under extreme conditions. At this moment, I merely want these people out of my Home. They are being temporarily removed from my employ. I'll reserve my final judgment pending further investigation. At the moment, we're taking necessary precautions. Do you have a problem—a friend on that list perhaps?"

"Can I be honest with you, Mr. Patterson?"

"Please."

"It'd be my pleasure to escort a few of these jokers off the premises. I just wish Jack were here, so I could throw him out."

Faintly amused, Kip glanced at JD. "You just have to know what to say to people," he commented and shifted his attention to the desk, lifting a notepad. As he started jotting messages for Angie, he commented, "When Angie arrives, give her this note. Should Dr. Frances call before her arrival, ask him to come straight here. When he arrives, page Mr. Mulden. If any of these others call, I'll expect you to page me." Tearing off the sheet, Kip handed it to Mike while looking at Jason. "If you'd rather not be a part of this, I'd understand."

"I'm in," King said flatly. "But ... you think I could call home before you disconnect the phones? My folks are probably getting a little worried."

"I'd appreciate it if you don't mention your recent promotions or make any reference to our endeavors over the phone, but do place the call," Kip commented and looked to JD. "Any questions? Anything I've missed in your opinion?"

"The phone idea's a good one, but I suggest we don't maintain a blackout for very long or we're liable to create a helluva mess and shake up the phone company in the process."

"Probably right," Kip considered briefly. "One hour," he decided abruptly and held Mulden's gaze. "Possible?"

Mulden glanced down the list, deciding and nodding, "No problem. You don't have anybody who resembles Godzilla or King Kong up there, do you?"

"It's all in how you talk to people, remember?" Kip commented with a faint grin. "Lure them out with sweet talk if you must, just get them out and contact Short and Franklen to make certain they remain out."

"You said you don't expect trouble," Mike commented, pensive. "What happens if trouble starts?"

"You know the number for the Randall Police. Use it. As of now, these people are trespassing on private property; deal with them accordingly. If Bill Bickerman or Carolyn McAnthony calls for me, tell them I'm not taking any calls this evening. If either comes to the door—" Both carried a key. Doubtful either would come, but could he afford to take the chance? "See that they do not enter any door and have them advised that you are acting under my direct order and will have them arrested accordingly. Any other questions?"

"There are a few more radios in the security station," Mike commented, looking to JD. "Maybe we should stay in contact. You can let me know who I might expect at the doors."

"I'll pick one up," JD agreed, looking to Kip. "Might be a good idea for you to carry one, too."

"Certainly faster than the intercom," he agreed. "I'll need a few minutes to dispatch the phones. You could leave one here for me if you will."

"Is Kelly staying with you?" JD asked directly, his gaze intent.

"I'm sending her home the moment you're out of the lobby," Kip answered without pause.

"Games?"

"We're saving you from an early ulcer," Kip answered, smirking and shrugging.

"Day late and a dollar short, old friend, but thanks anyway," Mulden said and turned his gaze to Mike. "I'll need a set of keys."

When exactly he'd collected the keys in the Private suite, Kip couldn't recall, but he lifted them from his coat pocket, separated the switchboard room key, and removed it from the ring, handing the remainder to JD.

"You sure you won't need any more of these?"

"Doubt it," Kip answered and glanced at King. "Make your call." Looking to Mike, he commented, "Escort the young woman from my office and see that she reaches her car without incident, will you?"

"Will do," Mike said with the first honest hint of amusement as his gaze darted to Mulden.

Enough said, Kip started across the lobby. Without a doubt, Mulden was relieved to have Mike escorting Kelly from the doors—

"One more question," Mulden said haltingly, and Kip looked over to find his peculiar gaze. "What the hell am I supposed to do with this?" he asked while holding up the yellow marker and donning a spark of amusement.

"Shit," Kip uttered, remembering. "Thought you might want to cross off the names of those no longer employed—narrow your margin, so to speak."

Mulden reached over, touching Kip's elbow to halt him before they parted to pass on either side of the staircase. "You know, removing these people could be the least of our problems. Have you considered how you'll keep them out?"

His gaze abstracted, Kip considered only a moment, meeting JD's sober gaze. "Let's hope my expedition is successful and I find enough evidence to issue a warrant or two."

"Where are you going to be?" JD asked simply despite his complex gaze.

"Doing a little research. You can reach me on the radio if the need arises."

"You're really not going to tell me."

"I really don't know," he answered honestly. Frank had said only the old fruit cellar, and the mere thought gripped Kip's stomach. For an instant, he considered canceling the plan and taking JD with him to the basement. The residents. Securing the Home held priority. As he parted from Mulden and strode into the alcove, Kip suffered an uncomfortable feeling that at any moment, all hell could break loose with eighty-eight lives suspended in the shallow balance. Unless he shut down the phones to avoid any incoming orders from his nemesis, last night could truly repeat itself. If the lives of Elsa Taylor and Vincent Seratti could be so easily forfeit to upset the prince's equilibrium, God knows how many other lives could be sacrificed in the wake of that damned Will, either to scare him off or frame him for murder.

God help me, if I don't find something in those damned archives...
***

Kelly had heard enough through the doors to realize Kip hadn't lied when mentioning 'no lack of interest.' The tension building all afternoon quickened through her system as she listened to the rather drastic measures Kip outlined in quick spurts. Something was seriously wrong here, and she wasn't about to walk away.

Pushing through the door just as the security guard reached for it, Kelly met the man's gaze. "New orders, Mr.—Dorsen, is it?"

"Mike," he offered while backing a step, catching the door for her.

At the reception desk, a dark-haired young man, possibly no older than seventeen or eighteen, rested, punching numbers into the phone. Calling home. In a split second, Kelly sized up the quiet atmosphere, reviewed the procedures she'd overheard, and decided. Looking at Dorsen, she commented, "You need a receptionist."

"We have one coming, Miss. I've been asked to see that you get to your car—"

"So, I heard," she said simply and slipped off her coat, noting his staggered gaze. She probably should have changed before jumping into her car. A little late to worry about that. "When Mr. King finishes his call, I'll man the desk, at least until your receptionist arrives."

"Miss, I'd—"

"I'll speak to Mr. Patterson when he returns from his mission," she said quietly, lowering her voice as several middle-aged people emerged from the doorway across the lobby. Only three of the four wore coats; the fourth, sporting a white cap of permed hair, wore a paisley dress and a light sweater, smiling as she walked with the others to the elevators. For some odd reason, the sight of that elderly woman stepping into the elevator on her own power lent Kelly a thought of Richard's lofty proclamation this morning. Belatedly, she realized Richard's misconception. Undoubtedly, he imagined a private house with a half dozen residents. She'd love to see his reaction to this Home, which closely resembled a grand hotel or resort, not even close to a state-funded hospital.

She reached the desk just as King replaced the receiver. His gaze skipped to her and halted. Cute kid. Brown eyes, a scruff of windblown dark hair, a nice smile.

He vacated the chair behind the desk and held out his hand. "Jason King, ma'am."

"Kelly Mulden," she offered and clasped his hand.

"Yeah, I know," he said with a flash of white teeth, a sheepish smile. "Your brother seems pretty cool, but uh … aren't you supposed to be ducking out about now?"

The phone emitted a first ring, sparing her from more than a wink and smile as she reached, collecting the receiver and sidling behind the desk. "Whistlebrook Nursing Home. Can I help you?"

In her ear, a rather surly voice growled, "My phone line just went dead. This is Earl Bingem, 202."

"Will you hold a moment, Mr. Bingem?" Another line had already lit on the phone base. In the space of five seconds, she identified another resident. "We've just become aware of a technical problem," she told Mr. Bingem. "We'll have it cleared up as soon as possible if you'll bear with us."

This was about to become one very hectic hour, Kelly realized as she engaged another button. Glancing toward the glass doors as Dorsen locked the panels behind the departing visitors, Kelly offered, "Whistlebrook Nursing Home, Reception desk."

***

Within the switchboard room, Kip concentrated briefly on transferring the system to manual and relaying a single outside line through the switchboard to the reception desk extension. In record time, the chain of tiny lights turned black, and Kip flashed an instant of nostalgia as he considered the angry shouts of residents whose calls had just been terminated. Unless he found concrete evidence against Carolyn McAnthony, getting chewed out by six or seven dozen octogenarians would be the least of his concerns. Assuring himself that the system would function, he watched the incoming line disengage. Jason had finished his call. Kip watched a moment longer. The incoming call light ignited as anticipated, and a subtle beep registered before the blinking light steadied. For the next hour or so, Mike or Angie would be extremely busy on the phone.

Returning to the lobby in time to see none other than Kelly Mulden holding the reception desk phone to her ear, Kip wondered what might have already gone wrong.

JD met his gaze and shrugged. "Figured we could use the help," he said lamely.

In a candid, operator voice, Kelly stated, "Please bear with us. We will place your call as soon as possible." She lowered her finger and pressed another lit button on the phone base. "Good Evening. Whistlebrook," she said curtly, flashing Kip an amused glance. "I'm sorry, we're unable to transfer your call at this time. We're experiencing technical difficulties due to inclement weather."

Kip turned an annoyed glance to JD and barely parted his lips.

"Don't even say it. She was eavesdropping."

"Oh, grand." How many others might have stood around a corner as he'd outlined the plan for Mike? He barely flashed the thought before assuring himself that the executive hallway remained the only point from which someone might have overheard more than murmured voices. Analyzing and forming strategies had always been his strong suit; he paid others to implement his plans. Shaking his head, Kip accepted the radio from Mulden, commenting, "One hour. Do hurry and radio me when you're through."

"If you want to stay on top of this, you'd better take a copy of this list. We're using the numbers rather than names."

"I won't need the list," he said honestly and flashed Kelly a wink, forcing himself to turn from her before she could disengage another call. The archives. Nothing else held priority at this moment, but tomorrow...

Passing through the brief hall to reach the kitchen, his thoughts lingered on Kelly and tomorrow, refusing any other thought as he passed through a utility closet, shortcutting his route to the rear hall and basement entrance. Too aware of the rapid banging in his chest, Kip strode the last paces to the oak door, absently glancing toward Mrs. Feeney's door down the hall. For an instant, he considered checking her suite. His stomach gripped with a pang of fear. Visions of his mother's funeral—and countless others—sent a wave of vertigo spiraling in his skull.

Could he afford to take the time to search for evidence? At this very moment, more residents could be in serious trouble, and he certainly possessed the means to determine who could be in trouble naturally. His blasted sixth sense.

No. The archives.

If he intended to turn this around, he needed physical evidence.

And therein lay the serious doubt, Kip considered as he stood gripping the doorknob. The paper chase. He'd watched the declining numbers for years. If the Home had ever run into serious trouble, he would have bailed his mother out of jeopardy.

A game, damnit. The paper chase was a fucking game, and McDaniels was a party to that hoax. But to what extent? And toward what end?

Two people were dead. Murdered, for God's sakes.

Could he afford to consider any part of this endeavor a game?

A treasure hunt. One of those wretched games where one was led around by riddles and hints toward some ultimately dangerous end. The paperwork. For several hours in Madison's office yesterday afternoon, he'd read over the financial reports. The *genuine* financial reports. And most of the information Madison held coincided with the data he'd compiled on his own over the past ten years.

Embezzlement. As soon as Mulden had spoken that word, Kip had realized the insanity of that charge, as well as the investigation, and yet, a DEA agent lingered in his company, compliments of Denton McDaniels. FBI agents followed him every time he stepped out of the Home, and that had begun four or five days ago, with suited gentlemen posing as paparazzi. They'd lingered in the hotel lobby as early as Friday morning. He assumed, then, that they'd found him Wednesday or Thursday. Embezzlement charges? JD hadn't heard anything about a murder investigation, but he'd mentioned something else. Laundering? As in m*oney laundering?*

DEA agent. Was the mention of money laundering part of a ruse enlisted to gain JD's participation or a serious consideration? Laundering. As in laundering drug money?

He had to play this out.

The archives.

Twisting the basement doorknob, Kip uttered a curse and pulled the door open, only slightly surprised at the soft fluorescent light already reaching up the wide staircase. He hadn't opened this door in years, and with a sudden wave of vertigo, he nearly stepped back and slammed the door shut. No single clear memory accompanied his tension. A sense of darkness and fear spiraled through him, gripping his muscles into quick knots.

"Damn it," he uttered softly, jolting himself in the echoing silence. Not silence.

Too clearly, the hardwood floor creaked overhead as someone passed through the second-floor hall, and a constant hum of a generator rose from the staircase. Inside him, a more distant sound stirred as Kip forced his army boot onto the first step. Unconsciously, he groped and touched the metal railing, skidding his fingertips on the metal as he continued his descent...

Sobbing. He heard someone sobbing. Faintly, the sound came to him within the droning hiss of steam and vibrating generators.

'D-Do It!' *the cry echoed within the shadows.*

Palm flat against the wall, Kip lurched to an internal sound and stood reeling. Disoriented, he awoke to a lightheaded sway, realizing belatedly that he'd held his breath, apparently long enough to suffer a pain in his chest and the heady sensation of oxygen deficiency.

"Shhhit," he hissed and dragged a calming breath into his lungs, clearing his focus of an abstract mist.

He'd walked only as far as the first corner, an intersection of narrow halls, narrower than his memory allowed. Despite his tunnel vision and sense of nostalgia, the hallways glowed in light. Surprisingly bright light. Blinking against vertigo, his attention riveted on the bold black print contrasted on the white wall directly in front of him. LOADING DOCK A and in smaller print, Kitchen Entrance. If those signs had existed a lifetime ago, he didn't remember them, nor the bold arrows pointing toward the staircase. Or the orange neon glow spilling across the paneled ceiling in the junction. EXIT. And somehow it was all wrong. As if he stood in another place, another time, he suffered the distortion of an alien world with gray painted cement floors and white-washed walls. Not this. Not brightly lit walls with clearly designated directions to guide him through the maze. What had he expected?

"Damnit." He knew what he'd expected. *A cave. A black cave with stone walls and endless tunnels of damp, mildew smells and black, shadowy entrances.* His mother had made changes. She'd replaced the single-watt bulbs dangling from cobwebbed copper pipes and wires. Fluorescent tracking stretched the length of the corridor, with every fourth long tube lighted, no doubt connected to an auxiliary generator.

Not ten-or-fifteen-year-old changes. More than twenty years prior, Marilyn had adhered to some fire or health code and reconditioned the basement. If not the changes, he vaguely remembered carpenters and electricians traipsing through the upstairs entrances at all hours of the day, and his mother ordering him to stay out of everyone's way. He must have taken those words to heart. He couldn't recall ever descending those steps to investigate the fruits of their labor, but Kip remembered wanting to satisfy his curiosity. Something had stopped him, then, as it threatened to stop him, now.

At a static crackle, his muscles lurched before he recognized the voice issuing from his pocket. "Stand by, we're going up now. Maintain radio silence until further notice. Checkpoints acknowledge. Base One out."

Annoyed with his foolish fright and appreciating JD's decisive tone, Kip forced himself onto his feet as three different voices acknowledged Mulden's command. "Station One clear... Station Two clear... Station Three clear..."

With a flashing thought of Kelly Mulden manning the phone, Kip stepped into the bisection, turning his attention to his own quest. A fruit cellar. And although he couldn't remember a specific fruit cellar, the coldest storage rooms would be located along the external walls.

"Damn it, should have done this last night—brought Frank along," he uttered. And he could just imagine telling Frank that he had no idea where to find a fruit cellar. Or anything else concerning the sub-level floor of Whistlebrook.

Damnit, Frank—

Collecting himself, Kip started toward the right, if for no other reason than simply because the administration wing was located to the right, along with the elevator shaft that would allow his mother easy access to her archives. He should have taken a moment to call Simon. Simon Jenkins, the new maintenance supervisor, could have led him through this maze. Only vaguely, Kip recalled an introduction—probably at Fitzpatrick's or in the Oak Room. Too late to consider shortcuts. By the time he reached Jenkens, and the fellow arrived...

Too many lives hung in the balance.

Digging the unpretentious key from his pocket, Kip paused to check the locks on several doors en route to the elevators. When he stood in a wide section of a corridor, he cursed his stupidity. He could have ridden the damned elevator one floor down and shortened his trip—at the same time, he stood in silent appreciation of Marilyn Patterson. Whistlebrook had truly 'moved with the times.' Probably not even a temperamental service elevator existed at any of the loading docks. Every door stood clearly designated as a storage cell for anything from canned goods to office supplies.

Well-stocked, he verified, by opening a door across from the elevator. Undoubtedly, in the further reaches of the Home, doors would be labeled: Linens, Medical Supplies, Maintenance. Doubtful he'd find any old laundry rooms with industrial-sized wringers rotting away. In a distant memory, he recalled some mention of an auction and her 'unloading' a lot of obsolete appliances and equipment. She enlisted laundry services now.

He recalled a blood-pressure-flushed face and a meaty palm squeezing his hand, while offering to review the linen service contracts.

Not even a whole week had passed, but it felt more like a lifetime.

Absently, Kip turned, reading the bold print on the wall parallel to the elevator doors. She couldn't make it easy. No designated ARCHIVES rested on the list written on the wall. MAINTENANCE OFFICE. LOADING DOCK A. MEDICAL RECORDS. Records? Indeed, records, medical or otherwise. *Thanks, Mom.* At least she'd provided a direction, though he doubted he'd find the 'archives' clearly marked, and with a lurching dread, he realized the improbability of finding the records at all. What had Frank said? 'I could save you some time ... direct you to the files.'

On the outside chance that he could be wrong about life, Kip found the Medical Records room, not surprised to encounter a locked door and cursing himself for giving Mulden his keys. Had he believed, even for a moment, that he'd experience a genuine institutionalized basement, Kip might have held onto the damned keys, but this? To discover actual hallways?

Only a hint of mildew and stone scents lingered more in his mind than in the halls.

Shaking his head, Kip brought out his wallet. When all else fails, pick the lock. *Thanks, Brother Nathaniel,* Kip mused as he lifted a laminated card and a slight metal wire from his wallet. He hadn't consciously tucked that wire in his wallet after picking his mother's office lock three days earlier. Either a fear of locked doors or too many memories...

What was a kid to do when faced with a prefect who chased him out of libraries and made his life hell when catching him alone in his dorm? Utility rooms and storage rooms had become his safest havens from that sanctimonious cretin.

I could have become a great cat burglar, Kip mused as the doorknob turned in under ten seconds flat. Returning the card and paperclip to his wallet, he shoved the door open and reached around the corner, running his palm along the smooth wall, finding the light switch.

After the organization and meticulous nature of his mother's realm, the sight before him knocked him slightly off balance. Cardboard boxes and crates stood head high, with vaguely recognizable file cabinets behind mounds of overflowing paraphernalia. This wasn't a room of Medical Records, not by any stretch of imagination. A single track of fluorescent light stretched across the ceiling, barely offsetting the shadows between undefined aisles. Apparently, Marilyn had never gotten around to putting these 'records' in order. By the ragged edges of several visible boxes, these records were dated. Possibly back to the Home's sojourn as a Boarding House.

'Carried some of those old trunks down from the attic,' Frank had said.

On a closer, more thorough scan, Kip recognized at least a half dozen trunks dating from an era of steamboats and railroad travel, and abruptly, he understood the nature of the tiny key he held within his sweated palm. Not a door key. A trunk key! One that had seen a lot of use in recent months, judging by its silver-edged contrasting with its oxidized patina.

With the nature of the information and Marilyn's frame of mind, Kip doubted she'd have placed the trunk front and center, but she'd need easy access. Wading into the aisle to the left, he ruled out several trunks simply because the boxes mounded on top were too large for a woman of his mother's size to wrestle. Shifting stacks of smaller boxes, he stooped at several trunks, checking the locks, attempting to insert the key. The room hadn't seemed significant at the onset. Still, as he trespassed into the fourth cluttered aisle, tasting dust and aged paper, he became sharply aware of time passing, unconsciously listening for Mulden's voice breaking 'radio silence' with a progress report.

The silence in the room seemed more suffocating than the scents. Only a distant hum of generators and furnaces reached into the room. Almost grateful for the scrape of cardboard and grit, he countered his thought when a landslide stirred a wave of dust. Resounding, the thud of ancient books slamming the floor at his feet, muffled within the close, cardboard walls. Stifling a sneeze, he stood, likewise restraining a curse while waiting for the dust to settle. If she had all this damned information—and had any incriminating evidence—she would have gone to the police!

'I love you too much to stop you.'

"Bullshit," he stated and lurched at his resounding voice. At the same instant, his attention snagged and held on a mound in the furthest corner. And why did that box rest so precariously on the end of that trunk? A single touch might start another landslide of the half dozen average-sized boxes crowding the trunk. Automated, Kip stepped over the clutter in front of him and reached the corner. Stooping, he shifted a precarious crate to the floor before reaching for the lock. A ragged piece of dry-rotted leather covered the worn brass lock, but on closer inspection, the fine streaks of shiny brass confirmed his suspicion before he fitted the skeleton key into the keyhole.

He'd found Marilyn Patterson's archives.

Barely breathing his victory, Kip pushed to his feet and quickly lifted the boxes off the trunk. He imagined his mother arranging these smaller boxes into a comfortable chair and using the flat top of the steamer as a table. The lock turned easily; the lid lifted without a hitch. The initial smell of mothballs and old linen contradicted his victory. Without pause, he slipped his fingers into either end of the opening and lifted the internal tray.

Jackpot! Or was it 'Bingo' as Frank Culver would say?

In the deep interior, over a dozen ancient manila folders—each one bulging and frayed at the edges—served as the only slight visual deterrent. The folders might be from another era, but the information contained within would be anything but. Settling onto his knee, Kip lifted one at random, only amused by the ancient, worn notations concerning a long-deceased resident and the frayed edges of the flap.

"Bingo," he uttered as a snapshot slid out and hit the floor alongside his knee.

Chapter 16

B ase One. West exit. List 5, 9, 10, 16. Repeat. List 5,9,10,16. Clear. Acknowledge."

"Station One, acknowledge. Clear... Station Two, copy that, Base One. Clear... Station Three, got it. Base One. Clear..."

Leaning against the trunk, Kip rested with a forearm across his knee, a single photo dangling from his hand, his misty gaze staring vacantly at a ragged corner of a box beyond his knee. Frank had been thorough, and where his investigation had failed, professionally prepared reports had supplemented his findings—no doubt, compliments of Denton McDaniels' private investigators. Page after page, photo after photo, Kip absorbed the details, compartmentalizing and analyzing. 'Impact assimilation,' those were the words he'd used long ago in a rare moment of self-explanation to Marsh Baxel. Impact assimilation—the ability to impact information and absorb every detail at a glance. Facts, figures, discrepancies. Even photographic images, he would add, now, as he rested, gazing beyond the photo.

The evidence was there, in livid yellow highlights and penned in questions in margins, in black marker circles on glossy photo finishes. Marilyn Patterson had them—all thirty-two of them—that much, she'd surely known before her death. An invisible web had woven through the Home and spun around her as fiercely as a spider's silk thread. Only one part of the conspiracy remained missing. And clearly, he heard an echo of her outrage in that letter he'd found in the Family Album. 'If you are responsible for this. Stop it!... God knows I love you too much to stop you.' Not merely words spoken in a failing mind, an oxygen-deficient mind in the throes of dementia. She'd been sincere. And cognizant.

And because of her fear that he'd masterminded and orchestrated this conspiracy, she failed to take the proper steps to remove this parasite.

Shaking his head with a sting of tears, he dropped his sweated forehead to his forearm, bracing on his raised knee. She truly had died believing he wanted Whistlebrook—her legacy—destroyed. She'd died never knowing how much he'd needed *her*—not the *Home*. She'd spent the last three months of her life surrounded by traitors and liars, surrounded by deceptions that she believed he'd conceived.

Not even the anger would come, now. Not the outrage Kip should feel for Carolyn McAnthony—a key player, not the spider to weave this wicked web. Only pain pulsed against his mind as he realized how alone, how horribly *alone* his mother must have felt, and whether he'd masterminded the plan or not, he felt the weight of his guilt gripping every fiber of his body. If he had once—just *once*—dropped his guard and told her he loved her—needed her, he knew what her reaction would have been. As in every other moment of his life, she would have forgiven him a million inadequacies. They might never have shared a close relationship, not even a strong friendship, but she would never have believed him guilty of such a vicious attack on her life.

Oh God, Mom, why? Why didn't you pick up the goddamn phone? Why didn't you call in the Feds or the fucking Justice Department and try to prosecute me?

Why the hell didn't you just once *trust* me? I was *mad* at fifteen. I was *hostile* at seventeen, but at twenty I wanted to come home! And your note* *said,* 'Thank you for letting me know you're all right. I've been worried out of my mind. Write soon! Love Mom!'

A dozen years later, and I still remember that goddamn note!

Not, 'When are you coming Home?' *Not,* 'Come Home. I miss you. I need you.' *Not even,* 'I'd like to see you.'

You dropped me a line, as if we were casual acquaintances reconnecting after a year's absence. I went on a four-day binge, and three days later, I smashed my first corporation. I put fifty-nine people on the unemployment line, sold blueprints to recoup my losses, and sent a wrecking crew to do some landscaping. Goddamn it, Mother, why did you have to protect me instead of love me? We could have stopped this madness! We could have eliminated this parasite!'

Should have. Could have. Nothing would change the past. His mother died believing she'd spawned the devil's son just like that old bitch had always said...

If Nanny Briggs came down here. With his thought, he shuffled a few steps into the shadows, not fool enough to think he couldn't be seen. The voices were barely audible, now—muffled sounds—but he understood the different pitches, and Dr. Cullugan's voice came almost steadily, now. Heaving a breath, he began sidling along the wall. Nanny Briggs told him about monsters, trolls that lived under bridges like the one in the back lawn. Trolls that liked little boys even better than Billy goats! Ghouls, too! He wished he hadn't thought of the ghouls. Sidling through the shadows, his attention swung front and back, peering and darting into the cobwebbed beams overhead and searching the shadows. Mommy said there were no such things as monsters and ghosts, but Nanny Briggs—

Dr. Cullugan's voice became clearer now.

Less than a half dozen steps from that strip of light, he halted, listening to the low lulling voice. "Just relax, now. That's it... You'll be a little woozy for a little while... You'll have to rest... You have a room in town, don't you...? There now. That's it. Lie still now..."

Confused, he listened to the moaning reply, recognizing that sluggish sound, like the old folks moaning even after they were given pain medicine to stop their wailing or cursing. What would Mommy need a room in town for anyway? She was going away! Going to Greener Pastures! No! She couldn't leave him here with Nanny Briggs! Taking the last paces in a hurry, he reached the door and slid his fingers into the thin opening, starting the door open—

His body froze. His mind jolted, riveted—

"Base One to Kip! Acknowledge, Goddamn it!"

His muscles gripped in a knot; Kip lurched with a painful jolt. Disoriented, he swung his sweated head off his arm, his focus darting off boxes. His ragged breaths awoke him to the scents of paper and dust. *What? What! Who had screamed at him—who?*

"Goddamn it! Kip! Acknowledge!"

Mulden! *Mulden?* "Damn!" he heaved sharply, aware of tremors rolling through his system, his heart racing. *A coronary!* More like an anxiety attack, he realized as he fumbled in his pocket. How long had Mulden been calling him? Only vaguely, Kip remembered hearing the voices., Bases and Stations communicating between long silences. Clumsily, he lifted the radio within speaking range, collecting his thoughts—*poise*—before breathing, "Problem?" Mulden's voice had been tense, angry. Alarmed? Kip's muscles gripped in another wave of anxiety.

"Why the hell didn't you answer—never mind! Mission accomplished, but we have a few problems developing at the main entrance—only starting with Chief Cartel of the Randall P.D. How are you making out?"

Distractedly, Kip found the photograph bent in a fierce grip. *Bingo*, he thought absently. "What other problems?"

"Well, let's see, now," Mulden said in a mocked, pondering voice. "We have a hysterical blond who looks like a Barbie doll. There's a New York Attorney with a consortium of four. Two gentlemen who I believe are with the Federal Bureau of Investigation. A ranting stockbroker? From

California, I trust. Two other gentlemen, whom I haven't had the pleasure of meeting, but they look like mafia hitmen to me. They're staying awfully close to a guy who looks like a don, except he doesn't look Italian. Oh, and there's a brunette out here with the looks to give my sister and Barbie a run for their money. I think that about covers it. Unless we throw in the fact that four capable-looking elderly people have just come down the steps looking for a bomb shelter. They're pretty damned sure Whistlebrook's being invaded by Commies. One seems to think Henry the Eighth has a battalion out on the fucking lawn and another's clutching a little dog that looks like ToTo. I think you might want to postpone your research for a little while. Acknowledge."

Acknowledge. Morgan. Brad Sinclair? Marsh? Federal Bureau. Mafia? Brunette? Marion McDaniels-Smithfield?

"Shit," Kip hissed softly, not quite aware of his finger holding down the transmit button until the silence registered. "Shit," he said again and snapped his finger off the transmit button.

"If that's considered an acknowledgment, it leaves a little to be desired, old friend. Where are you?"

Not at all certain, Kip scanned the stacks of envelopes arranged in cluttered stacks on boxes and the floor. A shiver rolled beneath his jacket and flannel shirt. Sweat lingered cold on his palms and forehead. Abruptly, he registered the weariness tugging at every fiber of his body. Mentally—physically tired, he shook his head absently, lifted the hand with the photo, pressing his fist against a pulse at his temple. The last damned thing he needed was a migraine.

"This is *not* a good time for radio silence, Kip," JD stated.

How many other radios were operating? How many different locations would hear what he said? No static or chaotic voices had accompanied Mulden's voice, but Mike should be in the lobby, and he held a radio. "What's your location?" Kip asked lamely.

"My favorite stomping ground," JD said clandestinely, possibly considering the open frequency. He was in the kitchen.

Deciding, Kip commented, "Stay where you are. I'll be there in a moment." Snapping off the radio before Mulden could respond, Kip looked again at the picture as his fist dropped from his temple.

Numbers do not lie. Photographs could be altered, but this one, like a dozen others, appeared authentic, and the likeness was unmistakable. This—nor the others—were photos Frank had taken with his 35 mm. The images had been professionally developed, and a professional, accustomed to writing concise reports, had compiled the information. 'Rendezvous' rather than 'meetings' at chic restaurants, several Pittsburgh parks, the Stadium, the Cathedral of Learning, and other Pittsburgh landmarks. In each photo, Carolyn and her blond comrade appeared to enjoy each other's company.

Why? Why would Carolyn McAnthony go to such extremes to bury the Home? That question had accentuated his search, and the photo in his hand contained the answer. The face had changed, and he might not have recognized her at all if not for his recent introduction to a beautiful brunette. His gaze trailed down, his hand lifted the photo that caught Carolyn in a casual pose on a recliner; the house in the background was inevitably the dwelling she shared with investment banker, Charlie McAnthony, whose name had stopped Kip from signing a document in Madison's office.

Frances Logan. That was the name attached to the photograph. Francesca Logan, the former wife of Joseph Logan, whose name Kip would have recognized on impact. A man who'd recently been appointed to the President's Economic Committee. A competitor in investments on a national and international scale. Charlie McAnthony and Joseph Logan had attended Princeton together, old buddies. And Goddamn his older half-sister for investing so heavily in Carolyn's future. Goddamn her. Goddamn Francesca McDaniels-Logan, who, fifteen years ago, with her dye-black hair and heavy makeup, had come into the Home and apparently declared war on Marilyn Patterson for producing an heir to her father's fortunes. No wonder Denton McDaniels had failed to uncover this complex web. Far too easily, Kip imagined Franny—Franny fifteen years ago—Francesca, now—sabotaging her father's effort at every turn.

Had Marilyn Patterson recognized her, or had the investigation ceased with Joseph Logan? Either way, the connection led to him. Franny had entered the home fifteen years ago, and Kip remembered her following him around then. She'd disturbed him then, always turning up, always appearing behind doors. She'd entered his bedroom. To collect him for a doctor's appointment, he remembered absently. She'd attempted to seduce him, then, shoving his hands from his shirt buttons, playing a finger down his chest, studying him with her blue eyes so cluttered with thick fake lashes and wads of makeup. For Marilyn's benefit, no doubt, Franny had dressed and acted trashy. And she'd come here under another name, no differently than her younger sister had come Saturday. Marion, with her dark hair and pale blue eyes. If not for seeing Marion, Kip might never have recognized Franny—Francesca—but the connection solidified.

Francesca, the daughter of Denton McDaniels. She'd attended Maria Van-Alts School of Dance thirty years ago.

What had he said to Denton McDaniels only a short time ago? 'My mother didn't trust you any more than she trusted me.'

September, he realized absently. The date on the private investigator's information. September. The month that his mother had forfeited her search and surrendered any attempt to stop him.

Marilyn had resigned to seeing the Home destroyed, resigned to dying, and determined to thwart him from the grave. She'd made the connection with several powerful names. McDaniels. Logan. McAnthony. Her son. And the combined forces against her, the financial acumen and clout alone, had overwhelmed her into forfeiture. His mind and body thick with guilt and pain, Kip collected the folders nearest him, which contained information on the few key players, including Bill, Janet Cross, and Margie Morone. He returned the others to the trunk. When the time came, he'd resurrect these folders and file the appropriate charges for mediocre extortion and conspiracy. Currently, only the key players concerned him. Securing the Home, safeguarding the residents, and finding Mrs. Feeney. Those were his primary objectives. No other ... not another funeral would he attend to satisfy Francesca McDaniels-Logan's need for revenge.

Returning the linen tray and closing the trunk lid, Kip replaced the boxes as he'd found them, covering any traces of his presence. As an afterthought, he turned and straightened the landslide that he'd stepped through a lifetime ago. More than once, he found himself pausing, holding a box to halt the sway in his skull. Too much. Far too much. Beneath his jacket and shirt, he shivered while swiping his sleeve to wipe sweat off his forehead. If not for the weight of his discoveries, he might find his physical ruin somewhat amusing. Ironic, if nothing else. His mother, the formidable Marilyn Patterson, had lived with this deception for a year, despite having concrete evidence of deceit for three months. And in under a week, he neared physical and mental destruction. Not amusing or ironic, he countered. He was falling apart. And he paused to realize that his mother might have anticipated this end when carrying out her original plan to hold him here for three lousy days. Financially, she couldn't have beaten him on a bet. Mentally, she'd tipped his shallow balance and beat him hands down.

"You win, Mom," he uttered as he tucked the four folders into his jacket, swaying even as he connected the zipper. *Game over. I'm not the son—or the man—I've claimed to be. I'll go through the final moves—eliminate the opposition. After that, I'll follow the outline you left for me and ensure that the Home perpetuates in capable hands.*

Stepping into the hall, Kip touched the wall while shutting off the light and pulling the door closed behind him.

As much as a year ago, she'd discovered subtle discrepancies and begun to question him. As much as six months ago, when concocting the plan with John Madison as an unwitting partner, she hadn't eliminated her suspicions. Three months ago, she'd put him in league with her enemy.

Starting toward the elevator, he halted at an unnatural sound—a rattled sound—a sound of a small child on the brink of a scream, and the image blasted into his mind's eye.

From the metal prongs, a dripping red glob suspended. And it wasn't paint—not paint at all. Blood—blood dripped off the wicked scissor prongs, splattering the metal table and jittering foot! But the thing caught in the prongs jittered too, and in flashing milliseconds, he recognized the outline of a tiny human head between the blunted metal prongs. A tiny bloodied arm swung in open space, aglow under the wash of blinding light. A single leg—a single bloodied leg jiggled above the tray, and in a blinding flash, he understood why that first glob had stricken him dumb—a tiny leg—a tiny red leg! MOMMMY! *His silent scream echoed through his reeling mind.* MMMOMMMY! *The plop resounded in a vacuum as the obscene red glob dropped into the metal pan. A sound escaped his constricted throat. He saw Dr. Cullugan turning, the face lifting at the far end of the metal table.*

"Oh-my-God—" *Dr. Cullugan breathed, his voice amplified as he turned from the table, bloody hands, gaping bloody forceps extended—*

Choking and gasping for breath, Kip staggered backwards along the wall. Images flying through his mind, he knew only a need to run! *Run! Get away! Far away!* Spinning and stumbling, he staggered on rubbery knees, setting his boots in motion, hearing an echo of footsteps, voices calling to him ... *Stop ... Kippen, stop!*

Not stopping! Have to get away! Not stopping ever!

What part of his mind controlled his flight, he would never know. Visions of arms and legs flying apart, splatters of blood echoing through his mind, he ran blind, heaving gasps and stifled cries, stumbling and throwing himself off the walls he dinged with his shoulders. At the bleary image of enclosed steps, he ran clumsily, sucking breath, banging his shins and knees when his boot soles skidded. Whether he held folders or his own entrails, he ascended the steps with his arms folded about his waist, slamming the door with his shoulder, spilling out onto a worn carpet, and scrambling clumsily afoot. His breath collapsed. A cry held captive in his constricted throat. The rear hall! He'd found the rear hall! The kitchen! Someone in the kitchen! *Help me!*

Slamming and staggering through the swinging door, Kip stumbled three paces. His tear-blind eyes locked on an image before him, and his only clear thought—*Mr. Beers wasn't wearing a white smock! The hands weren't bloody! No forceps!* He'd launched into the safety of the old man's arms—

"Jeeesus! Kip?"

Caught at the shoulders, Kip collected his feet under him, trembling and lurching for a clear breath. Head swinging, heart racing, he heaved, needing to vomit—wanting to vomit. A kaleidoscope of sparks flew in his mind's eye as his entire body threatened to cave. In mindless breaths and heaves, he stammered, "N-na-ne-ever ah-uh-gain-n! Na-ever ever gu-go no-o da-down th-tha-there! Ne-evvver!"

"Goddamn it! What happened? Catch your breath! Down where? Is someone—? Damnit, Kip, what the hell happened!"

Oh God, not Mr. Beers! JD! JD Mulden? Rescuing him? Have to reach JD! The cafeteria! Dying! Feel it!

"Kip! Talk to me! What the hell *happened!* Are you hurt? Did you run into somebody? Did we miss somebody?"

Images scattered in his mind, bloody images. Panic and fear blazing neon in his confusion, Kip stood catching a clear breath, blinking against a wash of tears. Not thirteen! Not the school cafeteria. Not four years old! Afraid of monsters ripping babies apart in the basement!

"O-oh God," he heaved, realizing he stood shaking like a dead leaf in a strong wind, caught between an adult JD Mulden's grip on either of his shoulders. *Never again! Whatever the hell had just happened...* "Never again."

"Where the hell were you? What happened?"

Shaking his head, Kip collected enough to wrench from Mulden's grip. *Never again!* He took only four clumsy steps before an image of a tiny, torn body blazed in his mind, not the mind of a four-year-old. He understood that image. His breath caught and held as every muscle constricted through his limbs. He blew a thin breath, took another few steps to lean against the refrigerator. His head tipped, hitting the refrigerator door with an audible thump that reverberated through his pulsing skull. "Damn," he grunted.

"Don't even start that shit again," Mulden warned while clasping his shoulder. "You'd better start talking and tell me what the hell's going on. You're still shaking, and you look like you saw a fucking ghost. If there's another problem, you'd better let me in on it fast. The natives in the lobby are getting restless."

Shaking his head, Kip released his locked grip on his waist, and the folders skidded from under his jacket, descending and scattering on the floor at his feet. "E-evidence—guilty," he struggled. "All o-of them. Damn it."

Mulden hadn't released his hold. Nor did he move toward the folders. "You knew that before. And you weren't rattled ten minutes ago on the radio. What the hell happened?"

At the mere thought, Kip shook his head and shuddered, pulling away, pushing off the refrigerator, sidling out of Mulden's grip. Abstractedly, with a funhouse effect, he identified Jason King standing across the room, guarding the entrance nearest the lobby. Swinging away, Kip sidled past Mulden a second time and staggered a step, catching his balance on the long metal counter. Dragging a breath into his aching lungs, he buckled forward, flopped his elbows on the counter, and clasped his thumping head between his hands. He was still trembling. His knees threatened to buckle beneath him. No doubts remained; he was coming apart physically and mentally, and if his mother were alive, he could tell her, *I'm having my nervous breakdown now, thanks.*

"Are you gonna tell me what's wrong, or should I just get Dr. Frances down here?" Mulden asked carefully, without a doubt, enlisting Mark as a threat.

Shaking his head, Kip heaved, "Not yet." *Soon, though,* he would need Dr. Frances, and, no doubt, Dr. Carmine. "Any—any changes? More problems?" he managed.

"Your attorney. Sinclair," Mulden started hesitantly. "He talked to the Feds, and I think he's working on Chief Cartel. Something about legal grounds—harassment—circumstantial evidence. He's one fast-talking son of a bitch. Your ... stockbroker? And I think I'm using that term loosely—is working on the mafia don. And that term is also used loosely. Mike and Angie managed to get most of the residents either headed back to their rooms or into the lounge. Your blond looks like she's going to rip the hair out of your brunette, and I have to tell you, old friend, my ulcer's coming along nicely. On the whole, the fire's dying down."

"I should have taken a walk on the Boardwalk a week ago," Kip uttered and ran his fingers through his sweated hair before pushing off his elbows. Swaying, he slapped his hand down on the table. No illusions here. His mind floated in a dizzy circle.

"You know, Kip, déjà vu is one thing, but this is getting out of hand," JD said temperately, his hand resting idly on Kip's elbow, steadying him. "You look about as lousy, now, as you did fifteen years ago. You planning on losing your cookies any time soon?"

"Thinking about it," Kip said lamely, not half as amused as he tried to sound. "I'll l-let you know in a minute."

"Fifteen years ago, you had physical problems," JD said absently. "Any chance you're suffering a few, now?"

A hernia. Kip shook his head slightly, drawing a clear breath and straightening more, finding JD's gaze, then glancing at the folders on the floor. "How about picking those up, and we'll go to the office. You can radio Mike from there."

Mulden hesitated; conflicting concern and curiosity lingered in his considerably aged face as he turned to collect the folders.

Moving around the table, Kip reached the sinks, leaned on his forearms, and splashed cold water on his face. Hot and cold, he still shivered madly within two layers of cloth, and for a crazy second, he wished he'd eaten so he'd have something to throw up. Nothing to throw up. His stomach rattled and rolled, gripping in a painful knot as a tiny bloody body flashed in his mind's eye. Jolted, he shook his head, pushing off his forearms and groping for the dishtowel Mulden had offered. He held the cloth to his face as he willed the image away.

Death. So much death. Violent death. But those were babies.

Shoving the thought aside, Kip flashed Mulden a glance that gained him a more troubled glimpse, then motioned toward the executive wing. "Let's get this over with," he commented.

"What exactly are we about to do?" JD asked.

"You can use the phone and tap your sources to find out if those Federal agents are legitimate. Then we're calling a meeting in the office," he shoved through the executive wing door, continuing in automation. "Once we determine the proper authorities, we'll see warrants issued to arrest all thirty-two names on that list. The four contained in those folders are priority. Emphasis on Cross and Morone—" He halted abruptly, his attention divided between a need to catch his balance on the wall and a hundred threads of information tangled inside his mind. "Something, damn it." Something was still wrong. *Or was it paranoia? Paranoia and mentally induced physical ruin.* Uttering a curse, he continued his unsteady stride, aware of Mulden keeping pace, prepared to catch him if he collapsed.

Chapter 17

Someone had found the good sense to close the French doors to the lobby. Sounds of thick anxious voices muffled through the curtained-covered glass. In a startled double-take, Kip entered the secretarial pool in time to see Kelly Mulden replacing the receiver on Carolyn's phone. Her startled gaze barely hinted at relief before concern flashed across her lovely face, and she darted a glance at her brother, parting her lips.

Recovering from his surprise, he nodded faint acknowledgment, calling on every ounce of his learned fake poise to comment, "Do hope it's not been too hectic for you, luv."

"Kip, what's—"

He continued past her desk, walking into the alcove toward the office door as his stomach gripped in a horrible spasm. He was a fraud; his entire life was a grand illusion, or perhaps a delusion.

"How about seeing if you can round us up a couple cups of coffee in the lobby, sis."

"JD, what's—"

"On second thought. Jase, you've been in that madhouse a few times. Think you could do it?"

To the sound of Jason's "You got it, JD," Kip strode into his mother's office, the queen's domain. Illusions, delusions, deceptions, and was it any wonder he was a fraud? *A fraud on the brink of insanity?* Shaking his head against his internal sounds, he moved behind the immense desk, settled into the comfortably thick leather cushions, tipped his head back, and closed his eyes. A mistake. An awful mistake. Behind his closed lids, the image of a maimed infant erupted, dripping its blood into a metal pan. His eyes snapped open, clearing only after Mulden's involuntary start. Within his concentrated focus, Kip watched his old friend's surprise turn to a more wary concern.

"Afraid of falling asleep?" Mulden tried to taunt.

"I may never fall asleep again," he said absently, honestly.

Mulden reserved a comment, settling into an opposing chair and separating one of the envelopes at random. "Mind if I have a look before I make that phone call?"

"By all means," Kip said vacantly as his focus drifted toward the long, heavy drapes. The steady hum of voices from the lobby carried faintly; more steadily, the hum of rain drumming on the porch roof created a lulling rhythm. Rain on Christmas. His mind floated, catching on the shuffling pages.

Each and every one was guilty. All thirty-two names. The scope of their guilt ranged radically from payoffs of a lousy hundred dollars a month—unaccounted for by either alimony, lottery, or bingo winnings, and as constant in some instances as trips to the market—to possibilities of extortion to the tune of a hundred grand. Most were pawns, merely eyes and ears. A handful, including Janet Cross and Margie Morone, were far more critical—rooks or bishops, if this were a Chess game. Whether Janet or Margie had become chess pieces of their own accord or were blackmailed into service didn't matter. Janet, whose husband had died in February of 1972, had assisted in his painless demise. Of that, Kip harbored no doubts.

The man's health had declined too rapidly even for a stroke victim at the ripe old age of 48.

Margie's case wasn't unusual either, and given the circumstances, Kip would have dismissed her about five minutes after the duty nurse had found the elder Mrs. Morone. The charge nurse had found the elderly woman splayed on the floor of the medical supply room. A set of stolen keys remained in her hand; her body turned blue from a lethal dose of atropine, with a dozen bottles cluttered on the floor around her. Police investigation or not, Margie should have been dismissed.. One or the other of those two had administered lethal doses to Seratti and Taylor, and remembering Janet Cross avoiding his gaze in Madison's office, his money lay on her guilt. A guilt that would inevitably be her undoing when she faced a police interrogation.

The others—from a janitor with a high school GPA of .94 and an IQ of 69 to a physical therapist with an unhealthy infatuation for the sulky races an hour away—all strategically placed throughout the Home to collect information and listen to the idle rambling of failing minds. Readily, Kip imagined those anonymous names reaching Franny via Carolyn. From a single name, the head of the octopus could be pieced together. Those residents who fit the profile—financially solvent, heavily dependent on the Home for a reasonable amount of time—had become targets. At random, Carolyn had tapped her husband's sources to create dummy bank statements and reroute checks or bank drafts that had never entered Whistlebrook's accounts. Deliberately hit or miss, the accounts were paid in full or simply left unattended. Which was Bill's contribution to the plan. And what did they promise him? Whistlebrook on a silver platter? Whistlebrook to call his home—his Home.

"Thanks, Jase," Mulden uttered.

"No problem," King answered lightly.

Absently, Kip glanced at the boy, noting and appreciating the concern he witnessed on the young man's sturdy face. "It's been a long day, hasn't it?" Kip asked absently as he accepted the cup.

"Seems like it," he agreed lightly. "Are uh ... are you okay?"

"After a day like today, I believe you could use a vacation," Kip said without affect and shifted enough to slide his wallet from his jeans. Extracting several hundred, he considered only a moment and removed the entire fold of bills, handing it to Jason. "Take a week off. That won't get you to Tahiti, but it should make your vacation fun."

Jason started backing away, waving away the bills. "You already tipped me plenty—"

"Don't annoy me at this late date," Kip said evenly and held the boy's worried gaze.

"Take it, Jase," Mulden commented. "He has more money than brains, and he always had more of those than he needed, too."

"I ... shit, man," King said hesitantly, flashing a wary glance off Mulden and back. "I didn't stick around for the money, ya know?"

"I should have you arrested for being too fucking righteous," Kip said heavily and flicked the wad of bills to land on the corner of the desk. Lifting his coffee, he shifted his chair and gazed toward the curtained window. "Go home and have a Merry Christmas, Jason. I appreciate your assistance."

"Pocket the cash, kid," Mulden advised. "I'd have been up shit-creek tonight if you hadn't been there a few times."

"If I go home with all that, my old man's going to think I took up a new profession," King said hesitantly.

"Have him call your new employer," Mulden said lightly. "And consider it a Christmas bonus."

Kip tuned out the words, but his thoughts of King lingered. As was the case with all Whistlebrook employees, Marilyn had hired him personally, as she had hired the thirty-two names on that list. Thirty-two mistakes over the course of thirty years? One hell of an average. One error per year.

Most were like King: righteous, dependable, and energetic. Those were her requirements for employment, whether hiring a janitor or a physical therapist.

Unconsciously, Kip lifted a hand pressing his palm to his temple, leaning heavily on his elbow on the armrest. Too much thinking, analyzing. Even on his most strategic ventures, he'd never scoured the multitude of information he'd covered over the past three days. Was it any wonder his head pounded like a little man with a jackhammer had crawled into his skull? "Damn it," he uttered, and tipped his head to spy JD. "Are you finished?"

"Not quite. You want to simplify this and point out the evidence?"

"It's a paper chase," Kip said evenly. "Pay close attention to the bank statements. Add up the eighteen payoffs of the current employees, and you'll have the fluctuating amount of money Carolyn removes from her main checking account and deposits into a floating account under her maiden name, which, I might add, contains about a quarter of the missing funds over the past five years. Either in bank drafts or cash, she disburses funds to keep ears and eyes wide open. Elsa Taylor, of the Richmond Taylors, is one of the current targets. Her real name is Elesia Avancourt, the heiress and widow of the late Edgar Avancourt, a tailor by trade who built a multi-million-dollar clothier franchise. Few surviving relatives. Her son holds Power of Attorney. She fits the profile." Tiredly, Kip's attention wavered from Mulden's studied gaze. "Payments made to the Home never reached the proper accounts. If we move quickly, we can catch Carolyn or Bill with a few improperly endorsed checks in hand."

"You don't have any doubts, do you?"

"None," he answered honestly and looked again to Mulden. "I make my living adding, subtracting, and spotting discrepancies. Carolyn and Bill have been embezzling for several years. Bickerman buried himself with his outrage over the Will. He shouldn't have been aware of those missing funds. My mother never availed him of facts or figures. Doubtful, she even mentioned her suspicions. She didn't trust him half as much as he believed."

"Knew I didn't like that son of a bitch," Mulden said with genuine anger and shifted forward, glancing at the phone. "If you're satisfied with this evidence, then I'll make that call."

With a glance at the phone base, Kip barely started an affirmation before realizing the futility of trying to place any call. A single line through the reception desk. "Shit. I suppose I should repair the phones." And make an appearance in the lobby. He may get lucky, and there would be a couple of mafia hitmen out there. Quick and painless.

Just don't let them miss a vital organ, he considered, pushing himself heavily from the chair. Not even the lousy half cup of coffee was sitting well on his empty stomach, and a long-distance hike to avoid the lobby and reach the switchboard wasn't feasible.

"You really aren't feeling too great, are you?" Mulden asked as he sidled a step, prepared to catch Kip from another unnatural sway.

"Not too," he admitted while catching his balance. "Fucking weather's probably killing me," he said absently and veered to the second door. In and out of snow for the past week, wet more often than dry throughout the day? If not the mafia, pneumonia might take him out clean. By the time he reached the French doors, the voices outside had grown steadily louder in tempo with the pulse at his temple.

"Maybe we ought to take the long way," Mulden commented. "You can reach the switchboard room from the kitchen, can't you?"

Clasping the door, Kip ignored the suggestion and pushed the panel open to the sound of Morgan throwing a loud, angry snipe at Marsh. Something about her having first 'crack at him.' Catching her eyes, Kip barely acknowledged her before scanning the odd combination of faces in small clusters at various points in the room. Mulden's 'mafia don' wasn't the most difficult to spot; he rested on a settee near the door, alongside Marion McDaniels-Smithfield. Two impressively large, suited gentlemen stood at strategic points, one leaning casually against the wall, the other positioned to shield the don from the glass doors. Not at all amused at Mulden's misconception, Kip stood momentarily looking into the gray-blue eyes across the room, and it was no longer a surprise that it had taken nearly a minute to reach McDaniels on the phone. A minute for their trusty butler to relay the call to Randall. The arrogant bastard had probably flown in this morning for the reading of the Will, probably initiated that surveillance—

"Kip!" Marsh stated, breaking from his group a step ahead of Morgan.

Brad Sinclair, whose physical stature might account for half of his ability to sway others toward his end, stood slightly behind Baxel with his consortium of legal underlings spread out behind him. He started forward without preamble, a pensive set to his lips and visible furrows across his bushy, graying brows.

At some recent moment, John Madison had arrived. He stood in a small circle with Chief Cartel, another uniformed officer, and two men who were likely Federal agents. One, Kip recognized in a half second as his indiscreet escort in a movie theater. At least the fellow no longer wore loafers with his polyester slacks. *Or* that asinine knit hat.

"Kip! We have to talk!" Marsh started with an almost comfortable panic blazing in his dark eyes.

"I don't recall sending out invitations," Kip said dryly, his focus skipping off Morgan, who pushed Marsh aside to advance.

"Oh, baby!" she blew into Kip's mouth as her thick fur-coated arms slashed out to fold across his shoulders. "Missed you!" she breathed as her tongue darted. "So, sorry!" She hissed as her blond hair fell about her arms and their faces.

"Kip! Before you blow! Let's talk!"

Getting handfuls of black fur on either side, Kip recoiled from Morgan, looking into her watery blue eyes and hurt, startled expression. On her, those expressions were contradictions, magnifying tiny lines about her heavily made-up eyes and long lashes. Blonds. Always blond with blue eyes. They came into his life as regularly as the funerals of a lifetime ago.

"Oh, baby, you look so awful," she whined. "I should have come with you! I'm so sorry!"

"You shouldn't be here, now," he said in a low, dull tone; his gaze held steady on her darting, searching eyes. Only five months ago, he'd met her, like so many others, at one of his frequent hangouts in L.A. A casual romance? Coincidence that she had come on to him, as surely as the brunette only a week earlier in a crowded hotel lounge? Or was she yet another pawn, placed to monitor him? Ironic, either Denton McDaniels or Francesca Logan could have hired her. "You're taking an unnecessary risk, aren't you, Morgan?"

"Baby, what's wrong? You—you look so—"

"Your rhythm was off Saturday, Morgan, and it's off now," he continued. "As well it should be under the circumstances." She'd been speaking to Carolyn, screaming in her ear. Screaming words meant for him to hear? Carolyn had seen him coming, Morgan had shouted, 'Fly out there and pull your hair out.' Did it matter? "Prostitution's against the law, baby," his voice dripped with the anger rising through his mind as her perception donned, offering more verification with the apprehension enhancing in her posture. She started pulling away. He held her by the coat. "Going somewhere?" he asked evenly.

"Yo-ou sound so—so mad!" she stammered, collecting her voice.

"You really shouldn't have come. You should be home packing your bags, but since you're here, I'd like you to meet a couple of my acquaintances." His gaze shifted to John Madison's group; Kip's attention landed on the Federal agent from the theater. "I could use your assistance," he stated in a voice to transcend the dozen paces. At the same time, he sidled, nudging Morgan with him, turning her, leading her. Face to face with the curious agent, he stated, "Keep an eye on her, will you? Her name may or may not be Morgan LaMont, and I'll explain everything to you shortly."

"Mr. Patterson," Sinclair said as he came alongside him, conveying a warning in his gaze. "If I might offer my condolences."

Condolences were the last thing Sinclair would like to offer. "We'll speak in a few moments, Brad. Thanks for coming—" His words cut short as his attention caught and held on Denton McDaniels, already risen from the settee and stopped, now, a step behind Morgan.

"Lad, if I might have a moment?" McDaniels said simply, his cultured features a complex menagerie of faint smiles and deep worried lines.

Odd, Kip felt only numb as he looked into the familiar pale blue eyes. He'd inherited those eyes, as empty and enigmatic as his own. What should he feel? Contempt? After thirty years? After fifteen years of silent observation? "I don't think we need to speak," he said evenly and drew his hands away from Morgan's coat, turning and nearly running into Ed Cartel. Not numb. He wasn't numb. He felt suddenly as if he stood in the Oak Room with mourners closing in about him, thrusting condolences and hands at him, suffocating him. His heart racing, his foundations threatening to crumble, Kip forced himself to maintain his poise like never before.

"I'd like a word with you."

About Frank? Or murder? "Is it urgent, or could you give me a couple of minutes, Captain?"

Cartel studied him for a second, then glanced about at the tense circle of strangers. His attention skimmed over Sinclair's imposing physique and cool, persuasive gaze before he decided, "It'll keep a moment."

"Thank you," Kip said and sidestepped from the group, only vaguely aware of JD following on his heels, keeping pace with him, probably staving off the masses. Without another word, Kip passed alongside the steps, found the key in his jeans, and fumbled the switchboard room door open. Stepping into the room, he settled into the chair and turned his full attention to returning the system to its original status. Several lights ignited even before he settled into the comfortable chair. His focus trailed to the corkboard, where the faces of three happy-go-lucky children and a schnauzer were proudly displayed. How he envied those children and the woman who rested in this chair for six or seven days a week, and perhaps the father of those toothless wonders.

"Morgan's a part of this, too, isn't she?" Mulden asked carefully.

Kip nodded absently. "Undoubtedly," he answered honestly. "Not a key player, but I don't want her stopping at a payphone on her way to the airport." With his thoughts returning to the circumstances, he leaned forward and pressed the in-house connection to open the monitor.

Leaning back, he spoke quietly, "If I could have your attention, please." He paused only a heartbeat. "I suppose I should introduce myself for those of you whom I haven't spoken to. I am Kip Patterson, Marilyn's son. As of five o'clock this afternoon, I became sole owner and proprietor of Whistlebrook, as well as the single administrator. First, I'd like to apologize for the inconvenience you've experienced over the past ninety minutes. The phone lines have been restored.

"To the staff, herein remaining, I should like to apologize personally. I know the burdens I've placed on you this evening. Extenuating circumstances governed my actions. If you bear with me, I'll speak to the nurses currently in charge of each ward within the hour.

"To the residents, hello," he said absently, collecting his momentarily scattered thoughts. "I've spoken with several of you recently. The pleasure, mine, I assure you. Some of you may not fully understand my following discourse; however, I believe most of you will. The prince has secured his castle. His kingdom and all who dwell within are safe. Do sleep well, my respected friends." Leaning, he touched the intercom and settled back in the chair, smiling faintly as several buttons lit on the board in front of him.

An illusion, a delusion, but a few would relax for the time being.

Pushing to his feet, he looked to JD momentarily disoriented by the faint honest grin and laughter in his hazel eyes—his sister's eyes. Kip's attention faltered downward to the four folders held on Mulden's hip like a stack of high school texts. Next order of business. He motioned Mulden outside and into the hall, paused long enough to lock the door, and turned toward the lobby. On second thought, he'd rather not enter that mob a second time.

Reversing his course, he motioned to JD. "Let's take the long way," Kip commented absently and headed for the kitchen.

Going through the motions, merely going through the motions. His mind and body automated, Kip passed through the kitchen, faintly aware of two orderlies filling serving carts with evening snacks of gelatins and puddings. Life goes on. Whistlebrook's general routine hadn't been too badly disrupted by the chaos. As he stepped into the executive hallway, he glanced at Mulden. "If I don't get a chance later, thank you," he said lightly. "I take it you didn't have an easy time in the wards."

"Not too bad under the circumstances," JD said distractedly.

"Before you place your call, I'd like to speak with my attorneys," he commented offhandedly.

No other words passed between them; Kip avoided the secretarial pool and passed through the more direct route into his mother's office. Settling into his mother's chair, he tapped the intercom, reached a flustered Angie, and suggested she send Madison, Sinclair, and Baxel into the office. Leaning back heavily, he pulled a legal-sized notepad from the center drawer, fished a pen from the tray, and began doodling absently.

When all three entered—Baxel flushed with his blood pressure elevated—Kip motioned them each into chairs. "I take it you've introduced yourselves?" he asked.

Madison sent a respectful glance at Sinclair, and Sinclair acknowledged in like fashion.

Without further pause, Kip began the verbal brief, outlining his present situation and the course of action he intended to pursue. Between salient points, he jotted the names on the list—those still in Whistlebrook's employment—along with brief notations concerning the evidence against each one. For Marsh and Brad, his rapid-fire statements were neither unusual nor surprising. Neither attempted to take notes throughout the dialogue, and John Madison realized the futility when Kip ignored his attempts to intervene or cross-examine. At some point, John grasped a revelation that he was receiving a concise and complete summary, and his attention fixed.

At the end of seven minutes, Kip tore off the legal sheet and handed it across the desk to Sinclair, meeting his studied gaze for the first time. "Possible?"

Sinclair ran his focus down the page, then looked over. "As much as I'd enjoy prosecuting each and every one of these imbeciles on general principle, I'd imagine this is the swiftest means to the end."

"Kip, are you positive about these mercy killings?" Madison asked tensely.

Leveling a cool gaze on Madison, Kip nodded. "At least two people were murdered here last evening, and unless I'm terribly wrong, the local police will—if they haven't already—receive an anonymous tip that I'm responsible for those deaths. Correct me if I'm wrong.. Under the circumstances, if I were convicted, Whistlebrook would be seized and sold to compensate the respective families for the damages. Not only would I spend the remainder of my life incarcerated, I'd do so, penniless, and *that*, John, is the penultimate goal of my nemesis."

"You're not wrong," Madison said deftly, his lined face far more pale and aged than even a half dozen hours earlier.

Kip looked at Sinclair. "You spoke to the Federal Agents outside and Ed Cartel. Prognosis?"

"From what I could ascertain, the federal agents are here for your protection. The Police Chief intends to question you concerning an accident earlier this evening, but I sensed an underlying intention behind his visit. He may suspect foul play," Brad barely paused. "I suggest we don't waste time. We have these warrants issued and begin drawing up the affidavits." He looked at John Madison. "I'd imagine you could reach the District Attorney at this hour, and if you'd be willing to supply office equipment, my assistants could draw up the documents."

"You've removed eleven from the grounds," John said thoughtfully and paused only a moment. "What of the others? Can you be certain they'll be stopped from entering before they can be apprehended?"

"My security men have been alerted. If those Federal Agents are legitimate," Kip looked to Mulden, who leaned at the window a few paces from the desk. "You could speak to them, brief them, and gain their assistance in covering the entrances. Possible?"

Mulden had been listening. His expression held none of the usual casualness. In fact, he still appeared genuinely worried. "They're legitimate, Kip," he said evenly. "If you're right about all this—and I don't doubt that you are—I don't know that we can afford to trust them without running a serious full-scale investigation, and that would take more time than we have. We'd better try handling this internally. My opinion, for what it's worth."

"It's worth a great deal," Kip commented and decided. "We'll stick to the original plan." Unconsciously, he lifted his hand, pressing his fingertips against his temple to offset the steady drumming pulse. "Other questions?" he asked Madison.

"KJ, I think we'd better talk," Marsh said with a subtle glance toward Mulden.

"Obviously, you've met Mr. Mulden," Kip said evenly, his gaze level on Baxel, conveying his understanding, reassuring him.

"No questions," Madison said and looked over to Sinclair. "We'll use my office and contact the D.A. from there," he commented, then to Kip. "If anything should develop, we'll contact you here. As for those Federal Agents—for your protection, I think you might reconsider keeping them on hand. At least until we've attained these warrants."

"I'll post them at the main entrance," Kip agreed and met Sinclair's gaze. "Brad, I appreciate you coming. I don't imagine Peg's too pleased."

"Frankly, she was furious with me for not breaching our arrangement earlier and coming to Randall a week ago ... but we'll discuss that later." Pushing off his chair, he glanced at Madison while rising. "At the moment, it appears we have our work cut out for us."

"KJ," Marsh said as he stood up. "I'm not sure what that business with Morgan was all about, but I don't think she's a part of this. She's been a mess for the past few days—"

"I'm sure she has," Kip said dryly, deciding. "Wait in the lobby, Marsh. I'll have her released to your custody. Find a hotel, then contact me. Do see that she's not out of your sight. She's not to use a phone for any reason until I inform you otherwise. Understood?"

"Kip," Mulden intervened. "Leave her on ice for now. She'll give the Feds something to do."

At a studied glance, Kip understood Mulden's ulterior motive. His professional skills and instincts were functioning, his message clear. Proceed cautiously. Let no one out of the net until the facts can be sorted and the players in custody. "Fine," Kip said and addressed Marsh. "Wait in the lobby. We'll talk again shortly."

Ignoring Marsh's annoyed glance toward Mulden, Kip leaned and touched the intercom, reaching Angie a second time and directing her to send Ed Cartel into the office. Disengaging the button, he sank back into the chair, allowing himself a moment to close his eyes and massage his temple.

Going through the motions, removing the enemy. The sooner he finished with Cartel ... Denton McDaniels. Absently, he realized he hadn't mentioned Francesca McDaniels-Logan—not to Mulden—not to the attorneys. Carolyn, Bill, Cross, and Morone—all thirty-two names, but he hadn't once mentioned Franny, and neither attorney had questioned why McAnthony and Bickerman would want to see the Home destroyed ... both accepted the financial aspect as a motivator.

Opening his eyes as Cartel crossed the office, Kip motioned to a receiving chair while shifting from his comfortable lean. "What can I do for you, Captain?"

Settling into the chair, his gaze intent, his pronounced lines indenting his jawbone, Cartel began simply, "You can start by telling me who might have wanted to run Frank Culver into a ravine and end by saving me a lot of time and telling me where Edna Feeney is."

"Frankly, Captain, I hoped you could answer either of those questions," Kip said honestly.

"I've had a few strange calls over the past four hours, boy. Don't try my patience. The only reason you're not already in custody at this moment is out of respect for your mother."

Naturally. "On what grounds would you arrest me, sir?"

"You had three deaths here last evening. Some might find that a little peculiar."

"At this moment, sir, I have twenty-six terminally ill residents in various stages of decline," Kip said evenly, his gaze unwavering on Cartel. "Perhaps, you'd care to elaborate on your suspicions?"

"What can you tell me about Frank Culver's accident?"

"Obviously, a helluva lot less than you could tell me," Kip said in a controlled annoyance. "Have you verified that it wasn't an accident?"

"I have a witness who claims to have seen a late-model pickup leaving the scene of the accident. The color and make of a vehicle parked outside at this moment."

"I don't imagine your witness came to you in person or identified him—or herself, by any chance?"

"Were you in that vehicle earlier this evening?" Cartel asked.

"In it, yes. At the scene of an accident, no," Kip answered honestly, studying Cartel's concentrated gaze. Unconsciously, he wondered how close Ed and Marilyn might have been. "Just how many of these 'calls' have you received, Chief?"

"Enough to wonder who wants you behind bars," Cartel said succinctly, his dark eyes intent. "Where's Edna?"

"I've been asking that question for the past eight or ten hours, and unless you fully intend to arrest me, I'd appreciate your help in trying to locate her, which, alarmingly, was Frank Culver's mission before his accident, and I'm using that term loosely," he said evenly. "Before leaving Madison's office this afternoon, I asked Frank to check her house on Adderly Lane. If she wasn't there, he was to return here to search for her."

"Where did you go after leaving the attorney's office?"

"I attended a dinner engagement at Le Chateau," he answered honestly. "Which you could verify with either a phone call to the manager, or you could step into the lobby and speak to that dark-haired female. Aside from this anonymous caller, were there any other witnesses to Frank's accident?"

"No," Cartel said lightly. "I posted a man at the hospital to talk to him as soon as the doctor gives his okay."

Kip nodded absently, his headache thumping angrily. Refocusing on Cartel while trying to press the erratic banging from his temple, he commented, "My security team is extremely understaffed." Lifting his gaze to Mulden for the first time, he decided abruptly, "Possibly you could show Chief Cartel to Frank's apartment above the garage. He has a rather elaborate base station with several unique views of the Home. If Mrs. Feeney left the Home, it would appear on the tapes. I assume she was in her suite last evening. I remember hearing her television when Frank and I passed her door around nine or ten. If you don't see her leaving, then by God, turn this Home upside down and find her."

"What are you going to be doing in the meantime?" JD asked carefully.

"Obviously, dealing with a half dozen other problems and praying no others develop," he said honestly. "Is there anything else I can do for you, Chief? Or are you still inclined to arrest me?"

"Just don't leave the Home without talking to me first," the chief decided.

House arrest. "Fine," Kip said and started to rise, intending to offer Cartel a handshake. Whether a momentary sway in his skull or the buzz of the intercom halted him, he settled back onto the chair and groped, hitting the appropriate button on the phone base. "Yes?"

"Mr. Patterson, Dr. Frances is on ext. one."

The familiar sensuous voice lent him a second momentary sway—Kelly Mulden had a fantastic phone voice. "Thank you," he said and lifted the receiver, depressing the line. "Doctor?"

"Are you in a position to speak freely?"

Oh damn. Kip barely glanced at Mulden and Cartel, both starting for the door. "Yes?"

"Problem, son," Mark said with an audible tension. "Your suspicions about the meds were right on. Unfortunately," he paused, dreading his words. "I've called in Dr. Sheffield. If you still have the doors under guard, will you see that he gets in? I need him on the second floor. At least two residents are beginning to show signs of decline. I've begun procedures to counter the effects, but before you ask, I don't know that I'll be successful," he paused again. "I've closed off the med cabinets on all three floors. We'll need to call in the authorities."

At least two residents... "Damn it," Kip uttered absently. "Anything else, doctor?"

"Kip...? Did you hear what I said?"

"I heard," he said heavily, his mind suddenly alive with red images and spinning faces. Leaning on his elbow, he clasped his weighted head, holding his breath unconsciously.

"Kip?"

"I'll—I'll send JD up as soon as I can, doctor," he strained softly. "Take care of the residents. The proper authorities will be notified within the hour."

"Are you alright, Kip?"

"Fine," he said absently and dropped the receiver into its cradle. Not fine at all. One more meeting, one more conversation, and then all hell would break loose, and let the chips fall where they may. His affiliation with Whistlebrook would be finished. Pushing the intercom button to reach the reception desk, Kip awaited Angie's clipped, "Reception Desk!"

"Send in the white-haired gentleman. See that he comes in alone," he ordered.

"Yes, sir," she snapped.

Kip leaned back, shaking his head, forcing himself to remain calm despite his shivering.

Going through the motions, removing the enemy, Mother.

Chapter 18

Listening to the drumbeat of rain striking the windowpane, Kip heard the office door creak open and opened his eyes as Denton McDaniels paused and scanned the office. Even within the shadows, Kip recognized the distressed yellow and swirls of blue overlaying his arrogant features. Distress and intuition warred against the disheartened nostalgia in his eyes. McDaniels had visited this room before now, and like him, this man—his biological father—stood in awe of Marilyn's presence emanating from the soft light and delicate beauty.

By force, it seemed, Denton pulled his thoughts together and started forward, his attention drawn toward the desk, ultimately to Kip as a soft, wary smile touched his lips. A deceptive smile. His eyes conveyed more than a hint of tension and speculation; the sallow, yellow hue shrouding him accentuated his anxiety. "I'll apologize in advance for deceiving you when last we spoke."

"To what manner of deception are you referring, sir?" Kip asked in a deadpan tone, and God help this man if he answered in any way other than with the location.

"I had your call transferred from Boston to a hotel near the airport, as I'm sure you know."

Vacantly, Kip studied the gentleman's mature features. First impressions were accurate. McDaniels wasn't an old man, but rather, a premature gray. With very little trouble, Kip imagined Denton McDaniels in control of the fortunes Marion had mentioned. Motioning toward the chair that the chief had occupied, Kip commented, "You've asked to speak to me. I'm listening."

McDaniels moved cautiously, lowering but not relaxing. His hunted gaze dominated, but his faint smile remained. "I'm truly not your enemy, lad," he began carefully. "The two gentlemen accompanying me are here for your protection. Both are trained field agents, officially retired from Central Intelligence. Their qualifications are—"

"Are you responsible for the Federal Agents as well?"

"Indirectly, I'd imagine so," he said evenly. "Your safety means as much to me as it did to your mother."

"Let's not have any misunderstandings, sir," Kip said without affect. "Your life, your safety, means nothing to me. Frankly, we are on the brink of becoming lifelong enemies regardless of what you may believe."

McDaniels maintained his poise, impressive in his calm, indifferent expression. "On what is that decision contingent?" he asked perceptively.

Faintly amused, Kip commented without a hint of humor. "On what you'd like to tell me about Francesca McDaniels-Logan and her obvious hatred for an illegitimate heir to your dynasty."

More curious than surprised, McDaniels asked, "Possibly you should tell me what you've learned in the past few hours?"

"Tell me, did you personally receive the information your investigators uncovered, or did you have the information sent directly to my mother?"

"Financial reports, I received and reviewed personally before sending the information via courier to your mother," he answered as if he'd rehearsed his response. "I know there's a list of thirty-two suspects in your mother's possession."

"Personal data?" Kip asked without moving from his comfortable lean. "Did you review that information as well?"

"You've connected my oldest daughter to this conspiracy, lad. Let's not fence this issue. How did you connect her? Who—may I ask—is her liaison within this facility?"

"I find it difficult to believe that you don't already know her liaison. Even more difficult to believe that you didn't discover her deceit before this moment. Frankly, you could have created this entire ordeal. You certainly have the financial and personal influence to assist your daughter in her efforts."

"You're referring to McAnthony," he said evenly. "Chuck McAnthony and my former son-in-law were college friends. An association I did, in fact, become aware of during the investigation; however, it's unlikely that either McAnthony or his wife is a part of this."

"On the contrary, sir," Kip said without affect. "Carolyn is very much a part of this, and a warrant is being issued for her arrest. Figures don't lie, and you were aware of her guilt as much as six months ago, which justifies my concern for your integrity. I believe this concludes our audience—"

"I don't believe your mother anticipated how swiftly you would either uncover the evidence or act accordingly," McDaniels said smoothly, his manner noticeably more tense. "I took the liberty of waylaying your attorneys. There can be no warrants, lad."

"Excuse me?" Kip asked without conveying his immediate alarm. Against his temple, the thudding pulse magnified in tempo with the rain; his stomach flinched with a sudden drop. Far too easily, McDaniels had spoken those words, and his gaze had become complicated, complex. A matrix of colors swirled around his entire persona.

"There's no conspiracy, lad," he said carefully. "And I regret my participation in this elaborate hoax." His attention wavered for the first time, a pulse in his cheek, a sigh in his tone as he firmed his gaze. "It is a hoax, lad. There was no conspiracy, though I'm sure you'll have a difficult time believing any of this." He dropped his focus, opening his lapel. Lifting an envelope from the fold, he held it for a moment. Shaking his head, he leaned, sighing again as he skidded it across the felt mat. "You'd better read that, lad."

Another Goddamn letter from the grave.

Kip gazed at the envelope that stopped with a corner extending over the lip of the desk near his knee. Another Marilyn Patterson pre-postmortem diatribe. Shaking his head, he shifted in his chair, his focus wavering toward the sheer curtains and the fading sound of rain. Rain is turning to snow, undoubtedly. God knows, he felt cold suddenly—bitter cold.

"Lad, I think you'd better read that before I continue—"

Shifting and leveling a glare on McDaniels, Kip commented, "I believe you'd better leave, sir, and do take whatever precautions you feel necessary. You will be hearing from my attorneys, and I should remind you, I'm not without a little means of my own—"

"There is no conspiracy, Kippen—"

"I'm not a nice person when I'm tired and angry, sir. Leave, or I'll have you physically assisted—"

"Read the letter, lad," Denton said evenly as he pushed from his chair. "I'll step outside; however, I have no intention of leaving until we've spoken again." Sidling around the chair, he strode to the door, stepping out without a backward glance.

For another long moment, Kip stared at the envelope, then leaned and lifted it. Ripping the end, he extracted the two folded pages, shaking his head absently as he read:

Dearest Kip,

By now, you must surely dread hearing from me. As I recall, you once accused me of writing too little and not nearly often enough. I'd imagine you regret that complaint now. I have written you a total of six letters—including this one.

If you've received even half of them, and the fact that this one I'll place in Denton's care, you will know a great deal about your past—my past. Our history. You will have also learned a great deal about Whistlebrook in the process. You always loved a good story, and I was never able to tell you any good stories. You depended on others for imaginative dialogue; however, as I mentioned earlier, we Pattersons are creative. If you have uncovered a conspiracy and are about to take action, I am entrusting this letter to prevent you from doing so. There is no conspiracy, Kippen. The files you received with Frank's help were designed—contrived by me with a great deal of help from Denton —to appear authentic. Don't blame him, darling, I'm extremely persuasive and convincing when your welfare is at stake. Don't hate me, darling. I do know you. I knew you wanted nothing to do with Whistlebrook. Changing your opinion was not to be an easy task. Called for drastic measures. I'm sorry for deceiving you, darling, but I needed a reason to have you remain in Whistlebrook, and I knew how you could never resist a good mystery. And you always wanted me to play games with you. I never had time for games, to my latent regret.

Whistlebrook is—as Whistlebrook always was—a Home full of sorrow and stories, idiosyncrasies, and anomalies. If I've kept you here under false pretense, do accept my apology, darling, but I truly believed it was time for you to face your fears and hatreds, to battle those—your only true enemy. Please don't blame those who've been unwitting players in our little game; not even your biological father knows the extent of my deception while authenticating this game we've played. (Don't try using the evidence I've created, darling. Though I know how convincing it is, believe me, those bank statements are fake.) Edna—Mark—Frank—John—all unwitting partners, darling. Had they known what I was up to, I doubt any would have approved, much less participated. I do hope you haven't been too hard on any of them, and please, darling, don't hold Carolyn or Bill responsible for any of this. Neither is guilty of embezzlement or fraud, but I so needed a few villains on whom you could concentrate. Both are only loyal to me and to the

Home, therefore to you, darling. Carolyn, God love her, has tried many times to resign, but I don't know what I'd have done without her more often than I care to consider. She has been my right hand, and Bill, though he's a pompous drag at times, has been my left hand—also a valuable asset to Whistlebrook. He's a fantastic administrator. Don't write him off unless you're facing a severe personality conflict.

Well then, Darling, I do hope you've enjoyed playing this game as much as I've enjoyed creating it. Take a few days, relax, put Whistlebrook into perspective, and if you are willing to accept your rightful place in the executive wing, do so with your eyes open to the steady losses—natural losses both concrete and abstract. I would so love to know what your decision will be—what you are thinking at this moment. Despite what you choose to believe, I do love you, darling. If you can't be happy here, then by all means, darling, do what you must and have no regrets.

Love - Mom

A game? A Goddamn Game?

How many times had he believed that at the onset? *A goddamn game*—the game she'd never taken time to play with him.

"Damn you," he uttered and tipped his head, brushing at his bleary eyes, crinkling the pages, turning his vacant gaze toward the window. A game. No conspiracy. Only the conspiracy she created to entertain him, to put him on a mental roller-coaster, driving him half mad with his search for answers.

"Damn you," he uttered again as a bloody image rose inside his mind and his muscles constricted against the internal vision. In the same instant, he saw the face of an old man lying beneath a burgundy drape. Mr. Calfactor. But then, Elsa Taylor, aka Elesia Avoncourt. Vincenzo Serratti. Lonnigan? A game?

Edna missing? A game?

Leaning forward, Kip lifted the receiver, punched a button for an outside line, and then dialed the number from memory. On the fourth ring, the familiar husky voice answered, "Mr. Fitzpatrick? Kip Patterson here." He paused only a half-beat. "This afternoon, when you phoned me at John Madison's office, the information you relayed to me..? Was that information correct beyond any doubt?"

Fitzpatrick hesitated, unnaturally. Seconds dragged by before he answered in his thick voice. "Certainly, young sir," he lied poorly.

"Bear in mind, sir, I am in the process of opening a coroner's investigation. Should either of the autopsies prove otherwise, you will face conspiracy charges, and that will be out of my hands."

Fitzpatrick hesitated again, tension transcending the line. "Young sir, you might reconsider calling the authorities. I've wrestled my conscience, but let there be no further incidents, and we'll keep this between ourselves."

Only one thought came clear in Kip's mind. Fitzpatrick hadn't fabricated either his information or concern; more likely, his moral outrage created his hesitation on the line. "Thank you, sir. I'll postpone further action at this time." Leaning, he dropped the receiver into its cradle and rested momentarily, staring at the phone. The conspiracy might have been an illusion, but two people were prematurely deceased. Frank Culver was in the hospital, and Edna Feeney had vanished.

'Six letters — including this one.'

He'd received only five letters: two via John Madison, one in the Wallendorf, one in the Family Album, and one from Denton McDaniels. Where would she have left the sixth letter? Where would she have put that letter, or with whom had she entrusted it? No mention of John Fitzpatrick in any of the letters and only a single reference to misused medicine fifteen years ago. Mark Frances hadn't just fabricated his concern or the present situation. At least two people had been murdered, and Janet Cross knew something about those murders.

Goddamn it, no game. Regardless of this damned letter, something—someone was threatening the Home.

His mother never had time for games; it was doubtful she would have spent the past six months or a year creating a conspiracy—a game. No game. Two people were dead. Frank hurt. Edna missing.

Who were you playing with, Mother, who damn it? Not me. Not after all these years.

Who then? Denton McDaniels? She'd placed this letter in McDaniels' hands, a failsafe to halt legal action if Kip meant to enlist the authorities and take positive action.

None of this makes sense, damn it! Who were you playing with? Who would want to destroy the Home? Or did you fully believe I was your enemy? That I meant to ruin you?

Bill had known something—something about Dr. Blake's records—something to worry him when three residents took rapid turns. Enough to wonder if Kip had visited the wards before those declines.

'Someone in this room is your enemy.' Part of her illusion? Or had those words been written in earnest? Could she have known an enemy truly existed inside that room? Janet Cross? Margie Morone? No mention of either in this final letter, but Marilyn had included their names on her list, and their files were in the archives, clearly designating their questionable past experience with husband and mother, carefully placed in the evidence. Neither had received financial stipends to warrant their position in that batch of contrived evidence. They were the only two suspects on that list who hadn't received financial gratuities. 'Not even Denton knows the extent of my deception... Bank statements are fake.' No bank statements in either of the nurses' files.

Numbers don't lie.

How many times had he considered that fact?

Often enough to realize the truth, that the numbers added up far too clearly, too neatly. Each and every number added up—accounted for—excluding Cross and Morone. A money trail, a trail that his mother knew he'd follow to link the alleged conspirators. No money trail led to

Cross or Morone. They were loose cannons in the group, their past relative to a secondary conspiracy—the *genuine* conspiracy.

At the wrinkle of sound, Kip glanced to the door as Denton McDaniels entered far more cautiously than a few moments earlier. Thoughts spinning, head thumping, Kip continued his vacant gaze as the man strode forward and settled onto the arm of the opposite chair.

"If you've read the letter, perhaps we could speak again, now?"

"Tell me, sir, what makes you think I should trust you any more now than ten minutes ago?"

"Your mother's letter should have clarified my position—"

"You've lied willingly—or unwittingly—time and time again. Absolutely nothing you tell me, now, could convince me that you are in any way a man I should trust."

"Despite my deceitful participation in whatever you've endured these past several days, I should tell you—had I not believed there was justification, I never would have entered willingly into this charade. I didn't fall for your mother's whimsy when she enlisted my assistance in this affair. In thirty years, she's never been one to play games. I do believe there's something shady happening in this Home, but why she repeatedly deceived me—and you—I have yet to learn."

"How much about her plan do you actually know?" Kip asked evenly.

"I know that she created a conspiracy, and over the past week, I've followed a verbal script with an underlying twist. The inception of your old friend was my addition. She once suggested to me that, should anything happen to her, I was to provide you with a bodyguard." He shrugged, his expression anything but indifferent. "She spoke those words rather flippantly, as if she might consider that event an amusing addition to her plan. I was neither deceived nor amused at her suggestion. A very real threat to your personal safety exists, and despite my efforts, I haven't discovered who might be responsible for it. In effect, lad, I haven't lied to you. Most of the information I forwarded to your mother was more authentic than she believed. Numbers were altered to provide the paper chase you've discovered; however, on the whole, those documents were created from originals which I've kept in Boston."

"Did you plant your daughter here fifteen years ago, sir?"

"Plant her, no," he answered succinctly. "Francesca discovered my connection to your mother when she attended a funeral service of an acquaintance of mine--you might remember, Linc Montgomery, although I believe he lived here under an assumed name." He shrugged as if the anonymity game were commonplace, then continued. "Frankly, Francesca's discovery came only shortly after my own. I knew when I saw you, you were my son; however, before that time, I hadn't even considered the possibility. Rather than return to her husband and graduate school, Francesca came here—a fact I discovered several months later."

"She and Carolyn have remained friends," Kip commented.

"Your mother was furious when she learned Francesca's maiden name," he said with a faintly amused shine in his eyes. "When last she'd seen her, Franny was a gangly nine-year-old with braces and pop-bottle glasses." He barely paused, but the lingering sorrow touched his pale eyes despite the subtle amusement. "I'm not sure, even now, whether your mother was more angry at me or my daughter—the latter regarding her flirtations with you, I came to learn eventually." By his tone, he shrugged. "To answer your question. Yes. Carolyn and Francesca have remained friends. Through my daughter, Carolyn became Mrs. McAnthony, a relationship which outdistanced Francesca's marriage."

"You realize, the combined evidence—fabricated or otherwise—tends to incriminate your daughter," Kip said lightly. "And nothing you've said counters that possibility."

McDaniels hesitated, speculating silently for several seconds. "You've spoken to Marion," he said carefully.

In a flashing revelation, anger flamed in Kip's mind. *Not Marion, damnit! Franny!* Franny with her dyed brunette hair and carefully applied cosmetics. Franny seducing him in the bathroom and testing his memory of her? Franny in the candlelight, outlining her history, not the history of a younger sister!

"You do realize who you've spoken to," McDaniels said carefully.

"More deceit," Kip commented in a dead tone.

"Frankly, lad, she came with your best interest in mind. She was aware of my investigations. She knows a great deal about my business affairs. She knows I've been worried, and I believe that concern magnified in her eyes due to her friendship with Carolyn. She, too, knows there's something very wrong in Whistlebrook. As I understand it, she attempted to warn you of possible danger."

"Where's your youngest daughter? Marion?"

"No part of this, I assure you," he said quietly. "Marion resides in Europe with her husband and his family. She's quite content to be a wife and mother, and before you ask, yes, I am positive regarding her innocence. She was, in fact, investigated at the onset, a fact you alone are now privy to—"

The intercom sounded with an offensive buzz. Kip glanced down to find several buttons on the phone base lit up. Leaning forward, he depressed the intercom. "Yes?"

"I wasn't going to bother you, but JD's on line two. Bill Bickerman's on line four, and uh, Dr. Frances is on line three. He says it's urgent, and there's a Dr. Sheffield is giving Angie and Mike a hard time at the front door."

Shit! "Have Mike let Dr. Sheffield in," he said and pushed the third button while lifting the receiver. "Mark?"

"You're as difficult to reach as your mother. I thought you'd like to know, I have two of the three stabilized. Also, I took the liberty of investigating who prepared those solutions. Of that list you have, it seems Janet Cross might have had a hand in this. She stopped on two before leaving today. One of the girls here recalls seeing her coming from the supply room."

Not surprised, Kip commented, "Thank you. Dr. Sheffield just arrived. He should be up there in less than five."

"I'll keep you posted." Mark disengaged the line.

Belatedly, Kip heard the distant alien voice calling for assistance over the Home speakers. Gripping the receiver, he pressed line one, his voice calm when he asked, "Problem, JD?"

"Thought you'd like to know, Edna left in a cab around 12:30 last night or this morning. Ed's having the driver tracked down. We gave them the Home's number for him to call... This is some setup Frank has over here. How are things on your end?"

"I don't have time to explain all the details. Have Ed send a squad car to 315 Adderly Lane and have him issue a warrant on Janet Cross and Margie Morone. I believe one or the other sabotaged the Home before leaving this afternoon," Kip answered evenly. "For the moment, ignore the other thirty names on that list."

"Maybe you better take the time to explain that," Mulden stated.

"Later," Kip stated. "Finding Edna is a priority." He disengaged the button, pressing the line to reach Carolyn's desk. "Kelly?"

"Right here," she said smoothly.

"Connect me to Angie, if you will."

She barely acknowledged him before Angie stated, "Reception desk."

"Is Mike there?"

"One moment, please, he's letting Dr. Sheffield in—Here he is. Mike, Mr. Patterson."

"Dorson here."

"I need you to contact your security team. Rescind the orders regarding that list. If Morone or Cross should arrive, detain them and deliver them to the main entrance. No others on the list should be considered an enemy. Understand?"

"Yes, sir."

Kip disengaged the line, pressing line four. "Bill?"

"What the hell's going on over there? Who is that woman manning the phones, and while you're telling me that, explain to me why I've spent a half hour trying to get through the switchboard. And what the hell's the meaning of having me turned away at the doors—"

"We have a problem, Bill. Come over. I think we should talk. I'll see that you're let in." Kip pushed the button to reach Angie's desk. "Let me talk to Mike again."

"Mike, it's for—"

"Dorson, here."

"See that Mr. Bickerman comes to my office when he arrives. Are the attorneys still in the lobby?"

"They've gone into the lounge, sir."

"Fine. Thank you." Kip stated and disengaged the line. Dropping the receiver into the cradle, he leaned back, unconsciously studying Denton McDaniels. "No more games, sir. Is there anything else you can tell me about your investigations or suspicions?"

"If I understood the last several moments, you've discovered the threat. How, may I ask, has the Home been sabotaged?"

"In the past three days, I've lost four residents, Mr. McDaniels, and if not for taking countermeasures earlier this evening, I'd have lost at least three more. My mother's game has been costly, and I can't help but wonder what her ultimate goal might have been. Or exactly why she risked the lives she obviously placed in jeopardy by not acting sooner on her suspicions."

"My God," McDaniels said quietly, his calm wavering unnaturally.

By instinct, Kip's muscles gripped in alarm, his vacant gaze solidified into sincere scrutiny. "What do you know, sir?"

"Before I helped your mother remove you fifteen years ago, there were at least four questionable deaths," he paused, his attention riveted. "You weren't responsible for those deaths, were you, lad?"

"What do you know about those?" Kip asked without affect.

McDaniels' face screwed up with his concern, his focus darted before landing in deliberation. "I know that your mother felt you were responsible for those deaths, and she never pursued an investigation for fear of the answers she might receive. And all of this suddenly makes a great deal of sense." He paused again, only for an instant, his gaze steady. "I believe this entire ordeal might have been contrived to answer that question at long last. By devising a means to keep you here and forcing you to examine all aspects of the Home, she pressured you to search your past.

"Those incidents ceased after you left, Kippen. If not you, then...? Janet Cross—if I remember accurately, she was here at the time of those incidents. I have a perfect memory for numbers and dates, a hereditary ability I passed on to you, as I've come to realize. Do you know why she might have wanted to frame you for those crimes?"

Mrs. Ramsey. That was the woman who'd ultimately changed his life and touched off a series of confusing events fifteen years earlier. In haunting echoes, Kip heard her screaming as he'd listened to a thousand other similar distress calls, and by instinct, he'd raced to her room, found her clinging to her bed. He'd heard the call button resounding within the room and echoing from the nurses' station down the hall. Someone should have responded to that signal.

"No one answered the call button," he remembered absently. That sound had pulsed beneath the elder woman's cries, in tempo with his heartbeat throbbing in his ears when he'd tried to cushion Mrs. Ramsey's fall and ripped his intestines in the process. "Tubes, catheters... She was filled with cancer," he said absently, his focus trailing toward the sheer curtain.

A stomach tumor bloated her to an enormous size. Catheters, IV lines...

"She never should have been out of that bed." *But Janet Cross had put her in a recliner and left her there.* "One of her caths had flooded," Kip remembered the smell, an ungodly smell of urine and bowel. The rancid scent had slammed him as he'd neared that open doorway, and Janet Cross had known about that cath, had refused to answer the call button, ignored it while she finished her lunch. "Mrs. Ramsey died. She died less than two days later. That day, I gave myself a hernia when putting her back in bed," Kip remembered vacantly, his thoughts drifting. "And maybe I did think I killed her. God knows, Janet Cross screamed at me, and a rumor started that I'd killed Mrs. Ramsey." His focus cleared, firming on Denton McDaniels. "The woman was dying of cancer, and Mrs. Cross was punishing her for making a mess. And the only one who might have believed Janet Cross's accusations was Janet Cross herself, who—had I reported to my mother—would have lost her job, and likely her nurse's license for mistreating a resident."

"Why didn't you speak to your mother?" Denton asked carefully.

"As I said, I gave myself a hernia." And he remembered, "I'd have been forced to report that as well, and I might have truly felt responsible for Mrs. Ramsey's dying. God knows, every death affected me badly," he shrugged, shifting his gaze, again considering his mother's staged conspiracy. A conspiracy she created—to stop him from the grave if he were responsible for the crimes of fifteen years ago. Not a bodyguard, she'd tricked McDaniels into placing someone in a position to stop her son from a repeat performance. All the letters, geared to tip his emotional and mental balance—to pressure him into action. She might have alerted Bill Bickerman as well, alluding to the possibility of foul play should Denton's watchdog fail to prevent a repeat episode. "She certainly didn't think very highly of me, did she?" Kip said in an empty tone.

"She loved you, lad. I don't think she could bear the thought of facing what she might have done to you had she pursued this in her own lifetime."

Passing Denton an indifferent glance, Kip leaned forward and engaged the intercom, reaching Angie. "Send Brad Sinclair and John Madison into the office, will you, and if Bill arrives, waylay him briefly."

"Yes, sir."

As Kip released the button and settled back, the intercom engaged. Tapping the button, he asked, "Yes."

"Kip, Jason's out here, he wants to come in a minute—he says it's 'sort of' important."

"By all means, send him in," he commented and released the button a second time, settling back into his mother's chair. Odd, his head no longer pounded; he felt only tired now. Exhausted and still unnaturally cold. That chill would never lift, not here, not in Whistlebrook, not in Randall.

At the tap on the door, he commented, "Come in. It's open."

King entered hesitantly, a metal-capped dish in hand, a faintly worried grin touching his weary features.

"Didn't I send you home a while ago?"

"Well, yeah, guess you did, sir, but uh... Well, I went back to check the schedule, see if I'd have to call off, and I sort of ended up helping to deliver the snacks to a couple of floors. Anyway—" He advanced to the desk and glanced nervously at the lidded plate. "You haven't eaten much. I found this in the fridge, and I got to thinking. Mrs. Feeney left you plates in aluminum foil like this last week. Anyway, I know you've been worried about her, and this plate wasn't in there this morning. I mean, it has roast beef, and that was on this evening's menu. Mrs. Allison might have made it up for you, but..."

But Edna was more likely the culprit.

Kip accepted the plate, sliding it onto the mat in front of him, lifting the lid. Thin-sliced roast beef, cooked carrots, and a hearty portion of mashed potatoes. Jason had taken the liberty of heating the contents. A rich aroma simmered off the steaming plate. Replacing the lid, Kip reached past the plate and lifted the receiver, punching the numbers for Frank's home. At the strange voice, Kip hesitated, then asked, "Is Mr. Mulden nearby?"

"He just went over to the Home with Chief Cartel."

"Thank you," he said without betraying his annoyance. Replacing the receiver, he looked up at Jason. "If I send you home now, should I expect to see you again in a half hour?"

He smiled faintly, "Doubtful. Think I'm getting tired."

"Go home, then, and thank you again," he said simply.

"Welcome," he said simply, glanced off McDaniels and back to Kip as he started to turn. On impulse, he stopped and sobered, "Could I call tomorrow? I mean, I'd really like to know about Mrs. Feeney. She's a neat lady."

"By all means, call," Kip said evenly and looked to the door as Sinclair stepped into the room a step ahead of John Madison. Both attorneys wore their curiosity as well as their distrust of McDaniels in open display. They passed Jason without more than a glance.

"Suppose I should apologize to both of you. It seems I've been had," Kip began simply and shifted his full attention to Madison. "My mother played an elaborate hoax on all of us, John, and though I won't outline the details, suffice it to say, if either of you were to contact a District Attorney, we'd all face serious repercussions." His gaze shifted between the attorneys. "We were misled and fed a great deal of fabricated evidence. Only two warrants will be issued—both in connection with the manslaughter charges I outlined earlier." Barely pausing, he leveled his gaze on Sinclair. "Return home on the earliest flight, Brad. Book a return passage for the first week of January. I'd like you to visit with Atty. Madison's and begin proceedings to place Whistlebrook on the open market. I want it liquidated, and frankly, I don't give a damn if it's purchased as a nursing home, or if it's sold for strip mining—we still hold all mineral rights. Atty. Madison has market analysis figures along with an in-depth inventory relating to the merchandise contained within these walls—"

"Kip," Madison interrupted. "Why don't we discuss—"

"There is nothing I care to discuss, Atty. Madison," he said simply. "You asked me not long ago why I didn't take positive action regarding the loopholes within the Will. Consider this positive action. I'll expect you to cooperate fully." Glancing between the attorneys, he commented, "It's been a long day, gentlemen. We'll be in touch." Looking to McDaniels, he commented, "Unless you intend to bid on the estate, I doubt we'll have a need to remain in contact. It's been an experience making your acquaintance. Do have a splendid holiday and do stay the fuck out of my life hereafter."

The intercom interrupted at that precise moment. "If you'll all excuse me, now," Kip said simply and leaned, lifted the receiver, tapping the intercom. "Yes?"

"Kip, JD and the police chief want to talk to you," Kelly said smoothly.

"Send them in, then go home," he said simply.

"Kip?"

"Goodbye, luv. Do have a splendid holiday." He replaced the receiver on whatever she was about to say and returned his vacant gaze to all three halted men. "I've asked you politely to take your leave, gentlemen. Should I have you assisted?" Glancing between the attorneys, he commented, "Should I learn that either of you is discussing my affairs with—for example--the gentleman beside you or any other outside party, I will have you charged for violating your legal oaths. Now, get out."

Both attorneys glanced at McDaniels, then at each other, as they began to accept his command.

"Lad," McDaniels started.

"See that your entourage leaves with you, sir. Or we'll have a serious problem in the very near future."

Across the room, the door opened under JD's push. Ed Cartel followed on his heels. Both were in a hurry; both were startled by the men moving toward them. Stepping aside, Mulden barely glanced at them as he passed, his expression gripped in annoyance. "Would you care to tell me what the hell's going on, now?"

Without moving from his comfortable lean, Kip watched the attorneys and McDaniels file out and waited until Cartel closed the door before looking to Mulden. "It's now time for the cavalry, JD," he said simply and caught Cartel's gaze as the man approached. "I've had at least two homicides in the Home, Captain. Autopsies should prove that at least two of the three people who died here last evening were intentionally overdosed. I'd like you to call in your respective detectives and teams to investigate. My supply rooms need to be dusted for fingerprints, and my staff needs to be questioned about the activities of Janet Cross. I don't imagine it could be proven, but I have reason to believe she was responsible for several premature deaths fifteen years ago. Do what you need to do. I'm authorizing Mr. Mulden, my acting Chief of Security, to see that you have full cooperation."

Barely pausing, he looked to JD, "After you found Edna's departure time, did you happen to continue reviewing the tapes to learn if she might have returned?"

"She didn't," he answered simply. "We ran through every tape until about eight this evening."

Apparently, the assistant kitchen coordinator had prepared the meal for him. "Nothing more on the cab driver?" he asked absently.

"Not yet," JD answered. "What's going on?"

"I'm tired," he said simply and again looked to Cartel. "Very shortly, I'm putting Bill Bickerman in charge; however, unless you have objections, Captain, I'll resume my command from the recliner in my mother's private rooms. If anything should develop and you need me, have Bill come to get me. Questions?"

Cartel considered a moment too long.

Angie's voice succeeded the announcing buzz. "Sir, Mr. Bickerman's arrived."

In one fluid motion, Kip pushed up and out of his chair while depressing the button. "Send him in," he said as he caught himself from an unnatural sway. Spotting Mulden's tense gaze, Kip commented, "See that all our guests are escorted out. Visiting hours and office hours are officially over. Have Marsh call here in the morning." Stepping from behind the desk, he looked again at the police chief. "You can use this phone to make the necessary calls. Regardless of the hour, I'd appreciate hearing from you before you leave."

Without another word, he sidled past Cartel and strode to the door. He stepped into the hall, nearly running into Bill Bickerman. "I'm resigning my position," he said simply. "You are hereby reinstated as Chief Administrator. Assist Mr. Mulden and Chief Cartel. Keep in touch with Dr. Frances and Dr. Sheffield; however, do not interfere with them. Should you have a moment to speak with Dr. Frances, please have him prescribe and send down a mild pain reliever. I have a bitch of a headache. I'll be in Marilyn's rooms."

"What's going on here, Kip? Who the hell are all those people in the lobby—and lounge—and what the hell am I assisting Chief Cartel with?"

"Despite what you may have been led to believe, Bill, I'm not—and never have been—responsible for an evil deed in Whistlebrook. You would have been better off questioning the staff about Janet Cross's visits to the medicine cabinets last evening. Now, if you'll excuse me?"

Not awaiting a reply, Kip sidled past Bill only to come face to face with Kelly Mulden around the first corner. Looking into her hazel eyes, this once, he felt nothing—or perhaps, he felt something. "Do go home, Kelly. Have a long chat with your fiancé. I'm sure he'll forgive you for your poor judgment and infatuation. What might have been will never be. Have no regrets. I am asking you, now, to leave and not return. And my decision has nothing to do with either your fiancé or your brother. Find your happiness, Kelly, and have a wonderful life... Excuse me," he said and sidestepped, pulling his gaze away as her eyes filled with tears.

Yes, he felt something—something dead inside of him as he walked across the secretarial pool and entered the hallway. Ignoring the sounds of muffled voices from the lobby, he continued down the hall into the PRIVATE suite.

Chapter 19

Knees close to buckling with the pain ripping through her limbs, Kelly settled back into the chair at the reception desk. She'd meant to knock on that door and check on Kip's physical state. He hadn't been well. Whatever this madness, it was not boding well for him, not mentally or physically. She'd meant to make sure he ate whatever Jason had delivered to him. She doubted he'd eaten anything despite his visit to Le Chateau. Too clearly, she'd glimpsed the manager arrive at that corner booth and overheard his discreet inquiry over the meal. Kip hadn't eaten. He needed...

Unconsciously, she dragged a tissue from the box on the secretary's desk and wiped at the trickle of tears rolling down her cheeks. Like a hammer slamming a nail, his vacant words resounded, punctuating each syllable, although he'd never lifted his tone.

She needed to leave. She needed to go back to Baltimore—

The inner door opened again, and in a blurry glance, she identified JD emerging. Embarrassed by the tears, gripped with the pain knotting her stomach, she pushed off the chair, fumbling with the tissue and tipping her head. JD was far too perceptive to be fooled.

He hand clasped her elbow as she started for the door.

"Hold on, sis," he said in his natural deep pitch. "What did Prince Charming say to you?"

"It's—" She swallowed a sob and tried to steady her voice. Maybe she was tired too. Too tired to handle another single thing, much less an older brother's heartfelt concern or I-told-you-so-lecture. "Nothing, JD. It's—"

"Kell," he interrupted in a far more gentle tone. "He can be a bastard, but whatever he said this time—Don't take it to heart. He's uh... I think he's pretty hurt underneath the anger right now. I can't explain at the moment, but I promise, we'll talk tomorrow."

The words were meant as comfort, but somehow, they made her feel worse and even more foolish. "I'm going home, JD," she said with a firm rein on her emotions. Those words, 'Go have a chat with your fiancé ... have a wonderful life.' slapped her again and nearly caved her resolve. She managed to meet JD's worried gaze. "We'll talk tomorrow," she agreed.

He hesitated, momentarily studying her eyes before he nodded and withdrew his hand. "Just hang in there, sis. Once this shit's sorted out, he'll come around."

"JD." What could she say? The finality in Kip's words, the resignation in his empty tone. Suddenly, she felt worse for him than for herself. As if she'd absorbed the pain he refused to feel, the ache settled into her stomach, inexplicably intense. Words, the vacancy in his words struck deeper than the words themselves. "Tomorrow," she repeated, firming her conviction as much for herself as for JD. Tomorrow, Kip would need company, and if he thought he could dismiss her with such flippant disregard, he had another thought coming.

Apparently satisfied, JD nodded and flashed a glance to the coat rack near the door where her coat hung. "There's an emergency exit down the hall, here. How about I help you avoid that madhouse out front and see you to your car?"

"The exit's appreciated," she admitted with a collected breath. "I don't need an escort, though. I have a feeling there's more than enough security out front."

"Humph, that there is. And likely to be more,"

"What's really going on here, JD? Do you know?"

"Not yet, but I intend to find out soon," he said simply and held her coat in gentlemanly fashion.

Of all her brothers, JD most resembled their father in manner as well as appearance, carrying himself with unparalleled confidence and strength, and only more impressive now that she understood his position. Accepting his conviction, donning her coat, Kelly received his escort into the private hall and needed travel only two doors before registering the overhead neon designating an exit. The Home was more like a maze, designed to keep a body guessing, if not disoriented at every turn. Only once, she flashed a glance toward the PRIVATE room, only fleeting a thought to follow her heart and breach that solid door.

Tomorrow.

Tomorrow, she would track down the elusive Mr. Patterson and have it out with him once and for all. How dare he tell her to go back to Richard and reduce her feelings to a childish infatuation? Did he, like her brother, still consider her a child or worse, see her as one? Fleeting a thought of the heat flashing in his gray eyes a time or two, she countered her own thought, a thought to carry her to and through the emergency exit.

Only the cold air whipping across the narrow flight of iron steps blasted the thought away. The air had chilled considerably, turning the salted sidewalk crispy under her high heels. She should have accepted JD's escort; her heels were no more sensible now than last week when JD had assisted her in their parents' driveway. At least the vapor lights on the 20-style, cast-iron lampposts offered a degree of safety to circle the side of the house. As she'd noted more than a time or two, the Home's grounds were meticulously maintained and groomed, with manicured pine hedges and barren shrubs lining the walkway that circled the home. Even before she reached the front of the Home, she heard the voices on the front porch and the pulsing red and blue lights of at least one police car breached the pines, piercing the pockets of lights.

Luckily, she'd parked her car to the right of the front door, tucked at the fringe of the main parking area. Without a need to duck and run, she veered left at the main sidewalk. With her long coat shielding her from the wind, she continued toward her car, intent upon bringing her keys from the deep pocket. Had she thought ahead, she might have changed into more sensible clothes—like jeans and boots—but there hadn't seemed enough time. Once and for all, she'd needed to confront him, and despite his last words, she couldn't regret participating in the earlier madness. At some point in the morrow, JD would have a lot of explaining to do, but one thing he needn't bother to admit. Kip wasn't guilty of whatever had initiated the investigation into his activities. And that alone was a relief.

Too lost in thought, Kelly never heard the car door opening opposite her driver's door, never noticed the Datsun parked in the more shaded slot alongside her New Yorker. At the glimpse of motion, her instincts ignited, and she pivoted, prepared to fight despite the absence of a weapon. High heels flashed through her mind an instant before she identified Richard in the glow of parking lights. Her reaction had startled him. He stood poised, frozen, an empty hand lifted, clutching open air where her upper arm might have been a second ago.

Drawing a startled breath, Kelly relaxed only until she saw the hostility carved into his handsome face. In the simulated day glow, the tension formed dark craters in his sculpted features, turned his mouth into a rigid grim line, and enhanced his drawn brows.

In slow motion, he lowered and withdrew his hand, maintaining an arm's length distance as he began in his so-familiar lofty tone. "I knew I'd find you here."

The tone pricked her, as alarming as it was irritating. How dare he speak as if accusing her? "Shouldn't you be halfway to the Carolinas by now?"

His gaze fanned past her, spanning the lighted porch and elaborate entrance of the home.

At night, Kelly had noted hours earlier, the Home resembled a castle or an immense Victorian mansion rather than a nursing home, and she needn't follow his gaze to know what Richard gleaned. Instead, she read the pulse at his cheek as he brought his attention to her. "Richard—"

"At least it makes sense," he said snidely. "Why you would be drawn to someone like him if this is the little geriatric home you mentioned—"

"I don't recall mentioning a thing, Richard—other than his mother passed away—"

"Oh, that's right. You led me to believe your old friend was suffering a hardship over his mother's loss," Richard continued in a low, lofty tone. "You left out the part about her owning one of the largest geriatric homes in the state—the equivalent of a private hospital—and how your dear brother's old friend was about to inherit millions." He said with a soft edge. "I had to hear that over the radio. Although I can't imagine why I didn't realize sooner, what with his thousand-dollar suits and shoes. Why settle for a measly doctor when you could land a multi-millionaire—"

In a split second, Kelly's temper flared, her hand flew, lashing across Richard's cheek with a resounding slap.

He reacted as well, a split second later, catching her wrist, yanking her to land against her car door, crowding her.

Too angry to consider the threat in his posture, Kelly snapped, "How dare you!"

"I'm calling it the way I see it, darling," he stated in his more irritating arrogance. He portrayed a position of indifference, but beneath his calm exterior, his jealousy flowed like hot lava. "You deliberately led me to believe that your brother's old pal needed consoling, running here behind my back to what? To warm his sheets?"

If not for his hand still holding her wrist, she might have lashed out and slapped him again. Within the heavy cloth, the force of his grip registered, and for the first time, Kelly considered her predicament. She'd always sensed something beneath his veneer of sophistication, had chalked it up to arrogance, or the practiced indifference and distance every doctor must surely perfect for his mental health. This was different. This was Richard unleashing a hostility she hadn't anticipated. Either a backbone. Or violent streak.

A fleeting thought of landing her high heel on the toes of his leather ankle boots sped across her mind, but practical sense won. This was Richard. Whiny, self-righteous Richard, whose lofty southern temper couldn't hold a candle to her Irish ire. "Richard, I'll say this only once. Let go of my wrist."

"Or what, darling? You'll scream and bring your brother or Patterson to your rescue?"

That thought hadn't crossed her mind. "What the hell's wrong with you, Richard?"

"You're mine," he snapped. "And it's high time someone talks some sense into you," he continued loftily. "I'm willing to forget this entire ordeal. I can certainly see the appeal." Again, his head tipped in such a way to scan the Home.

With the improved light on his features, she read the expression clearly, the disbelief and fleeting outrage that, whatever his family's social and financial position, it couldn't compare with Kip Patterson's status.

His focus returned, sharp and intense. "No one walks away from a Whitman, let alone a gold-digging showgirl—and you can rest assured, I'll put an end to that once we're married. There'll be no wiggling your behind and shaking your breasts in other men's faces."

With the sudden gust of wind and Richard leaning closer, as if he meant to kiss her, Kelly caught the distinctive scent of whiskey on his breath, and that, too, wasn't completely unfamiliar. 'Just a nip to help me unwind. You wouldn't believe the day I've had ... just need a little help getting to sleep.' And she should have realized those signs in that last line. He fell asleep at the drop of a hat, although he might be stopping off for a nip along the way. Lord knows, she'd seen vodka bottles in his liquor closet, a fully stocked closet at all times.

"Damn you," she said softly, perhaps startling him by her calm, quiet tone. "Just damn you, Richard."

"Oh, that's rich, darling. Damn me? For what? For not being duped by your little charade here? For not falling for your innocent routine? We both know you've slept around even before this, but I won't stand for it, Kelly. I won't be made to look the fool by you or anyone else—"

In an oddly casual tone, the young voice interrupted. "Everything all right over here?"

In a quick glance, Kelly identified the young man who'd been flanking JD throughout the evening. He'd approached from the parking lot, likely spotting them on route to his vehicle. From where they stood, she couldn't see the porch, and it was not likely anyone from the porch could see them. Dangit. The last thing she needed was Richard striking a teenager, and one glimpse of his lifted, angled head, his dark eyes flashing to the intruder, and Kelly grasped the danger.

"Everything's fine—" Kelly barely started while intending to tug her hand away.

Richard's grip firmed, not unlike how he'd held her under the awning several hours earlier. "Move along, boy. This is none of your business," Richard spoke in his inherently lofty tone.

Whether the tone or Richard's posture alerted him, King took another step closer, commenting, "JD just sent me to get you, Miss Mulden. If you need a few minutes, I'll wait—"

"Tell her brother, she'll see him at home," Richard said aloofly. "The lady and I—"

Enough! "The lady and you—nothing, Richard," Kelly snapped and, in a quick, angry move, freed her hand, starting a sidestep toward her back bumper. "You need to sober up—"

"We're not finished here, darling. You and I will reach an understanding, and I'm not going anywhere until we do," Richard stated while sidling to block Jason's advance. "I really don't want to make a scene here, but I will if I must. I was willing to grovel for your family's benefit, since you forced me to come to this asinine little town, but it's just you and me here, now."

Maybe he was crazy. Buckled to the pressure of his residency. Or drunk as a skunk. Either way, she was about finished with this. And thinking of Kip's words—his suggestion for her to take this idiot back and have a wonderful life? Maybe all men were crazy! Maybe she'd swear off men completely—

"Now, get in the car," Richard stated as if addressing a child—or worse, a mutt. "I've about had it standing around in the cold to talk some sense into you. I rented a room earlier. We'll continue this discussion—"

"You've lost your friggin mind, Richard," she decided. "For the last time, this discussion is over. I'm not—"

Surprisingly quick, he stepped forward and reached for her arm, a move she barely evaded and deflected, spinning further away in a dancer's move despite the heels. Clumsily, he swiped air and staggered a step, which only outraged him into a swift recovery. Apparently forgetting their audience, he snapped and advanced, "You're getting in the fucking car—"

Apparently, the teenager had taken combat training—or he belonged on a wrestling team. In one quick move, he tripped Richard, broke his fall, and sent him staggering to the opposite end of the snowcapped cars. Perfectly balanced, he stood between Kelly and Richard, facing Richard as he commented, "I'm escorting the lady inside, mister. If you'd like to talk to her, you're welcome to join us and wait in the lobby until she talks to her brother."

"If you think—"

"Or I can shout over to that porch and bring a couple cops over to sort this all out."

Richard might be drunk, but he wasn't stupid. The words halted his started advance.

She didn't like him much, but she still felt something for him. Irritated, Kelly snapped, "Just go, Richard. Go sleep it off and call me tomorrow. We'll talk then." When he was sober and possibly rational. One way or the other, he needed to accept the facts and move on before any of her other male protectors discovered this latest encounter. Before he could say more, Kelly touched the teenager's letter jacket sleeve. "Let's go, hon." If nothing else, she needed to find out what her brother wanted, and she had a bad feeling that it involved Kip.

Hurrying just a little, she lengthened her stride despite the salted wet sidewalk, and they'd nearly reached the porch stairway when Jason cleared his throat in a cough, slowing.

Quietly, he admitted, "I sorta lied, ma'am."

She likewise slowed her stride, finding his sheepish smile awash in the bright entrance lights. "About?"

"I'm not sure who that guy is, but uh... That's the second time I've seen him try to corner you today, and uh... I know he isn't your brother. Figured he'd know JD, though, if I mentioned him."

"And?" she coached, fleeting a glance to see the blond woman and dark-haired fellow passing through the glass doors, emerging onto the porch. A half dozen men lingered near the entrance, their conversation ebbing with the new arrivals from either direction.

"JD isn't looking for you. At least not that I know of," the boy admitted with a quiet, musing tone. "Probably be a good idea to stick around inside for a little while, though, until I can make sure that guy's gone."

Whether she was annoyed or grateful, Kelly couldn't decide, but sizing up the uniforms and suits, she chose not to object, nor change direction. The blond, Hollywood-styled, sized up Kelly with a scowl as they passed, and suddenly, Kelly was just too damned weary to deal with any more confrontations.

Without first or second thought, she strode into the administration wing, shrugging out of her coat before reaching the secretarial pool that she'd occupied for the past few hours. If nothing else, she could hang out until JD returned. Twofold, she could find out what had triggered Kip's mood and receive a genuine armed escort to her car. If Richard got himself shot, it would be his own damned fault.

Settling behind the desk, a thought of Kip's last words assailed her again and lifted a sting to her eyes. In a single day, she'd dumped her fiancé, kindled a potential love affair, and lost the man of her dreams. Had to be a record of some kind. At least she'd discovered the truth about her former fiancé. Cancelling the wedding was the best thing to happen all day... Aside from seeing the heat flashing in those dark gray eyes.

Chapter 20

For a long moment, Kip stood gazing at his two suitcases, reconsidering his decision to remain one more night within Whistlebrook. He could snatch a page from Edna's book, call a cab, and deliver himself to a hotel. If he left his answering service number, anyone concerned could contact him outside the Home without necessarily learning his location. In the morning, he could board a plane and follow his earlier thought to distance himself from the Home. With a brief stop at Frank's security office in the rear corridor, he could add a glitch to the rear camera feed and depart incognito. By the time anyone learned he was gone, he could be halfway to Australia.

Why bother leaving, now? Besides, he hadn't lied to Bill. His headache had returned in force, and the damned chills ran from his crown to his toes.

Uttering a curse, he sidled, lifted the blanket Mulden had worn last evening, and moved into the recliner. Should have called Mark himself and had the good doctor send a few extra-strength aspirins down from one of the supply rooms—or he could have checked Marilyn's desk. No office should be complete without a bottle of aspirin. Unless of course, it was the office of the infallible Marilyn Patterson.

Probably never suffered a lousy headache in your life, did you, mother?

Dragging his boot over his knee, he freed the laces—then halted abruptly.

'Ask Edna about our first interview'

Marilyn had written those words in the first letter, the letter Madison had turned over to Kip on Friday afternoon. He had asked Edna on Saturday, but he hadn't heard anything remotely humorous about the tale she'd told. Edna Feeney, Mark Frances, John Madison, Frank Culver. Those were the people she'd told him to trust. Was there a secondary message in those words? No, damn it, all part of her damned *game! All* unwitting participants in her fabricated conspiracy.

Kip leaned back, not bothering to remove his boot, lifting a hand to press his palm against his thudding skull. *Let it alone—let it all alone—it's finished.* At long last, she'd forfeited the game and revealed her goal—along with her feelings toward him. Those letters might have been written to forward her game; however, the emotions behind them had struck a chord. She neither trusted him nor wanted him here, now, any more than she'd wanted him around fifteen years ago. Bad enough she'd accused him of financially accosting her and her domain. *But to believe him capable of murder?*

Closing his eyes against an unnatural sting and burn, he barely considered uttering a curse when a flash of a bloody fetus singed his mind's eye. His eyes snapped open; a curse caught on a breath. Never sleep again. He might never be free of the vision this odyssey had released from the cobwebs in his brain.

An abortion clinic—*Goddamn it*—Cullugan had run an abortion clinic in the basement.

Did you know that, Mother? Is that why you believe I could be a killer, too? Following in your footsteps? Did you condone that little sideline? Save and care for the old—maim and kill the young? Possibly, you felt sorry for those young women. Maybe your own little mistake made you sympathetic toward those unwed mothers? Probably wished you'd had someone like Cullugan on your side a little sooner! What was that ring of contempt I heard in your letters concerning your father—finally had a male heir? *Wouldn't let Cullugan ditch me for you, eh? Male ego—was that it? Resented him, too, didn't you?*

On and on, his thoughts raged, and with each passing second, his anticipation of Whistlebrook's end grew. Liquidating seemed such a shallow end to this madness. Possibly, he would waylay the sale, evict the residents and place them in other facilities, auction the contents one piece at a time, then stick around and oversee the strip-mining personally. What a thrill it would be to stand between those pillars and look at a gaping hole where this Home had stood.

Ironic. Three days ago, Kip remembered, he'd been willing to walk away and leave the Home standing, unscathed—a sacred perpetual shrine to Marilyn Patterson's memory.

Three days ago, I trusted you and respected you, Mother.

Three days ago, he would have been happy to leave the past buried and walk away, glad to be free. Ironic, he wanted it torn down one brick at a time, now.

I want it—and you—removed from the face of the earth, and I don't particularly give a damn what happens to the residents. They'll be better off in a real facility. I don't owe them—or you—a damn thing.

He would start the strip mining in the center of the basement. He could imagine standing on the hillside and watching the towers fold toward the center like a cardboard construct. Dynamite should do the trick. All the parapets and windows would burst.

Too bad this is a holiday,' he mused silently. *'I could have the place evacuated in a week.*

A subtle rap of knuckles on wood interrupted. Annoyed, Kip lifted his attention sideways, commenting, "Enter at your own risk."

Hesitantly, the door opened, and JD paused a half step before sidling inside and closing the door. Leaning against the panel, he tipped his head with a speculating gaze. "Want to tell me now, what the hell changed your mind about those thirty names?"

"Have you ever had visitations from a ghost?" Kip asked in a leaden tone. His focus drifted off Mulden, fanning across the room to land on the glass dome. "I have. It's an interesting feeling—these postmortem conversations. Rather one-sided, but then, nothing's free of a few minor flaws." *Except, of course, Marilyn Patterson.* "Enlightening—these postmortem ditties."

"The mafia don's your old man, and he delivered another letter," Mulden said simply.

Kip looked up, not surprised. Indeed, he and McDaniels shared some biological likenesses. "I wonder, if I were to cut my hair shorter and use tonic. Do you think I'd keep my hair styled?"

"You're in a mood," Mulden observed rather casually. "Want to tell me what all your mother told you this time?"

"Frankly?"

"Please," Mulden said.

"She fabricated this entire ordeal, right down to the last detail, and she positively despised her one mistake in life—namely, yours truly. Which, ironically, I was willing to live without knowing." Unconsciously, Kip fished under the blanket, groped in his jacket pocket, and lifted out his cigarettes. He couldn't remember when he'd last indulged. A while, obviously. A near-lethal dose of nicotine filled his lungs and started a brief coughing spell.

"You still look like shit," Mulden observed. "And I doubt you're under that blanket for appearances. Why don't you kick that chair back, and I'll see if I can find you some aspirin?"

"If you're truly interested in being a friend, trot down the hall and see if you can find my bottle of scotch or bourbon. They should be in the kitchen somewhere. I gave up on aspirin."

"You've already tried some?"

"Actually, no. The scotch is probably closer at hand, however, and you might stop along the way and turn up the heat on this wing. My dear mother never believed in wasting fuel in this section. Cold air's just the thing to keep the blood flowing—which I'd often found rather amusing. The executive staff generally ran their regal asses off just to avoid frostbite."

"Hate to break it to you, my friend, but the temperature in here isn't the problem, and I think I'll try finding the aspirin while I'm getting the scotch."

Stopping for a moment had been a mistake, Kip considered as Mulden strode out. Had he remained in the office, he might have battled the chills and headache a little longer. Uttering a curse, he manipulated the blanket to cover his knees and halfheartedly considered removing his boots and pulling his icy toes into a fold. Mentally and physically ruined. He'd driven himself half-crazy in search of concrete evidence to free his dear mother from her postmortem fears.

"Bitch," he uttered and dragged off his cigarette. Before quite releasing the exhale, he started coughing again, and it occurred to him as he struggled to untangle himself from the blanket and stood up staggering with the force of a hacking cough—he truly was getting—or had gotten sick.

Standing in the center of the room, he swayed against a slow reeling in his floating skull. Not just exhaustion or starvation, although, in reflection, he couldn't recall eating much over the past few days. Not since Friday evening with Mulden. His stomach had been upset ever since seeing Mr. Calfactor, or sooner. He remembered not feeling too great on the dance floor with Darcy, but then, he'd been drinking. A natural reaction to death.

No illusions—

He'd only begun having problems with funerals after Mrs. Ramsey—after getting a hernia—after Mrs. Ramsey. *Damnit!* Everything had begun or ended with Mrs. Ramsey and Janet Cross. *Or had it?*

His thought halted. Something was wrong—something was still wrong. Someone had bugged his mother's office, her PRIVATE phone. Janet Cross might be responsible for the mercy killings, but she couldn't have bugged the phones. *Why would she?*

McDaniels had been genuinely surprised, and that fellow was responsible for Mulden and the other agents, none of whom were allegedly responsible for a phone tap.

Impulsively, Kip reached into his pocket and lifted out the transistor. At what point he'd ignored the mechanism, he couldn't readily recall. He'd simply carried it with him, secure in the knowledge that his conversations wouldn't be recorded. Fingering the on-off button, he studied the makeshift device. An uncomfortable feeling crept into his pulsing skull as he fitted a thumbnail into the plastic groove. Without much effort, the device fell apart between his hands, and too quickly, his discomfort turned to anger as he recognized the transistor parts. A genius had in fact constructed the mechanical board. About thirty years ago. Kip's thumbnail found the single loose wire protruding from the tiny speaker. The only thing this device had blocked was the mechanism in his brain that demanded caution and privacy, and no solace derived from the thought of his mother falling for that same illusion.

Uncomfortably, his gaze shifted around the room, his thoughts backtracking over the various conversations in the past twenty-four hours. Frank Culver. Frank had deliberately deceived him, intentionally offered him this false sense of security knowing damn full well someone would hear every spoken word. From speaking to Mulden about his affiliation with the DEA to describing the plan to temporarily shut down the Home and remove the internal parasites, someone had remained privy to every word.

"Damn," Kip uttered as the full depth of deceit welled inside his mind. Whether his mother had contrived this conspiracy or not, something—someone—had conspired against her, and the damned trickling losses in the Home weren't a natural result of inflation or a failing economy. Someone had been bleeding Whistlebrook, and Frank Culver knew who—

Without knocking, Mulden started in, halted, and riveted his startled attention off the recliner to Kip as he spun toward the motion. JD's slight surprise eased into relief. "Thought you were going to kick back and relax," he commented as he continued into the room, offering a glass of water along with a packet of aspirin. "Think you better settle for these and crawl back under that blanket, old friend." His endnote trailed as he noticed the dismantled radio between Kip's hands. In a split second, he, too, recognized the parts and lifted a concentrated gaze.

"Thanks," Kip commented in a dead tone, his silent communication conveying more than words. Turning from Mulden, he strode into his room. With no trouble at all, he found a pencil and a notebook on his enshrined desk. Stepping from the room, he'd already begun writing on the pad. Mulden met him partway, reading over his shoulder at an angle. 'Get to the hospital. Talk to Frank. Find out who the hell he's working with. Find out who he was going to see or coming from seeing on Adderly Lane! When you know—call me here!'

Mulden took the pad and pencil, barely glancing at Kip as he wrote, 'What are you going to do while I'm gone?'

'Something I have to find,' he answered on paper and met Mulden's gaze directly, speaking aloud for the benefit of whoever was listening. "You look beat. Why don't you go home and get some sleep? I'm sure Chief Cartel can tie up loose ends here, and if anything comes up, I have your number."

"You sure you'll be alright?" Mulden asked with a sincerely concerned gaze and a disconcerting tone.

"Fine," Kip answered in a dead tone. "Thanks," he said sincerely.

"Don't mention it," Mulden said and handed him the packet of aspirin, his gaze darting to the water glass on the console with a silent suggestion. "See you tomorrow."

"Not too early," Kip said offhandedly while tearing the packet open.

Mulden hesitated long enough to be certain Kip intended to take the aspirin, then offered the thumbs-up sign and moved to the door.

Kip watched the door close before lifting the water glass. He would have preferred his scotch, he halfheartedly considered while swallowing the aspirin. Then, too, maybe not.

He barely considered his search and started lowering the glass to rest on the television when his attention snagged on the glass dome. 'Dancers and hats... Be sure and take the dancers and hats ... personal effects One of the letters in the base of the Wallendorf where he would have found it while taking his mother's advice to remove the dancers. Another in his hat collection?

Could it be so easy?

Clattering the glass on the television, he moved again into his room and strode to the beaded doorway. Silently, he shifted the strands and gazed at the plastic-covered shelves. The best books were always on the top shelf. Slipping his hand under the plastic, he started at the right and slid his palm under the stack of hat brims. Nothing could be that easy, he realized absently, and pulled off the plastic. To hell with the wiretap.

Let the bastard come find out what I'm up to.

Bringing the first stack of hats off the shelf, he began separating them, lifting one after another from the meticulous stack, checking the inside of each cap before flinging it onto the checkerboard quilt. Nothing in the first stack. He brought down the next and continued flinging hats onto the quilt. Baseball caps with league emblems, riding caps, railroad caps, beanies, tweeds, cashmeres, and a red angora inside a plastic bag. Barely glancing at the red blur, he started tossing the plastic bag and halted abruptly. Impulsively, he ripped the plastic and brought out the bright red ball of fur, and within the fur, he caught a glimpse of white.

Bingo!

Hello again, darling,

Not knowing when exactly you may be reading this or if you'll read it at all certainly has its pitfalls. I'm going to assume you've found this while reminiscing, and you've already read my actual Will. Hopefully, you've taken my advice, removed our dancers and hats, and had the lot shipped to California. I imagine you looking out over your ocean view, tasting salt—I so loved the taste of salt water on a warm breeze. Suppose I never told you I ventured out to California to see you. I came as far as your front door before chickening out. Spent a lovely afternoon kicking myself down a sandy beach. I had no right to intrude on your life at such a late date. I think I missed the beach second only to the man I left in Boston.

In a way, darling, I envy you that you've chosen a life away from Whistlebrook. I dared not force history to repeat itself and shackle you to the Home as my father shackled me from his deathbed. Believe I hated him for that. I truly loved your biological father. Think now, he might have risked the public scandal to take me as his wife and claim you as his son. But I'm off the track, again, aren't I? I've left this letter where I'm confident you'll find it eventually in your need to feel Whistlebrook.

As I sit here, holding this angora, I don't know what grieves me more, realizing how much of your life I've already missed or realizing how much pain you must hold inside of you. Do you remember this hat, darling? If you're reminiscing, I'm sure you do. It's certainly not the hat a little boy would wear, but then you weren't particular about style when Edna gave it to you. Despite the horror on your face, you were so incredibly beautiful. Oh, but how empty your eyes that day. I thought I'd lost you forever—thought you'd wandered off the grounds. I was never so terrified in all my life. You'd been gone for nearly two full days when old Mr. Beers finally found you in the fruit cellar. I was half out of my mind by the time he brought you to me. You were suffering from trauma and malnutrition when he found you. To this day, I don't know what terrified you, but I'd imagine Mrs. Briggs had something to do with it. I know only that you were left with horrible mental scars, and I think I did lose you forever. As much as I love Edna for bringing you from that trauma, I've always envied her, and I suppose deeply, I've cursed this Home a million times for demanding so much of me when I should have been the one holding you and comforting you. So many things I can't explain about the circumstances, things I wouldn't write to you even now. Suffice it to say, Whistlebrook had problems when I took the helm. I should be only grateful to Edna, who arrived in our lives at a time when I dearly needed a friend and confidant and you dearly needed the love she poured out to you.

Ancient history, I suppose, but I've had more time on my hands to reflect, and so many regrets, so many mistakes I've made. In any event, darling, I hope you are in California reading this. In which case, you've put Whistlebrook on the market without regrets and accepted the course of action I outlined in that dummy option. Don't hold John responsible for tricking you. I assure you, he wasn't a willing partner in my deception. I had reasons that, if you are in California, no longer matter. You've put the past behind you, and there it should remain. Do not return in search of explanations.

Since I am obviously not there, I find myself in a paradox now, not knowing what I should and shouldn't tell you. If you are still in Whistlebrook, then you may have already received a partial picture, and you've chosen to search for answers to several serious indictments I've made concerning several people in the Home. Oh, darling, I don't know how to continue without hurting you or confusing you. If you are in California, then you've simply received the actual Will and moved on. If you are in Whistlebrook, then you may have yet to receive a packet of information I've put together for John Madison to give you preceding the public reading of my Will. The information contained within is fabricated, Kip. If you've tried to act on the evidence presented to you, then you may have already been stopped. In the same respect, I do hope you try to act on the evidence presented. Only then could I be certain that you were not responsible for the problems fifteen years ago.

How I pray you are in California and oblivious to the plan I'm in the process of conceiving. I was just never certain, darling. Residents were dying. You were giving up on life, thinking only of death and dying. I couldn't make them stop dying for you, and I couldn't stand by and watch my thirteen-year-old son withering away to nothing. To this day, I know only that after I sent you away, the Home returned to normal and you regained your health. And I'd do it again, even knowing it was the final straw between us. My God, how I fear for you even now, darling. If you are in Whistlebrook, then history may be repeating itself. Something, someone might still be trying to hurt you, or you may be trying to hurt yourself. Never knowing for sure has driven me half insane these many years, but I've loved you far too much to open those old wounds.

If history is not repeating itself and you are still in Whistlebrook, if you have, in fact, taken the helm and there have been no repercussions of any kind, know only that I have been a fool these many years and think kindly of me when you can, my darling. I have loved you unconditionally.

All my Love!

Mom

Brushing tears off his cheeks, Kip uttered a curse, crinkling the pages in a crushing grip. Not a letter of vast insight or proclamation. Just another safeguard and final farewell if none of her other memoirs had reached him before his departure. Or was it? If he'd taken her first advice and returned to California directly after reading the Will, if John Madison had not broken that seal and delivered each of the letters into the respective hands of her chosen beneficiaries. What then? What if he'd opened this letter while looking out his panoramic view of the Pacific? She'd said enough to start him thinking all over again, said enough to make him question her 'plan'—her deception. She'd said enough to bring him back and have him approach Madison for the 'packet' he might not have received. The damned letter was retroactive. She would have brought him back regardless of his initial reaction to the Will.

"What the hell do you want from me, mother?" he asked aloud, his dead tone sending a chill down his spine. *A confession? An admission of guilt for fifteen-year-old crimes? Is that the ultimate prize of this game?*

To have me ultimately confess to murder, which you apparently wholeheartedly believe I committed?

"Damn you," he uttered as his watery focus lowered to find his hand still clutching the red angora in his left hand. He couldn't recall Edna giving him the hat, but then, Edna Feeney had given him so much more than Marilyn Patterson. She'd been his mother.

Unconsciously, he brushed the back of his hand over his eyes and stared at the letter crushed in his fist. His mother had alluded to the day of Edna's arrival. Coinciding with the time of his rescue from the basement? Edna's story. Her arrival hadn't made a single reference … *or had it?* What had she said about him not talking? Surely, he'd been talking by then. He wasn't a toddler when she arrived. *Nearly four, for Chrissake.*

His thought halted with the bloody image flashing through his mind. Holding his breath, he saw Dr. Cullugan turning toward him, saw red dripping forceps and a face lifting in shadows—

"No," he heaved softly despite his accelerating heartbeat. "No. Damn it." *Not Edna!* Edna Feeney could *not* be that face in the shadows, but already he was moving. Like a sleepwalker, he passed from his room through the living room and into the hallway. *Impossible!* Edna couldn't have been that woman he'd seen and heard giving up her child, allowing Dr. Cullugan to work his evil deed on a living child. *Impossible.* She'd been like his mother! She'd become his mother when his biological mother had abandoned him.

The kitchen had been swabbed. The smell of disinfectant lingered inside the room, filling the shadowy light with a cloying hospital smell. Oblivious to the constant low drone of fan motors and the soft rushing sound of heat blowing through the registers, Kip passed through the room. Silently, he strode into the rear hall, aware of distant sounds, voices, or footsteps overhead, an elevator in operation. Only two hanging 20s-style lampshades sent a shallow light from one end of the hall to the other. His attention wavered on the open cellar door, vaguely recalling his hysterical flight only a short time ago. His mother had sent him into the basement—sent him to her damned archives. Had he followed her plan, he might have gone down there with Frank Culver—Frank who'd offered a fake jamming device ... and what then? What would have been the outcome had Kip accompanied Frank to the basement? Had she suspected Frank? Could she have known about the jamming device? Did it matter? Frank's partner had obviously reneged. Possibly, Frank had intended to blow the whistle.

What mattered at this moment was finding Edna, and prickles lifted under Kip's collar with a feeling that he might, in fact, know exactly where to find her. His heartbeat slowing, he approached the open door cautiously, doubting his good sense. Possibly, he should go to the office and enlist one of Randall's finest to accompany him. Uttering a curse at his paranoia, Kip hesitated a moment longer in the open doorway, again cursing his foolishness. The only monsters and ghosts were those within his mind, and once and for all, he needed to exorcise them. Bracing for another dose of mental whiplash, he started down the steps, unconsciously holding his breath as if he honestly expected something—or someone to catch him.

Dr. Cullugan was long gone, dead at least twenty years along with Mrs. Briggs, but as he descended the steps, he heard echoes of their voices. Mrs. Briggs raising her acidic screech while wielding her wooden spoon, and Cullugan—Cullugan shouting his name down a gloomy corridor, chasing him with those bloody forceps held open like bloody claws or jaws.

Shuddering, Kip stood at the bottom of the steps, momentarily disoriented in the fluorescent glow. Not far. He turned slowly, passing the railing slowly, unconsciously peering into the shadows beneath the staircase. What had he expected? To find himself crouched in those shadows as he'd crouched an eternity ago? Always hiding in this damned house, if not from Mrs. Briggs, then from Dr. Cullugan or a thousand other horrors.

Unwittingly, Kip stopped at the first intersection of light, scanning the rear wall for the fruit cellar where he'd hidden. The fruit cellars and wine cellars of an earlier era bordered the exterior walls, where the earth had created natural insulation. The halls had indeed changed, and unless he'd turned himself around again, Marilyn had ordered the rooms sealed as tight as tombs. Uncertain, he looked down the long corridor with its smooth gray cement and glowing white plasterboard walls. Several doors broke the solid chain of white, and without consciously counting the openings, Kip walked past four closed doors before halting at the fifth. Rather than clanking and clattering generators, a low, steady vibration hummed through the corridors, and only intermittent shadows lingered between one string of fluorescent bulbs to the next.

Drawing his focus to the door, Kip fleeted a thought of needing his locksmith skills before the knob turned easily in his grip. In bold print, at eye level, he read, 'Storage Room One.' As he had in the archive room, Kip slipped his hand along the inside wall while searching the immediate shadows, only to find the light switch had no effect on the darkness within. Shoving the door further open, he identified a stack of boxes and the corner of a metal cart. A janitor's cart. *Or was it the short metal cart from a lifetime ago?*

Smells of musty stone and damp mortar awakened in his senses; his heartbeat quickened with a breath. Even expecting déjà vu, the flood of memory startled him as he imagined a bright circle of light and Dr. Cullugan's silver hair ablaze above his hunched white shoulders. The smell of blood flooded his senses, overwhelming his mind, as if the scents—like the horrors—remained an aura within the room. Blinking against the image, Kip shoved the door open further, allowing more light into the room. Not a metal tray. Not an image from the past. A janitor's cart stood in the middle of the room. And the smells trapped inside the room hinted at the contents of industrial-sized drums of disinfectants stacked along the furthest wall.

Nothing here. He'd been wrong. Barely breathing a sigh of relief, he started backing from the doorway.

"Don't go, sweetie," the voice whispered from the darkness behind the door.

His muscles jumped, but relief spilled through his startled mind as he shoved the door inward. "Mum!"

Chapter 21

As a bright beam of light shot into his eyes, Kip released the doorknob and lifted a hand to block the glare. The door snapped shut behind him, and he drew a short breath, startled by the bleary red glob dangling in front of him. His muscles cramped, he nearly sputtered the curse to realize he still held that damned angora hat. Faintly amused at his unruly fear, Kip started a grin, allowing himself an honest relief as he remembered who held the light.

Edna. That voice belonged to Edna, despite the eerie whisper, but what the hell was she doing down here in the dark? Even hoping to find her, he'd only halfheartedly considered success. Had she come down here to reflect?

"Uhhh, do you think you could lower that light just a little, mum?" Kip asked while squinting beneath the red beanie hat. Barely, he identified a blurry spot of pale blue slacks and sensible flats, rubber soled white shoes. Edna's shoes. Less than three feet in front of him? He lifted his attention toward the light, and what he believed he saw couldn't possibly be real.

Edna Feeney? Holding a gun?

"Uhhh. Mum?"

"I so hoped you wouldn't remember this room, sweetie," she said in a familiar sighing, resigning voice, the same voice she used on him a million times to chasten him for some 'foolish stunt' or another. "I guess I always knew you'd remember eventually, though, sweetie. You've always been so incredibly bright."

At this moment, Kip doubted that statement more than ever in his life. Only confusion spiraled in his mind as he squinted at the gun barrel aimed steadily at his waist. Edna Feeney would not—could not be holding a gun on him as she spoke with such a weary, resigned voice, a voice that had always professed her love for him even if he wasn't perfect in every way.

"You didn't find the plate I made up for you, did you, sweetie?" she asked in a hollow voice.

"Uh—" *What plate? Food?* She worried about him not eating while holding a gun? A horrible thought gripped him in a sudden well of pain and horror. She'd made him a plate—as she'd been making plates for him throughout his life. "You—?" Did he really need the answers? She held a gun—an undoubtedly loaded gun—and he hadn't even once considered that she might be responsible for a single crime. His mother, his only real mother. He'd feared to find her dead at the hands of a maniac, but here she stood. Confusion swam through his reeling skull as he stammered, "I-I—"

"Oh, Kippen," she said wearily. "How I prayed you would just accept that option and go away from here. Oh, but your mother was a clever thing. She was always so clever—so in control—and how I hated her for the way she treated you. Even now, from the grave, she's manipulated events to suit her. She wanted you to stay here, you know? She wanted you to take over this Home and follow in her footsteps. It was all a trick, you know, sweetie? She's tricked you into staying here. Tricked you into looking back on your life here. Tricked you into falling for all these old relics. I almost knew it was a trick. Knew she was manipulating you. I couldn't let that happen, you see, sweetie? I just couldn't let her trap you here," she said with a slight hitch in her voice. "I had to do something to make you see that you don't belong here."

"Y-you had Janet...?" He couldn't finish that thought. His voice stuck in his tightening throat. Edna Feeney could *not* be responsible for all this—not *murder* for God's sake!

"They were going to die soon, sweetie," Edna said quietly, sorrowfully. "Poor Mrs. Taylor has been suffering for such a long time. The others, too, and I know how you always hated to see them suffer. I think you felt more relief than grief when they died, but that was no life for a boy. No life at all for such a wonderful little boy. How sad you were—so awfully sad. Always wanting to hear a story. How you loved to listen to those old crone's tales." Her voice trailed momentarily. The flashlight beam wavered just a little, lending him a clear view of the pistol beneath a red haze of angora suspended from his lifted hand. "Irish McGuire was your favorite storyteller. How he could spin a tall tale for you. Always filling your head full of tales of glory days."

Pain. A horrible pain gripped Kip's chest as he anticipated her words. Already his head shook, denying, rejecting even the possibility. Despite himself, he strained, "Irrrish?" *No! Do not tell me you killed him!* "Youuu—you didn't ha-ave her...?"

"He was suffering so, dear," she said consolingly. "There at the end. Well, no, sweetie, I could never lie to you," she said tiredly. "He was suffering, but that wasn't the only reason I had to hurry him along. Oh, sweetie, can't you see what they were doing to you? First your mother, then—then *he* came into the picture all those years ago. Between them, you didn't stand a chance. I knew when he started coming around, he'd try to manipulate you, too."

"McDaniels," Kip said heavily, understanding coursing through his stricken mind. "Irish and Denton McDaniels."

"He was using Irish, prying your life story from that poor defenseless old man, and I knew what he was up to, sweetie. I know how that kind operates. They use people up and spit them out, just like your mother. It was no wonder those two fell in love. Between them, they were going to hurt you. I-I couldn't let them get away with that. You see that, don't you, sweetie?"

"Oh God," he uttered as his watery gaze fell into the shadows between them. "D-did y-you kill her?" he asked in a strained, deadened tone. His heart raced with fear and dread.

"Don't be ridiculous," she snapped in a voice filled with reproach. "How could you even suspect I'd do something like that? She was like a sister to me!"

Confusion rippled through his mind. Edna sounded angry that he could believe she killed Marilyn Patterson after admitting she killed Irish? "I-I'm sorry," he uttered as reality began to sink more fully into his mind. She was insane, and with a wrenching ripple of déjà vu, he knew this wasn't the first time he'd witnessed this flaw in Edna Feeney's matronly manner. A feeling—a too-familiar feeling of fear crept across his mind. *Briggs. Cullugan. Oh God almighty!* In an instant flash, he remembered the brittle limbs scattered on the basement floor at the base of the steps, and blood pooling around the gaunt, lined face. He'd seen that old crone there, twisted at the base of the steps, before his mother whisked him away. Then Edna Feeney had replaced Briggs in the kitchen.

"Oh God," he uttered. "You killed ... Bags."

"She hurt you," she said simply. "How could I let her go on hurting you once I learned what she was doing? I could never regret helping her down the stairs, sweetie. Not after all the welts I'd find on you. And you wouldn't even scream when she hurt you. You never screamed. You were such a pleasant little thing—"

"An-nd Dr. Cullugan," he said in a dead tone.

"I had to protect the others," she said in an estranged, distant voice. "You were so little. But you saw what that monster did in this room. I had to come back. I had to know if they'd found you, if you were alright. I was so—so afraid for you—afraid that butcher would hurt you," she barely paused and lightened her tone. "You were such a beautiful little boy." Her voice drifted again.

"M-um," he strained softly. "Give me the gun, now."

"I can't do that, sweetie," she said in a firmer tone. "Really, dear, you're not a little boy anymore," she said as if chastening him again. "We did a fine job of raising you, your mother and me. If only she hadn't hurt you so. You've grown up into an angry man, sweetie. A dangerous man, I think."

"Mum, please," he uttered softly. "Give me the gun."

"I'm going to retire early after this," she said in a sighing tone. "I'm going to need to go away for a time, I think. First, losing your mother—now, you. I never thought you'd turn on me, sweetie, but after the way you treated Bill, and all those questions you asked when you came to hear a story. After you left, sweetie, I did a lot of thinking, and I realized what you wanted to hear. You wanted to know what went on in this room, and you were carrying that old, brimmed hat that Irish gave you. Your funeral hat," she said almost reflectively. "Not here hardly a week, and already you were attending another funeral as if you were born to the task of mourning, and maybe you were, sweetie. I couldn't stand seeing you attending all those funerals. It wasn't right, not right at all, and I told your mother so once. I think after that, she made you go only to spite me. Sometimes I think she hated how I doted over you and how you flourished on every second of it. I think she went out of her way to prove her power over you. It wasn't right, Kippen. She should never have been so hard on you—then *he* came into the picture," she said again with a scathing disdain.

"I knew when you two came back from that funeral—her, all rosy-cheeked and bubbly over seeing *him* again after all those years, and they talked about you, too. She wanted to tell you, break it to you somehow. She felt she'd robbed you of those early years by never telling you the truth about your real father. She even talked about selling Whistlebrook. He was a widower by then, and he tried to tell her he still loved her. A *crock!* That's what it was, and she was going to ruin your life over it! I couldn't let her do it then—just like I couldn't let her do it, now. You were *my* son, too! How could I stand by and do nothing?"

"Janet Cross," Kip understood as he lowered his hand, letting his gaze fall deeper into the shadows, away from the intense beam.

"She was a feisty one, that Janet. I remember when she first came to work here. Started her in the kitchen just like all the others, and I remember how she'd go up to visit her husband at every break. She'd take his dinner tray up, personally, and after her husband passed on, I helped her get hired onto the floor, you know? It was as if God Himself had a hand in putting everything in order. He showed me the way. First there was that business with Janet and that heavy woman. I don't even recall her name, now—"

"Ramsey," Kip supplied, feeling very tired, very old. "Mrs. Ramsey."

"I should have known you'd remember," she said in a playful voice, and Kip imagined her little smile in the shadows—that little smile of approval and fond praise. "When I found out about that rumor she'd started about you? Well, I can tell you, I had a talk with that Janet. There you were looking so peaked after that experience, not eating right, flinching when you moved too fast. But I can see, now, that was a blessing in disguise. When you were still under the weather after that funeral trip, and your mother so set on packing it in and going to Boston? There it was, plane as the nose on my face what I had to do. If she thought you were suffering serious repercussions from the funerals? Well, she certainly couldn't present you to that *uppity* father of yours. How would that have looked? An illegitimate son would be bad enough. You didn't need that stigma on top of everything else. I couldn't let her hurt you like that, too, not after all the other humiliations she forced you to face."

"S-so you had Janet m-murder several residents and intended to have me framed—"

"I certainly did not intend to have you framed, sweetie. Lord sakes, no," she said with flat out reproach. "I didn't want you in Boston. Why on earth would I want you in a state prison? I simply wanted to keep you here, and of course, I wanted her to stop forcing you to attend all those damned funerals. With your belly on the fritz anyway, a few small doses of syrup of ipecac did the trick."

She sounded almost proud of her accomplishment, and Kip suffered a sinking, wrenching disdain growing in the pit of his knotted stomach. By the time her words started again in a sigh, Kip thought he might like to throw up without any synthetic aid at all.

"Your mother certainly was a clever thing. I just didn't count on her thinking the worst of you, blaming you for those mercy killings. She did, you know? She loved you, sweetie, but she certainly didn't know you very well, and you had grown more distant than ever. That JD—after seeing you two together, I decided then, you truly would be better off away from the Home. You'd make new friends. Have a real life. I promised myself then, sweetie, I'd see that you never had to come back here. You'd never be trapped like your mother was trapped all those years."

"You're going to kill me, aren't you, Edna?" he asked without a hint of the anger or fear crashing within his mind. After a lifetime of listening to stories, he knew when the end drew near, and she'd nearly talked herself out. "That's why you waited down here, expecting me, as it were. You intend to kill me, now, and have me framed for the murders you and Janet committed."

"Janet's grown soft and addled," she said distractedly. "By now, I believe she's drawing her final breath."

His stomach pitched with the implication of her words. She killed—or was in the process of killing Janet Cross even as she stood holding the gun on him? "Suppose you ran Frank off the road, as well," he said without affect. "Crossed you, I'd imagine. Perhaps, he saw you re-enter the Home today? Threatened to expose you—"

"Nothing so fabulous," she said as if slightly amused. "No, actually, sweetie, Janet ran him aground. I believe he might have seen her phone me from a station near the courthouse. Must have decided to follow her. She was frantic when she called me again from her house. I hope he's not too seriously injured. He's been such a dear all these years. If he'd not doted over your mother so—as *all* men doted over her—I might have given him serious thought. Oh, but your mother could turn the men's heads. It's certainly no surprise she ended up in the family way without a proper title. Only a surprise, she didn't give you a brother or sister—"

"You were never married, were you, Edna?" he asked evenly, his gaze shifting in the light, watching the gun barrel waver slightly. "You fell in love and conceived a child, but you weren't married—"

"I was young and naive," she said crossly. "And *that*, sweetie, is one story you don't need to—"

"Tell me a story, mum," he said softly, watching the barrel swing slightly with her tightening grip. "If this is to be my end, allow me to hear one more story."

"There's no story," she stated with a noticeable edge in her voice. "I fell for an older man—a *married* man—as I learned too late. I'd come from a backwards little town looking for a better life. I came as far east as Randall before my money ran out, and I took a job slinging hash at a diner in town. I fell for his sweet talk and sophistication and found myself in the family way. Ironic," she said cynically. "He was one of the partners of your mother's legal firm, and it's no wonder at all when I mentioned a child, he sent me here to that butcher Cullugan, and he was a butcher," she seethed in a low husky tone. The barrel no longer jittered in the steady flashlight beam as if the force of her rage firmed her hand. "But then, he had a distraction, too, now that I think of it. A little boy wandered in while the monster was performing his little deed for me, and when he went running off after that child, I was left lying on a table to look at what he'd done to me and my baby. I wanted to hate that little boy—I wanted to hate him in the worst of all ways, but those eyes of his."

Those eyes of his were watering, blotting out the light and image of the gun barrel. "I'm sorry, Edna," he said softly, his voice thick with honest emotion. "I am sorry, mum," he strained as he shifted his blind eyes toward the light, knowing what she must have seen in that metal pan. "I-I never knew. I never remembered—"

"Oh, sweetie, it wasn't your fault," she said in a wavering, consoling voice. "You were so little and so inquisitive. I couldn't help but come to love you as if you were my own."

She'd killed her own, he realized lamely, and by her manner, she'd suffer no regrets when pulling this trigger nearly thirty years later. That she'd once loved him no longer mattered. He was not a child—no longer her child. A man—a dangerous man—and she intended to see that he paid for the crimes of a child.

"I so wish you'd gone back to California, sweetie," she said with a weary sigh. "Your mother didn't know you well, but she knew how inquisitive you always were. She knew you'd want answers if she kept you here long enough."

"Suppose you wouldn't believe me if I told you, I've put Whistlebrook on the market," he said absently. "That I've already made plans to follow the outline she provided, and I fully intend to return to California and my own life."

"I would so like to believe you, sweetie, but it's already too late," she said resignedly. "I know Ed Cartel's upstairs."

"I've been worried about you," he said honestly. "When you didn't come to Madison's office this afternoon, I was afraid something had happened to you. I'd left several messages for you."

"I did hate to make you worry, sweetie, but I couldn't very well attend that reading. I'd hoped that if I stayed away, you'd simply turn everything over to the attorneys to handle. I didn't want to give you any second thoughts. Foolish, isn't it? All that worrying and there your mother had it all worked out, knowing you'd remain here if she made you stay for just a little while." She sighed again, resigning. "I so hoped it wouldn't come to this, sweetie, but I can't let you live here. You were always such a sad, lonely little thing. You couldn't be happy here. You'd grow old alone like your mother and me. I just can't let that happen to you, too, sweetie. You understand that, don't you? You're already such a cold, calculated man."

He understood she fully intended to shorten his life to save him the pain of living—and in her way, this would be just another mercy killing. At the same time, he understood the irony and suffered an uncontrollable annoyance. "You're wrong, you know, mum?" he said with a faintly bitter edge. "This isn't foolish. It's almost funny. Both of you seemed to have aimed for the same goal. Had you bothered to consult one another, you might have saved yourselves a lot of grief—and inevitably, my life. You didn't want me here. She didn't want me here. Truly, ironic—the trouble you've gone to, when you might have merely coordinated your efforts. Or tried an altogether unique tactic and merely asked me what I wanted." With images of his distant past swimming into the compounded images of his recent past, Marilyn Patterson's game, Edna Feeney—dear Edna's atrocities—his anger and frustration boiled to a head.

His focus shifted in the blinding light. Finding the gun barrel in his blurry peripheral vision, he started to lift his hand as if to wipe his face. An instant too late, he understood that Edna Feeney truly considered him dangerous. Barely, he pivoted. Time slowed with a thundering click. His palm barely touched the barrel as the preemptive click became a blast of sound and burst of white light. Staggering backward, he lost his shallow grip on the gun as white-hot pain ripped up his side, slamming his skull with as much shock as disbelief. A cart skidded behind him, not stopping his clumsy retreat. She'd shot him! Edna Feeney—his adopted *mother* had just violated his flesh and bone in the worst kind of way. One hand lashed out to stop his fall. His other shot blindly to douse the fire raging at his waist. Ball bearings squealed, metal pans tumbled in an echoing clatter—both sounds far too distant as he fell in an uncollected heap.

"Oh! Now, see what you've gone and made me do?" Edna's voice carried into his reeling mind, a voice he remembered, so familiar in its gentle scolding. "Oh, sweetie, I didn't want to hurt you so. Why couldn't you just have eaten your dinner? It would have been so much easier. You could have just gone to sleep. Now, just look? I'll have to tell them how you locked me up down here—how I found out what you and Janet were up to. Oh, I didn't want it to be like this, but don't you fret, sweetie, I won't let you suffer. No, I won't."

Through white splashes of internal light, Kip saw the beam of light moving, only now aware of his survival instincts igniting, lifting him partway off the floor. The beam of light wavered over him as he struggled for a clear breath. Through an unemotional blur, he saw his hand buried beneath a panel of an army jacket. No time! No time to think about that hot sticky flood or his chilled fingers. Edna was moving, sidling toward the door, fumbling with either the flashlight or the gun. *Cocking that gun! She would fire again!* "Mm-mum!" he heaved. "N-no—"

"Sweetie, I-I can't l-leeeave you like this. I j-just *can't*," she stammered in a voice breaking into a sob. She'd found the door, a gap of light opened, silhouetting her image as she started pulling the door wider. "I-I lovvve youuu, sweetie, I dooo—"

In a split-second decision, he shoved off his palm and dove into the deeper shadows. The flashlight beam shot after him, spilling light against a tangle of rusted metal legs and stone wall ahead of him. In a blind scramble, he started onto his knees.

"Edna! No!"

Losing his grip on the table, Kip pivoted and sank onto his hip as his mind rejected the sound of that voice. Someone had just spoken from the hallway. Or was it the hallway? His bleary focus followed the staggering circle of light. He gazed at the side of an industrial barrel, reading the bold print of a disinfectant as if he might learn the secret of life. He was dead—that could be the only reasonable conclusion. The bullet had killed him, and he only believed he rested on his hip, holding his bleeding waist.

"It's over, Edna," that soft lulling voice echoed into his stricken mind. "Put the gun down, now, dear. Just drop it."

"Wh-wha-wha—" Edna stammered as the beam of light swung erratically over the barrel.

"Very slowly, ma'am," a second deep, tense voice commanded.

JD Mulden's voice? A ripple of relief floated through Kip's mind as he drew a ragged breath. *Not quite dead yet. Not if JD stood outside that door and that other voice?* His mind playing tricks. Delirium, surely. Blinking spots and dragging a hand over his eyes to swipe away a blur, Kip sank against the wall, watching through a swaying focus as Edna's silhouette turned slowly.

"Th-this cc-can't beee," Edna stammered softly.

"Put the weapon *down*, Edna," another thick, familiar voice ordered.

"I-I can't. I can't let my baby suffer," she said in a collective breath and firming voice.

"Edna! It's *over*!" Marilyn Patterson said sharply. "He's *not* your baby! He's our *son!*"

In the doorway, Edna froze momentarily. From his position on the floor, Kip watched the gun waver. Nothing of the reality touched his swimming senses. He'd slipped off that shallow edge—physically—mentally ruined. Marilyn Patterson could not stand outside that door. He'd buried her—even imagined her snapshot on the Family Album opposite her father's photograph. What was she up to, now, this crazy bitch? *Turning that gun. Turning the weapon! Not toward him! Not into the hallway! She turned the gun upward*—upward toward her mound of dark fishnet-covered hair!

"Nooo!" he cried as he gathered himself and started off the floor. At the blast of sound, Kip froze. In stunned horror, he watched Edna propel toward the white light. In slow motion, she slumped against the industrial gray door, slamming it wide open as she sank, leaving a red skid down the steel as she crumbled.

"No," he breathed as another voice cried a horrified denial. "No."

No, that wasn't Edna Feeney lying on the gray cement floor. No, not his mother's voice breaking into a cry of horror. No, this simply was not real, but as he sank against the wall, he had a feeling, a horrible feeling that at least part of what he perceived was very real.

Chaos erupted outside the door. Voices rose in a confusing pitch over the sound of running footsteps. Shaking his head in denial, Kip dragged his hand to his inflamed side, feeling the pulse of his heart by the throb of blood spilling against his palm. Not real. Edna Feeney couldn't have shot him. She wasn't lying over there. He'd buried his mother. Even the infallible Marilyn Patterson couldn't return from the grave.

"Huh uh," he heaved as much in pain as denial. Only vaguely, he grasped spasms rolling through his muscles. His mind lurched to a burst of silhouettes, which could, indeed, pass for ghouls or ghosts, flooding the lighted space in front of him.

"Kip! Oh, Christ!" Mulden's husky voice thickened as his image swelled into the circle of light spilling across Kip's bleary vision. "Where are you hit—shit! Shit!" Mulden snapped as his hands tugged at Kip's arm. "Get a stretcher down here!" he shouted over his shoulder, then pivoted his attention more anxiously. "Just hang on, man!"

"T-To wh-what?" Kip heaved and froze as an image of Marilyn Patterson came into the brilliant circle of light. *Oh, she was still beautiful.* Her silvery-brown hair aglow in a halo, her soft blue eyes shone in an ethereal, shimmering white light. A smile quivered into Kip's mustached lips as he found her slender, shadowy face. The face of an angel. Pure white.

"Smart ass," Mulden hissed in a shaken, low voice.

"Oh, baby, Oh God, I'm ss-so *sorry*," Marilyn spoke as her hand fluttered toward him, touching his face.

Whatever Mulden was doing hurt! Grunting a breath and moving in pain, Kip dropped his focus from his mother's image as a wad of cloth jammed at his side. Staggering his attention to JD's distorted face, he strained, "Th-that hu-urts."

"No shit, man," Mulden said, forcing his amusement. "That's what happens when you get your ass shot."

Shaking his head heavily, Kip agreed. "N-o shi-it." His fuzzy gaze swam to find Marilyn's face hovering nearby. If he wasn't dead, he was going to die soon. Why else would Marilyn Patterson be here to help him on his final journey? As Mulden started to move him, Kip heaved, "No—"

"Come on, man, we gotta get you lying down," Mulden nearly pleaded. "If you're not in shock, you're getting awfully close."

No doubt about that. Even the crisscrossing flashlight beam or beams had begun to fade. Faces and voices swam in a confusing collage. Catching his breath, Kip swam in fading light, only vaguely recalling Mulden's order to 'hold on.' He was holding on—one hand gripped JD's in a thumb lock. Not ready to die—he wasn't ready to let go and take that final journey, no more now than years ago. Mulden had been there then, too, gripping his hand, chanting inaudible words as other hysterical voices razed his spinning senses. Déjà vu. A nightmare. So many nightmares. He might believe himself nightmaring now, if not for the pulsing pain and Mulden's firm grip. "D-Dying, J ... D."

"I wouldn't let you die fifteen years ago. I'm not letting you die, now," JD stated in a thick voice. "Kelly would never forgive me. She's in love with you. She's been in love with you forever—"

"L-Lo-ove her, too," he struggled as black shades began closing on Mulden's bearded features. "T-Te-ell her—"

"You're going to tell her yourself," Mulden stated and threw his head sideways. "Where the hell's that stretcher!"

"On the way!" Jason King's young voice carried into Kip's fading consciousness.

"Just hold on, baby. You have to hold on," his mother's quivering voice floated into his mind. "You can't—you can't let go—please, baby—don't let go."

"Mar-i-lyn?" Mark Frances's voice lifted in an unnatural pitch of shock.

"Do *something!* Mark! Help himmm!"

Too much. Way too much. Kip forfeited his hold, letting himself sink into a comfortable blackness. *Game over. You win, mother.*

Chapter 22

Whether the explosion vibrated the floor beneath her heels or transcended the airwaves, Kelly lurched with the resounding blast, her scalp prickling and lifting. She knew. Before the first static sounds broke radio silence, she knew Kip was in trouble. Every muscle wound tight, she launched off the chair behind her temporary desk and headed toward the smoked-glass doors to the lobby. Static sounds echoed, mechanical voices shouted in the static, not unlike those hectic moments when she'd manned the reception desk a short time ago.

The chaos lent a whole new meaning to shit hitting the fan then and this moment was not much better.

Not the lobby—uncontrollably, she spun and kicked off her high heels as she raced down the short hall. That explosion had come from further away, deeper, as if detonated at the heart of the ancient foundations. A gunshot. Not dynamite. But in her raging, racing senses, she suffered devastation.

By instinct, drawn by an ethereal pull, she burst through a swinging door, barely identified the vast kitchen, and continued between the industrial-sized ovens and refrigerators, rattling hanging pots and utensils with the wind in her wake. Through another door, she passed and knew her direction by the short cries and shouts echoing from an open door halfway down the Victorian-style hallway. Like the lobby, this passage featured ancient paisley wallpaper and wainscotting that shone to a rich mahogany patina. In tunnel vision, she recorded every detail while racing past the gilt-edged frames and oil paintings. Fleeting, she thought crazily of an ancient hotel, and flashed an instant thought of Richard's superior snide comment about taking care of a few geriatric patients.

Whistlebrook was as far from a simple nursing home as the Waldorf Astoria was from a Super 8.

Senses spinning, she sped through the door, down the steps, and nearly ran into the doctor—Frances—as he raced from a connecting hall. His stricken blue eyes flashed off her, he skimmed his hand to halt her stagger, and kept moving. Barely, Kelly recovered her step and took chase, aware of a gurney nipping her heels, and gray walls, closed doors flying past. They needn't go far. A dozen strides ahead, several bodies stood, oddly halted, blocking a doorway, filling the hall. As if wading through quicksand, time slowed. She recognized Jason King, his young face paled and eyes glassy, another of the security guards turning from the doorway.

Droning, she heard her brother's voice. "Wherrre's thaaat stretcher!"

King turning into the doorway, "Onnn the way!"

All things at once, Kelly registered a woman's voice crying desperately, "Hold onnn! Please, baaabbby. Don't let gooo!" She bumped into the doctor and caught her footing, aware of Jason clasping her arm to break her fall. Halted, her focus fell and landed, froze on the crumpled body at the door. By the clothes—the sensible shoes and bland skirt, the plump body—Kelly identified the woman from the funeral, an older woman who'd ridden in the limousine and clung to Kip's side throughout that ordeal. If only through JD, Kelly knew the name, Mrs. Feeney, but something had happened to her head—

"Mar-i-lyn?"

"Dooo something, Mark! Helllp himmm!"

Kelly's attention pivoted, locking on the light illuminating a circle at the deep end of the dark room. At least two uniformed men stood outside the circle, but three bodies tangled together as if playing the game Twister. One splayed awkwardly under another with a woman kneeling on the opposite side. Later. Much later, Kelly would identify her own instant recognition and shock. Still, in the quickening seconds, she knew only terror as she realized JD hovering over Kip, snapping commands, holding a wad of his own jacket to bulge at Kip's center. And Kip not moving.

Time sped up then. Dr. Frances sprang into motion, shuffling JD and Marilyn Patterson aside as he barked orders at the two aides who swept past Kelly, manipulating the gurney and launching medical equipment off the cart. Breaking through the shock, she lurched, wanting, needing to go to him, but halted even before JD touched her arm. Under the harsh white light, he appeared to be asleep, not unlike a day passed when she'd found him in his mother's office, eyes closed, head resting in the high-backed cushion. He was sleeping then. Not sleeping now. His mustached lips remained curved even when the oxygen mask covered his mouth and nose, barely jostling his handsome face. His neon curls remained scattered, no differently now than when he'd bid her farewell. Shell-shocked, she'd settled into the chair in the secretary's desk, unable to face another living soul with the pain ripping through her. But that didn't compare to the devastation holding her frozen, spellbound, as the doctor cut and ripped the cloth to bare the red flood at Kip's center.

"Kelly," JD's voice barely registered, little more than a whisper at the edges of her stricken mind. "Kelly?" And as if he knew she couldn't hear, wouldn't respond, JD drew her under his arm, holding her afoot, firming, "He's gonna be okay."

Lifting her blind gaze, she found her brother's hazel eyes straining, possibly needing his own words as badly as she needed to hear them. Through a tunnel, she heard the doctor's droning voice, starkly aware of the activity, the voices, the unnatural stillness outside the circle of light—a jittery light beam barely held in place by a police chief.

"He'll be okay," JD repeated firmly, enlisting his police and military training to appear calm and steady. "Let's get out of the way, now, so they can do their job."

Saving his life. They were saving his life. Unwittingly, she drew back into the shadows with JD's help and stood helpless as the trio of medical professionals worked in quick, steady motion. Lowering the stretcher, shuffling an oxygen tank, lifting the long, lean length of blue-jean-covered legs and army boots, and racing him from the dark room, into a fluorescent glow of hallway with the ghostly image hurrying behind. Following, Kelly barely glimpsed the plump woman crumpled in the hall before JD blocked her view and hustled her after the receding bodies.

Halting, several paces away, JD turned her under his arm, keeping his hold on her shoulder as he looked down at her, his face as strained and pale as she'd ever seen him. "Kell, are you okay?"

This wasn't possible. None of it. Not Kip on that stretcher, not the woman on the floor, not the apparition racing after that stretcher. Shaking her head, feeling like she'd waded into a nightmare, she found JD's more critical gaze. "Wh-what the hell happened, JD? Who—?" Two gunshots. She'd heard two shots. And in delay, she suffered the shudder, barely flickering a glance toward the doorway, glimpsing the sensible shoe. That woman was dead—

"Kelly, I'll take you upstairs and we'll... I'll call dad to come get you."

"Where are they taking him, JD? I need to go. I need to be there." Of nothing else was she more certain, and after a moment, her brother seemed to grasp that detail.

"Give me a moment, then. I think they're just taking him upstairs. There's a hospital ward in here. We'll catch up to them," he drew a collective breath. "Will you wait here a sec?"

Nodding, she trailed her gaze toward the long corridor. The gurney and company had turned a corner down the hall, likely to the elevators that opened in the lobby.

From the other direction, the teenager arrived, appearing shell-shocked and pale. "JD," he began, but his brown eyes stared down the hall, his brow furrowed beneath a sweep of loose brown waves.

"How about staying with my sister for a moment, Jase? We're following that stretcher in a moment."

"Oh-uh-okay," he stammered, collecting his balance with the order which JD had likely anticipated, giving the boy a job to help him settle.

Who helped whom, Kelly couldn't decide as she clasped the boy's hand and squeezed while JD strode back toward the collection of officials. Trained military, trained police. JD carried himself with an unmistakable, unshakable confidence as he joined the men at the open door. The voice was low, subdued, but Kelly caught enough of the words to understand. Her brother had taken control, addressing the police chief as an equal, ordering a crime scene team and a coroner. Internally, Kelly shivered, and by Jason's spooked gaze, he'd overheard as well.

Intent, the boy stared up the hall, then brought his gaze to her. "She—she shot him," he said absently. "Mrs. Feeney. She fuckin' shot him."

Kelly clasped his hand more firmly. "He's going to be okay." *He has to be!* No other thought held more firm.

"She—she shot herself, too," he said absently. "He—we tried to stop her, but she just…"

"It's okay, honey," she uttered, and if ever she needed to hug a body, never more than now. Tugging, she brought the teenager into her arms, and who held who remained a mystery as their tremors joined.

Down the hall, JD finalized his business, promising the chief he'd be on an upper floor or at the hospital, providing they weren't life-flighting Kip to Pittsburgh. "Either way, I'll get in touch with you."

Rather than follow the direct path, JD veered them into the cove of the staircase, staying a step behind and close in case either stumbled, and only after reaching the carpeted hallway, clasped Kelly's back, wondering, "Where'd you leave your shoes, sis?"

Belatedly, she looked down at her stocking feet and donned a faintly troubled smile, belatedly recalling, "In the hall, I think, near his private—near his private suite."

"If you two could wait here a minute, there's a back elevator to the wards," he spoke in a calm, controlled voice, a voice trained to deal with shock victims. "Give me a minute to find your shoes and find out where they took him. I'll be right back."

Later, maybe later, Kelly would consider the absurdity of standing in a hallway, waiting for her brother and listening to the distant wail of sirens, echoing voices, and an occasional loud, angry shout. The gathering in the lobby hadn't dispersed entirely, or they'd returned. Vaguely, Kelly recalled sitting at the secretary's desk, waiting and hoping the crowd would leave so she could escape with what remained of her dignity. Now, she would be glad to depart with her sanity if the coast was clear. But she wasn't going anywhere until she found out where Kip was taken, and as if JD knew his time was short, he returned before her patience snapped. Only the thought of leaving Jason alone had held her in place.

He hadn't wasted time, nor wasted any now, barely pausing to hand over her dangling heels before starting them toward the opposite end of the corridor. "They're down this way."

And over the PA system, a lyrical voice echoed, "Dr. Sheffield, Code Blue. Oncology Ward—room 105. Repeat, Dr. Sheffield, code blue, room 105."

"There's a shortcut," Jason supplied, proving his mettle yet again, stepping more lively as he led the way into a bisecting corridor.

They were nearly trotting by the time they rounded a corner, and only Jason failed to become disoriented when the carpet turned to sterile tile and bright fluorescent lighting. The Oncology Department, the gold embossed letters announced on the smoke-glassed doors and through the doors, the ambience transitioned again to become as homey as a living room in a mansion with carpeted floor, end tables and lamps, plushy cushioned settees and loveseats. Only one chair of the half dozen was occupied.

The hauntingly familiar woman rested on the edge of the seat cushion, poised as if prepared to launch. In casual navy slacks and a light blue pullover sweater, she appeared as elegant as if she wore a ball gown. Her shoulder-length auburn hair remained caught in a loose ponytail, and wispy curls framed her lovely face. Aside from the furrows in her brow and fear in her eyes, she appeared as beautiful and sophisticated as the prima donna framed on her bedroom wall. Kelly had seen that photo only last evening, right before Kip had shattered the doorframe in this woman's closet.

Marilyn Patterson. Alive and apparently well, and suddenly, Kelly suffered an almost uncontrollable urge to yank the woman's hair from her head. How dare she? How dare this woman fake her death and drag Kip through hell for the past week! Now he lay on an operating table—another woman was dead—and how many others nearly so.

"Marilyn," JD spoke as if they were old friends, his voice low and controlled as he stepped ahead, offering his hand.

"JD," she said with a hint of sorrow as she clasped his hand.

"How is he? Did Mark say?"

"It's... He's bad," she said with a quiver in her voice, the tears rising in her eyes. "Mark doesn't want to take him anywhere until they stabilize him. He—he was losing so much blood again."

Again? Again, Kelly confirmed, remembering an incident years ago, an incident in Randall High School cafeteria that had marked the end of Kip Patterson attending public school. The rumors had run wild, but by then, Kip and JD had become best friends and likely the most famous pair of teenagers in Randall. JD for his athletics, Kip for his nickname'

Undertaker,' which JD had transformed from a derogatory term to a name to be feared and respected. By the time Kip had nearly bled out on the cafeteria floor, every sensible female in the high school had vied for his attention. And Kelly had hated every one of them for being thirteen to her measly eleven.

"He's one tough son of a gun, ma'am," JD continued quietly and settled onto the settee with her, keeping her hand in a sure sign of acceptance and comfort.

"You're not going to ask," she said in a quivering voice, blinking her long lashes to clear the veil of tears.

"I'd love to, but the answers can wait," JD said soberly. "Eventually, I think Chief Cartel will be up here to talk to you, and there could be some fallout with the FBI. If you want my suggestion, don't talk to any of them without John Madison or one of those other attorneys present. I don't know the legalities of all this, but I'm sort of betting it crossed a few lines."

"It—it didn't," she said sorrowfully, dipping her wet eyes. "I had to... I had to know, JD. And there was no other way. No way to bring him home."

"Helluva gamble, ma'am," JD said with a mere hint of temper.

Her Irish rising couldn't compare with her brother's, and Kelly needed only an instant to decide, this was Marilyn Patterson, Kip's mother, risen from the grave. And he'd likely be thrilled after the hurt and anger passed. Blast it anyway!

Settling onto another chair, Kelly concentrated on donning her shoes, belatedly trembling with a thought of Kip not surviving to be thrilled. If they lost him, if he died because of this woman—no. She could not, would not—

The solid door opened, swinging slowly inward on a mechanical arm, and one of the aides—or nurses—emerged, flashing a quick scan before veering to Marilyn. "Ma'am, Dr. Frances sent me to tell you, we have him stable."

Marilyn and JD rose in sync. Kelly climbed onto her high heels, stepping forward in automation.

"The bullet?" JD asked. "Through and through?"

"I can't say, sir, but Dr. Frances and Dr. Sheffield are both working on him. They'll be out as soon as they can."

"Thank you, Denise," Marilyn said, and the young woman appeared slightly flustered before nodding and hurrying back through the door that hadn't quite closed. Sighing, Marilyn settled back onto the settee as if the moment had exhausted her.

"Marilyn, could I call someone for you?" JD asked from his towering height. "Maybe John Madison or that fellow—Denton McDaniels? I think he's still in the Oak Room, along with a few others."

The phone calls weren't necessary. JD barely finished speaking when the voices breached the doors and the shadowy images appeared on the glass. Even through the door, the administrator's voice came clear, huskily proclaiming, "I assure you, sir, I'll get to the bottom of this."

And a moment later, the disheveled fellow took three steps into the room, and stopped, swayed, and dropped. If not for the aging sophisticate in his wake, the stocky fellow would have landed on the floor. Instead, the handsome elder man caught and lowered him, but by no small measure, his gray-blue eyes fixed and held, stunned, at the sight of Marilyn Patterson. Absently, the man lowered Bickerman to the floor with Jason King's quick assistance, and appeared oblivious of his catch while rising, still staring at Marilyn as she rose slowly.

"I don't often suffer delusions, nor do I believe wholeheartedly in apparitions," he said somewhat hesitantly. "I do hope that's not about to change."

"Oh, Denton," Marilyn uttered, huffing softly. "I'm so sorry."

Fleetingly, Kelly recalled seeing this elder gentleman a week earlier, one of many sophisticates who'd attended Marilyn's funeral and the dinner in her honor. Belatedly, Kelly grasped the resemblance in the man's facial features, eyes, carriage and his entire demeanor.

Without more than a heartbeat pause, he stepped past the fallen man and reached Marilyn Patterson, enfolding her in his arms, holding her slender body against his as he ducked his head, capturing her lips in a desperate kiss.

Breathless, the words were whispered as their lips unlocked. "Oh, Den. What I've done to him? To you."

"Hush, love. There'll be time later. Just tell me what's happened here? Where is he? The police—an ambulance—my agents went to find out—" His attention pivoted and riveted on JD. "What's—"

"It was Edna—" Marilyn interrupted in a soft, quivering voice, ignoring the moaning man rousing beyond her line of sight. "It was Edna all along, Denton. I-I don't know if she ordered those deaths fifteen years ago, or she killed them herself. But she killed them ... because of us."

On the floor, with Jason stooped and steadying him by the shoulder, the administrator squeaked another sound and swooned, looking up at the apparition with his mouth gaping, his eyes as round as silver dollars as he fingered his glasses, absently trying to seat them on his thick nose.

"Because of us?" McDaniel's said quietly, curiously.

"I-I remember the day I told her about you, about seeing you again after all those years," she continued softly, her eyes shimmering with unshed tears. "I was so happy. And torn," she admitted. "I wouldn't have wished Evelyn ill. You know I wouldn't."

"Of course I know that, darling. That thought never crossed my mind," he said carefully, still bewildered. "Where's Kippen, Lynnie? What's happened—"

"Sh-she shot him," she spoke in a hushed, pained voice, and the tears leaked down her cheeks as she continued to hold onto her lover, her apparent friend. "She blamed us. She's blamed us all these years for wanting to be together. She blamed us for destroying him. She—she was crazzzy,

Den. Talking crazy. I-I didn't know she was down there, I honest to God, didn't know. I never suspected. But I was so scared for him. He sounded so—so desperate and weary. I had to stop this. I was staying with Frank in the carriage house above the garage…"

And she continued to pour out the story in short bursts and huffs. "Ed—Chief Cartel came to check Frank's security cameras and I heard Kip leave the suite. I was afraid he'd do something or find something and he was alone. I had to do something… I confessed to Ed … and made him stop JD from leaving. Then we came in the back doors, and I saw Kip enter the basement. I feared he'd find Edna's body in the basement—he was desperate to find her… But she was waiting for him. I don't even know how she knew he'd look for her there. But she was waiting for him in one of the old fruit cellars. She was sooo crazy, Denton. She shot him … and planned to frame him for murder."

And by JD's dark hazel gaze, this wasn't the first time he'd heard this story. With Marilyn Patterson, he'd followed Kip into that basement and stood in silent witness outside that door as his favorite gourmet cook had told Kip her story, and her reasoning for killing him. *In self-defense,* so she'd meant to claim.

"How? How bad is he hurt?" Unmistakably, fear resonated in the deep voice as clearly as Marilyn Patterson's voice strained against sobs as she admitted her uncertainty.

And in those moments, Kelly decided she liked them, both of them, and if half of what she heard was true, Kip had suffered a greater loss than even he'd imagined. Out of love for him, Marilyn had kept her distance, manipulated into believing the worst about herself and him. But somewhere in the back of her mind, she'd known the lies, and only the thought of him in danger—physically and mentally—had forced her to send him away.

"We couldn't risk him, Denton," she huffed and sobbed. "We just couldn't risk losing him, and now I might have killed him."

Her fear and pain were palpable, and not even Bickerman, who'd landed on one of the settees, dared to speak or moan as the lovely woman broke within her lover's arms.

"We're not losing him," McDaniels said in a low, firm voice. "I won't hear of it."

Unwittingly, Kelly clung to the conviction in the words, daring to believe the fellow was capable of either seeing into the future or negotiating with God.

The moments passed in painfully slow motion, but the waiting commenced with McDaniels ushering Marilyn back to her chair and Bickerman recovering enough to sputter a greeting to Marilyn. Once again, the woman apologized for her deceit and drastic measures, and Kelly watched, somewhat baffled by how quickly the man accepted the circumstances and capitulated to her authority. A formidable woman, as Kip had professed days ago. Even in her despair, she held command, a trait her son had inherited from both of his parents, obviously. Even suspecting the turmoil behind his gray eyes, Kelly had never imagined the extent of his sorrows.

Not surprisingly, JD retook command, taking Jason aside and suggesting the boy call his parents from the phone across the room. "By now, kid, they probably think you've been kidnapped, and anyone within ten miles heard all the sirens racing in this direction." Not leaving anything to chance, JD accompanied the boy to the phone and stood aside, prepared to take the phone when the need arose—as it did when Jason bungled the explanation. Taking the receiver, JD calmed the adult Kings, reassuring them that Jason was fine but suggesting one or the other parent come to the Home to collect the boy. "He's still pretty shook, sir—"

"I'm not leaving," Jason rousted to demand. "Not 'til we hear something."

The boy's father was on his way, and JD assured Jason, "Whether you're here or home, kid, I'll make certain you know as soon as we know that

Kip's out of the woods." And placing his own call, JD offered a similar calm call, suggesting, "If the roads aren't too bad, maybe you and mom could come hang with Kelly." And he needn't bother to add his concern over the possibilities.

As he'd placed the call, Kelly had drifted her gaze to him and belatedly focused on the blood stains on his fingers, on his shirt. She joined him at the phone, taking the receiver from his bloodied fingers, adding. "Better bring JD a clean shirt, Mom. And another coat," she added with a thought of his heavy sweater in the basement. And as an afterthought, added, "If you could grab me a change of clothes too, I'd appreciate it."

"Honey, are you alright?" Patty asked hurriedly.

"I—" She had no idea how to answer that question. The love of her life lay—possibly dying beyond the mechanical doors—and she'd never even had the opportunity to tell him, he was *still* the love of her life. She'd spent a lifetime waiting for him, not unlike the couple across the room who'd spent a lifetime apart, forced by inconceivable circumstances to live their separate, solitary lives. McDaniels had been married. "I'll be okay," Kelly decided for her mother's benefit, not at all sure that she would be. If Kip didn't survive.

Replacing the receiver, she turned and nearly lurched out of her skin with the apparition in front of her, halting her. As much as she would have preferred hating this woman, the pain and depth of sorrow in the pale blue eyes derailed Kelly's hostility. "Ma'am—" *Excuse me!*

"Miss," she spoke quietly, calling on a compelling reserve and poise to offer her hand. "We haven't had the pleasure of a proper introduction, but I understand you're JD's little sister. Kelly—isn't it?"

"It is, ma'am. Kelly Mulden," she offered cordially and accepted the firm clasp.

"You're every bit as lovely as I imagined," she said softly, her eyes warming for a moment as a weary, faint smile curved her lips. "I so look forward to getting to know you, dear."

"Likewise, ma'am," she said automatically, refusing to consider the last words Kip had spoken to her, the finality in those few words. 'What might have been, will never be … leave and not return.' Those were the words he'd spoken. But the despair in his voice had touched her more deeply than the command. He'd appeared desolate, as if the world had collapsed around him, and if she believed he meant those words as anything other than a means to remove her from harm's way, she might have suffered a mortal blow. He'd appeared so weary and resigned, almost defeated, and that alone had worried more than hurt her.

"That plate." Jason's words sliced through the quiet like a sharp blade, a question and a statement. The weary brown eyes lifted, riveted on JD, as intent as ever a moment passed. "She meant to poison him. And I delivered it to him. I could have killed him—"

"You didn't, Jase," JD stated firmly. "And you had no way of knowing what that plate contained—"

"It's still on the desk. If someone—"

"I have the lab techs taking it for analysis," JD confirmed. "And if you haven't chosen a career path, pal, I'd be glad to put in a good word at the police academy of your choice."

The first strained kink of a smile curved the young man's lips as he decided, "Think I'll pass, but thanks, JD. Some other smart guy recently told me to forget a tech school and go after a business degree."

No one needed to guess who that smart guy might be. Even Kelly had to smile slightly as JD shook his head morosely and commented, "Figures. Beat me to it again."

With the quick squeeze on her palm, Kelly woke to their lingering handclasp and offered a slight return grip in an offer of comfort and reassurance. By whatever means, Marilyn seemed to understand their shared concern, and looking into the older woman's eyes, Kelly realized the bond already formed. Marilyn Patterson was every bit as formidable as her list of accomplishments boasted, from civic engagement to political influence, and from this woman, Kip had inherited his fortitude.

Nodding in silent acknowledgement, Marilyn retracted her hand and turned her attention to JD, touching his sleeve as she asked, "Do you think we might have a word in the hall, honey?"

He agreed by action, moving Kelly and delivering her to the settee alongside Jason, while promising. "I'll be right back."

"I'll be here," she acknowledged offhandedly, leaving no doubt that she wasn't leaving this room before she received news of Kip's condition. With a mere glance at the antique Regulator clock on the wall, she nearly stopped. Surely, it was later than midnight, but even in a double take, the hands remained pointed 12 and 1. Barely a new day. and this one would be longer than the last unless those swinging doors opened again, sometime soon.

"Mr. McDaniels," Bickerman, the administrator, began hesitantly, apparently deciding the older gentleman might be the authority in this room. "Do uhm... Do you think...? It doesn't seem possible that Edna..."

"You've heard as much as I, lad," McDaniels idled, pushing off the chair he'd settled into. With an ease born of sophistication, he crossed the close space to reach the phone and settled onto the chair next to it. Lifting the receiver, he punched the keypad and leaned back, far from comfortable.

Chapter 23

E avesdropping had never ranked high on Kelly's list of faults. Still, it was difficult not to overhear at least part of the conversation, and Kelly had resided at the reception desk long enough to identify the names and faces of the visitors. Even as she matched the name Marion to a stunning brunette, she remembered the blond, Morgan, Kip's latest lover in an apparently long line of tall, beautiful blonds. He'd broken up with her, either right before returning to Randall for his mother's funeral, or sometime in the past week, and Kelly couldn't blame that lovely woman for flying across the country to attempt reconciliation, nor that scathing glance as they'd passed at the entrance. From behind the glass doors of the administrative wing, Kelly had heard Kip addressing his former lover and wondered now if there was truth to his accusation. And was that woman somehow part of whatever investigation had brought JD to Randall?

With time to think inside the secretarial pool, waiting to make good on her escape, she'd pieced together part of the trouble within the Home. A conspiracy, no doubt. Embezzlement. Fraud. But at whose hand? Edna Feeney.?

The mere thought exploded the sight of that woman crumbled in the doorway, and Kelly caught herself holding her breath momentarily, blinking and focusing on the oriental swirls of color on the floor past her knees. Still, the image lingered, from the splatter and streak of blood to the crimson flood matting the black, tattered fishnet and streaked gray hair. Oddly, the woman's face had remained intact, tucked at an odd angle on her slumped body, eyes wide open and staring blankly across the floor as if to spy Kip sprawled across the room.

Shaking her head as if to halt the distressing reel of film, Kelly drew breath, grateful for Jason reaching, clasping her hand as if he understood her sudden terror. Looking over into his likewise distressed eyes, Kelly suffered a pang of regret. This young man might never be the same. Not after this evening. Not after seeing that woman shooting herself. "Are you all right, hon?" she asked quietly, wondering suddenly if he'd stood in witness to the carnage.

"I'm not real sure, seriously," he said with an attempted smile. "Doesn't seem real."

"You were down there. When this happened, I mean?"

"Not close," he admitted, his brown eyes drifting momentarily. Shaking his head, he forced a more reluctant smirk. "JD wouldn't let me get close," he continued quietly. "As soon as we heard her speaking, he sent me down the hall. Mr.—Mr. Patterson tried reasoning with her. He kept her talking. He... She was holding the gun on him, and he just kept her talking like he wasn't even shook about the gun. It's no wonder he and your brother are friends," he said with a hint of his genuine admiration. "They're both like—unshakable. Even ... shit, even afterward. They were joking and shit."

"Joking?" she asked, either needing that tiny bit of hope and relief. If they were joking?

"Yeah, like it was no big deal. But they both knew different," he added as his voice shook slightly, and his eyes strained against a quick shine. "They're like two of the coolest dudes I ever met."

At that admission, Kelly smiled just a little, judging the accuracy and agreeing silently. JD, with his courage and valor, and Kip, with his natural suave sophistication and business savvy. Cool dudes. Both would be amused by that assessment.

With the gentleman coming in front of her, Kelly's attention riveted, lifting to find the familiar gray-blue eyes already appraising her. Kips' father. The likeness remained obvious, and she wondered how she'd missed that detail several days ago when dining in the Oak Room. Older, perhaps, but the sculpted features, shape of the eyes, and patrician nose remained definitive and refined, and the natural curve in the gray-flecked pale brown mustache was an indicator. Softer, though. This gentleman appeared somehow softer, more approachable, and warm. "Sir."

"Just Denton, miss, if I could be so bold. Denton McDaniels."

"Kelly Mulden," she offered while clasping his hand. "Just Kelly,

"A pleasure, my dear," he commented with a quick clasp, then extended his hand and offered his name to Jason, adding. "I understand you were instrumental in assisting to secure the Home this evening. Commendable, and appreciated, lad. My son seems to have a talent for choosing his friends wisely."

"Uhhh, thank you, sir," Jason managed, not oblivious of the compliment, and maybe just a little surprised to be considered a friend.

"If either of you should need anything, don't hesitate to ask," he offered and excused himself to speak with the administrator, apparently, taking command to suggest quietly. "If there's someone you could call, Bill, perhaps, we could have a pot of coffee and cups delivered here? We might all need some before too long."

"Oh. Oh, of course, sir," the man collected visibly, apparently needing direction and a job with his features still strained in confusion.

Marilyn's resurrection hadn't boded well on this fellow. Out of sorts, he needed an extra second to find his footing and reach the phone, then struggled with the details before deciding and placing a call. He might work well at hospital administration, but the evening had taken a toll.

Kelly refrained from rising and taking the phone before he managed to reach an apparent nurses' station on the second floor. She'd never toured Whistlebrook, not nearly as familiar as JD with either the layout or the mechanics. From what little she'd seen, it resided somewhere between a fully functional hospital, a nursing home, and an apartment building. Only in quips, she'd heard references to private residences with nominal care, to critical care and intermediate care wards. Over a hundred full-time residents and nearly that many employees occupied this monstrous structure, and suddenly Kelly gained a whole new respect for the woman who'd managed to fake her own death to... *To what?*

What exactly had the woman accomplished by this elaborate scheme?

Other than getting her son shot by a madwoman?

Shivering, Kelly studied the clock as if reading tea leaves or willing the hands to move faster. Only another ten minutes had passed since she'd last checked the time. Not even twelve thirty yet. How long? How long did it take to repair a gunshot wound? He was stable. They had him stable, according to the nurse who'd stepped out at the onset. Surely by now they should have an update. He would need stitches, but how long would it take?

Unwittingly, she folded her bare arms across her breasts as if to hold herself together. Belatedly, she became aware of the goose bumps rising on her arms and legs, the chill reaching into her bones. She'd known. Whether she'd heard that gun explode or merely felt the moment of impact, she'd known the strike and wondered, now, at the connection. As if an invisible thread held them, she knew he hovered on the brink of death and closed her eyes, willing the thought from her mind. 'Don't you dare. Don't you dare die on me,' she demanded and pleaded silently. 'Don't you dare leave me!'

And so began a litany of demands, praying he heard her, praying to the God above to give him strength, to reject him at the pearly gates. 'He's not ready!' she demanded. 'You can't take him.' Not when she'd finally found him, her knight in shining armor, her prince charming. The Prince of Whistlebrook. 'Come back to me, dang you! You can't leave now.' Not when she'd waited a lifetime in her mind. But what if...?

What if this was her comeuppance for dumping Richard? For sending him packing for the holidays?

No. Surely God couldn't be that cruel. She hadn't ditched Richard to hurt him, but moreover to save him from a lifetime of misery, which was what she would tell Richard when he called.

If not Kip, then no one. That revelation had slammed her decision home. If not Kip Patterson, then no one.

The raucous at the door drew her from her whirling thoughts, and Kelly was only grateful for the interruption.

Jason's parents were the first to arrive, and apparently, JD had filled them in and calmed their fears. Without reservations, they entered and zeroed in on their son. Before he was partway off the settee, they smothered him in an embrace, tugging him into a tight circle of relief and comfort. Proportionately large, like an average linebacker, the elder Mr. King managed to enclose both his son and petite wife within a fold of his sturdy arms, but tears shimmering over both his and his wife's eyes as they backed up enough to judge their son's physical state.

"Uhhh. Sorry. I—"

"Let's get you home, kiddo," his father said firmly.

"I have my truck. I didn't mean to get you up—"

"We'll be leaving your truck here for tonight, buddy."

"I'd sorta like to stick around until we know he's okay."

After a brief pause, a silent exchange between the broad fellow and his slight wife, whose eyes betrayed her fear for her son, Mr. King decided, "Guess we're all sticking around then."

"Really, Dad, you don't—"

"We're staying, buddy," his father interrupted with finality, and Kelly slipped off the settee, availing the chair to accommodate them. Hastily,

Jason offered the introductions, and by no surprise, the Kings withheld any judgment or accusations, accepting the names in stride despite their reservations under the circumstances. Even Bill rousted enough to receive an introduction and seemed not to notice when both Kings eyed him dubiously.

Kelly caught the quick glances between parents and son, wondering just how much Jason might have confided about his employment under Bickerman's authority. Likely enough for them to consider holding Bickerman at arm's reach and not trusting even his forced, strained smile.

Her own parents arrived with slightly more confidence and slightly less zeal, taking the forward steps to judge her present state to determine if she'd heard news, good or bad. Perceptive and still worried, her mother wrapped her in a quick, firm hug, and her father covered her shoulder and back in a quick clasp.

"JD said he's stable. Still in surgery though." Patty verified.

"They haven't come out yet again," Kelly confirmed, straining and holding back the threat of tears. Why was it harder to check the flood with both of her parents here? Or did their presence just make it more real? She could be losing him, might already have lost him, with as wicked a chill through her bones.

And as if reading her mind, Patty clasped her fingers, parting only a fraction. "You're freezing, honey. We brought you warm clothes."

Jarred proffered the overnight bag as Patty took a slight step back. Despite the hour, neither appeared tired nor frazzled, merely worried and in full command. With a mere flashing glance, her mother located the restroom door and asked, "Why don't you go on and change? I'll see about getting you a cup of coffee."

"We... There's coffee coming," she remembered and accepted the bag readily, although she doubted warm clothes would help. The chill had settled into her bones as surely as the fear had compounded with each moment. A mere thought of time passing, of news coming, started her into a frenzy within the small, private room. Hurried, she stripped from the flimsy dress and black nylons, vaguely recalling how meticulously she'd dressed for the un-engagement party, and remembering the flicker of heat in the gray eyes to skim over her. The interest in those chilly eyes, the smirk in the mustached lips ... *the oxygen mask covering that natural curve.*

Shuddering, she staggered into her jeans and cashmere sweater and leaned on the sink to pull on her socks, grateful for the pile-lined ankle boots. Warmer. Not warm. She might never be warm again if—no. She'd be warm. Just the heat in those beautiful gray eyes would heat her to the core just as soon as he woke up.

A nightmare, she could believe then as she gathered her flimsy clothes and stuffed them in her leather bag. Surely just a nightmare, But as she stepped from the restroom, she doubted the dreamscape. Marilyn Patterson had returned, sans JD. She stood clinging to Denton McDaniel's arm and apparently chatting with Patty. JD had apparently warned them—or they'd met the resurrected woman in the hall—but neither of her parents seemed to take exception to the second coming. The Kings merely appeared slightly confused, but far more concerned with their son between them; his mother clasped his hand in both of hers; his father's arm draped the back cushion and clasped the boy's opposite shoulder, anchoring him between them, which he appeared to take in stride.

Barely, Kelly set the bag on the nearest empty chair, breathing in the scent of fresh-brewed coffee as she started toward her parents. Near the door, Bickerman and two orderlies were busy filling cups from a large metal tray.

With the start of the mechanical sound, all motion ceased, and unconsciously, Kelly stopped breathing as she pivoted in slow motion, watching the doors swing open.

Rather than the orderly, the familiar, bearded doctor emerged, scanned the faces, and locked on Marilyn Patterson. His dark blue eyes riveted, he continued forward. Rather than the checkered shirt and jeans he'd worn earlier, he wore hospital scrubs, ill-fitting with the breadth of his shoulders pulling the cloth taut across his chest. The absence of expression on the face and grim line of his lips started Kelly's heart racing before he stopped. Automatically, his hand shifted and Marilyn's rose, capturing his fingers as she steeled her stricken eyes. "He's stable," he said shortly.

"Mark?" Marilyn breathed, pleading in that single word.

"He's stable," he repeated. "The bullet passed through, tore up more of his intestine, and nicked a kidney, but Dr. Sheffield managed to make repairs, and we stopped the bleeding. Luckily, we had that O-negative on stock. We started the transfusion, and his blood count is rising. He lost a lot of blood, Lyn. I honestly don't know if he would have made it to the hospital if we hadn't worked on him here. If you want, though, we should be able to transport him."

"Mark. Here—can we—can he.? Is it safe to move him, or can he stay here?"

"My opinion? We life-flight him to Pittsburgh as soon as we finish the transfusion, and we keep him under for the next three days."

"Ohhh," she moaned softly and seemed to need both the doctor's hand and Denton's arm to stay afoot. "He's that bad agggain."

"Lyn," Frances interrupted. "If we keep him calm—no. He's not that bad again. I'm less concerned with the wounds than his ... his reaction when he wakes up. We can keep him here if we can keep him calm—"

The second doctor emerged then, likewise wearing his green scrubs along with the cap, and he wasted no time, coming into the small conclave, starting, "Marilyn."

"He's alright? Truly, Jim? He's—"

"He should make a full recovery, Marilyn, but it is an if," the doctor said grimly. "God knows, the surgery went well considering bullets and living tissue should never meet, but the greater concern is his recovery." He barely paused. "I concur with Dr. Frances. If we can keep him calm, there's no reason why we couldn't keep him here. We've started him on

IV antibiotics, and I've already called to replenish our blood supply in the unlikely event he'd need another transfusion. All things considered, he's an extremely lucky young man."

"You're not suggesting inducing a coma?" Denton McDaniels questioned hesitantly.

"Not at all, sir," Sheffield answered with a side glance, apparently familiar with McDaniels' position in Marilyn Patterson's life. "Like Dr. Frances said, his recovery will depend on keeping him calm. And that means, around-the-clock sedation for at least the next three days."

"You don't intend to let him wake," Denton said grimly.

"Unorthodox, though it might seem, Den," Frances spoke with an easy familiarity. "It's either that, or like I said, shipping him to Presby or St. Frances before he comes off the anesthesia. Ergo, life-flight." He barely paused, his voice lowered, more careful as he looked to Marilyn. "Unless you know he's changed, Lyn, I'd rather not take the chance on him waking the way he did fifteen years ago. I doubt even I could hold him long enough to stop him now."

"I ... I don't know if he's changed, Mark," she said with a more disheartened tone. "Keep him calm."

Chapter 24

With JD beside her, Kelly stood alongside the hospital bed, as disoriented as every other moment in Whistlebrook. Despite the paisley-papered walls and genuine wainscoting, the room reflected the natural ambiance of a private hospital room, complete with the beeping monitor and IV bags dangling from metal poles. Splayed beneath a stark white sheet, a soft nightlight aglow above the industrial-style headboard, Kip more resembled a bisque sculpt than a breathing entity despite the air tube attached to his nostrils. His long, dark lashes remained as still as stone in the hollow below his eyes. Whether he was more beautiful than handsome in repose, she couldn't decide, but the neat neon blond waves spilling over the thin white pillow only added to his appeal. Quietly, JD commented, "This is f'n ridiculous, Ace. Déjà vu is one thing, but this is fucking ridiculous."

Confused, Kelly blinked at the sting of tears and found JD's glassy hazel eyes staring at the face above the spread of white linen.

As if in delay, he sensed her looking, and the grim set in his mustache tipped into a tighter smirk as he read her question. "I told him a week ago, the déjà vu was a bit much and I should have known then, it was about to start again."

"JD?"

"I never told you how we met," he said in a quiet tone, turning his gaze to the prone statue. "First day in Randall High," he continued. "I was on my way to the john, saw this dude flying past me from the cafeteria, ducking in ahead, and sort of holding his stomach. Thought he was a teacher or something—a dwarf maybe, since he was sort of short and wry and wearing a three-piece black suit, when the fad was bell-bottoms and tie-dye t-shirts. Had second thoughts about going in since I was jonesing for a cigarette, but then I caught a glimpse of his face." He shook his head slightly; a faded smile curved his lips. "If he was a teacher, he had to be the youngest substitute I'd ever seen. So, I went in and there he was, tossing his cookies in one of the stalls. I don't think he even heard me or saw me come in. He just kept gagging and throwing up until he was dry heaving, and he was close to crying, I think. He held it back, though, and came staggering out. I caught him from falling and helped him get to the sink. Handed him some paper towels. I ... I don't know what impressed me more, Kell, the feel of that expensive suit or his recovery. He slid down the wall and sat propped there, holding his stomach and heaving breaths, and I thought maybe I better pass on cafeteria food. So, I sat with him, thinking maybe I better help him to the nurses' office. Then he started talking, more to himself, and shaking his head and he just sounded so damned depressed."

He paused then, his gaze drifting over Kip's face, remembering. "When he realized I was still there, he looked over, maybe surprised to see me and he had some crazy eyes," JD said absently. "I think that's what struck me first. I don't think I've ever seen eyes that color, not before and not after, and he still has that look, almost as if he's looking straight through you."

Afraid to speak or move, fearful of breaking her brother's rare moment of nostalgia, Kelly wondered if JD knew how often he did the same thing, masking his thoughts behind a blank stare that could become a glare in an instant.

Drawing a sighing breath, JD tipped his head and spied her, not as oblivious as he appeared. "That's what drew you, huh, Kell? Tell the truth now. It's his crazy eyes that got to you right from the start."

"Maybe," she admitted with a soft smile, grateful for JD's playful tone.

"Humph. I knew it. You were a goner the moment I dragged him home."

"You dragged him."

"I couldn't let him start walking after chucking his cookies," JD shrugged. "He didn't come the next day," he said again thoughtfully, tilting his head to eye his unconscious friend. "He didn't come back to school for another three days, and by then, I'd heard more bullshit rumors than I could stand."

"They called him Undertaker," she remembered as she watched JD and recognized his grimace even after all these years.

"Kids are cruel," he said offhandedly. "Are now. Were then. He was different. Lived in an old folks' home, and he was always dressed well, even when he wasn't wearing three-piece suits. That he could run rings around most kids, mentally and financially, didn't help him gain popularity."

"You did, though," she remembered.

"Yeah, guess I did," JD said in reflection, shrugging despite his apparent tension. "There were a couple of real assholes on the football team, and I was never too keen on bullies." With a slight wry smile, he glanced over. "I sorta kicked the shit out of a couple big dudes in the gym locker and decided right then, I preferred his brains over their brawn. He ... he wasn't too keen on friendship, but I'm a persistent bastard when I want to be. Or so your prince charming is still fond of telling me."

"He... JD, he..." If she confided in JD, either her brother would be mad or relieved, and either could make her feel worse. Still, she needed to say the words, needed his opinion. And he was waiting, merely watching her intently. "He told me to leave last night. To go back to Richard and have a nice life."

JD studied her more closely. "And? Do you intend to take his advice?"

"I don't know," she admitted as she looked down at his sleeping face. The mere sight of him, even in this weird repose, still stirred her blood and stuttered her heart. He was so blasted handsome but that wasn't what drew her or held her even now. Meeting JD's gaze, she confided, "I really don't know why I love him, JD. I just know that I do. There's... I don't think there's ever been more than a week gone by when I haven't thought about him or hoped to see him," she barely paused, remembering. "I even tried to find him once. I called here a couple years ago. Right after I joined the Broadway troop. I don't know what I thought I'd do if I got his number, but I posed as an old girlfriend and lied a lot, claiming to have some of his stuff to return to him."

Amusement lit the hazel eyes. "Don't guess it worked, huh?"

"They promised to give him a message if or when he called and offered to take my number," she admitted and shrugged. "I couldn't very well leave my number."

"You asked me a few times," he remembered with a more musing tone. "And I wasn't much help."

"I was always afraid to bother you. You always... You've always seemed so damned stressed, and I thought it was that PTSD. We all did."

"Let you in on a little secret, sis," he said soberly. "It was. It took a long time to feel like I wasn't in-country, and by then, I'd already begun working with the DEA. I been thinking though, lately. I might shuck that and stick close to home for a while. I've been at this a long time, and... Hell, maybe it's time I get to know my kids. Maybe volunteer to coach their little league or something."

"Oh, JD," she touched his arm, drawing his full, sober attention, then threw caution to the wind and hugged him more fiercely than ever before. "That would be so wonderful," she whispered, daring to believe, to hope he was serious. "Have you told mom and dad?"

"Not yet, sis, so how about keeping it under your hat. If I can work it out, I plan to tell them and the boys on Christmas."

"Mum's the word," she promised and might have said more, her eyes bright with excitement until she heard the soft, uttered breath and registered the slightly elevated heartbeat. Her attention spun and held as the long lashes fluttered, trying to lift. The face tipped and lips parted on a wispy sound. Unconsciously, Kelly found his sheet-covered hand attempting to rise and vaguely recalled the mention of a soft restraint. Instinctively, she clasped the covered fist and held tight, forcing his hand still while whispering, "Shhh, honey. You're okay. You're going to be okay. Just lie still, honey."

"Damnit, he's waking up. I'll get a nurse, sis. Just keep talking to him and keep him still, otherwise he's liable to wake up swinging."

The lashes lifted, emitting a thin sheen of gray glass. No other sounds, not an iota of expression or emotion. Gray glass, but he looked at her, like a blind man, and the fist stilled under her hold.

"That's it, honey. Just lie still. Everything's going to be all right."

Whether he believed the words or understood them was a mystery, but he remained still, merely looking at her through a thin foggy sliver of gray glass.

Absently, her free hand lifted, and she brushed lightly at his hair, skimming the waves off his brow and remembering his similar touch beneath an awning under a pouring rain. Impulsively, she leaned and brushed a kiss on his forehead, and for the briefest moment, the light shimmered like quicksilver under the lashes. He might not be awake, but he was aware, and for that single detail, Kelly was relieved—and thrilled.

"You're going to be okay. We're going to be okay," she spoke softly, barely finished when a nurse, followed by Marilyn Patterson, hurried into the room.

No one tried to move her. Kelly felt his fist relax under her hand as the injection flowed into the IV line and took him under. His lashes sagged; tension slid from his handsome features. He appeared so young suddenly, vulnerable, like the first time she'd seen him mashed against their front door. But the expression then had evoked panic, and perhaps, sheer terror. She hadn't meant to release Max. She'd caught the golden retriever's collar, but then she'd seen her prince charming. Her heart slammed; her fingers released. Belatedly, she wondered if she'd truly scarred him for life against owning a dog.

What were the regulations about owning a dog in a nursing home? At least one of the live-in residents owned a dog. Kelly flashed a memory from her stint at the reception desk. The worried elderly woman had emerged from the elevator this evening, wearing a housecoat and slippers and cleaving a miniature Pomeranian under her arm. No regulations against dogs, just not one as large as a golden. Maybe a border collie—

What the hell was she doing? Thinking?

About moving into a nursing home at the ripe old age of 26?

Maybe they could build a little house on the hill—

Good God, that was even worse! She was already buying dogs and building houses and thinking about opening a small dance studio in Randall. And the last words he'd spoken to her. 'Find your happiness ... have a wonderful life.'

Well, dang it. That's precisely what she intended to do.

With him.

She'd waited fifteen years; she could wait until he woke up.

And if he thought JD was stubborn, Mr. Kip Patterson was in for a big surprise.

Resolute, Kelly remained at the bedside, aware of sharing the space with Marilyn Patterson and others, listening to the steady beep of monitors, watching his chest rise and fall beneath the sheets to cover him from the neck down. Under those sheets, he wore soft restraints across his chest, at his wrists, and ankles. She understood the need to keep him still, even understood the lasting impression he'd left after panicking and nearly dying several times fifteen years ago. They'd had no choice then but to keep him sedated and almost comatose, after one horrific episode when they'd tried letting him wake in the critical care ward.

Later, only later, returned to the waiting room, Kelly heard the story, related by JD, who had come back from whatever official business had taken him away. Her parents were still there, too, but the Kings had finally convinced their son to leave with a promise to return in the afternoon.

"I remember it scared the hell out of me," JD said in a nostalgic tone. "I wasn't even supposed to be in there, but his mom remembered me and let me go in. I didn't know I was the only guy our age that he'd ever taken into the home. She told them I was his brother... When he started waking up and went ballistic, I thought I was the cause, but I'll tell you what, Kell, it took me, his mom, and three nurses to hold him down, and he wasn't even halfway awake. He tore his stitches so bad, they had to rush him back into surgery—"

Marilyn had returned on that end note, slipping between the opening mechanical doors with Denton McDaniels touching her back, escorting her from the patients' ward, a ward generally reserved for cancer patients receiving chemotherapy. They'd moved him from the treatment room where they'd operated on him before letting anyone visit, and as Kelly had heard, Dr. Mark Frances intended to remain in the ward until they were certain of Kip's recovery.

Marilyn had heard enough. "You must be talking about his last hospital stay."

"I was," JD admitted with a faint grin. "Scared the hell out of me, and uh, I doubt we'd have any luck holding him down now if he decided to freak. He's still a lot stronger than he looks, and maybe a little faster."

"He struck you," Marilyn remembered as she returned to the settee where she and McDaniels had rested throughout the night. "In the suite, didn't he?"

"Knocked my lights out," JD said in a more musing tone. "He didn't bother to tell me he learned karate somewhere along the line. Gave me a nasty ass headache for hours."

"Seems to me, he has a puffy lip he didn't have at the restaurant earlier last night," Jarred commented. "Any chance that was your doing, son?"

"Once, I was willing to forgive and forget. Twice was a bit much," JD confirmed with a wry smirk, but the curve faded as he studied Kelly momentarily. "You look beat, sis. Why don't you go home and get some sleep? If anything changes, I'll call you."

That she might not have any right to remain slid through her mind, giving vent to second thoughts, but the idea of leaving him overrode the weariness and insecurities tugging at her mind. "I'd rather stick around," she admitted and found Marilyn's gaze across the room. "Unless you mind, ma'am?"

"Not at all, dear, but you do look tired," she noted. "Why don't I send for some blankets and pillows?"

From this waiting room, Marilyn had reclaimed control over the Home, conducting her private endeavors either on the available phone or stepping through the mechanical doors. As her first order of business, she'd sent her administrator home to get some rest. In the morning, she commanded, he'd need to return and man the office until his new boss was physically well enough to take the helm.

'But you...'

'It's his, now, Bill. Whistlebrook's fate will remain in his hands, dear, but do let's keep it running smoothly until he's well enough to make any decisions.'

Drifting, as if he lay on a raft beneath a heavy fog, he floated within the nebulous. He'd risen once, if not a dozen times, to find the hazel eyes hovering above him, as they hovered now. White light haloed the frame of dark waves; a smile curved in the lovely lips. Fleeting, he thought about tasting those lips, but his body lay as if mashed beneath an iron blanket. If he could move…but he'd made that mistake once too often, and worked out the details now. If he attempted to speak or even twitch, another white angel would descend and smack him with a hammer, sending him to hell.

Maybe not to hell. Perhaps, only into darkness, and he was rising, enough to grasp the details. If he moved, if he uttered a sound, an angel of mercy would arrive with a loaded syringe and send him into oblivion. Safer, much safer to lie perfectly still and focus exclusively on the face of an angel, his angel.

Kelly Mulden. The name came to him. A blinding epiphany to start his thoughts turning, his mind waking.

He lay on a hospital bed, in a vaguely familiar room, and in fleeting moments, he recognized the face of his mother, wondering if angels worried in heaven. She appeared worried with her knitted brow and damp eyes, her lips curved in a strained smile. Weird dream. More weird when reality struck and his senses swayed with the revelations. His mother wasn't meeting him at the heavenly gates. She stood in this room, as solid as the walls, as material as the IV tree hovering over his right shoulder. If he moved, he could make her disappear under a morphine fog, but he had a sense of something else he needed to grasp. And he wasn't a child. He needed to be awake.

Again and again, he saw Edna crumpled against the steel gray door, and no amount of mental tag erased that reality. Edna had shot him. The evidence burned at his center, threatening to awaken beneath the fog. With every ounce of willpower, he refrained from moving and slicing fire through his side. She'd shot him, and shot herself... at the sight of Marilyn Patterson materializing in the doorway.

Steadily, he rose from the raft, breaking through the fog and collecting the details of his last waking moments. He was not a child, not in need of drugged oblivion to remain still as his mind cleared, analyzing the visions and sifting through the recorded data before those moments in the basement.

How long he'd lain as still as a sculpt, he wasn't certain. Distantly, familiar sounds echoed through the corridors. They breached the closed doors, enough to know he remained somewhere in the Home, and this once, it wasn't either Kelly Mulden or Marilyn Patterson hovering above him. This time, the bearded face tilted at an angle to look down at him, studying him far more intently through familiar hazel eyes.

"How long, Kip?" JD asked in a careful tone. "How long have you been awake?"

"Long enough to ask," his voice cracked, croaking with the dryness. "For a drink ... and settle for water."

"Christ, it's good to hear you," JD idled. "But you probably need pain—"

"Water—JD," Kip rasped through sandpaper, starkly aware of bands on his wrists and chest, holding him still beneath the rise and fall of his breath. "No drugs."

"You really are awake—"

"Yes... And prefer to stay awake."

"Do you remember what happened?" JD asked carefully, not moving from his casual lean on his forearms on the iron rail.

"Edna," Kip confirmed, barely twitching a nod, blinking. "She ... she's dead."

Sorrow flashed in his eyes and tightened his grim smile. "Yeah, buddy. She ... shit. How much of this do you really remember? Do you remember going into the basement?"

"You were there, Tried to stop her, too," Kip confirmed.

"She was sick, pal. Probably for a helluva long time."

"She ... she killed ... several people."

"Yeah, she did," JD said grimly. "Maybe more than we even know about."

"I need ... to sit up."

"If I turn you loose, I'm liable to get booted out of here."

"Then find Mark Frances...and don't let anybody snow me under until he comes."

"I should probably get your uh ... your mom in here—"

"No," Kip said firmly. "Not ready for her. Just get Mark. And some f'n water," he croaked against the dryness in his throat.

"All right. Give me a minute."

In the interim, Kip closed his eyes, playing the wicked reel of film in his mind's eye. Edna, behind the bright beam, the gun wavering in her grip, the blast. She'd truly meant to kill him. but the reasons seemed too convoluted even in his woke state. Crazy, without a doubt, but crazy like a fox, intending to frame him, just as she'd framed him years ago.

Shaking only his head in denial, he froze at the sound of soles scuffing the tile floor, and his eyes shot open to find Mark Frances halting at the rail.

"Damnit!" Mark started, intending to turn.

"Stop," Kip croaked, and the *good doctor* halted, surprise etched in his dark blue eyes. "I no longer freak in hospitals," he strained. "Or panic over your title."

"You're awake. Fully," Mark grasped on the instant, relying on his own sixth sense.

The color was there, in his aura, the brilliant purple and indigo hues swirling and enhanced by the *good* doctor's concentration. Upon a time, those colors had scared the hell out of a little boy who hadn't fully grasped the meaning of the colors. The man understood, and a faint smile haunted his lips. "I don't need snowed under any more. Learned to cope, Mark. I could use some Tylenol."

The bearded lips quivered, the smile erupted. "Maybe something just a little stronger. I don't know what all you remember, but you're still in serious condition."

"Mm hmm, shot," he managed. "Remove the toseola, Mark. I won't come un-fucking-glued ... and maybe a Percocet if you're offering. Starting to hurt some."

"Christ, it's good to have you back, buddy," Mark huffed, and things moved more quickly then.

Shooting orders over his shoulder, Mark began personally removing the restraints, and in mere seconds—or so it seemed—the restraints disappeared and the bed lifted into a twenty-degree incline. Alas, a Styrofoam cup of water arrived, and Mark personally held the straw, cautioning. "Just a few swallows to start, Kip. You have close to a hundred stitches between your intestines, kidney, and liver. You really aren't out of the woods yet."

"Don't snow me under," Kip said more firmly, clearly.

"Don't give me a reason," Mark countered smoothly.

"Deal," Kip agreed, already suffering a strange weariness and sway in his mind. The mere glimpse of his mother—corporeal—stepping into the room sent his senses reeling, altering his equilibrium. Closing his eyes, tilting his head on the flimsy pillow, he succeeded in shutting out reality and dropping into a shallow sleep. Still, he understood the soft voices, the anxious words. His mother was alive; Edna was dead.

Kelly Mulden was here, covering his hand at his waist and sending odd tingles through his veins.

With everything inside of him gathered beneath the surface, he refrained from responding, positive of only one thing within the shallow awareness—if he cared for her at all, he needed to let her go. That revelation hadn't changed. If anything, Edna's final act and words only firmed the decision in his mind. He wasn't a person who could give her happiness. He'd decided long ago, he'd been born under a dark cloud, destined to destroy everything—everyone—he touched. Even his own mothers.

Kelly knew the instant Kip fell into a sound sleep, but she remained several moments longer, watching him and confirming what Dr. Frances had announced a short time ago. Kip was officially removed from the critical condition list, although he wasn't entirely out of the woods yet. The next several days were still crucial to his recovery, with a steady flow of antibiotics and pain medication on the roster.

With a lighter heart, Kelly met JD in the comfortable waiting room and shared the relief awash on his weary face. One long blasted night, she considered as she glanced at the Regulator clock. One night and half a day, she corrected.

"What do you say, sis, we go home for a while?" JD suggested. "I could use a couple hours on a mattress rather than that recliner. And you look about out on your feet."

"Sounds good," she agreed and barely glanced in search of her bag before remembering, their parents had taken it with them a few hours earlier. She'd refused to leave, and no one had pushed the issue. Like Marilyn and Denton McDaniels, who sprawled on the recliner, dozing for the first time, Kelly had remained, and JD had offered to stay with her when suggesting their folks head home for a while, although he'd claimed he needed to stay for official reasons.

He hadn't lied. Between visits to the private room, JD handled a multitude of official business, including speaking with local and federal authorities, directing a team of crime scene technicians, and likely consulting with the coroner. Marilyn had handled the arrangements for Edna, and Kelly had overheard the mention of a quiet, private service already scheduled for two days after Christmas. An autopsy wasn't necessary, nor any further investigation, as the cause of death was obvious and several officials had witnessed the entire ordeal. The powers that be, however, insisted on following the regulations regarding violent death. JD had offered an official written report to add to Ed Cartel's reports.

Walking through the quiet carpeted corridor, Kelly looked over to see JD stifling a yawn. He looked as tired as she felt, but no worse for wear. "JD...? Thanks."

Surprise etched across his brow. "For?"

She shrugged, "Being his friend, being my brother, staying with me."

"I had stuff to do—"

"Which you finished hours ago," she mused. "So thanks."

Smirking, he resigned, "You're welcome." Barely pausing, he wondered, "Are you okay to drive or do you want to ride with me and come back later for your wheels?"

"I can drive, and we could come back later in one car."

Disoriented, Kelly strode into the lobby, wondering how the hell everything could seem so normal and natural after the past dozen hours. Or maybe not normal exactly. Other than another receptionist, a silver-haired elderly woman, no one occupied the immense foyer. After the chaos of the past evening, she almost expected a barrage of reporters and authority figures camped in the entrance. "No press," she said absently while pulling on her thick coat, noticing another 'closed' sign hung on the smoked glass doors. On JD, her attention pivoted. "Tell me you handled that, too?"

"Didn't have to," he admitted. "Chief Cartel and a couple FBI agents held a press conference early this morning. Officially, the shooting was listed as a domestic dispute with an attempted murder/suicide. Most of the details are already buried."

"What about Marilyn's return?"

"That's a little more sticky. Right now, though, no one beyond those immediately involved is privy to her return."

He held the first glass door for her, and Kelly managed the second set, only vaguely aware of the fine flakes fluttering against her cheeks. "How's that even possible, JD? I'd think that would make national headlines."

"In New York or Chicago, maybe." He shrugged, smirking. "This is little old Randall." Unconsciously, he touched her elbow, offering her an added measure of safety on the steps, though it wasn't necessary.

Business as usual. The walks were salted against the onslaught of falling snow; the parking lot was wet. Not all of last week's snowfall had melted or dispersed under yesterday's rain. A gray mantle of iced snow covered the hillside and most of the bushes. They barely parted, with Kelly heading for her car in the visitor's area and JD heading for the employee lot, when they glanced toward the sound of a car door opening.

Her attention landed on the familiar blue Datsun and dark coat emerging from the driver's door. The car windshield was clean and wet, the wipers apparently keeping up with the snowfall with the help of the running engine. In a flash, the past evening rushed across Kelly's mind, waking her to the possibilities. JD might not know about Richard's half-assed assault—

"Goddamn it," his voice lowered to a deadly pitch, and Kelly needed only a flash to realize Jason King had likely enlightened him at some point during the night.

"Kelly," Richard said in a morose, hurried tone as he started across an empty span of pavement. "Please, darling, I just need to—"

Cutting, JD spoke as he veered to intercept the visitor. "You just don't know when the hell to quit, do you, asshole."

Richard halted, stuffing his hands in his pockets and adopting the least aggressive pose he could manage—and still appeared so blasted arrogant. "Kelly, please. I just want to apologize for last night. I know you must think me a cad."

Annoyed, more than either worried or angry, Kelly caught up to JD, halting him by his biceps. "Hang on, JD. I think I need to deal with this myself."

JD considered momentarily, his green eyes turned near emerald as he agreed tentatively, leaving no doubt how this would end if Richard acted a step out of line. "Five minutes, Kell."

She nodded and continued forward, meeting Richard halfway and leaving two arm's length between them. "Talk," she stated simply and glimpsed the annoyance in his brown eyes.

"I know I came on a little strong last night," he began timidly, but his bloodshot eyes betrayed him. "I'm afraid I might have said some things to offend you, darling, but I just—I can't stand the thought of losing you. I know it's no excuse, but I was in the hotel bar, and I had—Maybe I had one too many. And Christmas carols were playing. Surely, you know how I get when I'm tired. I just—"

"Stop there, Richard," she said flatly. "I'm sick and tired of your excuses and apologies, and you thinking that as long as you keep apologizing, I'll forgive you." Not awaiting his response, though he parted his lips, she continued, "For the last time, I am not marrying you. I wouldn't marry you now, or ever, if you were the last man on earth. You are a pompous, arrogant ass, and I can honestly say, I'm tired of making excuses for you or your holier-than-thou attitude. I am not, and have never been, a *showgirl*, or whatever other lewd ideas you may have about me. And I'm not the stupid bimbo you apparently want for a wife. Last night was probably the most honest you've ever been—"

He took a step forward, lifting his hands from his pockets as if preparing to scrub. "Sweetheart, please—we can work this out. It's natural for engaged couples to have second thoughts—"

"God, you truly don't listen to me, or hear a single word I say to you," she said, dumbfounded as she backed a step. "Listen carefully, Richard. The wedding is off. I am not marrying you. Frankly, I never want to see you again."

"Darling, you just don't understand," he placated, besieging. "I just can't stand the thought of you throwing your life away––our life away. I came here last night just to speak to you. Then, after seeing all this," he swept his hand to span the Home, adding a scathing glance. "I can understand you being drawn in by this. Your infatuation. I'm sure he's promised you the world, but surely you can see he's just using you—"

"Two minutes, Kell," JD spoke casually, and Kelly sensed him moving a step or two closer.

"You really are an asshole, Richard," she said wearily.

"I know I'm saying this all wrong," he tried. "But I love you, darling. I want—"

"I really don't give a fuck what you want, Richard," she said as she took a step forward. "What *I* want is you out of my life. Now and forever. Run home to your mommy and daddy doctors, and whine to them about what you want. I'm sure they can buy you a hooker to fulfill your mommy fantasies. I'm sick to death of catering to your sooo-important needs. Just go back to Baltimore and stay the hell away from me."

"Darling—"

JD stepped forward. "Mr. Whitman, your time is up," he said simply and dipped his hands in his pocket. By Richard's widening eyes and stumbling backwards, he must have thought JD was pulling a gun. Instead, JD produced his wallet and flipped open his official badge. "Consider this a warning. If I catch you anywhere near my sister—and that includes anywhere in Randall—or I hear you're hanging around her studio in

Baltimore, I'll have you arrested for harassment and stalking. Those charges will not look good on your resume, Dr. Whitman, and I can assure you, I'll see that they stick. This is a federal badge, not local or state. It would behoove you to get in your car and beat feet out of here, or I might incline to incur those charges immediately with an added charge of assault and attempted abduction. I have more than one witness who came forward about your attack last night. So do bear that in mind. And I probably should mention, that entire episode was caught on tape. It was pretty obvious you didn't intend a friendly chat."

Kelly had watched, as impressed by JD's calm presentation as she was surprised at how quickly the fear erupted in Richard's bloodshot eyes. An official charge—any of those official charges—would seriously alter his plans for his future, and just the threat of those blemishes on his stellar reputation would change his course.

"Should I continue, Mr. Whitman, or would you like some help to get to your car?"

"I-I—"

"Here in Randall, or in Baltimore, Mr. Whitman. I'll see you behind bars if I even think you're bothering my sister again."

Richard backed another step, flashing an incredulous glance to Kelly, starting, "I can't believe you're letting him threaten me—"

"Mr. Whitman," JD interceded calmly. "This is not a threat. You may consider this a promise. And if my sister wasn't so weary from staying up half the night worrying about a man who does love her, I'd escort her down to the local precinct and have her file the official charges right now. I suggest you turn around, march over there to your car, and get moving before she gets her second wind."

Richard didn't exactly march. More like stomped after he clenched his jaw and swung about.

For a half second, Kelly felt sorry for him, but the feeling passed. How could she have been so foolish as to fall for his poor puppy-dog expressions and pouting apologies? Shaking her head, straining to withhold angry tears, she avoided JD's glance a half second too late.

"Kell," he spoke as she turned away, halting her. "Please tell me I didn't just run off the love of your life."

Despite her self-loathing, she huffed a bitter laugh and shook her head. "Not hardly, JD. I just can't believe I fell for all his bullshit. I really thought I was smarter than that. I just—" She met his gaze, thinking about Kip and the words he'd spoken last night when giving her a send-off. "I just can't seem to get this right," she blurted and meant to continue her turn.

"Kell," JD stopped her again with his quiet, deep tone, and she found him through a blur. "What I said to that asshole, about Kip loving you. It. It wasn't a lie or a ruse. Last night, when he thought he was dying––hell, we both thought he was dying," He corrected. "He found breath and sense to ask me to tell you that he loved you. And sis, I know those aren't words he's ever spoken to another. For what it's worth, if you decide to pursue him, you have my blessing. He can be an asshole, but he's still one of the most decent men I've ever known."

"I..." She didn't know what to say; instead, she launched the few steps into JD's embrace. When she could find her voice, she managed, "Thank you again, big brother."

Chapter 25

Fresh snow collected on the bushes, nearly two inches thick on the railing outside. Only flurries still drifted beyond the porch roof, and those might have been blown off the pitched roofs. Further across the white lawn, a sprinkle of sunlight tried breaking through the barren branches of the Elms along the driveway. Wet salted pavement shimmered more like ice than asphalt, trailing away toward the stone pillars. On the stone pillars, his gaze halted momentarily, then drifted further to watch two tiny snow-suited bodies rolling across a span of white lawn beyond the highway barrier. Loneliness reared its ugly head, curling about his chest more painful than Jim Sheffield and Mark Frances's handiwork. Unconsciously tipping his head to cup a flame to a cigarette, Kip drew an unhealthy drag of smoke as his attention drifted across the white lawn.

'...A good place to heal old wounds.' One of his mothers had told him, though he couldn't identify the voice speaking in his mind. 'Whistlebrook has always been a good place to heal old wounds.'

Or to open new ones, Kip might add, now, as the winter wonderland evaporated to an image of Edna Feeney's silhouette launching backward, slamming, and sinking down the gray door. A sting of tears gathered in his eyes. He continued to gaze vacantly through the glass, feeling a chill wrapping around him, a shiver coursing down his spine. He hadn't cried at her funeral. Against Mark's wishes, he'd stood silently through the brief service as he'd stood through countless others. His mother's soft perfume flavored the air, more potent than the collection of flowers around the casket. Marilyn Patterson hadn't stood in the small crowd in Fitzpatrick's, but she'd rested in John Fitzpatrick's office.

'Damn her. Just damn her,' Kip might have uttered aloud.

"Are you ever going to speak to me again, Kippen?"

Even after a week, her voice still created a disorienting sway in his mind. A week ago, painkillers might have magnified the effect, but Kip was no longer floating on morphine, and a single Percocet couldn't alter his perception. She was alive. She stood somewhere not far behind him, and if he turned, he would read the pain and sorrow etched in every fine line of her still lovely face. No longer could he believe her image an ethereal mirage arriving to escort him on his final journey. With his mind clearing rapidly, he understood the extent of her deception, the details and explanations which Mark, JD, John Madison, and even Frank Culver had repeatedly outlined for him to solidify his mother's image.

She'd staged her death with the aid of John Fitzpatrick and Frank Culver. No others had known. With her vast knowledge of drugs, she'd contrived her own failing health and her inevitable death. With the aid of drugs, she'd fooled even the good doctor Frances enough to sign her death certificate, one which had mysteriously disappeared before becoming an official or recorded document. In the comfort of Frank Culver's domicile over the garage, she watched the cameras and listened to the chaos abounding in the home. And what a laugh they must have shared when Frank returned each evening with his updates. Kip could just imagine her reclining in one of Frank's masculine leather chairs, sipping coffee, nibbling on a pastry ... her lovely face a masterpiece of post-mortem poise, her soft blue eyes touched with amusement... And all the while, he'd swam in a wicked daze holding his heart in his hand and his stomach in his throat—thanks to Edna's little additions to the cups of tea and gelatin dishes she served him throughout those three horrid days. Marilyn was alive and well, and her little charade had nearly killed him—mentally and physically.

"Kip, I'd beg your forgiveness a million times if I thought it would help," she said softly. "I know the pain and horror I've caused you. God knows, it's a horror I'll carry with me for the rest of my life." Her voice wavered, thick with pain. Whether she thought of him, now, or Edna's demise—a by-product of her treachery—was anyone's guess. "I-I just couldn't think of any other way to bring you here. God forgive me, darling, I never wanted to believe you were responsible for those deaths fifteen years ago, but I never knew you well enough to be certain. I needed you here, but not if it meant I'd lose you either to insanity or prison. I tried, darling, I've tried for fifteen years to learn who was responsible for those crimes. I never suspected... God forgive me, I never suspected Edna, not even for a moment. She was like a sister to me. More your mother than I could ever claim to be."

"I'm leaving this afternoon," Kip said without affect. His gaze trailed across the white lawn, watching a whirlpool of white dust spinning against a thick elm trunk not too far from the porch. Unconsciously, he dropped cigarette ash into the crystal tray on the ledge. "I suggest you write another Will—a single Will and leave your entire estate to your choice of charities. Donate Whistlebrook to the state if that's your choice. Do not attach my name to any segment of your life—not in life or death, Mrs. Patterson, and do not attempt to contact me for any reason—"

"I understand your anger," she started in a strained voice.

"Do you really?" he said as he turned slowly and locked his vacant gaze on her watery blue eyes. A ripple of disbelief fluttered across his mind. In his mind, he saw her likeness on a photo, tucked into that ancient black book.

"I-I should have known you better. I should h-have trusted you." Her softly lined face pulled taut with pain; her drowning eyes emanated a depth of sorrow he'd never seen in his life. How frail she appeared suddenly—so worn and drawn—so desperate. "I-I *still* don't know you," she pleaded softly. "I'd so imagined this differently. Is it foolish that I thought you'd be overjoyed to find me alive? That you could truly love me enough to forgive me? That you might have found you didn't hate me as badly as it seemed over these many years? You're," she paused to choke on a lump and swallow, clearing her strained voice as her eyes darted over his face, searching. "You're standing there looking through me—as you've *always* looked through me. And oh, what you must be thinking to wear such a blank expression ... the things you must think."

Her hand fluttered to catch a tear rolling down her drawn cheek. Even at her age, her hands moved with a grace and elegance unparalleled by any of the elderly he'd ever known. Her salt and pepper dark hair, shoulder length, rested back from her face, held off to one side in a flowered comb. Soft curls lay on one small shoulder, defying her age, and a halo of sallow red and swirling yellow bespoke of her fatigue and high anxiety. When she looked at him again, her blue eyes had cleared of tears. Sorrow and pain—regret—shadowed the usual luster. "You truly do hate me. You hate me for every moment of your life, and I never fully realized how badly I'd hurt you until listening and hearing your voice through those wiretaps." She paused only a heartbeat, her gaze steadier than ever he remembered.

"I wanted to believe—needed to believe that somewhere in your heart, you could forgive me for the life I forced you to live, for the grief I've caused you, for the lies I've forced you to believe over all these years. I prayed that I'd not destroyed you—that I'd find out once and for all that we still had a chance to become mother and son." Resignation echoed in a familiar sigh; her eyes strayed over her desk and chair, her shoulders sagged only slightly as she focused on him. "I suppose if wishes were horses, beggars would ride." A sad smile touched her pink lips. "The papers you signed, Kippen," she said quietly. "Whistlebrook is yours, now. If you feel you must put it on the open market and liquidate the assets you inherited, that is your choice.

The transfer of ownership was legitimate regardless of the outcome of this event."

"I'm sure John Madison will be more than happy to reverse the transfers," Kip said vacantly. "Have him reinstate your name. I'll be more than happy to sign—"

"I-I suppose, in my heart, I knew you weren't responsible for any crimes, darling. Whistlebrook is yours," she said wearily. "Do what you will with it. I've kept a few bonds to maintain a modest retirement. As much as I dreamed of seeing you behind that desk and reveling in the changes you'd make," she paused, a flicker of a smile touched her eyes as she glimpsed the window. "I'd never thought of opening the walls and inserting a terrarium..." Amusement drained into dread as she continued, "I'll be leaving Randall, dear. I won't interfere with whatever decisions you make concerning the Home or your life. If you ever need me or find it in your heart to forgive me, you'll find me in Boston. I so love to watch the surf slamming into rocks..." Her eyes watered as she continued searching his face through a blur. "Hate me if you must, darling, but don't live your life alone and bitter as you have these many years—not because of my mistakes," she paused only a second, her expression torn with pain. "Goodbye, darling."

Watching her start to turn, Kip asked, "Why, damn you?" She stopped in a half turn, and her drowning eyes lifted to him. "Why didn't you *once* just ask me to come home?"

For a moment, she looked as if she might pivot and race away as she had a thousand times in his memory. Instead, she whispered in a strangled soft voice, "Would you have come, Kippen? If I'd asked you—or *begged* you—would you have come?"

How many times had he asked himself that same question? How many times had he battled himself for that answer while searching for answers in her menagerie of deceptions? More often than he could count, he realized as his vacant gaze fell from her strained, waiting face. Before that Will, before the option had stopped him, he'd planned to pack and board a plane to California. He wouldn't have remained in the Home any longer than necessary. In the event of his inheritance, he'd intended to have John Madison handle the immediate sale and liquidation of Whistlebrook. He never once considered remaining to take the helm, to control the castle, to open all the old wounds and haunts of his childhood. If not for the paper chase she created for him, he would have returned to California and placed Marilyn Patterson's abstract photograph in an abstract book—never consciously realizing why he always envisioned that black silk binder in his mind after a funeral. All the black spots would have remained forever in the dark recesses of his mind... as dead to him as the emotions he forced into that book a lifetime ago. If she'd asked him to come home, he knew abruptly, he would have denied her that single pleasure ... and might never have known why.

"I didn't think so," she said softly and turned, coming to him. Touching his arm, she drew his blind focus. "I needed you here, darling. I wanted you here more than life itself, but nothing short of my death would have brought you back. I couldn't ask, and I couldn't demand. I made that mistake years ago, and the day you walked out of this office ... You were just thirteen, and the anger in your eyes shocked me to the core. I tried to make myself believe it was a child's anger, that you'd eventually forgive me for sending you away, that you'd eventually realize I sent you away out of love... and not just a little fear. I didn't know what was happening to you, darling. I knew only that you'd lost weight. You hated Randall High even before that incident in the school... I wanted you to learn to live, darling. I wanted you to be around boys your own age. I wanted you to be happy."

"You believed I was a murderer," he said without affect.

"I believed you might have acted out of compassion," she said quietly. "At the cost of your own physical and mental health, darling, yes, I believed you could have helped a few of our terminally ill residents on their final journey and taken it upon your shoulders to free them from their struggle with life and death. I never loved you any less for that possibility. I can't tell you how many times I've stood in one of the rooms wishing I had the courage to turn a knob and stop the pain… but then, I suppose I don't need to tell you that.

"I remember when you were very small—no more than three—I'd carry you with me when I went through the wards." A faint reflective smile touched her lips and eyes. "Probably one of my first mistakes—believing you weren't old enough to understand what you were seeing. I should have known then that you were far more perceptive than I could ever hope to be … You always reached out to them. You wouldn't be satisfied until you touched their hands or stroked their faces. Even then, you possessed a natural gift to calm them, to put their fears to rest, and bring smiles to their frail faces. You loved them, and by the time I tried keeping you from the wards, it was too late. You'd sneak off to make your own rounds, and I don't think it was ever a coincidence—you always lingered a little longer with those who wouldn't be with us much longer."

Her eyes misted, shifting away in reflection. "I remember once, you couldn't have been more than six or seven. I found you standing on your toes alongside a bed in the East Wing. You were holding a patient's hand, and I don't remember your words, but I remember you wouldn't let go of that hand. You stood holding that hand until the resident passed away, then you ran from the room. I found you later asleep on Irish's lap."

Sighing, she looked into him, sadness lingering in her eyes. "I didn't know how to change our life, Kip. I thought about selling Whistlebrook a million times or more, but I couldn't do it. They were as much my family as you were… and every time I decided to sell, another arrived. I never had a family or a real home, darling. My father sent me away when I was still a child. I lived with my mother's relatives in Boston, and I came to realize they blamed my father for my mother's early demise. They blamed me as well. As soon as I was old enough, I joined a traveling dance troupe. I married young and became a young widow. By the time I met your father,

I was a bitter woman—successful, but bitter—and falling in love with him...? I suppose, strangely, I felt safe falling for him because he was a married man. I knew he'd never divorce his sickly wife and that certainly had its advantages since I had no intention of becoming a married woman for the second time. Any more than I planned to be a mother and put a child through the struggles I'd endured. I was a great one for fantasizing about what it would have been like if Hans were alive. I imagined a white picket fence and a modest little house." She smiled sadly. "If anyone had told me I'd become the mistress of this monstrosity, I'd have outright died laughing."

Her hand denting his jacket sleeve, she continued in a sobering tone. "As much as I know you hate me for what I've put you through, I should tell you, I didn't exactly conceive this deception on my own. When I arrived here thirty years ago, I found my aged father dying and the Home in serious financial distress. Frankly, dear, I merely recreated a crime that I uncovered thirty years ago. Our residents were not quite as frail then. Frankly, your grandfather was the oldest resident, very nearly senile by the time I arrived, and he was being robbed blind by his staff. I came here alone, and I was surrounded by deceit... I came very close to losing everything before weeding out the bad apples, beginning with my father's legal advisors, before finding John Madison...

"Honestly, darling, even if I'd wanted to take you away from here, I wouldn't have been able to give you a decent life. Within months, most of my profits from selling my studio had been eaten up by this white elephant. It took several years to straighten out the books and files and begin turning a profit, where I might have afforded to give you a real life. By that time, I was over forty... far too old to open a new dance studio, and that was the only other life I knew. I couldn't very well have become someone's secretary, and I would have needed to work to support both of us," she sighed, her focus trailing off him and canvassing the furnishings of her office.

"Ironic," she said after a moment, lifting her damp eyes. "I'd trade every moment I spent in this office for the chance to go back and become only your mother all over again. I might even try becoming a secretary or a cleaning woman, if I knew what I know now, but life doesn't quite work out the way we think it should. God knows, I'd have probably found a million more ways to alienate you even if the circumstances had been different. With time to think these past few weeks, I've come to realize I probably buried myself in work simply because you scared the hell out of me. I never knew how to be a mother. Good Lord, at thirty-five, the last thing I ever imagined was becoming a mother, much less a single mother. Times have certainly changed." Despite her stab at a smile, sadness lingered in her eyes as her hand slipped tentatively off his shoulder and lifted, touching down lightly on his hair, brushing an unruly wave over his ear.

"Do you know," he started in a low voice, halting her hand as if he might have bitten her. Only vaguely, he realized his dry throat and a faint tremor rolling through his taut muscles. Swallowing, he forced himself to begin again. "Do you know how long I've waited for that story? For *any* story to explain why you were so inclined to run from me?" he asked quietly. "By the time you sent me away, I was afraid to ask you for a time-check for fear of chasing you off on some urgent errand. I came to my own conclusions eventually, not the least of which you contradicted when you sent me to live a life of celibacy. Frankly, I came to believe you couldn't stand the sight of me, much less the sound of my voice."

Pain etched across her brow and swelled in her eyes. "I never knew how to speak to you, darling. I feared that if you found out the truth about your past, your real father, that you'd never forgive me. You were so—so damned vulnerable—and I feared I was responsible for that. I—I wanted to confront you. Always meant to tell you the truth when you were old enough to reason with. I hated living a lie."

Unwittingly, Edna's words flashed through his mind, wrenching his stomach. 'She was going to tell you... ruin your life...' "Edna stopped you," he said vacantly.

"God help me, as much as I know I'll miss her, as much as I know she was sick, I hate her," Marilyn hissed softly. "I hate her—and myself—for being such a fool and letting her come between us. If—if just once, I'd taken a good long look at how she captivated you from that very first day..." She sighed heavily, shaking her head as her hand skidded down his biceps and paused on his elbow. "I always believed she was good for you, that she was giving you things I couldn't possibly give you, and she came at a time when I dearly needed a friend and ally. I never once bothered to investigate her past. I never doubted her story about a husband and son." Her soft humph carried a bitter note. "Even now, I don't know which of John Madison's partners she had an affair with, or which one brought her here for an abortion. Or if it was just another twisted lie—a fantasy—like the fantasy she created when she spoke to you in her room. I should have suspected her that evening. I sat in Frank's apartment, wondering why she was lying to you, and I still didn't suspect her of a single crime."

At the mention of Frank's apartment, Kip experienced a flutter of anger through his system. While he'd been driving himself crazy searching for a conspiracy, she'd rested comfortably ensconced not more than six hundred feet from the kitchen door, listening to every audible aspect of his three-day blitz.

Unconsciously, he sidled from under her touch and backed a step to lean against the window frame. He hadn't lied to JD Mulden, after all. Marilyn Patterson had bugged her own office, along with every other room in the executive wing. Only after he'd made those calls from her private line had she enlisted Frank to replace the room bug with the wiretap. And when he removed the bug from her office phone, she'd enlisted Frank to plant a bug in the transistor that Frank had easily convinced Kip to carry around in his pocket.

'...Such a clever thing...' Edna's words echoed regarding Marilyn, and Kip nearly inclined to tell her, *You didn't know the half of it, mum.*

"Damn it," he muttered and flashed an angry glance at his mother before turning his attention to lighting another cigarette.

"I'm sorry, darling," she said quietly. "I-I do know how you felt about Edna, and I shouldn't speak ill of the dead, but damn it, Kippen, she betrayed us—both of us." Retracting her start of anger, she sidled to lean on her desk. Maybe intentionally, she put more distance between them, though she might truly need the desk for support. Her palms rested on the shiny top; her fingers gripped the wooden lip on either side of her hips. Her pleated wool skirt fanned over her knees, and as always, she wore a loose-fitting gray jacket with oversized pockets fit for carrying a wad of keys and her cigarette case.

If he listened, Kip might hear a clink of metal when she moved. Instead, he heard the click of a lighter, only vaguely aware of his butane igniting.

Breathing an audible sigh, she asked, "Since we seem to have reached a tentative detente, are there any other stories that you've waited too long to hear?"

None came readily to mind, and even her apparent willingness to divulge any answer—a ploy, no doubt, to maintain their detente—sent a wave of annoyance through his mind. He stood, needing the window ledge to stay afoot, his mind consumed in a nebulous as if he were the sole survivor of a natural disaster—an earthquake victim, perhaps, looking at the ruins of his house and life—and she leaned at the desk as cool as a cucumber, manipulating him, even now. Shaking his head with an exhale, he suffered a subtle twinge in his side and shifted his free left hand under his jacket. She'd gotten him shot—four people were dead—Janet Cross would spend the remainder of her life in a state prison after barely surviving Edna's attempt to poison her. Marilyn Patterson was considered deceased and so far, had made no public announcement to the contrary.

Only in Randall could she have pulled this off. Only in Randall, where she manipulated men like John Fitzpatrick and Frank Culver. Where she could swear Mark Frances, Capt. Ed Cartel, John Madison, and countless others who'd seen her a week earlier—including a DEA agent and several Federal agents—to secrecy. Legally, she'd broken no laws, never allowing her death to be legally documented, and even if the paparazzi caught wind of the story, she'd likely slant the tale to become the romantic heroine of this masquerade.

Despite himself, a faint grin crept into his mustached lips. As much as he wanted to truly despise her, how could he help but admire her? Maybe not only in Randall. God help Boston's elite if she carried out her threat to retire there, but only Marilyn Patterson could pull something like this and carry through to the last detail. "Damn it," he uttered.

"If there's something else bothering you, darling. I'd certainly try to clear it up for you," she offered hesitantly. "I've noticed, you do a great deal of private swearing when you're disturbed about something."

Oh, indeed, she'd remember hearing his absent cursing, a detail that had apparently annoyed Mulden in this very room. Shaking his head, he found himself wedged between annoyance and amusement. "You've certainly shattered my faith in private conversations," he said evenly and caught her worried eyes. "In fact, I may invest in a legitimate jamming device to keep on my person at all times, though I think I may try to find one with slightly less bulk."

"I won't apologize for the wiretaps, darling," she said smoothly without losing her concern. "Despite that unorthodox measure and my moral struggle over eavesdropping on your private world, it turned out to be a worthwhile precaution."

He understood her words well enough. Mark and JD had both tried convincing him that she held only his welfare at heart. Even Kelly, regardless of his effort to keep her at arm's length—which had damned near proven impossible when she stood within twenty feet of him—had attempted to reconcile him to his mother. If Marilyn hadn't eavesdropped, she might never have realized the defeat in his voice and decided to halt her deception. She might never have exposed herself to the Chief Cartel in Culver's apartment and sent an officer to stop Mulden in the parking lot; she and Cartel might never have seen Kip enter the back hall and followed him down the basement stairs. Thus, none of them would have stood outside the door when Edna began pouring out her story, along with her very real intentions of putting Kip out of what she deemed to be his misery.

Again, Kip considered his cluttered mind, all too easily feeling like a sole survivor—of the holocaust, perhaps, one not fully recovered from the trauma. "I really should hate you," he said in a dull tone as his focus cleared on his mother. "In just over two weeks, you've turned my life upside down, you've turned my past, my reality inside out, not to mention that I've just spent a full week in hell, part of it strapped to a goddamned hospital bed like a fucking lunatic. And you're standing there, looking absolutely no worse for the wear." He barely drew breath. "Goddamn it, what did I ever do to you to deserve all of this?"

"Maria Van Alt's School of Dance," she said quietly, only sadness in her eyes as she darted her gaze off his slightly startled eyes. Sighing, she focused steadily. "I suppose I should clarify that, or you'll surely think I've done all of this out of some warped need for revenge."

"By all means, clarify," he said dryly.

"I knew when you destroyed every memory of Maria Van Alt that you held me in contempt, that you hadn't put the past away, that unless I found a way to bring you back and allow you to vent your rage, you'd eventually turn your financial guns on Whistlebrook, and in so doing, might destroy the one thing in your life that you still loved. This was your Home, Kip. You were the Prince of Whistlebrook, as Irish dubbed you a very long time ago. I suppose, in all honesty, I simply wanted to give you Whistlebrook. But I wanted you to face your rage. Had I just given it to you, you would have turned it over to someone else or destroyed it without ever setting foot through the doors ... And years from now, you might realize what you'd lost. Compassion can be a curse, darling, and you were so filled with compassion before events turned you into a very bitter young man."

She paused momentarily, searching him. "I won't apologize for turning your world upside down. I think, despite everything, I've seen the first honest emotions in your eyes since you left here fifteen years ago. If you tear Whistlebrook down, now, you'll do so for reasons other than revenge or anger ... but honestly, darling, if you'll accept a little advice from someone who's been on this earth long enough to give it, you might consider sitting on the throne for a while before condemning the castle." With a faint smile, she pushed off the desk and came to him, lifting a hand to his arm. "You might also reconsider your indifference to Kelly, darling. She's such a lovely young woman, and she certainly is smitten with you."

Good God! Returned from the grave just over a week, and already she was trying to straighten out his love life? Not to mention, she'd heard every word he and Kelly had exchanged a week ago. "I am going back to my own life—my own world," he stated evenly. But he might not mind some company. *Damnit. She deserved better! And far more than a* one-night *or* few-month *stand!*

A subtle twinkle caught in his mother's soft blue eyes. She stood on her toes and brushed a swift kiss on his cheek. "Certainly, darling," she said as she slid away, patting his sleeve in assurance. "I'll see you before you leave then, darling. I have a few travel plans of my own to make." She started to turn, then paused with an afterthought. "You really should sit down, darling. Mark will be stopping by soon, and you did promise him you'd take it easy for a few more days."

Watching her walk toward the door, he suffered a quandary of distrust, positive he should bolt for the second door, leave his suitcases that he'd stopped here to collect, and board the first outgoing flight—destination unknown. She was up to something. He could feel it. She fully intended to manipulate him into staying, and that comment about Kelly Mulden...?

He certainly didn't need any help to question his blasted resolve. Just the thought of wrapping himself in her ethereal glow...

"Damnit," he uttered, turned, and dropped a long ash into the crystal tray on the window ledge. He understood his mother no more, now, than he had two weeks earlier. Lack of conversation was obviously not the only barrier between them. His gaze shifted through the glass, noting with disdain that it had begun to snow again, and he couldn't even remember why he'd detoured into this office on route to collect his luggage. Perhaps, he needed to look through this window once more and try to figure out what the hell happened a week ago. God knows, he felt like he'd missed something—like maybe the punch line of a joke ... or the meteor that crashed right before his eyes. "Shit."

At the buzzing sound on the desk, his muscles lurched, sending a shock wave tingling up his side. Cursing again, he turned and looked at the intercom button, doubting he wanted to answer that call. He let it buzz a half dozen times before moving forward and stabbing the button. "Yes?"

"Mr. Patterson?" Angie started nervously. "Sir, I hate to bother you, but there's a Mr. Louten out here—he'd like to see you."

Mr. Louten? The resident, *damnit*. "Send him in," Kip stated.

"Uh, sir? He went into the Oak Room. He asked if I'd ask you to meet him there. Something about his wheelchair on the carpet, I think."

"Fine," Kip said bluntly and released the button. He needed a reason to escape this office, and he probably owed Mr. Louten a proper thank you; after all, for whatever reason, the old man had tried to warn him of trouble. Inevitably, another of his mother's manipulations, but Kip couldn't hold Mr. Louten responsible for her deceit. Without a backward glance, he strode from the office, taking the shorter route to the lobby. Glimpsing Angie's smile—at him—he flashed a double-take. Perhaps he should be grateful she didn't jump out of her seat and run, but that smile only lent him greater cause to worry. Paranoia. If he'd suffered that condition before returning to Whistlebrook, he was close to a basket case now, searching for deceptions and conspiracies at every turn. He might never trust another single soul, if in fact, he ever had. . .

Lost in thought, Kip completed three steps into the Oak Room before the silent audience halted him abruptly. The baby grand erupted, and the quavering, rusty voices broke into song as Kip scanned the faces scattered about.

"For he's a Jolly Good Fellow..." Banners hung along the internal walls. Words ranged from 'Welcome Home' and 'Happy New Year' to 'Get Well Soon.' Marilyn Patterson had coerced them into this. She stood against the inside wall between Mark Frances and none other than Denton McDaniels. At one of the nearest tables, Mr. Louten smiled, but he wasn't alone. JD Mulden smiled somewhat smugly, though by a flashing side glance, he might be just a little preoccupied with the dark-haired Marion McDaniels-Smithfield, who smiled back at him even as she joined in the chorus. Along the inside wall, several of the kitchen staff and aides stood singing and fussing over a dozen filled trays of food ... and in a single glance, Kip knew he wouldn't likely try eating a single bite in Whistlebrook.

At the hand sliding under his jacket, he lurched, and half spun before his side pulled him to a jolted halt to find Kelly's amused eyes transforming into serious alarm. His nerves were shot, shot to hell as surely as his physical health. Backing away from her with a serious effort, he flashed an angry glance toward the trio on the wall, and already the voices had begun to falter, piano notes dwindling.

His name echoed from several directions at once, tones ranging from serious concern and alarm to honest surprise from JD's direction. His attention remained on his mother, seeing her perception dawning, her delight wavering into concern.

"This is not going to work," he stated in a dark, angry tone. "I'm not staying here. I am not taking over Whistlebrook, and if you so much as say another word to me, I'll not only have every resident thrown out on his ear, I'll have the whole fucking building dynamited before the end of the month—"

"Kip," Kelly stated sharply, drawing his angry gaze to her deep hazel eyes.

For an instant, his heart leapt with something other than pain. God, how he would love to—*no damn it*. He wasn't about to ruin her life, too! Too many losses! Too much pain already—

"She—she didn't put them up to this. They've all been so worried about you. This was my idea," Kelly said softly with a quiver in her lyrical voice, the start of moisture adding a shine to her eyes. Whether the twinkle of Christmas lights from the immense fir near the door, or an internal light sparkled, the colors prismed under her long lashes.

"And I sort of helped," Jason said from the doorway, looking as though he might block Kip's departure. And by Bill Bickerman's bold step alongside Jason, he might intend to assist.

"Actually, Kip, we all had a little hand in this," Bill said with a wary smile. "I know you and I haven't seen eye to eye, but as your assistant, I thought we might try starting over, and it is New Year's Eve Day. I couldn't see the harm in throwing you a welcome home party. The preparations did a lot for morale around here."

"Is that a fact?" Kip said in a monotone.

Mark Frances was the only one bold enough to step forward and stop a step in front of Kelly. "How bad did you pull your stitches with that stunt?" he asked simply.

"Not bad enough to stop me from passing through that door," Kip stated and sidestepped, turning and starting toward the two-man blockade. "Excuse me," he stated, leaving no doubt that neither a bullet hole nor a hundred stitches would stop him from moving either of them. When they stepped aside, he passed between them and strode toward the executive wing needing every ounce of his willpower to keep walking. Angie was no longer smiling. In fact, she appeared mortified and nearly jumped off her seat when he spoke. "Call me a cab and ring my mother's room when it arrives."

"Y-yes, sir," she stammered.

He was going home. Home to his own life. His world. If he tried, he could find a skyscraper in need of demolition, and that would just about satisfy his newest desire for destruction!

Epilogue

Lost in a desire for demolition, Kip only became aware of the body following him through the private corridor when he passed through the door marked PRIVATE and a hand halted the door from slamming in his wake. He turned enough to find JD's critical gaze. "Not one fucking word out of you either."

"Just a question," JD said as he stepped into the doorway and leaned casually against the frame. "How long do you intend to keep running from the past?"

"Not that it's any of your business, old friend, but I'm not running from a damned thing. I'm going back to my own life."

"Your life's here," Mulden said evenly. "You know it, even if you don't want to face it. I remember two weeks ago, sitting at the bar. You were sincerely pissed because you believed your mother wanted Bill to run the Home. What the hell do you want from her, old friend? A red carpet? She's gone to a helluva lot of trouble to get through that thick analytical brain of yours. So, it was a little rough going there for a while—but Goddamn it, man, she was right. You wouldn't have come back here if she'd gotten down on her knees and begged. You're so goddamned afraid of this place, you can't see straight.

"And I just don't get it—" JD hesitated as a strange light brightened in his eyes. "Or maybe it just hit me," he said abruptly. "Things really haven't changed much, have they, Kip? You're afraid of friendship—afraid you'll start to feel the pain of losing a friend ... afraid of having to mourn. It's not dying that scares you—It's death in general. It wiped you out as a kid, and it's still wiping you out."

"I can't spend the rest of my life mourning, goddamn it! Is that what you want to know? What you find so fucking incredible? That I can't handle another fifteen years—or fifteen minutes—mourning? Goddamn it, JD, is that so fucking hard to believe or understand?"

"You better do a little more serious thinking, Kip. And you might want to consider this long and hard before you make any major decisions about Whistlebrook's fate. You never asked to leave this Home. Your mother *sent* you away, and you've spent the last fifteen years hating her for that. So, who are you going to hate this time? And while you're at it, you better remember that before all that bullshit fifteen years ago, you *did* handle mourning. It was part of your life, a part you accepted no matter how many times you went through it. You accepted it, man," JD paused, his gaze steady. "And that's part of what sets you apart from anyone I'd ever met. You had your life together. This was your Home. Good or bad, you knew where you belonged, and if Edna hadn't interfered, you'd have been happy as hell to bide your time and take over here. You'd have stood at a thousand funerals if it meant you'd get to comfort that many elderly.

"Damnit, man, I did come here after you left. I spent a helluva lot of time shooting the breeze with Irish McGuire and trying to figure out what the hell happened. Maybe you were an arrogant shit to guys our own age, but you poured every ounce of yourself into your family, and these people were your family," he paused a heartbeat before continuing in a faintly annoyed voice. "So, you do what you want, old friend. Turn your back on your family. Convince yourself that death is the only thing you see when you look at those old faces, but I'll tell you, you're full of shit. You love each and every one of them, and it's not their death you're running from. It's their love—the same way you're running from my sister."

"I really don't like you a helluva lot," Kip said evenly.

"Yea? Think I've heard that before," JD said bluntly. "But then, in-laws aren't supposed to get along very well anyway."

"What the hell kind of life could I give her!" *Christ, did I say that?*

With a disgusted humph, Mulden pushed off the doorframe. "You really are so fucking smart, you're stupid," he commented. "But if you're asking for a suggestion, you might start by spending a few bucks on a ring, and you might want to build a modest house with a few extra bedrooms. You're probably going to start needing them about nine months after the wedding—" He stopped from a half turn and eyed Kip with a mocked sobriety. "And it better be nine *full* months, old friend, or I just might have to give you another bloody mouth or two."

"I can't give her a child," he said absently.

"Yeah? I'll believe that ten months after the wedding," Mulden said and started to turn into the hall. Something—someone—stopped him short. His face drained into a screwy innocence. "Uhhh—"

"I'm going to strangle you," a lyrical voice whispered into the room. "I really am."

Something other than fear accelerated Kip's heart, and an image of green eyes flashed into his mind even as JD's similar eyes looked in at him with a desperate innocence.

"I think she means it," he said evenly. "This might be a good time for you to rescue me for a change."

Hesitantly, Kip moved into the doorway and as he looked into Kelly's watery, angry eyes, an all-too-familiar rush of heat rose rapidly through his system. Had he taken a few extra seconds in the Oak Room, he couldn't have backed away from her. Even as his temper had flared beyond reason, he'd been drawn to her, and in an odd instant, JD appeared to be silhouetted against an intense white light.

Without consciously reaching the decision, like a miller to light, Kip sidled past JD and stepped into the dazzling white light, already drawn into her livid hazel eyes. "I'm not very good at apologies, luv," he managed, as he clasped her hands. "But I think I owe you a few hundred by now. Do you think we might just start over?"

"Only if you can honestly tell me that JD didn't pressure you into this," she said quietly.

"Who's he?" Kip asked as he tipped his head and tasted her lips, drawing her forward to lean against him before sliding his hands up her sleeves to rest on her shoulders. To his surprise, he realized his anticipation rising at light-speed as the warmth spread through him. Tipping his head, he whispered against her ear. "You really are beautiful, and if your offer still stands from a week ago, I wouldn't mind spending the next dozen or two years trying to decide if we're compatible."

She pulled back slightly and spied him, doubting, possibly hoping she'd heard him right, and her eyes sparked green fire. White light encompassed her ... a pure white light with rainbow glitter sparkling like tiny stars in a wild incandescent halo.

"I have a cab coming," he said quietly, looking down into her magnificent eyes. "How long would you need to pack for a warmer climate for about a week or two?"

"About ten minutes," she answered smoothly.

He considered for a second before realizing he wasn't cold for the first time in weeks. In fact, the temperature was rising quickly, and he could almost smell jasmine and earth scents. Strawberries and peppermint, too, he realized as he leaned into another kiss. A half hour for a cab? Ten minutes to pack? A few minutes or hours waiting for a flight south...? Deciding, he withdrew from the kiss, drawing her with him toward the PRIVATE door. His gaze slid down to the repaired lock, then lifted to JD's curious, mildly amused eyes. "Do me a favor, will you, old friend? Tip the cab driver well when he arrives and send him on his way. Ask

Caroline to book two seats on a flight for California—say between Sunday and Monday morning. Then keep that party going for an hour or two."

"My ulcer's flaring up again," JD growled.

"Have Jason get you an antacid on the house," Kip commented and backstepped into the room. Glancing down into Kelly's laughing eyes, Kip caught the door, deciding, "Better make it three hours, old friend, and put a bottle of antacid on my tab."

Maybe he'd found a cure for mourning after all, he considered while shoving the door closed on Mulden and looking into Kelly's livid hazel eyes. God knows, time hadn't healed all those old haunts...

'Whistlebrook has always been a good place to heal old wounds...' Mrs. Feeney's words echoed, and he found himself drawing Kelly against him as tremors rolled through him with the force of Edna's image resting on peach satin pillows. A black satin book opened inside his mind ... Family Album scrolled in gold embossed letters.

Exposure

Turn the page for a sneak peek!

Book Four

The beginning of the second Trilogy in The MacDade Brothers Mysteries!

Exposure

Chapter 1

Either winter had come early in the Blue Ridge or God frowned on her mission. Leaning forward, knuckles white on the steering wheel, Becca Sinclair could almost believe the latter. To either side of her Blazer, hazy apparitions wavered behind the white curtain, designating a tree or a briar bush. The blacktop had disappeared. Even if she wanted to turn around, she doubted she could manage a three-point turn without landing in a ditch, or worse, a gully.

"Just a little snowfall," Becca muttered, straining to focus between the wiper blades and thick flakes splattering the windshield. Just a few flakes, nothing to worry about. Six hours ago, she'd checked the national weather service. A little rain, snow flurries. Rain, she could handle. Snow, in moderation, on decent highways, would be a breeze. Traipsing through a blasted blizzard in unknown territory...? Searching for someone who might not want to be found...? Damn Alicia for putting them through this! And damn that bloodhound, Ms Vanburren, who had created the necessity! Someday, hopefully soon, Becca vowed to slap that temperance bitch and whoever had hired her. Whether she used a lawsuit or her hand remained the only question, but presently, her hostility toward Vanburren ran a close second to her disdain for meteorologists.

'Accumulation in the Midwestern states...'

Far more accurately than the professionals who were paid to make educated guesses, a tobacco-chewing gas attendant had mentioned, 'Wouldn't count on a dusting in the high country.'

"Radar tracking my—" *Ass!* "—butt," Becca corrected with a thought of the little man seated across from her.

"You see Santa, Aunt Becca?"

Glancing at the wide blue eyes studying her, Becca managed to smile. "Better keep looking, sweetie." Lucas Helms, four going on fourteen, forgot nothing, least of all a newscaster's stunt last Christmas suggesting that Santa's sleigh had been caught on radar. Between the snow and her mention of deer a few moments ago, he might fully believe they were nearing the North Pole.

Disappointed perhaps, Lucas resumed his vigil through the passenger window, straining against his seatbelt to see over the door panel. A little small for his age, he appeared even more fragile within the fuzzy collar and cuffs of his puffy winter jacket. Tussled from sleep, his white-blond curls sprang in erratic coils from his round pixie features. Physical size and delicate appearance were of no consequence. Lukes had more on the ball than most adults Becca knew, and to blasted hell with the system! Come hell or high water — or a blizzard — Becca intended to see this through for Lucas.

Far more determined, she downshifted to the lowest possible gear, peering through splatter in search of a marquee or main entrance. According to the blasted brochure, they should have reached the Lodge by now. 'Easy access to major highways,' the pamphlet had boasted.

Imagination? Or had the snow increased yet again, attempting to white out even the gauzy tree trunks to either side?

"Aunt Becca! A Weindeer!" Lucas shouted.

For an instant, Becca glimpsed a brown blur. Instinctively, she lifted her foot off the gas pedal, already touching the brake and pitching the gearshift into neutral as the animal romped into her path. A mistake! All four wheels slid on fresh snow as the animal brushed against the Blazer's front fender. Time slowed. Her hand swung, clasping a wad of Lucas's jacket and tugging as she shouted, "Get down!" If the animal came over the hood, through the windshield—! Every year, people die in just this situation! One-handed, Becca spun the wheel into the slide, her focus jetting. The animal pivoted away from the fender as tree trunks, so dim a moment ago, magnified a hundredfold. They were going to hit! Throwing herself sideways over Lucas, she braced for impact.

Endless, seemingly endless, the vehicle slid on its own slow momentum, the steady flip-flop of wipers and whirring engine amplified inside the car. Beneath her arms, she shielded the small body, praying his heavy coat would add protection, wishing she could fold him even smaller to cover him completely.

Jostling and bouncing, the Blazer skidded broadside off the blacktop. Weeds and branches scraped; the front end dipped and rocked. Seconds dragged into infinity before the stopped motion registered in Becca's racing mind.

With the first muffled sound beneath her, Becca shot upward, tugging Lucas from the fold. "You're okay!" she chanted as panic surged adrenaline through her veins at the sight of his wide blue eyes. "You're okay! You're okay!" No scrapes, no bruises! Not on his soft, round face. Her hands worked frantically, freeing his seatbelt, drawing him into her arms as she checked his denim-covered legs and boots.

"We w'ecked," Lucas uttered, likewise searching her face for damage.

Directly outside the passenger window, a tree trunk stood ominously close, possibly touching the door. Another stout trunk stood near the front right fender, but only spindly vines lay across the hood. Not broadside. They were not resting broadside. Through the white fuzz on the windshield, she spied another tree directly ahead of the left fender. They rested at a downward angle, neatly tucked between trees that had served as guideposts for the past half hour.

"Did we hurt him, Aunt Becca?" Lucas uttered while tipping his shaggy head, peering at her with a more worried frown on his soft, full lips. "Did we?"

In a quick scan over the shaggy blond head, Becca checked the immediate blanket of snow, hoping not to see the deer. No deer. "No, sweetie. I'm pretty sure he's just fine." Already, snow clung to the window at her side, and the wipers had wadded, barely clearing the splatters. Unless she could pull out of this ditch, they might not fare as well as the deer.

Fighting an internal panic, she forced a smile as she met his worried eyes. "I want you to sit here a moment. Okay, sweetie? I need to get out and see how badly we're stuck. Will you sit here for just a moment?"

"Yes, ma'am," he said quietly, letting her kiss his forehead and stroke his hair before he scooted and settled onto the passenger seat.

Hunkered down in the bucket seat, he appeared even smaller and vulnerable than usual, and for a moment, Becca could only look at him, her heart in her hands. After everything else in the past four months, nearly hitting a deer and skidding off the road in a blizzard seemed like an anticlimax in his busy mind. Too old, too weary, his blue eyes to study her. Reaching and scuffing his blond curls, heart aching, she pulled her coat closed to brave the elements.

As she tugged the door handle, the door nearly wrenched from her grip, torn by either the bracing wind off the slope or gravity, dragging her half off the seat. Slipping aground, she wrestled the door shut, already shivering as she pulled her hood over her head and stuffed her long blond strands under the fur.

She should have postponed this trip, regardless of how urgent it was. In another season, this mountainside probably produced a harvest of blackberries with the thick vines tangled around the wheels and snagging her jeans. Already, her ankle boots filled with snow as she trudged to the rear bumper. Ripped vines and snowy gouges marked the car's departure from the lane, in what appeared to be nearly a straight shot off a ledge. A steep straight shot. Too steep. If not for the vines...

She shook the image of an inverted car from her mind and drew a chilled breath, holding it a moment, praying to hear another engine or some sound of civilization. Other than the idling engine, the whistle-wind and her hammering heartbeat, nothing echoed within the serenity. Muttering a curse, she rounded the back bumper, spying the tires. At the right front fender, she halted, staring through the steady white streaks. Just past the tree trunk, the land plunged and vanished, but with the flakes and wind thickening, that could be an illusion. Drawing a calming breath, she assessed the size of the tree directly in her path, deciding that if she skidded while attempting to back out of the ditch, the wide trunk should hold them.

Already doubting her success, cursing the weather, cursing the reindeer, cursing even Santa Claus, Becca climbed into the car and stomped snow off her boots on the rubber mat. At least the car's heater worked. If they were stuck, they might remain inside until a plow truck or another hapless driver wandered along ... but if this was a blizzard, it could be days before a car came along. Even with a full tank of gas, she couldn't afford to wait that long.

Finding Lucas watching her worriedly, Becca forced a smile, attempting to keep her tone light. "Buckle up, sweetie. We could be in for another rocky ride."

"We're stuck, huh?" he asked simply, sounding more like himself than he'd sounded in several weeks, if not months.

"Hopefully not too," Becca answered while leaning to assist with his seatbelt. She'd never lied to him or deliberately attempted to deceive him. She wasn't about to start now. They were in a tight spot, and he knew it, which probably accounted for his sudden clarity of speech.

"Hold on, squirt," she said as she turned her attention to the steering wheel. Easing the gearshift into reverse, she twisted in the seat and touched the gas pedal lightly. All too swiftly, the tires spun, inching the car closer to the tree outside Lucas's door. "Come on, car..." she uttered as if she might coax the wheels to find traction. Instead, the car bucked and pitched. Relieving the gas, she drew a breath. They were not backing up the hill, and forward wasn't an option.

"Sit tight," she told Lucas while again bracing herself for the cold and climbing from the car. Slipping and sliding around the fenders, she inspected the position of all four wheels and verified the futility. They were not driving out of this predicament.

Running through a list of options, Becca returned to the warmth of the car. Either they remained in the vehicle and prayed for deliverance, or they started walking.

How much further could it be? According to the brochure, the Skyview Lodge was 'just ten minutes from State Rt. 652,' off which she'd turned more than a half hour earlier. Either she'd missed another turn, or the author of that claim had never driven this route in a blizzard. "Good thing we packed our snow gear, sweetie," Becca decided. "Looks like we're going for a hike."

Climbing into the backseat rather than standing in the snow, Becca rooted in the rear compartment as Lucas unfastened his seatbelt and climbed over the console to join her.

"We could make a snowman, Aunt Becca," he said with a hint of anticipation.

Becca smiled as she settled into the seat with her supplies. "We might need to save some of our energy for a little while, Dickens, but I promise, we'll make a snowman before this snow melts."

Satisfied, Lucas squirmed into the bulky snow pants, opening his ski jacket to fasten the straps over his shoulders. When Becca had bought the new suit a month ago, she hadn't counted on needing it this early in the season. The suit was a full size too large. Again, rooting in the open suitcase, she found a heavy sweater.

"Gonna be awful hot in all this," Lucas noted sagely as she slipped the sweater over his curly locks and tugged it down.

"That's my hope, sweetie," she said and fastened the nylon straps at his shoulders before reaching for his moon boots. Hopefully, the advertisers hadn't exaggerated about the warmth. She might not have planned on a blizzard, but she'd certainly taken a few precautions before setting off on this hapless journey. Removing her own coat, she pulled a bulky red sweater over her head, then rummaged in the back for her other boots. If she'd truly planned this adventure, she might have bought a pair of ski pants and winter boots for herself when purchasing the suit for Lucas. Nylon-lined leather might be fine for dancing, but it's doubtful her boots would hold the heat. Adding an extra pair of socks and pulling a pair of sweatpants over her jeans, she glanced at Lucas, who watched her pensively.

A year ago … just a year ago, he might have giggled aloud at her antics or rambled excitedly for her to hurry. He'd changed, and not for the better.

Attempting a smile to counter his sobriety, Becca tugged a knit hat over Lucas's silky curls and pulled his coat hood over his head. A frown touched his lips as she tugged the strings and tied a bow under his chin. "You might look like an Eskimo, sweetie, but you'll be warm as toast," she consoled before wrapping a thick, warm scarf over his nose and adding his mittens. Only his eyes and the bridge of his nose remained visible, but she needed little else to realize his displeasure. Hurriedly, she slipped into her coat, hat, and gloves, then stretched between the seats to shut off the engine and remove the keys. "All set, Lukes?"

His head bobbed, and he mumbled indiscernible words.

Stepping from the car, she remembered to lock the doors before collecting Lucas from the seat. Slipping and sliding clumsily, she held onto Lucas as she climbed the short hill. Already, the skid tracks had nearly vanished under a new layer of snow, and even afoot, visibility had narrowed to a ten-foot margin.

Muffled, Lucas called, "Mmm gonna walk, now, 'kay?"

"Okay, sweetpea," Becca said as she slipped him downward. The snow nearly crested his new blue boots. Taking his mitten in her gloved hand, she looked down into his bright blue eyes, wondering if this could be a mistake. At least in the car, they would be warm for a while … but to sit and pray for rescue when the Resort could be right around the next bend? She would take her chances on the road and pray her instincts were on the money. At all costs, she would get him someplace warm and safe. She hadn't spent the last four months battling every kind of idiot only to have them both lost in a damned blizzard!

Firming her resolve and lifting her neck scarf over her nose and cheeks, she spied the lane and the surrounding woods. With nothing behind them for at least three miles, uphill remained the only sensible option. Sooner or later, they would reach the summit, and even if she needed to carry Lucas on her back, she vowed they would reach safety.

"You ready, sweetie?" she asked, and his bright red head bobbed with a muffled assent.

Setting off at a determined pace, Becca kept a firm hold on the mitten, but far too quickly, she began to feel the cold as well as the worry. With the added complication of wind whipping snow and landing flakes in her lashes, she suffered more than a few second thoughts about leaving the safety and warmth of the car. At her side, barely reaching her hip, Lucas struggled in his small boots through the deepening snow, and by his stumbling, he was already weary of this adventure. Snow … in every direction, the whiteness hung as if suspended in a solid curtain. Barely, tree trunks appeared in the haze, offering only an impression of a road by the contour of the whiteness. With the swell of wind whipping between the trunks, leveling the terrain, she feared walking off course. Never, absolutely never would she look upon a snow scene and consider only its beauty, not when this one might very well be—

No! She wasn't about to buckle to that thought, not with the little fellow beside her, depending on her.

"How about I carry you, sweetpea?" she called over the wind. His head bobbed, and his squinted eyes lifted as she stooped in front of him. Removing one of her gloves, Becca wiped the flakes from his lashes and pulled his hood lower to shield his eyes. Forcing a smile into her eyes, she gathered him under the arms and hoisted him to her hip as she rose. "Not much further," she told him, willing herself to believe her words as she struggled forward, squinting against the whiteness.

Only in her head, Becca maintained a running dialogue of all the warnings she'd ever heard about people caught in blizzards. Keep moving, that was the only lesson she held to heart. If she stopped, if she even paused too long, they might not survive. Frostbite, hypothermia ... drowsiness would be the first sign of exposure. With her revelation, she noted the little Eskimo-covered head tucked against her shoulder and neck. "Lukes, you awake?" she huffed beneath the soggy cloth at her mouth.

A muffled response lifted her spirits.

How much farther? How much damned farther could this Lodge be? Already her back muscles ached from clinging to the overstuffed bundle, and her lungs burned from huffing and puffing icy air. Ten minutes felt like ten hours, and not a single indication of civilization in sight. Only the wind and snow remained constant, whistling and whipping to spike through the scarf, pricking her lashes and cheeks where the cloth had skidded away.

What in God's name had brought her on this asinine journey? What in God's name could she have been thinking to come on this 'adventure', not even bothering to tell anyone where she was destined or why. She should have at least mentioned it to Tony. Undoubtedly, Manetti would have attempted to talk her out of this, citing a dozen reasons, none of which would have made a difference. Even with Tony in her corner, they had lost Lucas a half dozen times through the blasted court system. She wasn't risking it again. For Lucas, she would brave the fires of hell or this blasted frozen tundra. One way or another, she would get them out of this! If she never did another thing right for the rest of her short, miserable life, she would see Lucas Helms was safe and happy. If that meant carrying him across the frozen Arctic, by God, she would see it done!

In the meantime, however, she couldn't afford to let him rest so quietly and still in her arms. Whether getting snow down his boots or the chilled wind was more deadly, Becca could no longer decide, but with a thought of him falling asleep, she rousted him anxiously. "Lukes! You awake?" she shouted against his hood, and his head jerked with a nod. "Think you could walk a few minutes, sweetie?" she asked while stooping again, slipping him onto his boots.

Bright-eyed, he peered at her beneath a shade of thick black lashes, bobbing his head and muffling his agreement.

"That's my boy," Becca said and pushed wearily to her feet. Already, her legs stung with a chill, and needles prickled her toes; still, she clasped his mitten and started a step. At a glimpse of motion — a dark shadow —Becca halted, her attention riveted on the hulking black shape advancing through the blowing snow. A bear! An immense black bear! Heartbeat accelerating, she forgot the cold. Not a bear! A wolf!

"Oh-dear-God," she huffed through chilled cloth. Frantically, she searched the nearest hazy trees, but even the murky outlines appeared far too straight to offer safety. No outcrop of low branches, not even a felled log or stick remained visible within the white blanket. Instinctively, she clasped the mitten, shuffling Lucas behind her, blocking him from the advancing beast as she began backing toward the nearest tree trunk. Heart hammering, she barely heard Lucas shouting at her back. Her attention remained fixed on the animal stalking toward them. As its pace slowed, drawing near, its shape defined, more that of a dog than wolf. An immense black dog, nearly as ice-encrusted as she and Lucas. Backing, she felt Lucas stumble and collect himself, sensing him scrambling to step back from her backward steps. "Stay behind me!" Becca shouted, not sparing a glance. "When I tell you — Run!"

Her words faltered as the animal stopped no more than a few steps away. She stopped as well, startled as the dog rocked backwards and settled on its haunches. With a far too vivid view of its long canines, Becca jolted as the dog threw back its snow-capped head and bellowed a bark to skip her heartbeat. Its bright brown eyes seemed to hold her in trance, and she suddenly knew what a deer felt when caught in headlight beams. Her heartbeat slammed a more painful beat as the animal yelped another quick bark. At close range, the thick black fur glistened with a wet shine, and its head canted as if in question. A Shepard mix, she guessed, but was it a wild dog as she feared? Or could this mean...? Could there be a house nearby? Was the animal poised to attack or ... or was it a savior?

Again, the animal tipped its head and let out a roaring bark amplified within the thick walls of snow.

"O-Okay!" Becca said as she slowly lowered into a stoop, keeping Lucas behind her, although he pressed against her back, undoubtedly trying to see around her. Tentatively, she held out her gloved hand. "Friend or foe?" she asked in a barely audible mutter, praying the animal would advance with its mouth closed.

Before she could worry too long or hard, another shadowy figure appeared beyond the animal, and her breath held a moment before a wave of relief washed over her. Unwittingly, her wet knee dropped, hitting powder. Human. This form was human. She barely started off her knee when Lucas shrank, hiding, now, huddling at her back, clinging to her coat. In a paradox, she rested, not sure whether to turn to collect Lucas or rise and greet this immense stranger whose image seemed to magnify to an incredible height and width. In front of her, the dog pivoted and leapt, bouncing like a puppy to reach the man's hip.

Weary suddenly, Becca rested, not attempting to rise as she identified the blue jeans and laced leather boots of a military design. Her gaze lifted, squinting to see the face within a dark woolen scarf and mirrored ski glasses. Snow-capped, he wore a black watch cap and parka with the furry hood tossed back.

"What the devil are you doing out here?" The deep voice breached the cloth with no trouble at all as he closed the distance, offering her an immense gloved hand.

"Taking — a — stroll!" Becca huffed as the hand tugged her afoot against a greater internal urge to rest. How dare this Eskimo giant sound as if he were accusing her of something — like stupidity!

"Good God — a child!" the deep voice cut through the wind like a base drum in a band.

Feeling Lucas pressed against the back of her legs, Becca thrust her hand instinctively to ward off the gloved hand reaching past her. Afoot, she barely stood as tall as this fellow's shoulder, and leaning as he was to reach for Lucas, she saw herself — or some rendition of herself — within his mirrored shades. "Slow down!" she demanded.

Straightening, he stood near enough to blow his condensed breath against her wet lashes as he snapped, "Is there anyone else out here with you?"

She shook her head in a quick jerk.

"Unless you want to freeze, I suggest you let me lift that child and we get a move on it! My cabin's a five-minute hike from here!"

There was a time, not too long ago, when Lucas might have accepted the stranger without much of a fight, but Becca knew better than to expect his compliance now. Despite her weariness, she cast the stranger a disheartened glance before turning and stooping again. In an instant, the little boy buried his face against her neck and flung his stiff, snow-covered arms about her shoulders. She lifted him with an effort, almost grateful when the immense hand wrapped easily about her upper arm and helped her afoot. Squinting into the glasses, wishing she could see the face behind this immense, capable hand, she heaved, "I have him. If you could just — lead the way?"

His hand remained on her arm, turning them both. Far more grateful than she cared to consider, she relied on his size and strength, trudging on leaden feet and stumbling against him.

Without a word of warning, he simply paused, and half turned, clasped the bundle clinging to her, and drew Lucas away as if he were a puppy. "Not much farther," the low baritone voice assured while manipulating the struggling bundle against his hip. "Settle, little one. We'll have you warm in a moment," his silky low voice promised as he renewed his grip on Becca's sleeve. "Your Mom's tuckered out..."

Becca heard the words, too weary to correct the mistake. A little farther, just a little farther, she coaxed her burning feet, heaving chilled breaths through the cloth and wishing she could just sit, or lie down for a few moments. Just a few moments of rest. But the hand at her arm whisked her along, drawing her up when she stumbled over hidden logs and tangled vines, keeping her moving.

With the snow whipping through her vision, the stairs appeared out of nowhere. She could barely lift her legs to ascend the planks. Just a little farther ... and as if magically, she slumped against a wall, seeing only shadows as the icy flakes and wind suddenly vanished with a snap and bang. Squinting, nearly blind with the whiteness, she could barely make out the image of her savior as the fellow stooped, sliding Lucas a-ground. The sound of Lucas's whimpered sob drew her from her momentary stupor. As she slid down the wall to his level, the needles burning in her legs and ankles snatched her breath in a gasp.

"Christ, you're half frozen — both of you," the low voice uttered, sounding nearly as worried as Becca felt. "Here. Let me help you," he spoke while his immense hands came, tugging almost gently to pull the wet cloth from her numb fingers. "Are you awake?"

Remembering how she'd spoken those exact words to Lucas, she jerked her head, squinting and blinking to draw the face into focus. No use. Her eyes hadn't adjusted. Only the red blur of the snow suit remained distinguishable from the other sights. She reached toward Lucas, attempting to clasp the bright red scarf. "Warm — get him — warm ... Lukes ... let him — help you, sweetie..." Something was happening in her head, so sleepy, so heavy...

QR Code

For the latest news and updates from

J. K. Grueber

visit:

Jkgrueber.com

"Thank you for reading!" J. K. Grueber